NOMAD SERIES - BOOK 1

K.A.FINN

Also by K.A. Finn

Nomad Series (Space Opera)

Ares

Nemesis

Perses

Chaos

Mania

Cronus

Talos (TBA)

Blackjacks Series (Paranormal Romance)

Breaking Phoenix

Reviving Davyn

Defying Shep

Defending Rhain (TBA)

Broken Chords (Rockstar Romance)

Broken Rock (Tate)

Fractured Rock (Gregg)

Split Rock (Tate # 2)

Crushed Rock (Luke)

Shattered Rock (Dillon)

Damaged Rock (Gregg # 2 - TBA)

Twisted Legends (Fantasy Romance/Folklore Retelling)

North Bound (Nick/Santa)

Shadow Bound (Damon/The Boogeyman – TBA)

I'm an Irish author who is addicted to writing romances featuring damaged, moody, book boyfriends searching for their happily ever after.

Visit K.A. Finn online:

www.kafinn.com
(trailers, excerpts, artwork, playlists etc)

Facebook: kafinnauthor

Instagram: kafinnauthor

Additional links: linktr.ee/kafinn

Cover design by Deranged Doctor Design

www.derangeddoctordesign.com

Published by Cooper Publishing

www.cooperbookservices.com

ISBN: 978-0-9932073-2-7

To my husband. Without your support and badgering
this book would never have been finished.
To my daughter. Without your encouragement and attention
this book probably would have been finished years ago!
To my parents. Thank you for all your support even though science
fiction isn't quite your cup of tea!
To my friends. Thanks for not disowning me. Apologies if I bored you
all to tears talking about the book!
To my two dogs. Thanks for keeping me
company on the long journey.

And finally, a big thank you to YOU for reading this in the first place.

ARES

NOMAD SERIES — BOOK 1

K.A.FINN

1

'Captain, we're nearing the location of the unidentified signal.'

Gryffin ignores his radio as he focuses on the training drone in front of him. The life-sized robot circles him, patiently waiting for his next move. Gryffin twirls the sparring stick in his metal hand. Another message sounds over the intercom, calling him to the command deck. So much for a few hours of peace and quiet.

With no time left for a proper fight, he launches himself at the drone. He dodges a swipe to the head and ducks under the drone's arm. Swinging around, he swipes the machine across its side. It retaliates by striking Gryffin squarely on the metal implant fused to his chest.

He grunts in pain and withdraws for a few seconds. The drone relaxes slightly. Gryffin takes advantage and fakes right. When the drone reacts, he jams his sparring stick into its side. Sparks of electricity spit from the wound, before the drone collapses on the floor.

Gryffin holds the drone down with his foot and yanks his stick from the machine. After placing it back on the rack against the wall, he drags the drone to the corner and dumps it with the other scrap. He grabs his t-shirt from the bench and climbs the spiral metal staircase to the upper level.

The crew members he meets on his way to the command deck, stand to attention as he storms past. As he walks, he glances down at his chest. The damn drone's lucky hit tore the skin joined to the W-shaped metal implant framing his chest. He ignores the wound, and pulls on his t-shirt as he gets to his destination.

The command deck falls silent when he enters. 'What have you got?'

'Take a look for yourself, sir.' His first officer, Klay, steps aside to give the captain an unobstructed view of the ship in front of them. The sleek silver vessel is clearly a long distance cruiser. A ship of that calibre so far from the border can only mean trouble. He clenches his jaw and digs his metal hand into the console in front of him.

'Foundation ship?'

Klay nods soberly. 'Confirmed.'

Klay steps back as the metal surrounding Gryffin's left eye glows deep red. 'So, the Foundation has officially arrived in the Sector. Greedy bastards must want to colonise.'

'I can't think of any other reason for them to be here, sir.'

Gryffin sits back in his command chair and quietly surveys the Foundation ship. He had heard rumours they'd entered the Sector, but this is the first time he's seen them in the flesh. He's vaguely aware of his crew moving at their stations around him. They're waiting for the order to strike. They've taken down bigger ships and he's sure they can overcome this vessel.

'Do you want to launch an attack, sir?'

'Not yet. Let them make the first move. Bring us closer to the planet.' The scarred battleship slowly manoeuvres into position behind the larger Foundation vessel. With cloaks engaged, *Ares* can approach the Foundation vessel without alerting them to her presence.

Gryffin doesn't have to wait long for the stern of the ship to open. He leans back in his chair and watches three small transports exit the cargo hatch of the Foundation vessel, unaware of their audience.

They're heading towards the surface of the planet.

So it's beginning — they've chosen their first colony to target. He smiles to himself. It's just their bad luck they decided to start with one of his. As soon as they set foot on the planet, their fate will be sealed.

While a part of him hopes they'll abort, he's itching for them to land. It's been too long since he's had a proper fight. Time seems to slow for him as the three ships on the screen move closer to the planet.

His purple eyes glow in anticipation of the upcoming battle. He rises to his feet. 'Ready the raiding teams. Time to go introduce ourselves.'

∞

Captain Jensen Roman peers around the corner of the building and narrowly avoids a bullet to his head. He doesn't have time to wonder about what went wrong. The talks with the town elder came to an abrupt halt when the ambush began. Three of his crew members have already lost their lives.

On his signal, the team opposite him break cover to race to the shelter of the trees, and hopefully towards the safety of the transports on the other side. As soon as they move, their attackers resume firing. Roman and his first officer, Evan Stanner, lay on covering fire. Once the team is out of sight, the two officers work their way around the other side of the town.

'You should have stayed on board, Captain.'

'No point mentioning that at the moment, Stanner. How long do you think it will take them to reach the transports?'

Stanner pauses firing to reload. 'Hard to say. Hopefully another minute at the most. Doubt they'd waste any time.'

Roman empties another magazine, then reloads as the three Foundation transports burst out of the trees from different directions. Two of the transports cover the third as it lands to pick up its valuable cargo. Roman, Stanner and two crew fire out of the open door as the craft lifts off the ground.

A lone bullet punches into Roman's upper arm as the hatch closes. The adrenaline pumps through his body and helps to dull the pain. Roman releases a few shots of his own, before the transport ducks behind the trees. He only allows himself to stand down once the convoy leaves behind the blue cloudless sky and enters the darkness surrounding the planet.

'Are you okay, sir?'

Roman nods and wipes his forehead with his sleeve. 'Minor graze. Persistent, weren't they?'

'I didn't think the locals would be aggressive. They seemed almost withdrawn when we spoke to them earlier.'

'Those shooters weren't locals. Our new friends appear skilled. And well trained. I'd say military of some sort.'

Stanner frowns. 'The Foundation Council failed to mention the existence of any military groups in the area.'

Roman looks at the bodies of the three crew members at his feet. 'I suspect they don't know.' He pulls his sleeve up and examines the wound. 'It appears someone doesn't want the Foundation here. We may be in for a bit of resistance.'

∞

Gryffin puts his gun back in its holster. He flexes his metal hand as he watches the Foundation transports disappear into the distance.

'Orders, sir?'

'Let them go.'

'Captain, we have to go after them.'

He turns his masked face towards Klay. 'And start a war?'

Klay waves his gun in the direction of the retreating Foundation ship. 'They started it by coming here. We'll just be ending it. We need to show them who owns this Sector.'

'It's not about ownership. It's about getting the Foundation to back off.'

Klay lowers his gun. 'So we let them escape? What was the point of all of this? We've wasted ammunition for nothing.'

Gryffin's metal fist clenches and instantly stops any further arguments. 'I wanted to let them know we're here. Now they know they'll have a war on their hands if they try anything. If we destroy that ship, we risk bringing the full power of the Foundation to our doorstep. Until we know more, don't touch them. Understood?'

'Yes, sir.' Klay glances over his shoulder at the town elder who is hovering nearby. Klay gestures at Gryffin. 'You're wanted, sir.'

'Extract everyone. We take off in ten minutes. Send the word out to the other ships. I want an eye on the Foundation at all times.'

The elder nods at Klay as he passes, but doesn't speak until Gryffin turns in his direction. The man shrinks away from Gryffin's presence. People always do. Although his crew never exit the ship without a metal mask hiding their features, Gryffin himself still manages to stand out — even with his metal arm hidden.

The man fumbles for a moment before he composes himself. 'I would like to thank you for your help. The last thing we need is Foundation leadership here. Will they come back?'

'We'll do what we can to keep them away.' Before the man can respond, Gryffin storms back to his transport.

He prefers to use the large black motorcycle whenever he gets the chance. He doesn't care that it's less convenient than the air carriers. Nothing can compare to the feel of every bump as the wheels travel along the ground. He swings his leg over the machine and wipes a smear of mud from the purple griffin painted on the side.

Some colonists customised the bike as a thank you for helping to push out a rogue group. The small mining colony on the outskirts of the Sector had been an easy target. With no weapons or defences to protect them, the rogue groups frequently attacked. That all stopped when the Nomad staked their claim. In exchange for a portion of the metal they process, Gryffin ensures their safety.

He starts the engine and kicks up the stand. With one last glance at the town, he revs the engine and accelerates down the dusty road leading back to his ship. He follows the winding trail through the forest, leaving a dust cloud in his wake. His mask helps protect his sensitive eyes from the dappled sunshine streaming down through the trees.

His mind races as fast as his bike. He needs to learn as much as he can about the Foundation threat. He hopes he didn't make the biggest mistake of his life letting the ship go.

∞

Roman stands on the bridge of his ship, *Infinity*. He runs a hand over his face and examines the large station filling the screen in front of him. Stanner joins him and crosses his arms. 'We received a communication from the Foundation Council,' Stanner reports. 'Their revised schedule will leave us little time to recover from the combat yesterday.'

Roman nods. 'I'm not surprised. The Council won't want to waste any time widening their net to gather as many colonies as possible. The ambush will only put increased pressure on us.'

He seriously doubts the Council thought anyone would retaliate. No one had ever fought back against the Foundation. Losing three members on the first away mission had shocked his superiors, but, if anything, it made them all the more determined to populate the Sector.

'No one could have known this would happen.' Stanner clenches his fists. 'The colonies had been warned in advance of these visits and told to co-operate. I don't know what they hope to achieve by attacking us.'

Roman nods. The disobedience is not going down well and even now plans are underway to ensure other colonies toe the Foundation line. He looks down at his hand and flexes his fingers, wincing as pain shoots up his arm. 'I do know one thing; we may not have seen the attackers in any detail, but I know they weren't the locals.'

Roman walks back to his seat with his heartbeat pounding in his ears. He sits heavily and rubs a hand over his jaw. 'Three lives lost so some lawless ship can mark their territory. I can't say I disagree with the Council's decision. We need to remove this group, fast. Did you check the scans again?'

'Yes, sir,' Stanner responds. 'Nothing showed up.'

'They must have used an illegal cloak.' Fighting a visible enemy is one thing, but if their attackers suddenly decide to increase the pressure, they could very well cause trouble. The rest of the fleet is months away at best. 'Enough thinking about it for now. We have a safe harbour for the next few hours.' The station where they planned to dock recognised the authority of the Foundation and had offered them a safe place to unwind for the evening.

'Sir, we're being contacted by the station,' Lieutenant Terra Rush reports. 'Pier Three.'

'Right.' He addresses Stanner. 'Settle her in for the night, Commander. Terra, summon the crew to the Rec Room.'

A few moments later, the thirty-three crew members stand to attention as Roman enters the Rec Room. An imposing man of over six-feet, Roman is well built with a strong, handsome face and cold, piercing blue eyes. His black hair is cropped tight to his head and greying slightly at the sides. At fifty-one, he is still fully capable of handling himself in combat and is well respected and liked by all his crew.

7

'You've got four hours R&R on the station. I want to remind you all this station is not officially part of the Foundation yet, so stay to the allocated common areas and keep your weapons with you at all times. Enjoy yourselves. Dismissed.'

The crew move in groups from the ship onto the station. Roman walks back to his office through empty corridors to start working through some reports. He has a conference call with his superiors in a few days, so he needs everything up to date by then.

After pouring a cup of coffee, he sits down at his glass desk and places his palm on the computer screen to activate it. Roman leans back in the chair and glares at the pile of computer pads on the corner of his desk, wondering if he can delegate some of the work to his crew.

Terra steps through the hatch leading from *Infinity* to the space station. Her close friend, Doctor Milla Collins, accompanies her along the corridor to the bar area. 'Oooh, I like that smell.'

Terra wrinkles her nose. 'It's certainly ... unique.'

Milla catches her foot on a loose bolt and stumbles. 'Did you see that? Damn station is trying to kill me.'

Terra laughs. 'Want me to alert Roman?'

Milla straightens her red leather jacket and pushes her shoulders back. 'Funny. Hey, looks like we've reached the party.'

They walk down the three metal steps leading into the bar and locate a seat near one of the windows at the far side. Milla leans closer to Terra to speak to her over the noise. 'I think a loose bolt is the least of their problems.'

Terra looks around the room and nods slowly. She runs a finger down the seam in the wall beside her. 'I can't remember the last time I saw metal welded by hand like this. And did you see the farms on the last colony?'

'Yeah, but you have to remember these people are about a century behind us when it comes to technology. They have no choice but to grow their food. There's no such thing as automated farming here.'

Milla grimaces as she watches a man at the next table spooning something grey and gooey into his mouth. 'Personally, I'd grow my food before I'd risk some of the pre-packed food-substitute rubbish they have here. Seriously, what the hell is he eating?'

Terra resists the urge to gag and looks away. 'Exactly. I can't understand the reluctance to join the Foundation. We'd provide proper food, housing and technology.'

'Eventually. Don't forget, the colonists would have to prove they have something to offer before the Council would grant such luxuries.'

Terra glances over at the man still fighting with his dinner. 'They'd have better food immediately. Surely that's an incentive without any of the other perks?'

Milla shrugs as she picks some plastic from the table edge. 'The Foundation did banish their ancestors to this Sector. The colonists even stopped using their family names because of what happened. Apparently, they only use one name for identification.'

'Seriously?'

Milla nods. 'Yep. According to the reports the colonists were so angry at being relocated here they disowned any family the Foundation permitted to stay on Earth. Being told you have nothing of value to offer the Foundation must have been pretty horrible. Can't blame them for being wary.'

Milla has a point. Even so, Terra believes this Sector would benefit from some help. The location is barely functioning and would certainly do with some Foundation support. Built decades ago, the large wheel-shaped station apparently hasn't been maintained or decorated since then. It belongs in a scrap yard.

Milla slaps the table and pushes her chair back. 'Well, I think it's time we do a bit of bonding with the locals. I'm off to the bar to sample some of the best this Sector has to offer. You game?'

Terra looks over at the makeshift bar and scrunches her nose. 'As long as you're the one to give me medical attention if something goes wrong.'

Milla smirks and pats her friend on the shoulder. 'Don't worry. I wouldn't dream of leaving you in the hands of the locals. Unless you wanted me to, of course.'

Terra laughs and waves Milla away. While Milla barges through the crowd, Terra pulls a small notebook and pencil from her pocket. She brushes her long dark braid off her shoulder and casually looks around the room. It's a pity Roman couldn't locate somewhere nicer to take their leave. Terra finds no new inspiration in the room so draws Milla's face.

She glances towards her friend, who's still trying to reach the bar. Next time they probably should bring drinks to the station. Her friend is getting swallowed up by the rousing crowd, but any concern for Milla disappears as the doctor forcefully elbows the other customers out of the way.

Terra smiles and shakes her head. This mission would be very long and extremely lonely had she not befriended Milla. They were both assigned to *Infinity* at the same time and the two women had instantly hit it off.

The petite, blonde doctor finally reaches the bar and places her order. Confident that Milla is coping with the locals, Terra glances around the room. Her colleagues stand out from the rest of the crowd in their crisp — and more noticeably — clean uniforms. She doubts many of the people on the space station have seen water or soap for weeks.

Terra sighs and turns to stare out the dirty window. She smooths a stray lock of hair back in place. At twenty-five years old she's one of the youngest and most inexperienced on the crew — something that's always in the back of her mind, pushing her to do better. When her parents died, Jensen Roman was the only one left who meant anything to her. Her father had served with him, so Jensen stepped into the role of surrogate father. She knows her posting to *Infinity* is due to his influence with the Council — though he denies it.

She absently wipes the condensation from the window and cringes when she sees Stanner walking towards her in the reflection in the glass. His steps seem a little unsteady; his movements sluggish, hinting he's had a few drinks. She doesn't know why Roman lifted the Foundation ban on alcohol while in the Sector.

'Hi Terra. You're looking lovely tonight.'

'Thank you, Commander.'

'We're off duty now, call me Evan.' He pulls up a chair across from her and places his drink on the table. He's an attractive man with short sandy blonde hair and emerald green eyes, but there is something about him that doesn't attract her. He's a dedicated officer and a friend, but nothing more — a fact she has told him on many occasions, but he keeps trying to win her affection, especially when there's drink involved.

Not wishing to have the discussion again, she decides to save him the embarrassment. 'Right, I'd better go see what's keeping Milla.' She stands up, but Stanner holds onto her arm.

'Terra, please relax for a minute. I haven't had a chance to speak to you lately.'

'It's fine, Evan.'

'No, I feel like I'm neglecting you.'

'Neglecting me?'

'Yeah, you know ... Hey, have a drink with me.'

'Sir — Evan. I need to go.'

'Wait.' He takes another mouthful of his drink and clumsily puts it back on the table. He leans towards her and knocks the liquid across the table and Terra. The alcohol runs down her red leather jacket, soaking into her white shirt and black trousers before dripping down onto her boots. 'Sorry, Terra. Let me clean that up.'

He reaches across with a soiled napkin, but she jumps away from him before he can touch her. 'I have to go. Excuse me.' Terra quickly weaves through the crowd and pauses for a moment as she tries to locate Milla in the sea of bodies. She finally spots her talking to a group of men. Terra pushes towards Milla and taps her on the shoulder. 'I'm heading back to *Infinity*.'

'Oh, Terra. It's been barely half an hour. You haven't even had a drink yet.'

'I'd die of thirst if I waited for you to fetch me a drink.'

Milla smiles sheepishly and hands Terra the glass of coloured liquid. 'Sorry. I got a bit distracted.'

Terra sips the drink as she glances over at the group of dishevelled men beside Milla. 'Them? Really? We're here to prepare for colonisation — not chase after men.'

'I can do both. I'm multi-talented. The people out here aren't so bad. Sometimes you have to dig beneath the surface.'

She looks at the men again and wonders how far under the surface you'd have to go before you found clean skin. Instead of commenting further, Terra points at the large beer stain on her shirt. 'Stanner spilt his drink all over me. I'm going back to the ship to change.'

'Okay, I'll come with you.'

'Don't be silly. It'll only take me a few minutes. You stay here. No point him ruining both our nights.'

'You sure you'll be okay?'

'Of course.' She hands her half empty glass back to Milla. 'Do me a favour. If you get a chance to spill something over Stanner, take it.'

'Hey, you don't even have to ask. It would be my pleasure.'

∞

After wandering the dark maze of corridors for over half an hour, Terra realises she's lost.

She doesn't even remember how to find the dingy bar. Somehow, she has ended up in an old section of the station, filled with rusty heaps of machinery and broken pipes spewing a haze of steam into the corridor. She pushes a plastic crate against the wall and sits down slowly. Time to finally admit defeat.

She takes her radio out of her pocket and tries it again. Nothing but static. She had checked the Foundation system before she left *Infinity*. Everything worked perfectly. Something must be blocking the signal in this area. She pulls a panel from the wall and searches for the cables running the communication system. If she's lucky, she may be able to boost her unit through it.

Damn Stanner. She blames him for this. If he hadn't spilt his drink on her, she would be gossiping with Milla right now. Stanner is probably back in the bar getting drunk while she's rummaging around in the dark for a cable. To top it all off, she's cold and the stench from the stale beer Stanner spilt on her clothes turns her stomach.

She finally locates the right connection. If her plan works, she should be able to piggy-back off their system and set up a link. A few adjustments later, she tries again with success. As she is about to relay her message, a sound in the background catches her attention.

She blocks out the other noises around her to concentrate on the new sound. She finally recognises it — three or four sets of heavy footsteps coming her way, fast. Terra stands up and reaches for her weapon out of instinct. She saw the type of people this location attracts. No harm in being cautious.

She crouches behind a mound of barrels. Hopefully, the shadows and steam will keep her hidden until she can assess whether they pose a threat. A group of five men step out of the haze and approach her hiding place. All are dirty, unshaven and, more importantly, armed. The tallest of the men halts the group and takes out a large knife, the one lone light in the corridor reflecting off its highly polished blade.

'We know you're here, girly. Don't make us search for you,' he says, but doesn't wait for her to show herself. He signals to the group and they begin searching the rubbish piled up along the length of the

14

corridor.

She quietly checks her weapon. Seven rounds. Should be enough as long as she's careful where she aims.

She slowly stands up and searches for something she can use as a distraction. With nothing else available, she places her hands on the large container in front of her. With a gentle push, it moves slightly against her. As it settles itself again, it rattles against the wall. Terra holds her breath, sure the men heard her. Luckily, they're making enough noise themselves by throwing pipes and barrels. She bides her time and waits until the leader steps closer to her before she takes a deep breath and pushes hard. The container falls off the rubbish with a crash and tumbles onto him.

She doesn't wait to see what happens. Before the container has settled, she fires her weapon and takes down the second man. The leader quickly pulls himself to his feet and grabs Terra around the waist. She shoves her head back and hears the satisfying sound of breaking bone. The leader roars in pain and lets her go. She kicks him in the stomach, sending him crashing into the scrap behind him. His friends quickly gather themselves and come at her.

Terra ducks behind some crates and fires at the men. They leap for cover and return fire. Terra holds her ground and after a few misses, shoots the third man in the chest. She ducks swiftly and narrowly avoids being hit herself.

That leaves two men and the injured leader. She checks her gun in the slim chance more rounds have appeared, but she only has two rounds for three targets. Terra grips her weapon tightly. There's no way she can take them all out. With no other option, she aims at one of the pipes running along the ceiling and fires. The steam rushes out of the pipe and fills the corridor. Using the steam as a cloak, she does the only thing she can.

Runs.

Admiral Avoca quickly jumps aside to avoid crashing into Admiral Balfe as he storms down the long corridor. Balfe gestures for Avoca to follow as he charges ahead.

Avoca curses to himself and obediently traipses after Balfe through the Foundation Council Headquarters. Corridor after corridor of pristine white walls and highly polished white floors go by in a blur as Avoca struggles to keep up. He can't help but search for some blemish, a scuff mark or piece of dirt on the ground, but there's nothing. Heaven forbid anything mars the perfection.

Out the window, Avoca can see yet more examples of the order forced on the populace by the Foundation. Lines of identical trees stand to attention along precisely laid paths weaving around equally identical houses. For once he'd like to see a random weed or a broken kerb. He'd even settle for a leaf on the ground.

But no. Everything has its place — including him.

Balfe opens the door to his office and ushers Avoca inside. Once safely behind closed doors, Balfe sits down heavily on his chair and curses loudly.

'Didn't go well then?' asks Avoca.

Balfe snorts. 'You could say that. Those bureaucratic idiots won't budge. They want the Sector — no excuses. The Council haven't got a clue. They perch on their thrones and assume they can have all their wishes granted with a wave of their hands. Common sense dictates a Sector full of criminals a mere hop, skip, and jump from here adds up to a dangerous situation, but colonising is not the answer.'

Avoca sits down opposite Balfe. 'What is left they could uncover?'

Balfe crosses his ankles and frowns. 'Any remaining test subjects died when the lab blew up. However, that doesn't mean something didn't slip through the crack. I'd feel a hell of a lot better if we went in with force. Less chance of stumbling across any incriminating evidence.'

'Do they want to pull *Infinity* back?'

Balfe shakes his head. 'The opposite, in fact. It isn't public knowledge, but I found out someone attacked *Infinity*, resulting in three dead. It appears a rogue group took a dislike to Foundation presence in the area.' He waves a hand dismissively in the air. 'This pathetic endeavour to turn the Council off colonisation had the opposite effect. They still want the colonies — even more so than before.'

Avoca rubs his hands over his trousers to warm his suddenly chilled fingers. 'So, that's that then. It's only a matter of time.'

Balfe pushes back from his desk. 'We've come this far, Avoca. Now isn't the time to lose our composure.' He brushes a hand over his hair. 'All we can do is hope no evidence of the project remains.'

∞

Her blood rushes loudly in her ears, beating in time to her pursuer's footsteps behind her. Apparently, the steam didn't hold them off for long. Terra runs faster, dodging the many obstacles in her way. She needs to find somewhere to hide until she can contact the ship.

Terra slows down at the fork at the end of the corridor and turns the corner, barely staying on her feet. She risks a quick glance over her shoulder to check her lead. The gap is too tight. They're going to catch her.

She forces her legs to move, but not for long. She runs full force into a solid wall of muscle in front of her. Her arms flail uselessly in the air as she tries to stay upright. Strong arms wrap around her waist and lower her gently to the ground. Her eyes and weapon move slowly up the stranger's tall body.

The man easily reaches six-and-a-half-foot and is dressed entirely in black leather with a hood hiding his features. A gun and a large handled knife hang from a thick black belt circling his waist.

She shuffles back, unsure whether he's a friend or foe. For all she knows he could be with the other three men. Through the shadows, his strange glowing purple eyes lock onto her for a moment before turning towards the men who have stopped behind her. They collectively take a step back and Terra can't blame them.

Even the surrounding air seems to have dropped a few degrees in response to the man's arrival. He may not have moved a muscle or said a word, but one thing is clear: Terra is more afraid of him than she is of the men chasing her.

She eases herself off the floor while keeping a close eye on her attackers and the stranger. Terra grips her gun, ready to shoot first if she has to. Time seems to freeze for her as the two parties stare at each other. Hopefully, the new man and her three attackers will decide to wrestle each other and provide her with the chance to disappear. With only one bullet, she doesn't have many other options available.

Unfortunately, the opportunity vanishes as the leader of the gang seems to discover his courage and slowly moves towards the stranger.

'I don't know who you are but this is nothing to do with you. That female broke my damn nose!'

The stranger lowers his hood to display a full metal mask covering his features. 'A broken nose is the least of your worries.'

The attackers pause for a moment. 'You're Nomad?' The man in black stays silent as the leader nudges his companions. 'You're all alone though, ain't you? Hey, Nomad, we'll cut you some slack this once, so how about you turn around and walk away now. She's mine. She owes me.' He steps closer to the Nomad and sneers up at him. 'Walk away. Now! We'll forget we saw you. You forget you saw us. Everyone's happy.'

The Nomad looks down at Terra for a moment before stepping over her, the creak of leather audible over the other sounds of the station. He stands in front of her like a guardian and silently looks at the group for a moment before speaking. 'I've got a perfect memory and she sure as hell isn't happy.' The stranger's voice sounds distorted due to the mask, which only adds to the air of intimidation surrounding him.

The men laugh. The leader takes another step closer and turns the blade in his hand. 'You're serious! In case you haven't noticed, three against one ain't great odds.'

The Nomad says nothing as he slowly takes off his right glove. His hand seems wrong, but she struggles to make sense of what she's seeing. He flexes his fingers and she realises he has a metal hand.

The group of men notice his mechanical hand at the same time she does. The leader's eyes open wide in recognition and the colour visibly drains from his face. 'Shit. Listen, we're sorry. We didn't know she was with you. We'll go. We can forget this ever happened.'

'As I said, I've got a perfect memory.' The Nomad suddenly leaps forward and pulls a knife from his belt. He slices it across the man's throat to open a large gash, then slams his metal hand against the second man's neck. Sparks of electricity run down the Nomad's arm, out of his hand and into the man's neck. The man convulses violently

19

before crumpling to the ground. The Nomad throws his knife at the third man, who follows his friends a second later with the blade embedded in his eye.

The brawl took three seconds from start to finish. If not for the bodies at his feet, she would have said she imagined the whole thing. He turns to face her and the purple tinted shielding over his eyes glows in the dim light. Her instincts kick in. Terra raises her gun and fires. The round hits him square in the chest, but he barely flinches.

Instead, he crouches down in front of her. 'That wasn't very nice now, was it?'

Before she can respond, he moves faster than she thought possible and jams a pressure syringe against her neck. The room spins around her and dark patches appear at the corners of her vision. His glowing purple eyes examine her as she passes out.

Gryffin has no idea what to do. He glances down at the limp body of the woman on the ground. Technically, he should kill her. First rule: no witnesses.

He turns towards the three other less graceful looking bodies. He had no choice but to kill them. As soon as he saw them, he knew they were slavers. They consider women a high-value commodity. The men would have sold the Foundation woman to the highest bidder. If he had his way, he'd personally wipe out all slavers.

He lifts up his t-shirt and grimaces. The wound is deep. A simple thank you from her would have been preferable to a bullet. Too many questions will be asked if he goes back to *Ares* with a bullet lodged in his chest. He'll have to take care of it on the station.

Ignoring the wound for the moment, Gryffin pulls his knife from the man's skull, wipes it on his leg, and slips it back onto his belt before he puts his glove back on. He quickly drags the three bodies to a nearby vent, pushes them in, and seals it back up by piling some junk in front of it. After checking the area for any other surprises and with no other distractions, he turns his attention back to the woman.

He has to kill her. He lifts his gun and points it at her head. Ten seconds later, he still hasn't pulled the trigger. All of a sudden an image flashes into his head of a dark red bloody hole in the centre of her forehead. He lowers his gun and curses himself. He can't do it, which leaves him with a problem. He'll have to take her with him.

Gryffin crouches down and examines her. As soon as he saw her crisp, clean uniform, he knew she was Foundation. The black trousers under long black boots with a white shirt and a fitted red leather jacket look uncomfortable and regimented.

He was on his way back to *Ares* when he heard the fire fight. When he realised the men were chasing a Foundation crew member, he lost interest and was about to withdraw. But then he saw it was a woman.

Curiosity took hold and he remained. She was a confident and fierce fighter. If she'd had enough ammunition, she would have won. He's astonished to see a woman in combat. He knows some of the rogue groups have female members, but none of them are trained like this Foundation woman. And among his Nomad, there aren't any women at all.

Before he can stop his hand, it reaches out to gingerly brush some strands of dark hair from her eyes. Her skin is flawless. Most of his men have at least one scar on their face. It was part of life in the Sector.

His leather-covered finger traces down her small delicate nose and along her jaw. Gryffin pauses at her full lips and pulls his hand back. He takes a deep breath to focus on his task, but it has the opposite effect. The delicate, almost fruity scent coming from the woman assaults his senses. He's never smelt anything like it — like her — before. Gryffin shakes his head and gets to his feet. *She's only a woman, Gryffin. Focus.*

He moves further away from her and her intoxicating smell. Gryffin pulls out his radio from his pocket as he keeps an eye out for any more visitors. A big part of him hopes more enemies appear out of the darkness. The adrenaline is still pumping through his body and the short brawl did nothing to help release the pressure. He's itching for a decent fight. He *needs* a decent fight.

Shaking his head, he pushes those thoughts to the back of his mind. He puts all his focus into staying in control, but it's not working. He can feel his enhanced eyes shift between their usual blue and aggressive purple. In a desperate attempt to remain focused, he punches the wall viciously and concentrates on the shooting pain in his arm. It works, so he activates his radio.

'Yes, sir.'

'We in yet?'

'A few more minutes, Captain.'

He pauses as he considers how to approach this. 'Klay there?'

'No, sir.'

Klay being out of earshot makes things a bit easier. 'Break into that system now. Find out if any transmissions went to a Foundation ship in the last thirty minutes.'

'Yes, sir.'

He shuts down his radio. Hopefully, Klay won't hear he's looking for a Foundation ship. He might get the wrong idea and want to start a war again. Gryffin looks down at the woman. He needs to move her from the area before the rest of the slavers come looking for their friends.

A chill runs down his spine at the thought of what the slavers would have done to her had he not been there. He only regrets their quick, relatively painless deaths. His anger threatens to spill to the surface again. It's not usually this hard to keep in control. Maybe he's tired? Cursing himself, he shakes his head. No, this is a bit worse than a lack of sleep.

His machine side is malfunctioning. The flaw in his programming is gradually getting worse. Everything had been working well enough until a few months ago. Like a virus, the fault or programming error

— whatever the hell Klay called it — began to spread through his control implant, forcing him out of his head, bit by bit. Between that and the searing pain the malfunctions cause, his future isn't looking too good.

His communicator sounds in his ear, pulling him out of his thoughts. 'What?' he snaps, taking out his frustration with himself on his communications officer.

The officer doesn't falter at his tone. Like everyone else on the ship, he's well used to him lashing out. 'Sir, no transmissions have been made from the station. However, there is a Foundation ship docked at Pier Three. Do you need me to send back up?'

'No. Send me the location of a vacant room near my signal. I'm going off comms for an hour.'

Gryffin ends the communication and waits for the plan to come through. He can't read, so hopefully the comms officer will remember to send a map instead of directions. Less than a minute later, the plan arrives on his unit. According to the information, it's not too far. Once he's removed the bullet, he can leave her safely in the room.

Unfortunately, unless he's going to drag her back by her arm, he's going to have to pick her up. The thought of anyone touching him, especially his chest, doesn't appeal to him. But she needs him to help her. It's been a long time since anyone needed him.

He reactivates his mask and before he can talk himself out of it, gently scoops her up in his arms. The feeling of her leaning against his chest isn't as bad as he thought it would be. He looks down at her briefly before he makes his way through the station.

∞

On the third attempt, Terra finally convinces her eyes to peel open. She looks at the smooth metal ceiling as she slowly assesses her body. There's no pain — nothing to explain why she's lying on a soft bed in a strange room. She remembers running from some men, fighting them and then ... nothing.

Something or someone moves to her left. Terra instantly stills her breathing. Memories of the fight in the corridor and her mysterious rescuer come back in a rush. The Nomad must have drugged her. She silently checks her gun and confirms her worst fears. Her last bullet was used on the purple-eyed man.

Terra scans the room but can't see anyone. She moves to the door opposite her and tries the handle, but it won't budge. The sound of running water comes from the doorway to her left so she cautiously moves in that direction. Might as well face whoever is in there. She reaches out to push the door open and freezes. A man — presumably her rescuer — is sitting on a small stool next to the shower digging into his chest with a knife.

'What the hell are you doing?'

He glances at her briefly, before he looks back down again. 'You should still be unconscious.'

She levels her gun at him. 'Sorry to disappoint. What are you doing?' she asks again.

The man remains focused on his task. 'You shot me, remember.'

'You were going to kill me.'

He grunts and shakes his head. Locks of dark brown hair hang over his down-turned face, hiding him from her. 'Of course I was. I took out three men who wanted to kill you just so I could kill you myself.'

'Yeah, well, forgive me if I don't believe you.'

'Put your gun down. I won't hurt you,' he says. 'Unless you're going to throw it at me, it's damn all use to you anyway.'

For some naive, stupid reason, she wants to believe his intentions. He had saved her after all. 'If that's true, let me see your face.'

After a brief pause, he sighs and lifts his head to look directly at her.

One word leaps to her mind — lethal. She knew he was deadly by the way he killed those men and his looks match that impression perfectly. She expected there would be something wrong with his

25

features; something to explain the mask, but he's still incredibly handsome.

Stray locks of hair fall over his face to slightly hide his deep blue eyes. A single black stud sits in each ear and a leather cord is wrapped around his neck with a pendant of some sort hanging from it. Screwed to the left side of his face is a large metal implant that trails down his forehead, surrounds his eye and ends at a point half way down his cheek.

Two scars mark his face: one curved scar running along his right cheek and another large Y-shaped one across the top of his nose and forehead. The large jagged scar across his throat explains the gravelly sound to his voice. Without the scars and metal, he could be described as model perfect but the flaws give him a darker, more dangerous edge. Nevertheless, she thinks he is stunning.

She dumbly stares at him as she struggles to form any coherent words. Terra scolds herself and tries to force her brain back on track. 'I guess I owe you a thank you for saving me back there.'

'Would have been better than a bullet.'

She cringes slightly at his words. 'I'm Terra Rush. And you are?'

The man furrows his brow and pauses for a moment. 'Gryffin,' he replies in a thick and husky voice before lowering his head again. 'The sedative I gave you causes dehydration. There's water in the other room. You should drink.'

Terra ignores his dismissal and silently watches as he digs the knife into his skin. After he struggles for a few minutes, she sighs. 'Let me do that for you. There'll be nothing left of your chest if you keep hacking at yourself.'

'I don't need your help.'

'That's a matter of opinion.' She holds out her hand for the knife. He slowly raises his head again and stares at her outstretched hand. 'For heaven's sake, I've already shot you. What else can I do?'

She knows he agrees when his shoulders drop slightly. 'Stand up so I can see the wound clearer.' He does as instructed and rises to his feet. Terra moves further into the room to face him and her breath lodges in her throat when she sees him clearly.

A thick, W-shaped plate of metal frames his broad, perfectly sculpted chest. The metal stretches from under each arm, down to his waist, and up the centre of his chest. Numerous scars pepper the skin surrounding the metal and continue down his arms. The large black wing of the griffin tattooed across his chest moves slightly as he takes a deep breath. The body of the creature covers his upper left arm with the other wing stretching across his back and the tail up the side of his neck.

He flips the blade in his metal hand and holds it out to her. She can't help but stare in wonder at the mechanical limb which stretches to just past his elbow and is roughly the same shape and size as a flesh arm.

'You just going to stare, or remove your bullet?' he asks.

'I'm sorry. I've just never seen a cyborg before. I didn't know they even existed.'

His hand lowers and she realises she's offended him. 'That came out worse than I intended.' She holds out her hand to take the knife from him. Terra searches the cupboards in the bathroom and finally locates a small and badly stocked first aid kit. Luckily it does have a pair of tweezers, so she places the knife on the sink behind her. She pulls on the rubber gloves and places one hand on his chest to steady herself, but he flinches and moves away like he's been struck.

'Don't touch me,' he growls.

Terra waves her arms in the air. 'Don't be ridiculous. How do you expect me to remove the bullet if I can't touch you? I can't magically teleport it from your body.'

His dark eyes lock onto her but he remains silent. Whatever his problem, he's clearly not going to be the one to back down. 'Fine. *I* won't touch you. Now, will you stand still so I can finish.'

Gryffin frowns but nods once. Terra pours some disinfectant over the wound before inserting the tweezers. 'So, have you always been …

like this?'

He clenches his metal fist and shakes his head. 'I don't do back-story.'

She blows out a breath. 'Chatty fellow, aren't you? You can't blame me for being curious.'

'Stop asking questions about me and remove the bullet or else I'll knock you out again and do it myself.'

Terra forces the tweezers into the wound a little harder than necessary. Gryffin grunts in pain and glares at her.

'So, why did you knock me out and bring me here?' she asks.

'Slavers always hunt in packs. More would have come and taken you. The sedative should have knocked you out for longer than it did. Mustn't have given you enough.'

'Judging by your first aid efforts, you're lucky I did wake up early.' She pauses as what he just said registers. 'Hold on — did you say slavers? Seriously?'

'Yes. That's why I had to kill them.'

The information sobers her. The Foundation warned them of the possible threats in the Sector, but never mentioned slavers. Then again, they also failed to mention attractive cyborgs in their briefings. 'Now I feel really terrible for shooting you.'

He shrugs and looks away from her. 'Sometimes it's best to shoot first.'

'Yes!' Terra exclaims suddenly. 'Found it.' She pulls the bullet from his chest and drops it in the sink. She cleans his wound the best she can by splashing it with the pathetic supply of antiseptic. 'You should live.'

She reaches out to place a bandage on him, but he steps back from her. 'Oh right. No touching. Bet that plays havoc with your love life,' she scoffs. His only response is to silently look down at her. She raises her eyebrows. 'Right. No talking or touching.' Terra shakes her head and throws the bandage on the seat. 'Cover that before it gets infected.'

Gryffin places the bandage over the hole and without a word of thanks, grabs his t-shirt from the back of the chair and pulls it over his head. He pushes past her and retrieves his jacket from the main room. 'Once I've gone, contact your people.' He points to a series of numbers stamped into the metal above the door. 'That's your location. Stay here until they come to collect you.'

'You're leaving?'

He pulls on his gloves and glances at her again. 'I can't be found with you.'

'I don't understand. You saved me — why can't you wait?'

He steps closer and his intoxicating scent of leather and soap assaults her. 'Do not move from this room alone. Understood?'

'Well, yes, but—'

Without another word, he opens the door and disappears.

∞

'You could have been killed! What the blazes were you thinking?'

Terra winces as Milla continues her rant. She can't blame her friend. Apparently, Terra had been missing for nearly two hours. Foundation search parties had been sent out to locate her, but instead they had found something else. A Foundation recon officer had been tortured and killed in one of the lower deck rooms. The crime scene was pretty horrific by all accounts.

If getting lost on the station wasn't bad enough, she had made matters worse by gladly telling everyone about Gryffin's rescue. Well, an edited version. She left out everything that happened after she woke up in the room. He clearly didn't want anyone to know what he looks like — the least she can do is respect his privacy after he saved her. She had hidden his knife under her coat, but completely forgot about the bullet in the sink. All she can do is hope Roman doesn't ask Milla to test it.

Even though she had left a lot of details out, her brief report had caused a stir on the station. Her best intentions seem to have been a waste of time. They knew exactly who had helped her.

She stares across at the landscape painting hanging on her wall in a vain attempt to push Gryffin from her mind.

'You're not even listening to me. Why do I bother?' says Milla.

'Sorry. I was miles away.'

'I can see that. I'm not going to repeat everything I said because you weren't listening.' She hands Terra a cup of peppermint tea. Milla's face loses all sign of its usual mischievousness. 'Seriously though, I can't help but worry, Terra. I know you can handle yourself but, as your friend, it's my job to worry about you. If that guy hadn't shown up when he did, you might not be here.'

Terra nods. Milla is right. 'I was lucky. Ouch! Hey, take it easy.'

'Oh quit complaining,' Milla says as she withdraws the needle from Terra's arm. 'The headache is probably a side-effect of whatever sedative he gave you. I'll rush your blood sample through testing so we can be sure.' Milla applies the ice pack to Terra's head. 'It'll help in the meantime.'

Terra pushes Milla's hand away. 'Quit fussing. I don't need that.'

'You promised to do as instructed. Otherwise, you'll be back in the med bay before you can put that cup down.'

'What happened to doctor compassion?'

Milla makes a face. 'It stays in the med bay, which is where you should be, but I'm not going to have that argument with you again. So, you think your rescuer killed the recon officer?'

Terra has been wondering that since she heard the news. She'd like to believe he wouldn't be able to commit such a horrific crime and then save her. In truth, she doesn't know anything about him. Maybe she just caught him in a good mood. 'I honestly don't know. I hope not. Sort of takes the heroism out of him saving me.'

At that moment, there is a knock on the door and Stanner pops his head around the corner. 'Roman wants us in his office now if you're up for it.'

'We'll be right there,' Terra responds

Milla looks at her and grins. 'Looks like we may get an explanation for what's going on around here.

Gryffin guides the small craft towards the cargo bay of *Ares*. As he approaches the location, the defences lower to allow him to pass through her cloaks. He could see his ship every day and not get tired of the sight of her.

Even though she was born out of many different, mostly stolen, parts of ships, Gryffin can't imagine a better looking craft. In this Sector, you had to adapt constantly or you died. The same applied to their vessels. Gryffin had personally acquired the latest addition — the cloaking system fitted to *Ares*. Over the last few months, the system has been copied and mounted on every ship in his fleet.

He flies over the large tiered viewing area at the back of the ship, lined with an array of different sized windows which house the central command deck, mess hall and his quarters. Her enormous metal sails rise from the top deck above the engine room, transport holds and the rest of the crew quarters.

His ship moves around the back of *Ares*, temporarily pushed off course by her large thrusters. He quickly guides the transport around the edge of the engine vents and up towards the cargo bay doors. A small smile pulls at his mouth as he passes under the watchful eye of his griffin symbol painted on the rear sail. Strange as it may sound, he hates leaving *Ares*. He considers her home — the only one he's really ever known.

Gryffin lands the transport in its allocated spot, then shuts down the controls and closes the outer bay doors. He opens the inner door and climbs out of the transport. The young officer on duty stops what he's doing as soon as he sees Gryffin and runs over to greet him. 'Sir, do you need any assistance?'

'No. Everyone back on board?'

'Yes, sir. You're the last.'

He exits the cargo bay, leaving the nervous officer staring after him. A few minutes later, he enters the command deck. He walks past the bank of computer screens and climbs up the steps to the control platform, where he expects to discover Klay, but he's not there. 'Where's Klay?'

'I thought he went with you,' the lieutenant at the helm says.

'On a solo mission?'

'My mistake, sir. When you were late, he mentioned he was going to locate you.'

Gryffin ignores the *late* comment. 'Is he on board now?'

'Yes, sir. All hands have reported in.'

'Take *Ares* away from here. Tell Klay the mission's done and he's to get up here now. He's in command for a few hours. I'll be in my quarters.'

The short walk along the corridor seems to take longer than usual, but eventually he's safe in his room with the door firmly locked behind him. Gryffin leans against the metal wall and rubs a hand over his face. He needs to be away from people for a bit. He's angry at himself and the last thing he wants is for his crew to be in the firing line when he's upset.

Why the hell did he let that woman see his face and tell her his name? Hundreds of people have asked his name. When faced with him, the first question was usually *'Who are you?'* He's never answered it, however. Not once, until her. It came out before he could stop it. He can't explain why he let his guard down. One moment of weakness and he's managed to put the whole damn ship and crew in danger. He shouldn't even have stopped and intervened in the first place.

No doubt she told the officials about him. Now they know he was on the station, which also means they know what he did.

The man he'd interrogated was a scout for the Foundation. As far as he could tell, he'd been in the area for a year gathering information on the different colonies and reporting back to the Foundation on their defences and numbers.

It took Gryffin three months to locate and track him down, but it had been worth it. After a one-to-one chat, the man confirmed his suspicions. The Foundation is going to make a move on the Sector. *Infinity* is here to recruit colonies and take away the independence people had come to enjoy. He couldn't let that happen, so after tracking him down to the station, Gryffin met him and did what he does best.

Having his group linked to the incident so quickly isn't part of the plan. Then again, neither is rescuing a Foundation member. He should be thinking about the problems he may have caused for his Nomad, but he can't stop thinking about her.

His chest tightens and he punches the wall to distract himself. The control implant in his brain is fighting for dominance. The programming heightens his aggression, turning him into a killing machine. Unfortunately, his creators didn't see the need to include an off switch. As a result, he always feels like a spring wound too tight, ready to snap at the slightest thing. Even now his eyes are more purple than blue — a sure sign he's not in complete control.

He pulls off his t-shirt to examine the fresh bullet wound. The shot missed his chest implant by a hairs-width. As long as he doesn't need repairs to the implant, he's happy. When he was in the lab, he endured enough modifications and repairs to last a lifetime. His captors carried out countless procedures to slowly modify him, cutting off bits of flesh to replace with metal.

And it wasn't due to any medical problem. It was done to cause him pain. The sadistic doctor in charge of the modifications wanted to see how the subjects would react to different pain stimuli, so anaesthetics were obsolete. He even went so far as to ensure the implants would neutralise any drug.

His chest tightens as the memories come back. He steadies himself against the wall and squeezes his eyes shut. He can feel the pain in his wrist even though it's no longer there. Feel the knife cut into his skin as they took his hand. Remember the smell of his rotting flesh as the open wound got infected, the poison spreading up his arm to his elbow, claiming more of his limb. Aftercare never rated high on the doctor's priority list. Gryffin forces himself to take slow deep breaths as he pulls himself back to the present.

He looks down at his relatively new arm. The limb may be the same shape as a real arm, but nothing can disguise the fact it's not flesh and blood. Like the rest of his implants, it serves as a constant reminder of a time in his life he'd give anything to forget.

Gryffin punches the wall with his flesh hand again and again, adding more dents to the already heavily damaged walls and not stopping until he leaves blood on the metal.

He flexes his fingers, letting the pain ground him. The sooner this day is over, the better. He showers quickly, wraps a makeshift bandage around his knuckles, then sits down at his desk to record his report. After he's finished, he realises he made no mention of Terra. It wasn't intentional. Maybe it's his subconscious telling him to keep it to himself. Who is he to argue?

∞

'I apologise for disappearing like I did before. We needed to search the station immediately,' the official informs them.

Stanner, Milla and Terra have gathered in Roman's office with the spokesperson for the station. Roman sits behind his desk with his well-practiced unreadable expression on his face. It's taking all of his self-control and training to keep his face neutral. He's still upset about the ambush on Terra. He'd be angry if it happened to any member of his crew, but to have it happen to her is more unsettling. He promised her father he'd take care of her.

The station spokesperson clears his throat while he waits for Roman to speak. Roman doesn't like the man. He reminds him of a rat; long pointed nose with over-sized ears and an annoying habit of twitching his nose. The thing baffling him is how a location in the state this one is in has a spokesperson in the first place.

Maybe attacks like this are commonplace so they needed someone to quench the flames afterwards. He doubts it though. The level of security has tripled in the station since Terra woke up and explained what happened. Checks were suddenly being run on every person and ship docking or departing. Something else must be going on besides a mysterious rescuer.

As much as he'd like to delay the man further, he'd also like to withdraw from the station as soon as possible. 'Start what search?'

The official sits back in the chair and mops his forehead with a tissue. 'Before I continue, can I be assured you will not let this incident damage our relations? This could destroy our reputation if word gets out.'

Roman bites the inside of his cheek, trying not to smile. Did he really think the station had a reputation to safeguard? 'I assure you the Foundation will do nothing to destroy your... reputation.'

'Good. Good.' He takes his handkerchief out of his pocket and mops his brow again.

Roman clenches his jaw. If this man doesn't start relaying some actual information, he is going to lose his temper. 'A Foundation representative is dead. Murdered on your station. Then an officer is attacked. I suggest you start talking right now.'

'Of course. My apologies, Captain. We completed a thorough examination of the crime scene and have only found one vital detail. Your man has an electrical burn to his arm.'

'He was electrocuted? How do you explain that? And what does that have to do with Lieutenant Rush?'

'The electrical burn, along with the way in which your woman was rescued, leads us to the conclusion that the Nomad leader is involved.'

'I need everything you have on this suspect. Give the information to my team when they examine the scene.'

'Of course. As long as I know in advance so I can arrange— '

'They're already on their way,' Roman interrupts.

'I would have appreciated if you had asked first.'

'The Foundation doesn't ask. You and these Nomad should get used to that.'

∞

Roman pours himself a cup of coffee and offers Stanner a chocolate muffin from his dwindling supply. Hiding his relief when Stanner refuses, Roman places the container on the highly polished wooden shelf that runs around the room. For a slight change of scenery, he sits on the couch in his office while Stanner occupies the single armchair to his right.

His people would need another few hours to process the murder scene. He had locked the ship down and sent two three-person security details with the processing team. After what happened to Terra, he isn't taking any chances.

'Is everything going to plan on the station?' he asks Stanner.

Stanner nods as he swallows his coffee. 'So far so good. The station agent is grumbling about the Foundation taking over, but he knows he has no choice.'

Roman grunts and takes a bite of his muffin. The official can complain all he wants. He has no choice but to allow them access to all information. 'Does Terra have any additional information?'

Stanner shakes his head. 'Nothing different from her initial report.'

'You pushed her hard? I know she went through a traumatic experience, but we need to be sure she's told us everything.'

'I pushed, sir.'

Roman nods. 'Well, the official seems less than eager to talk about this Nomad leader.' He takes a small bite of the muffin and tries to savour it as long as he can while the report loads on the screen in front of Stanner. 'Did you find anything?'

'Well, the Nomad group is led by a man called Gryffin,' Stanner reads. 'He's in his early- to mid-thirties.'

Roman frowns. 'Mid-thirties?'

Stanner nods. 'We are in the Outer Sector, sir. No rules out here.'

Roman shakes his head and gestures for Stanner to continue. 'Gryffin captains the Nomad flagship, *Ares*. Women aren't allowed under any circumstances, even on the ships as guests. They believe women bring bad luck to a vessel.

'Not much else is known about Gryffin and his Nomad. No one knows what they look like — or if they do, no one has spoken up. Like Terra reported, they wear a full-face metal mask when off their ships. There's only one photo of Nomad personnel on file. A colonist took it about a year ago.'

He turns the screen around so Roman can see the image. The colonist captured four men. Each one is dressed in black leather and any exposed skin appears to be covered in tattoos and piercings. Each man wears an almost robotic face with purple tinted eye shields and intercom links at either side of the mouth.

'Why the mask?'

Stanner scans through the report and snorts. 'Well, if you believe

38

this report, Gryffin has robotic elements to him. Reports range from a metal limb up to him being a full robot.'

That gets Roman's attention. 'Robotic? Did Terra notice anything robotic about him?'

'Nothing.'

'So, if they wear masks, we can presume the leader has distinguishable metal aspects to his face also. Any other intel?'

Stanner shakes his head and leans back in the brown leather chair. 'People don't defect, so there are no reports on how their ships operate. Without any other intel, we're in the dark, sir.'

'If we're in the dark, perhaps many of the colonists are too. We may be able to use that in favour of the Foundation. We can offer security they can't.'

'Yes, sir. I agree. Surely, the colonies will be eager for a bit of stability.'

'Report the findings to the Council. Any information they can dig up on this Gryffin and his group will be useful.' Stanner leaves him alone with the remains of his muffin. For some reason, he has no appetite for the rest of it. He can't say he's looking forward to meeting Gryffin.

∞

'I wondered how long it would take you to come and give your opinion on what happened.'

Terra steps away from the door to her quarters to let Stanner come in.

He sits down on the couch opposite her and shakes his head. 'I want to make sure you're okay. It sounds like you had quite a scare. I'm worried about you.'

'First Roman and now you? I'm all right.' She holds out her arms and slowly turns around. 'See. I can handle myself. You all seem to forget I went through the same initial training as you. Okay?'

Stanner stares down at his feet. 'I could have walked you back to the ship.' He meets her eyes again. 'I'm sorry, Terra.'

She brushes his apology away, hoping he'll leave. 'Yeah, well I didn't want to ruin your night.' *And you were the one I wanted to escape from,* she adds to herself.

Instead of leaving, he leans back in the chair and crosses his legs. 'I know you told Milla and the Captain this ... Gryffin guy didn't hurt you, but you can tell me the truth. I'm only here to support you.'

Terra wants nothing more than to have a hot shower and slip into bed. Continuing this conversation with Stanner is the last thing she needs. 'Hang on a sec. I am telling the truth. Where does this hurting me thing come from?'

'I wanted to make sure. He's a dangerous person.' Stanner narrows his eyes. 'He didn't do anything? No threats?'

Terra gets up, needing to put some space between herself and Stanner. She leans against the wall and crosses her arms. 'How many times do I have to say this? He didn't hurt me. Why is it so hard to believe he helped me?'

'You know what the Foundation says about the people out here. They don't do anything for free. What reason did he have to let you go?' Stanner turns and looks at her strangely.

'What?'

'Nothing.'

She shakes her head and laughs. 'You still don't believe me. What's so hard to understand? He didn't trick or threaten me. He didn't lure me into the area of the station. I got lost, got into trouble, and he helped me.' She crosses her arms and glares at him. 'So, are you saying he should have left me there? Thanks, Stanner.'

He gets to his feet and paces the area in front of her couch. 'I didn't mean that, Terra.' Stanner shakes his head and glances down at the table in front of him. He pushes some of the books out of the way and picks up a piece of paper. 'What the hell is this?' he demands.

Terra tries to grab the page from him, but he moves it out of her reach. 'Give it back, Stanner. It's private.'

'Private?' Stanner laughs harshly. He waves the page in front of her face. 'Is this him?'

Terra stares at the sketch unable to say anything. What possessed her to leave the page on her table? After what happened on the station, she needed to relax and sketching helps her unwind. She knew she was asking for trouble drawing someone as controversial as the most wanted Nomad Captain in the area but she couldn't help herself. She had to capture his face on paper while still fresh in her head.

He saved her life and in return, she betrayed him. She looks away from the picture and Gryffin's accusing eyes.

'I don't believe it. You told us he was wearing a metal mask. What the hell, Terra?'

'My picture is none of your damn business, Stanner. It's someone I met on the last colony.'

Stanner snorts. 'Do I look like I'm fresh from the academy? He's got metal on his face. You going to tell me there's more than one man running loose in the Sector with metal bits? I've spent the last half hour writing a report to the Council about this very person. It's Gryffin — isn't it?'

'Stanner, give it back!'

'Why the hell would you draw this and keep it from Roman? Why hide it?'

'I'm not hiding it.'

'So, I can give it to Roman?'

'No!'

Stanner steps right up to her. 'I can only think of one reason you'd have that reaction. You like him, don't you?'

Terra staggers. Her commanding officer catches her out in a big lie and his only concern is her attraction to Gryffin. He continues laughing to himself as he paces back and forth in front of the couch waving the page in front of her face. 'I knew you were hiding something,' he snarls, spit flying from his mouth. 'What the hell is going on in your head? He's a ... I don't know what he is. Even leaving all that aside, he's not Foundation. Never will be. How can you even possibly think like that about him?'

She turns quickly to face him. 'You really believe all the propaganda they feed us, don't you?'

He spins quickly and knocks her drawing pad off the glass table onto the floor. 'How can you say that? Of course I do. And so should you. You agreed when you joined.'

'Surely you must see it's not entirely correct. Their ancestors came from Earth like we did. They're no different from us.'

He storms over to the large floor-to-ceiling window beside her table 'Oh, come on. How can they not be different? The Foundation gives us all stability and structure. These people have been out here for two centuries with no governing body.'

Terra's mouth drops open. 'You should listen to yourself. They're not savages. They may not be used to the same structure, but that doesn't make them lesser people than us.'

Stanner turns away from the window and raises his voice. 'Enough! None of this matters. Best thing you can do is cease whatever this madness is and put things right.' He slams the crumpled drawing down on the glass table so hard her plate and cup rattle. 'You go to Roman with this picture in the next twenty-four hours or I will. If you do that, I may forget this conversation about your misguided ideas about this Sector.'

Terra walks to her door and thumps the control panel on the side to force it open. 'You get the hell out of my room now!'

'Terra, don't overreact.'

She crosses her arms over her chest. 'No, I understand perfectly, Evan. You decided to try your hand at blackmail. Leave now!'

'Think about what I said.'

Her only response is to close the door in his face and beat the metal where his head would have been.

Gryffin slowly paces back and forth on the rusty metal floor. The large overhead fans spin rapidly, rattling the lights hanging from the ceiling. He glances at the four men standing opposite him at the other side of the large, double-height room. Nomad line the mezzanine walkway circling the room. They've gathered to watch him spar these men.

He hates this part of his job. All new recruits had to battle for their place in the Nomad. It's been that way for hundreds of years and as much as he wants to, the Nomad would probably kill him if he scrapped it.

He silently assesses each of the men. They're young and a little too confident. They clearly think he's outnumbered. It is four against one after all, but he's not worried. It's not pride or smugness, but fact. He's a better fighter and he will win.

He's faced a lot of recruits like these — young men thinking they can win. Being a Nomad means more than having the ability to win a fight. He wants people who will fight for the Nomad whatever the odds, because they want to, not just to prove something.

Gryffin looks above him at the gathered Nomad. Credits pass hands as they place bets on how long the recruits will last. He suppresses a smile. None of them are betting against him. It would be a waste of credits.

Gryffin grits his teeth as the throbbing pain builds at the base of his skull. It spreads along the side of his head to reach his ocular implant. His vision swims briefly before it finally sharpens. He clenches his fists as the adrenaline rushes through his body to prepare him for the fight. He's still in control of himself, but it isn't a steady grip. The right thing to do would be to back away from this while he still can.

The decision is taken out of his hands as the largest of the four men suddenly lunges at him with the stick raised over his head. No amount of restraint can stop what happens next. Something clicks in Gryffin's brain and takes over, erasing all possibility of leaving. He stands firm as the man rushes him.

Gryffin waits until the last second to grab him by the arm and hurl him across the room as if he weighs nothing. The man hits the metal wall with a sickening crack of breaking bone before landing on the floor in a heap. The other men start their assault and rush at him all at once.

Gryffin sweeps the second man's legs from under him. He stands on his attacker's back and yanks the man's arm to the side. The man screams as his arm pops out of its socket. Like a predator after its kill, Gryffin targets the next one. He throws him over his shoulder and into the spiral metal stairs in the corner. Alone and face to face with Gryffin, the final man hesitates.

Without giving him the opportunity to run, Gryffin kicks him in the side of his leg and breaks his limb. Incapacitating the men doesn't stop him. He purposefully moves towards his first casualty. His ocular implant distorts his vision to blur out everything but his target.

Before Gryffin reaches him, a shot of energy hits him in the back, followed quickly by a second. He spins around and tries to charge his mechanical arm, but before he gets a chance, he is shot again. Gryffin falls to his knees and two sets of strong arms wrap around his upper body as they restrain his wrists behind his back. He fights against the restraints but is pushed to the ground and held down on his front by numerous bodies on his back. The metal restraints cut into his flesh wrist, but he doesn't stop. He can't stop.

They half carry, half drag him to a waiting cell and lay him on the ground. The Nomad hurry out and lock the door before he can rise. Gryffin scrambles to his feet and launches himself at the bars of the cell again and again. He fights to remove his restraints. Warm blood runs down his flesh hand onto the floor, but he doesn't care.

At that moment, the only thing on his mind is getting out of the restraints. Suddenly, a sharp pain hits him in the chest. He looks up at his captors and sees a gun pointing at him before the darkness claims him and he falls to the floor unconscious.

∞

Milla stares at the screen with her mouth open. Roman had ordered her to run a DNA test on the bullet found in the room with Terra.

Fully expecting the tests to reveal no DNA match, she had gone about her day and completely forgotten about the test results, only checking them a few hours later. The fact the system found a match surprised her, but when she saw the other results, she found herself frozen in place at the screen.

Finally pulling herself out of her daze, she contacts Roman, then sits at her screen and continues to stare at it until he arrives with Terra a few minutes later.

'I found this one loitering outside. What's so urgent, Doctor?'

Milla asks them both to sit down. 'I ran a test on the bullet from the Nomad that helped Terra and it showed up something …

unexpected.' Milla takes a long drink from her coffee, wishing more than ever she had added vodka to it. 'I'm not sure how to say this, sir.'

'I don't have all day to chat. Get on with it, Milla, or let me get back to work.'

'Sir, on second thoughts, maybe we should continue this in private.'

'For heaven's sake, tell me what you want to say. The results have apparently shown up something of interest so out with it.'

Milla pauses and tucks some hair behind her ear. 'Sir, I think it would be best to keep this off the record for a moment.'

He looks confused but doesn't argue. 'Off the record it is.'

She activates the screen on the wall, showing a picture of a striking dark-haired boy. 'The DNA from the round matches a missing person report from twenty-three years ago for a boy called Daegan Sawyer. His mother, Maggie, reported him missing after a transport accident when he was ten years old. No one ever saw him again.'

'I knew him. Well, his mother to be exact. His mother ... we were friends.' The realisation hits Roman's face all of a sudden. 'Hold on. Are you trying to say Gryffin is Daegan?'

'Yes, sir. The results are conclusive. There's more, sir.' Milla takes a deep breath before she continues. 'The DNA matches a member of the crew. It matches your DNA, Captain.'

'I don't understand.'

'Sir, Daegan or Gryffin, whatever his name is. He's your son.'

∞

Gryffin is pulled back to consciousness by the mother of all headaches. Through the pain, he's vaguely aware of voices in the background.

'How is he?'

'Think he's getting there. He should be coming around shortly.'

'Let me know when he does. We'll need to do more testing on him, try to discover the reason for the malfunctions.'

He tries to open his eyes, but his body refuses to do what he wants it to. Ignoring the conversation, he forces himself to breathe slowly through his nose. The cold metal floor presses against his face and the smell of blood hits his senses. He feels terrible. The implant still buzzes in the back of his head, but it's starting to give him back control of himself.

Bit by bit, the feeling returns to his limbs and after an enormous effort, he succeeds in moving his legs. It's a small victory but a victory at least. He tries to raise his head but doesn't get far, so slowly lowers it down onto the cold metal floor. Slow deep breaths help him push through the fog in his head.

Somehow, through the darkness, he hears one of the voices again. It's very faint and sounds like it's calling his name. It's a voice he recognises, so he puts all his strength into focusing on it and follows it back to consciousness.

Gradually it clears as he finally gets control of himself again. The pain in his head dulls to a more manageable level and he blinks a few times as his eyesight returns to normal, the edges of everything blurring slightly. As much as he hates the implant in his head, the only time his vision is perfect is when he lets it take partial control.

Still slightly groggy, he moves to rush his captor as soon as he hears the door being unlocked.

'Hold on, sir! It's me.'

'Chayse?' His voice is barely better than a croak.

'Yes, sir,' his aide replies. 'Take it easy for a minute. I'd prefer if you didn't kill me by mistake, sir.'

Gryffin tries to sort through what happened. He remembers being in the training room with some new Nomad recruits. They were about to spar but something happened. Gryffin squeezes his eyes shut and curses himself.

The damn implant had suddenly taken over and turned the recruits into enemies. He was sure they were going to strike him and his crew, so had to stop them. He hurt them...badly. The cocky newcomers may have thought they could win, but he had no intention of harming them.

He opens his eyes and looks at Chayse. He doesn't need perfect eyesight to recognise the worry on his aide's face. His stomach clenches as the increased silence confirms his suspicions. 'How bad is it?'

'Two concussions, a dislocated arm, broken leg, shattered ribs and a few bent fingers. But on the plus side, you got control again relatively quickly. And the recruits are still alive, so you did well.'

Gryffin takes a deep breath to push the queasy feeling aside. Not killing the men shouldn't be something he actually gets credit for. He reaches up with his metal arm and grabs onto the bars. It takes more effort than he'd like to admit to drag himself to his feet.

'Chayse, don't stand there. Help him.'

Gryffin doesn't look up as Klay walks into the room. 'I'm okay. Anyone else hurt?'

'You mean apart from you and the recruits?' Klay asks. 'No. Your wrist needs seeing to. It's a bloody mess again. On the plus side, this should be the last time we have to use those restraints on you. We're finishing testing a new set to restrain your whole arm instead of your wrist. Keep going like this and you'll lose your other hand.'

Gryffin doesn't listen to Klay. The state of his wrist is the least of his worries. Standing on his own would do him for now. He leans heavily against the cell wall before he finally stands upright. 'I'll be on the command deck in twenty minutes. Make sure the reports I requested are ready.'

'Afraid not. You'll be in the sick bay in twenty minutes. Don't even think about arguing because you don't have a choice,' Klay continues, cutting off Gryffin before he can speak. 'Patch your wrist and run a full set of scans first and then you can return to work. Not my rules. You want to argue with Rayde, go ahead.'

Knowing he has no choice, he nods. He doesn't have the energy to fight and Klay could continue like this all day. Gryffin may be captain, but Klay has the unofficial authority to make his life hell if he refuses medical treatment. Whether he'd tell Rayde he refused treatment or not is another story.

As the retired high commander of the Nomad fleet, Rayde's rules are still law. Gryffin considers the man a father figure. Rayde rescued him from the lab, trained him and worked alongside him until he retired last year and appointed Gryffin as the new high commander, Klay knows by threatening to go to Rayde, Gryffin will listen. He nods and takes a step forward, but has to grab onto the bars as his legs go from under him.

'Sir, stay where you are. I'll help.'

One glance from him has Chayse backing away. 'Don't touch me. Twenty minutes.' Gryffin practically stumbles into the cage-like lift which takes him up to the walkway surrounding the room. He steps out onto the walkway and leaves the room without another word.

His mind races as he clumsily winds his way through the ship, not really paying attention to where he's going. His footsteps sound loudly on the metal gantry floor as he tries not to crash flat on his face. Bracing his metal arm against the wall, he manages to stay upright as he slowly climbs a set of steps leading to the next deck.

He loses his footing at the top and lands heavily on one knee. Cursing, he looks behind him to make sure no one saw, but he's alone. The shadows cast from the light seeping through from the level below, are his only company in the gloomy corridor. Not that he's ever alone, thanks to the implant. The implant's buzzing continues in the back of his head like an annoying voice, nagging him, taunting him.

He pushes himself to his feet and forces one foot in front of the other. The gloomy interior of the ship matches his already foul mood. Like all Nomad ships, *Ares* had started her life as a standard cargo vessel, but after they had acquired her, she had been severely modified to suit their needs. Gryffin has a lot in common with *Ares*: both were unwillingly adapted and modified for battle, although she's coped with the alterations a lot better than he has. At least she doesn't malfunction and attack the crew.

Ares has served the team well and has done whatever they have asked of her, performing better than some of the newer ships in the fleet. He looked after her as best he could, but unfortunately she had suffered a bit over the years. When times were bad a few years ago they had to sell whatever they could in order to buy food, including pieces of her. The interior walls had been stripped of all metal panelling, leaving her steel skeleton exposed.

Now he's the one feeling exposed. He sits at the bottom of the next flight of steps and puts his head in his hands. He hates feeling weak like this. Having to rest before going up some steps is pathetic. He closes his eyes and his mind drifts back to the training room. Maybe he was a bit hard on the four men. They certainly weren't the worst recruits and he didn't give them much of a chance to prove themselves. Usually, he'd toy with them for at least ten minutes before breaking a bone.

Unfortunately for them, their place in the med bay was secured as soon as he lost control. Having the commanding officer beat a recruit on the first day didn't help cement any feelings of loyalty. Earning their trust after what he did won't be easy.

Eventually, he gets enough strength to stand and finally reaches his quarters. He locks the door behind him and pulls off his clothes before walking into the small bathroom — one of the few perks he has as captain. Unlike the rest of his crew's quarters, his are stark in comparison. No photographs of partners or family are hanging from his walls. No mementoes of special people or places line his shelves. He doesn't see the need or point in keeping useless objects as reminders. He's seen people lose all their belongings when an enemy attacks. You can't replace years of memories and trinkets once they're gone. He can't understand why people put themselves in that situation. He keeps what he needs from day to day — nothing more. After all, that's all anyone can plan for. The past is gone and the future may not come. All anyone has is today.

He turns the shower on and leans heavily on the sink while the water reaches the correct temperature. That last episode has left his wrist a bloody mess of torn skin. Klay's right — if he keeps using those restraints, he will lose his hand. He grabs a roll of bandage from above the sink and quickly wraps it around his wrist. It'll do until he goes to see Klay. He looks longingly towards the shower stall, the glass sides steaming as the water temperature increases. He steps under the spray and lets the hot water work into his sore muscles.

Terra takes a deep breath and knocks on the door to Roman's office. After a brief pause, he lets her in. As usual, he is sitting behind his desk, focused on the screen.

She casts her eye over the bound leather books lining the wall as she quietly waits for him to finish his task. Roman had challenged her to read the entire book collection by the time they completed their mission. So far she's read three. Only forty-odd left to go. She couldn't even pretend to read them, as Roman tested her knowledge of the novels.

Noticing his lone plant is withering, she picks up the jug of water from behind his desk.

'It might be best if you adopt that thing.'

Terra laughs. 'You're the captain of a ship. Why does a plant intimidate you so much?'

He glances up at her before looking back at his work. 'I'm not intimidated. We have the perfect relationship. The plant wants to die and I am allowing it.' He pushes his computer away and rolls his shoulders. 'How are you feeling?'

She smiles and sits on the edge of his desk. 'I'm good.'

Roman swivels his chair around and takes two cups from the shelf behind him. 'You had me worried for a bit, Terra. I'd appreciate if you didn't do it again.' He winks as he fills the cups with tea and passes one to Terra. 'So, in the future you'll keep a better track of where you're going.'

Terra rubs the back of her neck. 'That would probably be a good idea. I'm a Foundation officer. I shouldn't have lost my way.'

Roman peers into his tea and shrugs. 'Move past it, Terra. I'm glad nothing more serious happened to you.'

'Thanks to Gryffin. It would have been a very different story if he didn't show up. I still find it difficult to believe there are such things as slavers.' She removes a dead leaf from the plant. 'He saved me from being sold. Doesn't bear thinking about.'

Roman shifts in his seat and nods. 'His one and only honourable deed.'

'There's no proof of that.'

'He saved you by killing your attackers. Not exactly a vote of confidence.' Roman slides a module across the desk to Terra. The picture of Gryffin as a child fills the screen. 'An innocent ten-year-old boy disappears for twenty years, then reappears in a different Sector and is ... for want of a better word, a cyborg. What the hell happened, Terra? What changed the child into the fugitive in these reports?'

'I wish I had the answers for you. I can't imagine how you feel. You do have a son, however. Surely that's something to be thankful for?'

Roman shakes his head. 'Is it? Why didn't Maggie tell me about him? Maybe I could have ...'

'Don't do that to yourself.' Terra scolds. 'You've always told me there's no point regretting. You can't know if things would have played out differently if you were there. All you can do is start from this point with him.'

'We both know that can't happen. Besides, Maggie made her

decision. I have to respect that.' He laughs to himself. 'Gryffin.'

'Sorry?'

'His name. Maggie loved mythology, especially the griffin. I even bought her a platinum griffin pendant for our first anniversary. Surely it can't be a coincidence he chose that name.' He turns from the window and lowers himself into his leather chair. 'Well, I guess I'll never know. Now, Lieutenant, as much as I'd love to chat all day, you have work to do.'

There's no putting it off any longer. Knowing Stanner, he will hold to his side of the threat. It would do severe damage to her relationship with Roman if she didn't give him the drawing personally. Keeping the picture to herself for this long is going to cause enough problems between them without getting Stanner involved. 'Sir, I have a picture — a drawing of Gryffin's face.'

His face loses all signs of the mirth it showed mere seconds ago. Roman transforms from a father figure to a stern captain in front of her eyes. 'You have a what?'

She puts the drawing face down on his desk. 'I ... I drew this, sir, after the station.'

He leans back and crosses his arms defensively. 'And you're giving me this now because ...? Before you answer, you're doodling on my desk with your finger. You only do that when you're nervous.'

She quickly pulls her hand back onto her lap. There goes any chance of showing him she could do the right thing. 'Commander Stanner found it, sir.'

Roman nods. 'I see. Let me guess, he threatened to tell me if you didn't.' He stands up and looks down at her. 'I don't need to tell you how disappointed I am.'

She cringes under his icy blue glare. The bitter disappointment is clearly visible. 'No, sir.'

'You told me you didn't see his face, only the metal arm. You lied to me.'

'I apologise, sir.'

'I don't want to hear it! You're excused.' Terra reaches out to take the drawing. 'Leave it.'

Terra stands up and leaves the room. In the space of a few minutes, she's betrayed Gryffin and let her captain down.

∞

When the door closes behind Terra, Roman curses himself and wipes a hand over his face. Terra didn't deserve that. She lied to him and then kept the picture to herself, but she didn't disappoint him.

Emotions seem to be running wild at the moment. For some reason, Gryffin is throwing things off balance. What should be a simple colonisation is turning into a battle. Terra is even breaking the rules.

He picks up the picture and turns it over. As usual, Terra's artwork is spectacular and very detailed. His superiors will no doubt be able to use the likeness to help unearth the Nomad leader. Roman places the drawing face up in front of him. His mind wanders back to the one and only time he had met Maggie's eldest son. He had joined them on a family picnic at the beach when the boy was about nine years old. Roman rubs his eyes. It was only a few months before he disappeared for two decades.

Roman gets to his feet and stands at the window. He leans on the metal ledge and stares out at the blackness. If he sends that picture to the Council, they will use it to capture the Nomad leader and put him on trial for piracy. He would spend the rest of his days on one of the prison moons. If the Council thought he was an unusually high threat, he would be executed immediately.

Roman turns and looks at the drawing of his son. He then looks at the file of the murdered Foundation officer next to it. Son or not, Gryffin tore that man to pieces. Roman wouldn't be able to live with himself if he walked away. He would be doing the officer, the colonists, and the Foundation a disservice by letting this criminal go free.

Before he can change his mind, Roman scans the picture and sends it to Admiral Balfe.

He leans closer to the screen and studies the image of his ten-year-old son. He looks so young and innocent. What happened to him to turn him into the scarred murderer in Terra's drawing? If Milla hadn't run this test, Roman would have carried on oblivious to his son's existence for the rest of his life.

Maggie apparently didn't want him to be a part of his life. She'd made that decision from the very start. Roman will never know why she cut him out. The only thing he knows is he's going to respect her wishes. With only a slight hesitation, he deletes the results of the DNA test. It never happened.

∞

This is bad.

No matter how he looks at it, that one thought keeps popping to the front of his mind. Admiral Hank Avoca sits at his desk in the lavish office appointed to him, staring at the screen in front of him. Mere minutes ago, he had a good position in the Foundation, a loving wife, two fantastic children, and a secure future. But after one communication, he feels as if his whole world is starting to slip away from him. It's strange how things can spin upside down in no time.

The file on his screen had been unopened for years. At the time, the group decided not to delete it. A foolish idea, in Avoca's eyes. Why not delete it and be done with it? Why let the noose dangle in front of them? They overruled him, of course. They didn't think anyone would ever need to access it again. Why would they? The chances of survival were non-existent.

If that were the case, why had someone from *Infinity* accessed the missing persons report a few minutes ago? The crew would have no need to search randomly through files. As one of the further out ships, surely they would have more important things to spend their time doing.

Avoca pulls open the bottom drawer of his antique desk and takes out a large bottle of Scotch. His secretary gave it to him on his last birthday. For eight months, the bottle has remained in the drawer. He isn't a big drinker, enjoying the occasional glass with friends and family. He never understood people who would laze at their desks and drink alone. It never appealed to him.

Three glasses later, he doesn't feel as sad and pathetic as he did. He'd nothing to feel ashamed about — well, not on the drinking alone side. He could barely keep the door to his closet closed due to the amount of skeletons inside.

In fact, he is surprised they don't jump out and batter him regularly. So far, he's managed to live with the secrets and lies, but he knew they would come out sooner rather than later. What then? Well, his career would be over. His wife would divorce him and take the children. His life would be ruined.

Filling his glass for the fourth time, he considers his options. Not that there are any. He can't come clean about what he did. Disappearing isn't an option either. What would he say to his wife? *Sorry, we have to abandon everything we've known, vacate our house, leave friends and family. I have to run from something illegal and morally questionable I got involved in. And no, I can't tell you any more as it would endanger you all too.*

No, unfortunately, his only option is to keep his mouth shut and pretend to go with the crowd on this one. He's got contingencies in place to cover him, but that doesn't help settle the feeling of fear. Whether positive or negative, he's not alone in this mess. His colleagues will want to start the project again, drag him back into something he didn't really wish to be a part of in the first place. At the time, he understood the necessity and why they were doing it, but not anymore. There's no backing out though. If he pulled out now, it would do more than spell the end of his career. The other members of the group may even have him killed. If they thought he posed a threat, it would be a definite possibility. He checks the report again in case he made a mistake. A feeling of dread settles in his stomach as he accepts the inevitable. If the *Infinity* crew searched for that particular report, it can only mean one thing.

Daegan Sawyer is alive.

∞

Balfe sits back in his chair, clasps his hands in front of him, and smiles widely. The report from Roman is open on his screen. He couldn't have planned this better if he'd tried. By killing a Foundation recon officer, this Nomad brought himself to the attention of the Council.

That one act should be enough to force the Council to respond. All things going to plan, the full might of the Foundation should be heading towards the Outer Sector within a few weeks. He forwards his report to the Council. Now all he has to do is wait.

He pours a cup of coffee and looks out the window, over the grass to the ocean beyond. The large harbour, a stone's throw from the Council offices, houses his private yacht. He plans on spending his retirement on that yacht. First, he has to bring the Outer Sector back under Foundation control — fast.

His radio sounds, signalling another message. Feeling a little unsettled, he opens the transmission. His smile falters when he sees the drawing. His cup slips from his hand, spilling coffee on his desk.

It can't be. There's no possible way.

He gets up and paces his office. Not caring that it's only half-past-ten in the morning, he grabs a glass of vodka, downs it in one, then turns back to the screen.

Damn it. It's one of them. There's no mistaking that ocular implant. The metal was designed to link to the subject's brain and optic nerve. It was the first major procedure carried out and the one that claimed the most lives.

He examines the drawing closer. The individual design of the metal is familiar. He saw the subject after he had the implant screwed into his skull. A million questions fly through his head, the main one being how the hell did he survive? He should have died when the station exploded. Then it hits him: the project succeeded.

The sinking feeling he had a moment ago dissipates. The fact this man is still alive proves that. This Nomad leader is the result of years of work and he's sent the Council after him. Cursing himself, he clicks on his outgoing messages, hoping that by some strange twist of fate, his message would still be there. But it's not. For the first time, he wishes Foundation technology wasn't so dependable.

If he had received the transmission with the drawing first, he would have kept everything to himself. Give them time to see what they could resurrect from the original brief. Now, though, they were against the clock. The Council would want to arrest or kill the Nomad leader, but he needed him to complete the project.

He reaches for the decanter and after emptying his glass twice, he curses loudly and throws the glass against the wall. He can't believe this is happening. This Nomad leader is the very thing he doesn't want the Council to acquire, but, without knowing it, he had sent the Council after that very person.

If they capture him, Balfe is finished. The only way out is to get to him before the Council does. How is he meant to get the Nomad into custody without involving the Council? From the looks of the report, the Nomad leader would not be easy to capture. If he even got a sniff the Foundation was on his tail, he'd be next to impossible to catch.

There's also the chance of the Nomad leader coming after Balfe if he found out. No doubt he had quite a few bad memories of what happened years ago. If he decides he wants revenge of some sort, Balfe could be targeted. There's no way he would risk his life for this. Power is all well and good, but means nothing if he is dead.

Roman clenches his jaw and stares at the computer screen. 'I don't think that's the best course of action. Did you not read the report from the station officials?'

The no-nonsense face of his commanding officer stares back at him. His expression is completely unreadable as usual, apart from a slight twitch at the corner of his left eye. It's the only sign he's upset at Roman. 'Yes, Captain. I did read the report, but I'm beginning to wonder if you did.'

'Excuse me, sir?'

'I apologise if I gave you the impression you had any choice in the matter,' Balfe replies. 'It's an order, Captain. Are we clear?'

Roman struggles to relax his jaw. 'Yes, sir. Of course.'

'Good. Now I've sent you details of the bounty on his head. Use this along with the drawing you have. Do whatever you deem necessary to capture him. Keep me up to date with your progress. The Council has put me in charge of this matter, so only report to me. We must remove the Nomad leader before we can proceed with our plans, or do you suggest we let people take their chances with an outlaw running free?'

'No sir, I'm not suggesting that.'

'Good. Do not let us down.'

The screen goes blank and Roman pounds his fist against the desk in frustration. Do not let us down. Even though the *or else* at the end wasn't voiced, he heard it as clear as day. His career is on the line if he doesn't address the issue. And in this case it will be next to impossible to accomplish that. How the hell is he supposed to deliver Gryffin?

He rises from his desk and rolls his shoulders, trying to ease the tension that built up over the course of the conversation. Pouring himself a cup of coffee, he walks over to the small porthole and looks out at the lights running down the length of *Infinity*'s hull. He takes a long drink and grimaces when he realises the coffee is cold. He puts the cup back on his desk. Of course it's cold. The call with Admiral Balfe had lasted for half an hour.

As per protocol, he had recorded his report on what happened at the station, along with any information he had received on Gryffin. He didn't expect a reply so fast, and certainly not from an admiral. Usually, the reports are checked by lower ranking officers who then filter out the relevant information.

The fact his assessment hit an admiral's desk within an hour of it being transmitted made him uneasy. The murder of an officer wouldn't instantly attract the attention of someone like Balfe. What did they see that he didn't? He couldn't imagine what the Foundation was expecting *Infinity* to do. Collectively, the Foundation could overcome the Nomad, but alone he's not too sure.

Too much about this didn't add up. It is a risky and unnecessary move. Much like poking a stick at a hornets' nest. He runs a hand back and forth over his cropped hair. Orders are orders, though, and he will have to dismiss his doubts. He has never disobeyed an order and he isn't about to start now. He'd have to put his faith in the Foundation. Balfe didn't have to explain himself, or the reason behind why the Foundation chose to target Gryffin. Roman hopes, when faced with the decision, he will be able to carry out his orders and bring his son in.

∞

Without saying a word, Gryffin enters the med bay. He looks away from Klay and Chayse, ignoring the relief on their faces. He pulls off his shirt, lies back on the bed, and stares at the ceiling. He hates the fact he took so long to get himself together.

He runs a hand through his wet hair and focuses his attention on one of the metal panels on the roof as Klay and Chayse start working. As soon as they touch his chest implant he wants to scream for them to finish. Trying to push back the panic, he clenches his jaw as the two men carefully start attaching the cables to his implants.

They know he hates anyone touching him — especially his chest — and do their best to make the procedure as quick as possible. That doesn't make him feel any better. Most days he can detach himself from what they are doing, almost like he's separated himself from his body. Years of painful surgeries in the lab gave him plenty of practice, but not today for some reason. Today he's stuck firmly in his body as they shove needles and wires into him.

Klay moves to the computer screen as Chayse finishes pushing connectors into Gryffin's chest. Gryffin watches in morbid fascination as the cables disappear into his flesh to connect with his internal components. Klay is working in silence, but Gryffin knows it's not going to last. Every few minutes Klay glances at him as if he wants to say something but keeps changing his mind at the last minute. 'Are you going to spit it out?'

'Spit what out?'

'Cut the crap, Klay.' He winces as the scan starts, but not because it hurts. The idea of having information from his internal implants displayed on the screen makes him feel uneasy, vulnerable, and more like a machine than a man.

Klay looks up at Chayse. 'You're dismissed.'

Gryffin shakes his head. 'He's got a job to do. The sooner he does what he needs to, the sooner I can leave.'

'Fine. What happened on the station, sir?'

'It's in my report.'

'I meant the part that's not in your report. The part about the Foundation. And before you say anything, I heard the ensign talking to you.'

He clenches his fists. 'It's none of your damn business!'

'With all due respect, to hell with that, sir. If it affects the ship, crew, or you, it is my business. You went to that station for a particular purpose. You carried that out, then disappeared for nearly an hour.'

Chayse slowly steps away as he tries to make his escape, but one glance from Gryffin changes his mind. 'So you're keeping tabs on me now? Funny, I thought you all answer to me, not the other way round.'

'We do, but this is different. Did the mission go to plan?'

Gryffin clenches his jaw and forces the answer out. 'Yes.'

'Did he have anyone with him? Anyone see you?'

'I covered that when I said it went to plan.' He glares up at Chayse. 'Are you done?'

'Another few minutes, sir.' Chayse quickly concentrates on what he's doing.

Klay takes the bandage from around Gryffin's wrist and cleans the wound. The silence continues, but Gryffin knows better. Klay's not finished yet. Sometimes he can be like an irritating dog with a bone.

'Captain, I monitored your vitals while you were on the station. I noticed a spike in your heart rate and breathing for a few seconds and then everything returned to normal. You fought someone.'

Gryffin looks back to the ceiling and glares at the little round lights as if everything is their fault. That bloody wireless monitor behind his ear is becoming the bane of his life. They fitted it a year ago to keep an eye on his vitals so they'd know when he was about to lose control.

While it seemed like a good idea at the time, he's seriously having second thoughts now. It does help by either getting him to a cell in time, or the team secured away from him, but it also gives Klay a little bit too much insight. By monitoring his heart rate, breathing, and other vitals, he can pinpoint what Gryffin is doing.

He absently runs his hand through his hair, touching the small implant behind his right ear, tempted to rip it from his skin. Before he does anything drastic, he puts his hand firmly back on the bed beside him. No point endangering his crew because he's pissed off.

'Sir?'

He looks over at Klay again, remembering he had asked him a question. 'Yes. I fought someone.'

'And ...'

'And I won.'

Klay shakes his head and sighs. 'I didn't doubt that. What's that have to do with the Foundation?'

'Slavers were attacking a Foundation woman. I killed them.'

Klay stands up and paces the room. Gryffin glances over at the screen. The blurred figures would mean nothing to him even if he could see clearly, but he needs something other than Klay to focus on. 'Did she see your face?'

'I'm not answering any more questions.'

'You used your electricity, didn't you, sir?'

Gryffin clenches his jaw and tries to stay calm. Chayse stands at the other side of Gryffin, aware of the storm about to erupt.

'She saw you right? I mean, saw what you did, how you killed them?'

Gryffin says nothing.

'If you did use it, we're in trouble. You know that, right? Unless there's another six-foot-six man who can shoot electricity from his arm. What if they know you were there and you killed the scout? Do you have any idea of the shitstorm you could've landed us— '

64

Gryffin's broad black blade embeds itself in the wall inches to the side of Klay's head. As Klay stares at the knife open-mouthed, Gryffin sits up, causing the alarms to go off on the machines as some of the wires dislodge. 'I am still the captain of this ship!' The practiced lack of emotion in his voice is harder to maintain than usual.

Klay tears his eyes away from the knife and looks at his captain. 'I didn't mean any disrespect. I'm just confused you didn't kill her. It's procedure.'

'You stupid enough to argue with me?'

Klay stays quiet.

Gryffin addresses Chayse, not taking his eyes off Klay. 'Go!' Once he's gone, Gryffin steps closer to Klay. 'Don't ever speak to me like that, especially in front of the crew. You do that again and I'll personally put a bullet in your head.

'As for the Foundation, I know I should have killed her, but I couldn't. I'm not a god-damn monster. I completed my mission and that's all you need to know. We've had unwanted attention on us in the past. We'll deal with it, if and when it becomes an issue.' He pulls the leads from his implants and throws them towards the bed. 'Where were you when I was on the station?'

'Sir?'

Gryffin steps closer to his second-in-command. 'Where. Were. You?'

Klay turns away and begins tidying the equipment into drawers. 'In engineering, sir.'

Gryffin crosses his arms as he looks down at Klay. 'They told me you left to search for me.'

Klay keeps his eyes averted as he turns off the monitoring equipment. 'You were misinformed, sir.'

Gryffin grunts and picks up his t-shirt. As he's putting it back on, he notices Klay glance down at the tablet with the readings from his monitoring device. He grabs the tablet from Klay's hands and looks down at the information. 'This telling you I'm about to lose my temper?'

'No, sir. All your levels are normal.'

He gives the tablet back to Klay and looks down at him 'It's malfunctioning.'

Klay closes his mouth and looks away from him, admitting defeat. Feeling satisfied, almost like he's won a battle, Gryffin walks away.

Roman is not looking forward to this conversation. No getting around it, however. He may not be overly comfortable with his orders, but his crew aren't going to know that. Unfortunately, he needs to take care of one small matter before he can address them.

'I've been ordered to take Gryffin in.' Roman leans back in his seat and watches as Terra and Milla assimilate the information.

'Why are they interested?' Terra asks.

'Why?' Roman stands up and runs a hand through his hair, barely keeping all the stress from the last few days under wraps. 'I'll tell you why. They're interested because the Nomad killed a Foundation member. From the report I saw, *killed* is the wrong word. He tortured him before eventually ending his life. He's also being blamed for the attacks against us. They're after his head. Balfe wants us to deliver him and I can't find a valid reason not to do as ordered.'

'You're going to do it?'

'Of course I am, Terra. It's an order.' His voice softens as he sits on the edge of the table next to Terra. 'Listen, I know you may think this is unfair and Gryffin isn't a threat, but it looks like you're wrong. He squeezed the bones in the recon officer's legs and arms until every one broke. He left the mark of his handprint on each of his limbs. He then gouged out his eyes and stabbed him numerous times before cutting his throat.' The silence stretches on for a moment as Terra reads the report. He can see the doubt in her eyes and knows she will not be able to keep her feelings to herself.

'But, sir— '

He slams his hand on the table in front of her. 'Damn it Terra, this is not a debate!' He slides the incident report across his desk. 'It makes interesting reading. To summarise, all evidence points to this Gryffin person. Guilty or not, the Foundation wants to talk to him.'

'What do you need from us?' Milla asks before an argument breaks out.

'I need your silence. I don't want you to mention anything about the test results. They didn't happen, understood?'

'You mean the test results you deleted behind the ship doctor's back,' Milla says.

He fixes her with an icy stare, but as usual it has no effect on her. 'I'm not going to explain myself.'

'I guessed you wanted everything erased, so I double checked. The system's clean. Never thought I'd be reporting that to you.'

Roman flashes a small sad smile. 'You're not alone there, Doctor.'

Terra sits down on one of the chairs opposite his desk. 'So the plan is that you want us to lie?'

'You're not going to tell me you don't lie, Lieutenant, are you?' Her face drops at his comment. Roman quashes the pang of guilt that hits him. 'It's not that black and white, Terra. I don't think it would be wise to alert the Foundation to this. I don't want to open myself up to that sort of scrutiny. What if they decide to remove me from command because they believe I'm emotionally involved in this? At least if it's *Infinity* charged with the task, I can make sure he's taken into custody without causing any harm to him or his ship. There are other captains that may not be so gentle with him.'

Terra looks over at Milla, a questioning expression on her face. Milla nods at her. Terra turns to Roman and clears her throat. 'You have our co-operation and support, sir.'

'Good. Milla, can you excuse us for a moment?' He keeps his eyes focused on the view outside his porthole until he hears the door shutting behind Milla. 'Are you with me on this, Terra?'

'Of course, sir.'

'I mean it. I need to know if we capture him you'll behave yourself. The last thing I need is trouble from you. This whole thing is messy enough as it is, without having to worry about my crew adding to it. Keep away from him.'

Terra looks at the pictures of the recon officer's body again. 'He's a threat to the Foundation. I promise you won't have anything to worry about from me.'

'Dismissed.' He watches as she leaves the room without a backward glance, knowing she won't be able to keep her promise.

∞

'No way, Terra. Not going to happen.'

Terra sits down on Milla's desk. 'Please, Milla. You know I wouldn't ask unless it was an emergency.'

Milla snorts. 'Digging up information on the Nomad leader is hardly an emergency. If Roman finds out, he'll kill you.'

Terra lowers her gaze. 'I know. But I can't sit back and let this happen. Surely you must be curious about him too?'

Milla chews on her bottom lip. 'That's below the belt, Terra. You know I'm interested, but accessing his medical records is breaking the law.'

'Not quite. I checked his personnel records. When they couldn't locate him, the Foundation declared Daegan dead. Technically, it's not entirely breaking the law.'

'Right.' Milla crosses her arms. 'I'll remember that one when the Foundation arrests me for tampering with confidential records. Why is this so important to you?'

'Leaving aside what Gryffin did for me, he's Roman's son. I need to uncover what happened to him. And there's the whole cyborg mystery. What if someone did that to him against his will?' She pulls a small tablet from her pocket. 'I've managed to uncover something interesting.' Terra hands the tablet to Milla. 'According to this, Daegan or Gryffin has a younger half-brother called Brayden. There's five years between them. Maggie and her new husband, Brayden's father, died in a transport accident twelve years later.

'He was raised by his aunt and uncle for a while, then his paternal grandparents took him in, but after they died a few years ago, Brayden vanished. He left the colony and disappeared. It also seems someone erased Daegan from Brayden's records for some reason. There are a lot of secrets surrounding Maggie and her sons. We both know how much you love a real mystery. We need to do more digging.'

'Yeah, I like the way you said *we*.' Milla sighs and slumps back into her chair. 'If I get into trouble, I'll direct them to you — got it?'

Terra hugs her friend quickly. 'Deal.' She pulls up a chair and manoeuvres herself closer to Milla.

'What? You want me to do it now?'

Terra smiles. 'No time like the present.'

∞

Chayse looks at the information on the screen for the tenth time and frowns. It's not right. He doesn't know what, but something is off with the readings from Gryffin's last scan.

'What are you doing?'

'Commander Klay.' It's too late to hide what is on the screen. 'I'm looking at the results from the Captain's last scan.'

Klay pulls the pad away from Chayse and turns it off. 'I told you

70

not to look at that information.'

'I know, sir, but...'

'But you felt like disobeying an order?' He smashes the tablet against the corner of the desk. 'You may be a lowly aide Chayse, but the rules apply to you too.'

Chayse doesn't let the snide remark throw him off track. 'I'm aware of that, sir, but something seems wrong with the results. Some of the readings don't make sense.'

'Thanks for your expert opinion. I don't want anyone else looking at these. Do you have any idea what it would mean if these results got into the wrong hands? What it could mean for the captain?'

'Yes, I understand, but if there's something wrong with the captain, we need to help him.'

Klay stands right in front of Chayse and prods him in the chest with his finger. 'Now you listen to me. You are stepping way outside your area. You are Gryffin's aide, nothing more. Your job is to vocalise reports for him, make sure he's got food and weapons, train with him, and do anything else he needs you to. Leave the more complicated things to me.'

Chayse gets up and looks down at Klay. 'I'm a fully trained engineer, sir. I understand machinery.'

'I'm sure the captain would appreciate you calling him a machine.'

'That's not what I meant. I'm saying you should use my expertise.'

'I think I'll manage. I've known Gryffin a hell of a lot longer than you have. We've been in many battles together and I've patched him up more times than I'd like to admit. I know his implants. I know how unpredictable they are. Readings vary from day to day. You've got to trust I know what I'm doing.

'Hell, Gryffin does, and you don't want to start questioning him on how he does things, or you might notice your career, if you could call it that, is quite a bit shorter than you planned.' Klay walks towards the door. 'Hadn't you better check the captain's not hungry, or something like that?'

The doors close with an ominous clank behind Klay. Chayse drops onto his seat and rests his head on his arms. Klay's right. What the hell did he think he would achieve by questioning Klay? Klay is the first officer and he's a glorified errand boy.

From the first day he met Klay, he knew they weren't going to gel. He has no problem with Klay, but Klay has an intense dislike for him, and he has no idea why. He always did his job and never stepped out of line. Well, not until today.

Unfortunately, keeping his head down doesn't help him to stand out. Sure, he is happy with his role at the moment, but he wants to be an active member of the crew. He wishes to fight alongside the others and to put his life on the line for the colonies like everyone else on board. But until he proves himself, he's stuck where he is. Then again, his role doesn't give him much chance to prove himself. He leaves his room and strolls towards the command deck to see if Gryffin needs anything.

∞

She's breaking her promise. Terra never breaks a promise, especially when it's to Roman. She has no choice, however. How can she sit back and do nothing?

After her little chat with Milla, she had gone back to work and then retired to her quarters for the evening. That is exactly where she should have stayed. Instead, she is crouching in an access tunnel about to use her training to hide a transmission from the ship so she can warn Gryffin.

They uncovered a faint signal in the recon officer's personal unit. Someone had linked a unit to it and transferred data. With a bit of jiggling, she had been able to isolate this signal and boost it. She hoped the signal linked to Gryffin's ship itself and not the entire Nomad fleet.

Terra crawls through the cramped space and finally locates the correct interface. She draws her legs under her and pulls her tools out of the various pockets of her combat trousers. It would have been too suspicious to lug her tool kit around with her. Terra wipes her dirty hands on the leg of her black trousers and then uncovers the interface. She cuts open a smaller internal panel and clips in her modification. Once the module is locked into place, she sits back on her legs and wipes her face on the hem of her red t-shirt. If only her systems lecturer could see her now. He always said she was the top of the class and would accomplish great things. Disobeying orders and mutilating a Foundation system probably wasn't what he had in mind.

She glances over her shoulder, half expecting someone to catch her at any minute. She must be losing it. There's no other explanation for disobeying a direct order and then hiding a transmission. Then again, her orders were to keep away from him. Technically she's not going anywhere near him. As if that will make any difference to the captain.

Finishing her modifications, she takes a deep breath and opens the link. Now all she can do is wait and hope someone answers.

∞

'Sir, we're getting a strange transmission.'

Gryffin looks up from his screen. 'What do you mean strange?'

The communications officer frowns. 'It says, *Do you want your knife back?*'

Gryffin fumbles with his pad. Managing to keep his expression blank, he forces himself to focus on the pad again. It must be the Foundation woman. How the hell had she found their signal? It couldn't have been easy. Completely ignoring the firm *no* coming from his mechanical side, he gets up and climbs down the metal steps to the bottom command deck. 'Is it live or a recorded message?'

'Live, sir.'

'Transfer it to the unit in my office.' In an award-winning performance, he casually turns and leaves the room. Once inside, he locks his office door firmly behind him, but instead of turning on his unit, he stands in the middle of the room. For the first time in as long as he can remember, he doesn't know what to do.

He should ignore the message and alter the signal codes immediately, but he doesn't want to. Well, not until he talks to her to see what she wants. He can't believe he's thinking of doing this. He slams his hand against the module and turns it on with a loud bang.

What is he meant to say to her? He's led hundreds of negotiations, fought battles, and carried out hits. Why is opening a comms channel causing him so many issues? He takes a deep breath. 'You can keep the knife.' He grimaces at the stupidity of the statement. Not the best conversation starter but it's all he can come up with.

'Is the line secure?'

'Yes.' Four little words, but he recognises her voice. 'How did you find me?'

'You left a signal on the Foundation unit you tapped into on the station. I just boosted it.'

She may have made it sound like it wasn't anything unusual, but he knows different. It wouldn't have been that easy. In truth, he didn't think it possible at all, but she proved him wrong. Someone with her skills is wasted on a Foundation ship. 'You didn't do all that to give back my knife.'

'No. To be honest, I want to keep it. It might come in handy someday. The real reason for the call is to warn you. The Foundation thinks you killed one of our men. Add that to the three you killed when we first arrived and you've definitely caught their attention. They're sending us after you.'

Gryffin falters for a second. She contacted him to warn him. He doesn't know what he expected, but it wasn't that. 'Hold on, you lost three crew members during our initial strike?'

She pauses for a moment and the static crackles noisily in the room. 'Well, yes. They were killed by your team. Are you saying you didn't know?'

Gryffin clenches his jaw. No, he bloody well didn't know. His orders were clear when they engaged the Foundation. No kill shots — no exceptions. What the hell had gone wrong? 'Is it only your ship looking for me?'

'At the moment, but there are more heading towards the Port. There could be another ten vessels in the area within a few weeks. They want you, Gryffin. They've told Roman to use whatever means necessary to bring you back to Foundation space. I've never seen the Council react this way to an individual. For some reason, they see you as a significant threat.'

Gryffin curses to himself. If the Foundation reopens the Port and sends ships through, the Sector's going to be in a hell of a lot of trouble. Built over a century ago, the large, heavily guarded Port allows travel between the Sectors within hours instead of years. It was made to transport the unwanted civilians to this Sector and then locked down so they couldn't come back.

The gate had remained a silent threat in the Sector ever since. Everyone knew it was only a matter of time before it reopened. *Infinity* is the first ship to travel through it for decades. 'Why are you telling me this?' Gryffin asks.

'You did me a favour. This is my way of saying thank you. Because you helped me, the Foundation now knows about you. I'm responsible for that. I don't want anything to happen to you because of me.'

He's glad it's not a picture transmission. He knows shock is plastered all over his face. If one of his crew had contacted the Foundation without his permission, it would've been the last thing they did. Her captain would more than likely feel the same. She put warning him before her career. As a leader, he's not impressed by her lack of respect: as a person, he can't help but be grateful for her actions. That deserves some acknowledgement. 'I appreciate you contacting me.'

'It's the least I can do. I also wanted ... I guess I needed to ... It's good to hear your voice ... again. I should go. Stay safe, Gryffin.'

Before he can untie his tongue, the connection closes and her voice is replaced by static. He should have said something back to her before she went. Anything would have been better than the nothing he offered.

He sits at his desk and stares blankly at the screen. Ten Foundation ships won't be a problem for his fleet. His Nomad ships outnumber the Foundation three to one. The problems start if the colonies get caught in the crossfire. People could die because the Foundation wants him.

He picks at a piece of flaking leather on his trousers. Thinking he had killed four crew members would hardly warrant the Foundation sending a small armada after him. Until he finds out the reason for their interest, he's in the dark. As much he hates to admit it, he may need some help on this one.

Bray downloads the report onto the pad and closes his computer. He yawns loudly and pushes his dark hair out of the way. His reflection stares back at him in the blank screen. Even in the distorted image, the dark rings lining his hazel eyes are noticeable. He glances at his watch and curses to himself. He's late yet again.

He pulls on his navy trousers, grabs a t-shirt from the pile of washing on the ground, and stuffs his feet into his worn brown boots. After quickly gathering his work, he leaves his room and races through the ship.

He bursts through the door and pushes his shoulders back, ignoring the glare cast in his direction by Sayber.

'Glad you could finally join us, Commander Brayden.'

'I'm sorry, Captain.'

The leader of the Hunters holds his gaze for another painfully long minute before breaking contact. Sayber only calls him Brayden when he's in trouble. He stopped using his full name years ago when he joined the Hunters. Released from Sayber's scrutiny, Bray allows himself to relax slightly. As second-in-command of *Perses*, being late for yet another meeting did not set a good example. Punctuality has always been an issue for him. While on the control deck or leading a strike team, he is the best. The problems arise when he gets distracted.

At his core, he is an engineer. His promotion had come a year ago when his predecessor died. Being chosen by Sayber had surprised him as much as it did the rest of the crew. Rising that fast through the ranks hadn't even been on his radar when he joined the ship, but his fighting and leadership skills had helped him stand out from the rest of the crew. On the flip side, so did his tardiness. He'd have to rein in his off-the-clock engineering projects before he got kicked off the crew.

Sayber slouches back in his chair and brushes a stray lock of hair from his face. 'Now that we're all here,' he says while glancing at Bray, 'what's the count after our last run in with the Nomad?'

Hearing his cue, Bray loads his report on the main screen. 'He took out two ships. All but fifteen crew made it to the escape pods in time.'

As expected, Sayber curses and thumps the table, knocking over a glass of water. 'Are the ships a complete loss?'

Bray shakes his head. 'Unknown at the moment. I've sent *Artemis* and *Pallas*. They'll try to salvage what they can. The initial report should be in within the hour.'

'I suppose it's too much to hope we even scratched that damn Nomad's implants?'

Bray shakes his head, adding to his captain's foul mood. Taking things from Sayber's viewpoint, he can hardly blame him. Sayber has five years on Gryffin. Not that age means a damn thing when facing an opponent like the Nomad. Bray will never admit it, but he can't help but admire the Nomad leader.

Like Sayber, Gryffin commands the loyalty and respect of his crew members. The Hunters have quite a few colonies, but Gryffin controls the majority. Leading the Nomad, dealing with colonies, and captaining a ship at the age of thirty-something can't be an easy task. Gryffin deserves respect for that.

The feud has been escalating for years, each side giving as good as they get. Well, at least it looks that way to anyone outside the groups. In truth, Gryffin has the upper hand. How could the war be fair with Gryffin being a cyborg? The speed and ferocity of his attacks is unnatural. Retaliating with the same force is taking its toll on Sayber and the rest of the Hunters, not that Sayber would ever admit it. Unless something extraordinary happens, both men will no doubt continue until one of them dies.

'Bray, locate a Nomad ship. Any ship.' Without another word, Sayber marches from the room, leaving the rest of the command crew to worry about their situation, like Bray is.

∞

'What the hell are you doing here?'

Rayde steps out of the transport and strides towards Gryffin. 'Well, hello to you too, High Commander.'

Gryffin crosses his arms and faces his mentor. Rayde's ship, *Kratos*, arrived in the area about ten minutes ago and since then Gryffin has been on edge. Rayde only meets in person when something is wrong. 'What do you want?'

Rayde gestures towards the metal steps that lead from the cargo bay. 'Can't I pop in to see how you are?'

Gryffin doesn't respond. Rayde always attempts small-talk even though he knows Gryffin hates it. Rayde won't tell him the reason for the visit until they're alone. Gryffin leads the older man up another five flights of steps and along the corridor to his quarters.

Once inside, Rayde shrugs off his worn leather jacket and slowly walks around the small space. He casts a critical eye over his surroundings and raises an eyebrow at the numerous dents in the walls. Rayde lifts the corner of Gryffin's threadbare blanket, grunts,

79

and places it back down again. 'How you doing, son?'

Gryffin bristles at the term of endearment. 'Fine, sir.'

Rayde sits down on Gryffin's lone chair. 'Do you know how transparent you are? I could practically see the hairs on your neck rising when I called you *son*. You'd think after two decades you'd be used to it by now. And you don't have to call me *sir* anymore.'

'Old habits, sir.'

'I give up,' Rayde says, shaking his head. 'How can I help with your problem?'

Gryffin raises an eyebrow. 'Problem?'

'You put in a call to me. You only contact me when you have a problem. You also have that pained *hate-asking-for-help* face on. Come on. Spit it out.'

'You're here because I contacted you?'

'Of course! You need help so here I am.'

'I didn't expect you to come personally.'

Rayde holds out his hands. 'I was in the area.'

'The Foundation is after me; not the Nomad. They're sending their flagship plus another ten to capture me.'

Rayde blows out a breath. 'That's a lot of ships. You must have pissed them off. What happened? You always get on so well with everyone you meet.'

'They didn't warm to me.'

'I find that difficult to believe. How hard have you been hitting them?'

The metal bed creaks as Gryffin lowers onto it. 'That's the strange thing. We attacked them, but my men were ordered not to kill any of the Foundation. I've debriefed each of the team. They are adamant it wasn't them.'

Rayde scratches his jaw. 'What about the recon officer on the station? You did locate and kill him, didn't you?'

Gryffin nods. 'I interrogated him, but didn't kill him.'

Rayde raises an eyebrow. 'You sure about that? I've seen your interrogation tactics, remember? You can be a pretty vicious bastard when you want.'

Gryffin bites back his sharp reply. 'I held back, sir. He wasn't going to be walking, or even dragging himself out of the room, but I left him alive. I'm not going to do something stupid like kill a Foundation crew member. The last thing I want is to start a war. I ordered the raid on the colony to convey our message. Looks like they took it the wrong way.' Not for the first time he wonders if he should have trusted his instincts and removed the Foundation ship from the equation at the first meeting.

Rayde shrugs. 'Fair enough. I'm used to your shoot first, question later attitude. I'm a bit surprised you took another route. But I see you made the right decision — both on the planet and with the recon officer. So, if you and your men didn't kill them, who did?'

'I'm damned if I know. I'm getting the blame and that seriously pisses me off.'

'Yeah, and we all know that's not a great thing. I'll do some digging, both on the deaths and the Foundation as a whole. See what I can expose.' Rayde leans forward and rests his arms on his legs. 'You doing okay?' He gestures at the dented walls. 'Your walls aren't exactly a standard design feature. Should I be worried about you?

Gryffin frowns. 'I'm fine.'

Rayde snorts. 'Of course you are. By the way, I read Klay's report. It contradicts yours. Why did you leave your heroic rescue out? Something to hide?'

Gryffin curses to himself. Damn Klay. For some reason, he's determined to undermine him at every turn. Helping the Foundation woman wasn't a big deal. 'No, wasn't worth mentioning.'

'She lives?'

'Yes.'

Rayde pulls out his knife and polishes it with a cloth. 'Going against the rules. Not like you. As I said, do I need to be worried?'

'I had helped her. Didn't seem right to then kill her.' Rayde may be a father figure to him, but he'll never admit he'd been too soft to kill her. If he wants to hold on to Rayde's respect, it would be best to keep it to himself.

Rayde doesn't seem convinced. 'Listen, you need to keep your head on what's going on. The last thing you need are distractions, especially ones of the female variety. No good will come of it. You know there's no way she'd be interested in you long term. A Foundation woman and a Nomad — especially one like you — wouldn't work.'

Gryffin glances at the ground and hopes a large hole will appear so he can dive into it. 'I'm not distracted.'

'I hope not. All our ships are looking to you for leadership, not relationship advice.' Rayde leans back and shakes his head. 'You've put too much hard work into becoming what you are today. Feelings will only weaken you. Drag you back to where you were when we found you. I've had to watch you struggle with your human side for years. You're half machine, Gryffin. I don't want you to get carried away and forget that.'

No such luck. 'I won't.'

'So what's the plan?'

'Carry on with business as usual. If they interfere, persuade them to back off — with a bit more force if necessary.'

Rayde puts his knife down and nods. 'If that's how you want to play it. I'll keep an ear out and let you know if I gather any more intel.' Rayde leans forward to rest his arms on his legs. 'Implants okay?'

Gryffin shrugs. 'Same as always.'

Rayde grimaces. 'That's what I'm afraid of.' He stands up and puts on his coat. 'I'll see myself out. Keep your head down, son.'

Rayde closes the door behind him and leaves Gryffin alone in his room. The conversation just made him feel worse. He knows Rayde only has his best interests at heart, but his little speech didn't tick a lot of motivational boxes. He looks at his reflection in the powered down screen beside his bed. He is letting his human heart rule his partially mechanical brain and not with fantastic results.

He preferred it when Rayde sat as head of the Nomad. Too many lives rested on Gryffin's decisions now, right or wrong. The commander of five hundred crewmen spread throughout the Sector, including the old high commander and each of them looked to him for a solution to the Foundation problem.

∞

'There must be something seriously wrong with you.'

Balfe's face turns a strange red hue before he composes himself. 'You speak to all your superiors like that?'

Sayber pushes back from the screen and rests his boots on the table in front of him. He takes a deep breath before he does something stupid like smashing one of those boots through the screen. 'You may be an admiral, but you're not a superior. Not only that, but you need me a hell of a lot more than I need you. Correct?'

Balfe glares at the screen.

'Sorry, I didn't hear that.'

'Yes,' Balfe grinds out through clenched teeth.

'So, what do I gain from all this?'

'Satisfaction.'

Sayber barely manages to stop himself from falling off the seat laughing. 'Let me understand. You want me to impersonate Gryffin, bombard his colonies, and risk getting killed if he catches me, and the only reward is the satisfaction? You'll have to do a lot better than that.'

'I thought you and the Nomad are rivals? That you continuously fight for dominance? The Foundation wants to remove the Nomad leader from the equation.'

While it sounds like a great outcome, Sayber isn't an idiot. Once Gryffin is out of the equation, his Hunters will be next on the list, but short term it could work to his advantage. It is going to take a bit more than mere pleasure to convince him to piss Gryffin off to that extent.

'I'm sure you can come up with some form of monetary satisfaction for me. And agree to replace any ships he decides to blow out of the sky.'

Balfe clearly isn't keen on the demands. The range of emotions that travels across his face gives Sayber a kick. The Admiral isn't used to depending on someone else.

'Fine. One hundred thousand credits. But I expect results. And fast.'

Balfe signs off, leaving Sayber feeling more than a little uneasy about their new relationship.

11

Avoca silently watches the group of men around the table and tries his best to blend in and not be noticed. The best the Foundation has to offer have gathered together: four admirals with too many secrets and too much to lose, himself included.

Balfe bangs the table in front of him to start the meeting. 'I'm sure you're all curious to know why you've been called here today, although I would imagine some of you have already guessed.'

'No games. Get to the point Balfe,' Admiral Leeson jumps in.

'I'd watch your tone, Admiral.' Leeson looks like he's about to argue but closes his mouth. 'Now we're all paying attention... ' he says, glaring at Leeson. 'I've received some interesting intel recently. I'm sure you all remember Project Conscript from two decades ago.'

The stunned silence is all the answer he needs. 'I don't need to tell you it proved pioneering for its time. We were so close to having a viable product we could use. The dregs of society transformed into disposable and fully controllable soldiers to man our ships, colonise and control worlds, and protect our people. We have all lost friends and family when ships have fallen. I've just had to notify three families their loved ones had been killed while serving on *Infinity*. The Foundation *needs* this project to succeed. Unfortunately, the untimely destruction of the station put an end to that. Until now.'

'You're not suggesting we start it again?' Grafton asks.

'That's precisely what I'm suggesting.'

Grafton leans back in his chair. 'Twenty years have passed. Surely it's too late to begin from scratch?'

Balfe shakes his head. 'Not if we have a workable prototype.' Balfe sits back in his chair and turns on the screen. He brings up an image of a young boy with the number thirty-five clearly printed on the bottom of the screen.

The questions fly around the room until Leeson silences everyone by shouting above them. 'What are you trying to say?' he asks, wiping his glasses on the hem of his shirt.

'This one survived,' Admiral Balfe confirms. 'I have verification.'

The occupants of the room regard him in silence, as he also remains silent, apparently enjoying drawing out his news. Balfe is the unofficial leader of Project Conscript. Avoca doesn't like him — never did. The man is ambitious and utterly ruthless. Born sixty years ago on one of the smaller colonies inside the Foundation area, Balfe is known for trampling over anyone or anything in his way.

It had earned him the position of admiral at a young age, but also lost him the trust of his colleagues. He'd have no issue stabbing someone in the back if it served him. This ruthlessness makes him ideal for leading the group, but it also causes the other three men many sleepless nights. Avoca knows they have all collected information on Balfe's involvement, in case he ever decides to turn on them.

'Please tell me there will be no children involved this time?' Leeson says.

Balfe shakes his head. 'It appears the very things we chose them for, also served as their downfall: youth. They were not strong enough to survive the invasive brain surgery, except for this one,' he says, pointing at the screen. 'No, if this is to work, our focus must shift to the more resilient residents of the prison moons. We have access to numerous test subjects between the recommended ages of twenty and forty.'

'So, not only do we continue with Conscript, but we can also reduce our numbers in the prisons,' Leeson says. 'That will work in our favour with the populace.'

'Exactly.' Balfe clasps his hands in front of him. 'Can I presume you're all prepared to fulfil your previous roles?'

One by one they nod.

'So what now?' Leeson asks. 'All the test subjects were meant to have died when the station blew. How did this one survive?'

'I don't know, but we're sure as hell going to find out.' Balfe stretches back in his chair and crosses his arms. 'We all knew this could happen. When the Foundation started actively exploring the sector, the risk of uncovering our work increased. We should have had a plan in place.'

'Come on, Balfe,' Grafton interrupts. 'How could we have known anyone would survive the explosion?'

'There's no point arguing about what happened. The fact remains one survived, and from what the reports say, holds a position of power within a potentially dangerous group. That is what we should be concerned about. Especially if he's been in contact with a Foundation ship. If the truth comes out, we are on a one-way trip to a prison moon.'

'Perhaps we should forget the project? Kill this remaining test subject,' Leeson says.

'That's a bit drastic, isn't it?' Avoca interjects before he can rein himself in. He can't let them discuss killing an entirely innocent man to save all their necks.

Balfe shakes his head. 'Trust me. If he weren't the sole survivor of the project, I'd be ordering his execution. Unfortunately, he's too valuable. We lost all previous data with the station. If Conscript is to work, a flesh and blood prototype is necessary. We now have access to that.'

Grafton shakes his head. 'We don't have that. Not yet.' He pushes the computer across the desk. 'According to the original files, he underwent severe modifications, internal and external. The project enhanced his organs, his brain is fitted with computer chips that control various other implants, and his eyes ...' Grafton grimaces.

'Well, let's just say I stopped reading when I reached the section about his eyes being removed. The modifications were designed to create a more resilient, stronger and faster subject. He's had twenty-odd years to adapt to and improve on what we did to him. We shouldn't underestimate him. We have to expect he'll be a competent fighter.'

'I accept the project certainly has potential, but how do we even begin to search for him?' Leeson asks. 'He's not going to answer a communication from us and come running.'

'Leave that bit with me,' Balfe replies. 'Things are already in motion for his capture.'

The confident smile on Balfe's face turns Avoca's blood cold. What the hell has he got himself into?

∞

Gryffin hands the report back to Chayse and looks out the window at the front of the control deck. It takes his eyes a few seconds to readjust after focusing on the numbers on the screen.

There's nothing outside the ship but grey rock. The view hasn't changed for the last two hours and is likely to be that way for another few hours at least. *Ares* has been hidden in the centre of a small moon while they make repairs and Gryffin has hated every single minute of it. It feels too claustrophobic, like being buried alive.

He pulls his eyes away from the depressing view to examine Klay, who has climbed the stairs to the control deck. It must be bad news. Gryffin knows that expression on Klay's face too well. And it must be bad if he's willing to speak to him. He hadn't seen much of Klay since their last conversation yesterday. The commander had the sense to keep out of Gryffin's way, which suited them both. He's positive Klay lied to him but doesn't know what he's lying about. 'What is it?'

'We've received some disturbing reports. A Foundation ship is hunting us.'

'I know.'

Klay lowers the pad. 'How?'

'What difference does that make?'

'Sir, this ship has visited seven of our worlds and made enquiries... about you, mainly.'

'We carry on as normal.'

'Sir, we need to end this, now. If they ask too many questions, it will make the colonies nervous.'

'We'll deal with it, if and when it becomes a problem.' When Klay doesn't respond, Gryffin looks up and instantly knows something else is wrong. 'What?'

'Can we speak in private, sir?'

Gryffin nods and they go to a small room off the command deck serving as Gryffin's office. The metal desk, set of chairs, and computer are the only decorations in the otherwise empty box. It is set up for function, not comfort. He leans against the desk and gestures for Klay to sit on one of the metal chairs. 'What is it?' he asks again.

Klay pulls a folded piece of paper from his pocket. Even without seeing it, Gryffin has an uneasy feeling. Klay looks anxious, and for once it's not caused by Gryffin. It's caused by whatever is on the page. Gryffin takes it from Klay and unfolds it. 'Shit!'

'Yes, sir,' Klay says quietly.

Gryffin gets up and paces the office. His boots hitting the metal floor is the only sound for a few minutes. At least Klay has the sense to keep quiet. Gryffin resists the urge to pound his metal fist into the wall in anger. He barely suppresses a growl as he looks down at the pencil sketch of his face. This is his fault. He should have left his damn mask on. He let his emotions take over for a split second and this is the result. 'Where did you find this?'

'Sent by a friend. He found it stuck up at the station we were… at…' His voice trails off towards the end of the sentence.

'What does it say underneath?'

'The Foundation is offering a reward for your capture.' Klay clears his throat before continuing. 'The artist also signed the picture. It says Terra at the bottom.'

This time he can't hold back a growl. He knew it was only a matter of time before someone found out what he looks like and made it public knowledge, but he hadn't expected it would be her. 'Any bites yet?'

'Not a lot by the sounds of things. People seem to be keeping their mouths shut, thankfully.'

He's furious at himself. Probably would have been quicker if he'd put some cuffs on his own wrists and walked back to her ship with her. God, he's such an idiot. 'Game plan's changed. Uncover everything you can about the Foundation ship and crew.' Before Klay can respond, he leaves the room and heads for the training room.

He can't change what he did. Picture or no picture, the simple fact is he is a wanted criminal, and they need him out of the way before they start colonising. Unfortunately, the added publicity is going to screw them. Stepping off the ship could place everyone in danger, even on ally colonies. If the reward attracts even one of his trusted people, he'll be in serious trouble.

He hits the wall of the corridor, startling the crew member walking towards him. The young man stops and shrinks into the wall until his captain storms past. Gryffin clenches his fist tightly. The pain helps to keep the implant from getting too much control.

'Sir! Captain, wait!' shouts Klay.

'Can't hold back the *I told you so* any longer, Klay?'

'That's not why I'm here.' Klay drops his voice when another crew member hurriedly squeezes by in the cramped corridor. 'Sir, maybe we need to think about getting you off the ship. It's too much of a risk.'

Gryffin's eyes turn purple with fury at his stupidity. 'It's not the first wanted poster offering rewards for my capture.'

Klay takes a step back. 'I know that, sir. For the first time, though, this one has a pretty good likeness of your face on it.'

Before he can stop it, the electricity rushes down his arm. 'I'm only going to say this once. *Ares* is my ship. I'm not going anywhere.'

'But, sir, what about the woman?'

'Don't talk about her. Not now. Not ever.' He whips out his gun and pushes it against Klay's forehead. 'You need to remember who's captain on this ship. I know you've been reporting to Rayde. That you told him about the Foundation woman.'

'I...'

He pushes the gun tighter against Klay's head. 'I don't want you to talk. You report to me, not Rayde. The next time you contact him behind my back, I'm going to get really pissed off. Understand?'

'Sir.'

Gryffin watches as a bead of sweat forms below where the muzzle rests on Klay's forehead. The droplet runs like blood between Klay's eyes. He closes his eyes briefly when his vision swims. He needs to reach the training room before he does something rash. He withdraws his gun and gestures towards the Command Deck. 'Get the hell away from me. Now.' He turns away and moves further along the corridor, not stopping until he's in the training room.

The three crew members training there quit what they're doing as soon as he bursts into the room. 'Leave.' They quickly gather their things and make a speedy exit. He pulls off his shirt, grabs a sparring stick, and launches himself at the training drone.

∞

91

Chayse stands outside the training room door and takes a few deep breaths to calm his nerves. He's not surprised Klay nominated him to speak to Gryffin. He's probably hoping Gryffin will kill him.

Chayse glances down at his watch. It's been half an hour since the captain left the bridge. He should be a bit calmer — hopefully.

Chayse opens the door and cautiously looks over the railings into the room below. Gryffin is standing beside a smoking ruin of machinery, looking a bit more relaxed. Well, relaxed for Gryffin, which doesn't mean a lot. He's still breathing deeply and clenching his fists tightly, but he doesn't have the cold, dangerous expression on his face anymore. To be on the safe side, Chayse stays where he is until his leader acknowledges him. A person can't be too careful around him. If Gryffin wants to take him down, he could kill Chayse in a heartbeat.

At six feet, Chayse is shorter than his captain and while he always prides himself on being fit and healthy, Gryffin is pure, angry muscle. Chayse works out every day without fail to keep himself in shape — sometimes with the captain, but standing next to Gryffin he may as well have sat in the mess hall during that time instead of training. Then again, he's not stuck with an implant in his head which drives him over the edge unless he works off the aggression.

Gryffin looks up at him. 'So he sent you instead.'

'Yes, sir.'

Gryffin shoves the remains of the drone away with his boot. 'Find anything?'

'Yes and no.' He walks down the stairs, throws a bottle of water to Gryffin, and sits on one of the benches. 'It appears *Infinity* is searching for you.'

Gryffin wipes his face with a towel before he throws it on top of the drone at the other side of the room. 'I wanted you to tell me something I didn't already know.'

Chayse silently curses himself. 'Sorry, sir. The ship, not the Foundation, is looking for you. The order came to *Infinity* alone.'

'From who?'

Chayse glances down at the screen. 'An Admiral Balfe. Do you know him, sir?'

'Not by name. Got a picture?'

'It'll take some time to hack the personnel files. Why are they looking for you, sir?'

'Damned if I know.' Gryffin grabs his shirt and sits down at the other end of the bench from Chayse. He absently rubs along the raised skin against the centre of his chest implant — one of the few noticeable habits he displays when trying to decide what to do. 'Where's *Infinity* now?' Gryffin asks.

Chayse glances down at his tablet. 'They left Kel, so probably a week away from our location. They seem to be on their way to Taldor.'

That gets the captain's attention. 'Taldor's a Nomad world. Have they signed with the Foundation?'

'Not that I've heard. I know the Foundation are offering hefty bonuses for signing up. Colonies may be tempted.'

Gryffin grunts. 'Yeah, it's hard to say no when there's a bloody big ship pointing its guns at you.' He looks down at the ground for a moment before addressing Chayse again. 'Lock the door.'

Chayse pauses for a moment, suddenly feeling a little concerned about his safety. He slowly moves to the control panel and seals the door.

'I need you to do something for me, off the record,' Gryffin says. 'It has to stay between you and me.'

Chayse can't help but grimace. He doesn't like the sound of this. 'Of course, sir.'

'Put a trace on Klay. I want to know where he is and what he's doing.'

'The commander? But why?'

Gryffin's cold blue eyes focus on him. 'I threatened to put a bullet in Klay's head earlier for questioning me.'

Chayse ignores his rapidly beating heart and stands firm. Showing weakness in front of the Captain won't do him any favours. In fact, it will probably piss Gryffin off even more. 'Apologies, sir. I just thought you trusted him.'

'I don't trust,' Gryffin replies. 'Not usually.' He stands up and locks on to Chayse's eyes. 'Don't make me regret breaking my rule with you. Understood?'

Chayse nods as he realises the enormity of what his captain is saying. 'Of course, sir. Is there anything specific I should search for?'

Gryffin pauses. 'You heard anything about the recon officer on the station?'

'The one you killed?'

Gryffin curses and looks down at the floor for a moment. Sections of his metal arm glow bright red and he clenches his fist tightly. When he raises his head, Gryffin's facial implant is also lit, casting an eerie crimson light over his features. Chayse takes a step back and reaches for his weapon.

Gryffin glares at him. 'Damn it, Chayse, I'm not going to hurt you.' He runs his metal hand through his hair. 'I didn't kill the Foundation recon. And I didn't kill the three crew members on the surface.'

Chayse narrows his eyes. 'I don't understand, sir.'

'Yeah, well neither do I. Someone is framing me. Klay went AWOL when I was on the station. I need to be sure about him.' Gryffin takes his gun out of its holster and levels it at Chayse. 'I can't have traitors on my ship. '

'Of course not, sir,' Chayse says, stumbling over his words.

Gryffin leaves his gun trained on Chayse for another moment before putting it back in its holster. The captain pulls his t-shirt over his damp skin. 'Let's go have a chat with this Foundation captain. Try to persuade him to abandon the Sector.'

12

Avoca looks out the window of *Omega* and wonders how he managed to get himself into this situation again. After the meeting, he'd tried to disappear back to his ship before Balfe could approach him, but Balfe said he needed help and Avoca couldn't think of a valid excuse to not to assist him.

Because of his lack of quick thinking, Balfe led him onto his ship, *Omega*. Avoca looks out at the old freighter drifting alongside *Omega* and tries to ignore the feeling of dread settling in his stomach. He doesn't know why he's here, or what the freighter has to do with anything, but it can't be good.

The ship comes to a stop beside the freighter and shudders as they connect to each other. Balfe meets him at the porthole and quietly guides him onto the other vessel. Avoca jumps as the door of the hatch slams and locks behind them. 'What is this place?'

'Patience, Avoca.'

Balfe's grin unsettles Avoca even more. He doesn't want to be here. The freighter has an air of death about it which seems almost familiar to him, but he can't think from where. Hopefully, they'll do what they have to, and then he can return to his ship.

They reach the end of the corridor and Balfe takes the exit to the left, which opens into a large room. What Avoca sees in the room makes his blood run cold. 'If you could see your face, Avoca.'

The room is an exact copy of the old location. Cages line the far wall, each one complete with a set of manacles. Metal tables covered in a terrifying array of implements sprawl along the adjacent wall. At various points throughout the room, chains hang from the support beams, each one directly over a drain in the floor.

Sitting in pride of place in the centre of the room is something he hoped he'd never see again: the operating table. It reminds Avoca of a table used in a morgue. Drainage channels run along each side leading into another hole in the floor. Heavy leather restraints attach to metal rings welded onto the top at the head, neck, torso, arm, and leg positions.

Avoca can't think straight. Images of screaming people in the cages, in the chains, or on the table push into his mind. 'There must be another way.'

'Another way? What are you talking about? You agreed with me. Are you trying to tell me you're getting cold feet?'

Agreed? He can't remember agreeing to anything. Unless ... He runs a hand through his hair and sighs. Balfe took his silence at the meeting as approval. For the first time in his life, his silence has committed him to something he wanted nothing to do with. 'Have you found someone to work with us?'

Balfe nods and signals to someone at the back of the room. A man appears from behind a bank of computers and walks closer. As soon as Avoca sees him, his stomach rolls. At five-foot-eight, clean shaven with short cut sandy blonde hair and old-fashioned wire-rimmed glasses, the Scientist is more suited to a classroom than a deserted laboratory drifting in space. The man couldn't appear less intimidating if he tried. 'Good to see you again, Avoca.'

Avoca shudders at the sound of his voice, deceptively soft and timid. He may have been the foremost expert in cybernetics in his day, but years locked away in his lab had left his sanity in a questionable state. The one and only time Avoca had been forced to visit the lab had left its mark on him. The Scientist's test subjects endured hell.

Avoca always preferred to think of them as test subjects; thinking of them as people made the horror real. They were subjected to horrific processes. The Scientist enjoyed causing them pain, hearing them scream, seeing their blood running off the table and across the floor. He can still hear them cry himself. The Scientist had cut his subjects open and put them on display for the visiting Foundation to admire. Perhaps the Nomad leader himself was one of the unfortunate souls Avoca saw. He clears his throat. 'Are there any more subjects here?'

The Scientist shakes his head. 'I have cleared the old ones out. I cannot have anything distract me from *Thirty-Five*. He is the culmination of years of hard work.' He moves to the centre of the room and pulls one of the leather restraints on the table. 'These will need to be stronger.'

Balfe laughs. 'That restraint has been utilised for years. No one can break through it.'

'*Thirty-Five* will snap them as if they were string. I requested what I did for a reason. We did not come this far to have him escape. I want them replaced with heavy duty metal immediately.'

'Avoca will arrange that for you,' Balfe says.

Avoca pulls Balfe to the side of the room. 'Is it wise to involve him again?'

'He created *Thirty-Five*. Of course he needs to be involved again.'

'But he's so... the methods are... '

'His methods aren't an issue. The result is what's important.'

Avoca struggles to find a response. Torturing innocent people — innocent children — is a serious problem. It should not have gone on

97

for so long the last time. To willingly go down that questionable path again shouldn't even be a consideration. One word describes the Scientist: a sadist. Balfe paid him to inflict the most horrific pain on the test subjects and he didn't seem to care.

To avoid looking at the Scientist, Avoca slowly examines the cavernous space they are in. His eyes are instantly drawn to the large glass coffin-like box in the corner. 'I'm almost afraid to inquire, but what is that?'

Balfe waves a hand dismissively at the box. 'The Scientist's sister or girlfriend. I wasn't listening. She was in a transport accident about a decade ago which left her brain dead. He spent the family fortune on that stasis pod. It will keep her alive until he can find a way of replacing her brain with a machine.'

'You can't be serious? We're supporting him in this lunacy?'

Balfe barely glances up from his tablet. 'To be honest, I don't care about his reasons. All that matters is that, by working on his little project, he helps us with ours.'

Avoca nods, unable to think of a reply. He turns his back to the pod and faces the room.

'Are you getting cold feet?' Balfe asks again.

Cold feet? Yes. He wants to be as far from this place as he possibly can. 'No. I ... I'm surprised.'

Balfe smiles widely and slaps him on the back before gesturing to the man standing beside the operating table. 'The Scientist is looking forward to this too. I didn't want to advertise his involvement initially, but he's worked closely on this project over the last few years trying to perfect what he's so good at.'

'Years?' Dear God. The project must have been carried on for years behind the scenes. 'How many more have there been?'

Balfe puts a hand on his shoulder making him jump. 'No need to darken the mood with numbers. There's only one number we're focusing on and that's number *Thirty-Five*.'

'But—'

Balfe looks at him strangely, so Avoca shuts up. If he keeps pushing, he could be the next subject on the table.

'You with me on this, Avoca?'

'Of course.'

'Good, because you'll oversee the project for me. In person with the Scientist.'

'I have to return to *Omega*. Avoca, stay here and make a list of anything else our friend needs. Make sure you're back on board in an hour. *Epsilon* is on its way. They'll pick you up at the station a day's travel from here.'

Balfe turns on his heel, leaving Avoca with the Scientist. Avoca watches in morbid fascination as the Scientist picks up a rib spreader and oils the hinges. As discreetly as he can, Avoca wanders towards the small bathroom off the main lab and locks the door firmly before emptying his stomach.

∞

Roman stares out the window of his office, not looking at anything in particular. He has been burying himself in paperwork for the last few days to occupy his mind, but it's not working as well anymore. Damn it, he can't even concentrate on primary ship reports at the moment. One thing occupies his mind and one thing only: Gryffin.

He needs to locate him, but it has nothing to do with his orders. He wants to meet him. As much as he's tried to skirt around the issue he can't. He's a father and he wants to meet his son.

They have put pressure on some of the colonies; demanding, threatening, and bribing, but it hasn't brought them any closer to locating *Ares*. The ship is proving to be as elusive as reported. No one will talk about the Nomad, *Ares*, or Gryffin. Perhaps they are too frightened to say anything. Whatever the reason, he's hit a dead end. It's also starting to take its toll on the crew. It is not good for ship morale.

He focuses on the small world they are orbiting. Taldor is a farming colony with no defences, so it didn't take much convincing to sign up the colony to the Foundation. In truth, *Infinity* merely arrived in orbit and they agreed to sign. The official signing of the territory contract would take place at a formal dinner in an hour on the surface. Some homemade food and drink will improve everyone's mood. He locks his office and goes to his quarters to change before taking the lift to the transport bay.

Five hours later and the stress of the last week seems like a distant memory. The Taldorans sure know how to spoil their guests. The feast they have prepared covers ten giant banquet tables in the centre of the main hall. The tables are laden with homemade breads, wine, fruit, meat, and vegetables. Roman hasn't seen so much food in one place since family gatherings back on Earth. His mother's family took pride in trying to outdo each other every birthday, producing bigger and bigger parties for the children. He leans back in his chair, sipping a local wine and starts to relax.

'Captain.'

He looks up at the young woman standing in front of him. 'Yes?'

'I apologise for disturbing your evening, but we have a query on a section of the agreement. Would you be so kind as to explain it to us?'

'Of course.'

He follows her down the corridor leading from the main hall and continues through a maze of corridors until they reach a small room. She opens the door and gestures for him to enter before bowing slightly and leaving him alone.

Roman looks around the small space. It is an office of some sort with a small window on the wall opposite the door. There are three wooden chairs facing a large table against the back wall under the window with a view of the bright red moon bathing the room in its light. Seeing no apparent threat, Roman walks over to the chairs and sits down.

A moment later a tall, imposing man dressed in black leather enters the room. A metal mask covers his face and his purple shielded eyes immediately target Roman.

'Captain Roman. I'm Gryffin. I think we need to talk.'

13

Terra doesn't like this. Roman left the room with one of the locals twenty minutes ago and neither of them has come back yet. Not only that, but some additional guests have joined the party and these visitors don't seem right. She brushes her long curls off her shoulder and searches for Stanner in the crowd. The tall candles lining the edge of the room create pockets of shadow.

Her heels click on the wooden floor as she shuffles through the crowd. Many of the locals had donned their best finery for the occasion, eager to impress the visiting Foundation delegates, but Terra had kept it simple. Her fitted black trousers, high heels, and flowing, white silk shirt said simple but elegant. Milla had tried to convince her to wear a dress, but Terra had quickly quashed that idea. She didn't entirely trust these people so didn't want to take a chance. There weren't many hiding places for a gun in the two dresses she had brought with her.

Terra politely nudges past revellers and finally makes her way to the edge of the room. She pops a grape into her mouth as she surveys the crowd. The drinks table is the obvious place to find Stanner, but he's not here. She then sees him speaking to a local woman. Before she loses Stanner to this woman's bed, she pushes her way up to him. Terra has to shout in his ear to be heard over the local band, who are doing their best to make sure people back on *Infinity* can still hear them. 'Have you noticed them?'

He excuses himself from the young woman's clutches and offers Terra some food on his plate. 'You mean the ten or so men that came in from different directions? Yeah.' He checks his radio and curses under his breath. 'Someone's blocked all signals to *Infinity*. Looks like we're in for a spot of trouble. Stay with Anders and Mills. Keep to the Southwest entrance. I'll try to locate the captain. Be ready to move.'

She nods and wanders back across the room; mingling with any crew she passes to subtly let them know there might be trouble. After collecting Anders and Mills, they stand near the entrance and lean against the thick wooden door frame.

The new additions to the party have tried to blend in and while their attire matches the locals, it's clear they aren't. They're watching everything going on around them like hawks. She places her hand on the butt of her gun as she scans the room again for Roman. It's not like him to wander off alone. She hopes Stanner finds him.

∞

Gryffin walks up to Roman and stops a few paces in front of him. He ignores the weapon pointed at his chest. Before Roman can fire, Gryffin rips the gun out of his hand and crushes the barrel in his right hand. He tosses it over his shoulder. 'No guns ... yet. If I wanted you dead, I would have killed you as soon as you stepped off your ship. And, from what I hear, you're under orders to capture me alive.'

Roman stares at the masked man — his son. He should be doing something, but all his training has vanished from his head. There was no plan after he drew his weapon. His brain seems solely focused on the fact his son is in front of him. Roman stands idly in the corner as Gryffin examines him. The Nomad leader crosses his arms. 'What's wrong? Forget your well-rehearsed Foundation speech, Captain?'

'I... ' Nothing else will come out.

Gryffin tilts his head to the side and reaches up behind his left ear. His mask retreats and Roman comes face to face with his past. It wasn't clear from the drawing, but his son looks so much like Maggie it makes Roman's heart ache.

Gryffin crosses his arms and studies his adversary. 'You want to colonise the Sector but you can't even string a damn sentence together.'

Roman pushes his shoulders back. Gryffin is right. He's representing the Foundation. Any other personal feelings will have to wait until later. 'No mask?'

'Figured a member of your crew screwed that little secret up for me already.'

'Why did you help her?'

Gryffin shrugs. 'Kind of regretting it now.'

'You're aware of my orders?' Gryffin nods once. 'Are you going to hand yourself in?' Roman hopes for one fleeting moment he will not have to arrest his son.

'No.'

'So why are you here?'

Gryffin sits backwards on one of the chairs and drapes his arms over the back. 'I need to know what you want with me.'

'I'm ...' Roman clears his throat. 'I'm following orders.'

Gryffin grunts and shakes his head. 'You'll have to do better than that.'

Roman crosses his arms to appear more confident than he feels. 'You know why. The Foundation considers you a threat to the people of the Sector.'

'You don't believe that any more than I do. It has nothing to do with the population of the Sector. If the Foundation wants me out of the way before the rest of the fleet arrives, you'd be under orders to remove me any way you can. What I don't understand is why you are under specific orders to take me in alive.'

'In spite of what you may believe, the Foundation doesn't issue kill orders unless they have a good reason.'

Gryffin picks at the back of the worn, wooden chair. 'I've killed four of your people. I would have thought that would be reason enough.'

Roman pauses. Gryffin has a point. In other circumstances, the Foundation would have ordered his death. It's not like he hasn't proved he deserves his place at the top of the Foundation wanted list. That fact helps bring Roman's brain back online. The man in front of him is a criminal. 'So, can I take it you won't be coming with me quietly?'

'Quietly, loudly, same answer. No.'

'So what's the purpose of this meeting?'

'Friendly warning. To politely ask you to leave the colonies alone.'

'What about bargaining for your own freedom?'

Gryffin shrugs. 'I'm not worried about that. You come after me and people will die. That's a given.' Gryffin's blue eyes suddenly change to purple and Roman takes a step back. 'Leave the colonies as they are. The Sector doesn't need fixing.'

'The Foundation thinks differently. We will colonise this Sector. You can't stop it.'

'I like a challenge.' Gryffin gets up and walks to the other side of the room. He leans against the far wall and looks above Roman's head. 'I'm curious. What did you say to the Taldorans to turn them?'

Roman holds his position and suddenly feels slightly uneasy. Something has attracted Gryffin's attention, but there's no way he's going to break eye contact to see what it is. 'They knew a good deal when they saw it. No competition really.'

Gryffin activates his mask again. 'I guess I'll be seeing you again soon, Captain. By the way, I'd take two steps to the right if you want to keep your head.'

Confused, Roman looks up through the glass skylight to see a ship in the distance. It takes his brain a second to notice the streak of light coming from her and another second to jolt his body into motion. He jumps to the side as the missile hits the building and rains glass onto him.

∞

'What the hell hit us?' Anders shouts as the building shakes.

Locals scream and run in all directions. Terra scans the crowd and notices the late arrivals have their weapons out and are moving towards the exits. 'We need to vacate.'

'But what about the locals?' Mills asks.

'They're under Foundation protection, so keep them safe. Move to the rendezvous point.'

She doesn't wait for them to acknowledge and runs through the panicking crowd in the direction Stanner and Roman went. There's no way she's leaving until she knows Roman is safe. Using the crowd as cover, she dodges the men with guns and pushes her way out into the corridor as another missile hits the building. Terra loses her balance and falls heavily against the wall. She pushes herself upright and tries her radio again, cursing when she hears nothing but static. A bullet hits the wall to the left of her head. She turns around and fires, missing one of the armed men who takes cover around the corner. With no cover of her own, she lets loose another few rounds before running down the hall, straight into a large crater.

∞

Gryffin climbs over the support beam that crashed to the ground, splitting the room. The power to the building suddenly goes down, plunging them into darkness. His ocular implant adjusts, bathing everything in an eerie green glow. Roman is gone.

Gryffin turns on his radio. 'Klay, are our people clear?'

'Yes, sir. They're on the other side of the building.'

'Good. Hit the surface again, then put *Ares* down as close as you can. We're going to need a quick evac.'

He charges his arm as he enters the corridor and lets his primary implant take control slightly. His vision sharpens and the familiar and unpleasant buzzing feeling starts at the base of his head.

He didn't order the barrage for the Foundation's benefit. This colony is one of his and the fact they signed up so quickly with the Foundation pisses him off. They need to learn allies can't pull out of the agreement.

Gryffin looks through a hole in the roof and sees *Ares* hovering in the distance, ready to land and pick them up. He doesn't have much time before the Foundation figure out how to bypass their radio block. Once their ship gets involved, the chance of his team getting hurt increases.

He pushes his way through the rubble. It looks like *Ares* didn't hold back on this side of the building. There isn't much left of the structure and the level is starting to give way. For some strange reason, the Taldorans built the hall over the old mines, leaving a maze of tunnels under the floor. He can cause quite a bit of destruction with only a few missiles. He braces himself against the wall as another missile hits the building. 'Klay. Leave it at that for a moment. Have they found the store yet?'

'Yes, sir. The transports are being loaded with the weapons and medical equipment we provided. What about the food?'

'Leave it. Are we meeting any resistance?'

'A bit.'

'Don't kill any of the Taldorans. They're going to have enough to worry about once we leave.'

'What about the Foundation?'

'Can't help a bit of collateral damage. I'm on my way out.'

He signs off and turns the corner, stopping when he sees the large hole in the floor. It's then he hears someone shouting for help. He pulls his gun out and peers over the edge. When he sees who is down the hole, he curses to himself.

And like the last time, she is pointing her weapon at him.

14

Roman presses his hand to his side and curses when it comes away covered in blood. It could have been a lot worse. He tries his radio, but the connection is blocked. He has no doubt the Nomad are to blame.

Roman pauses to get his bearings and then moves towards where he hopes the rest of his crew will be gathering. Recent experience had forced him to put a contingency plan in place in case the Nomad decided to crash the party. Every off-ship trip they took lately seemed to end in gunfire.

By following the screams and shouts, he eventually finds the main banquet hall. In complete contrast to earlier, the laden tables are overturned; food scattered and trampled on the floor. A hand touches his shoulder. He spins around, his gun raised, but lowers his weapon when he sees Stanner.

'Thank God, sir. We've been looking for you.'

'The rest of the team?'

'At the rendezvous point.' He looks around the room and frowns.

'Terra not with you?'

Roman groans to himself. Of all the people to go AWOL, it had to be her. 'Gather a small security team. We've got to locate her before the Nomad do.'

∞

'You again?'

Gryffin crouches down and looks at Terra. 'You going to shoot me or you want out of there?'

She leaves her weapon trained on him for another few seconds then slowly puts it down. 'How do I know you're not going to kill me?'

He removes his mask and looks at her. 'Because I stopped to help you — again.' He holds out his gloved hand. 'Grab on.'

Terra slowly reaches out but loses her grip and slips further along the ledge as the ground trembles again. Gryffin tucks his gun into its holster, lies on the floor, and leans over the edge. 'C'mon, Terra.'

She reaches out again, but the edge of the ledge crumbles under her. Terra falls onto a small outcropping below.

They're running out of time — quickly. One more tremor could tip her into the mines below. The web of support beams would kill her before she even hit the ground. They're what he needs right now, however. He drops down into the pit and grabs onto the broken end of one of the beams. Gryffin pulls his lower body up, wraps his legs around the metal, and hangs on tightly by his feet. He lets go and straightens so he's hanging upside down. He reaches out to her again, but she doesn't move. 'Terra, hold out your hand. I can't reach you.'

She looks down at the gaping hole underneath her. 'You need to leave, Gryffin. The whole ledge is going to collapse.'

'Terra, hold out your damn hand!'

The ground shakes again and causes the far side of the crater to break away. 'Go, Gryffin!'

'Lieutenant, Foundation or not, I am a superior officer. When I order you to do something, you damn well do it!' It does the trick. He locks his eyes onto hers when she lifts her head. 'I am going to get you out of here, but you have to trust me.'

'Gryffin, please go!'

'It's *Captain* or *Sir*. Trust me. Now stand up, Lieutenant.'

Terra looks back at him again and nods her head. 'Yes, sir.' She slowly stands and braces herself against the crater wall as she gets her footing.

'Now jump.'

'But ... sir.'

'The only *but* I want is yours in the air. Close your eyes and jump. That's an order, Lieutenant!' he shouts.

∞

Sayber frowns and shakes his head. 'I must have heard wrong. Did you say he's firing on one of his colonies?'

Bray double checks the information to appease him. 'Yes, sir. It looks like he's not holding back. The town centre seems to be collapsing into the old tunnels.'

Sayber shakes his head again. What the hell is Gryffin playing at? If he kept this up, the Foundation would have a firm hold in the Sector before they knew it. He always questioned Gryffin's sanity, but never thought he would do something like this.

Sayber had been Gryffin's second-in-command when Rayde stepped aside. They always had a fiery relationship and it only got worse after Gryffin's promotion. Sayber wanted to push the Nomad more towards the old ways while Gryffin wanted to transform them to cheery traders and protectors. After a few years of tension, Sayber had finally made his move and tried to take control of *Ares*.

Gryffin wasn't surprised when it happened. They couldn't continue the way they were. Unfortunately, Gryffin had quashed the mutiny quickly and ruthlessly. Any of the crew who had joined Sayber, died at Gryffin's hands, but he had managed to escape with his life.

A year later, he had taken *Perses*, formed the Hunters and ever since they had been at each other's throats. Sayber knows Gryffin like a brother, knows most of his moves. But in all the years he has never once attacked one of his colonies. There must be a valid reason for him attacking the world. He leans over Bray, examining the screen over his shoulder. 'Scan the area. There has to be another ship there.'

After working on his keyboard for a few minutes, Bray's shoulders drop as he curses. 'Foundation. They're on the far side, hidden from the initial scans.'

Sayber nods. That makes more sense. 'The Taldorans must have switched alliances. I would imagine Gryffin's nose is out of joint. Hell of a punishment.'

Bray leans back in his chair, tapping his fingers on the screen. 'What do you want to do? Leave them to it or join in?'

Sayber smiles at the excitement on his first officer's face. 'Afraid I'm going to have to disappoint you — no time for playing with the Nomad at the moment. Let's leave them to it. Either they kill him or he kills them. No complaints from me either way. Set coordinates for the next colony on the list. Best get a head start while he's busy.'

∞

Gryffin's metal hand grabs on to her arm to halt her fall. The metal pipe creaks under their combined weight. She opens her eyes and locks onto his purple gaze.

He tightens his grip and hoists his upper body towards the beam, bringing her level with it. She wraps her arms around it as he pulls himself upright. Gryffin climbs up the side of the hole then reaches back down for Terra.

Without waiting to catch his breath, he yanks her to her feet and pulls her after him along the corridor. He practically throws her around the corner and pushes her to the ground as he contacts his ship. 'This is Gryffin. The southwest corner of the building has collapsed. Teams three and four, move to back up teams one and two. Gryffin out.'

She leans against the wall and tries to catch her breath. As much as she hates that he had to rescue her again, she wasn't going to complain.

He points to the corridor to their left. 'Go down there until you exit the building then veer to the left. I'll keep my teams away from you as long as I can.'

'Why not call them off?'

'I shouldn't have saved you — again. My men will have my command if they even know I'm talking to you. Now do me a favour and go.'

'Hang on. I warned you about the Foundation. Why am I the bad guy?' Gryffin pulls a piece of paper from the back pocket of his leather trousers. He opens it and a chill runs up Terra's spine when she sees the image on the page. It's the sketch of him she gave to Roman. How did Gryffin obtain it? 'Where did you get that?'

He pins her to the wall with his flesh arm while he shoves the sketch up to her face. 'The whole Sector is being turned upside-down because I helped you. And you thank me by drawing that! That's your name on the bottom isn't it?'

'Yes, but I had no idea this would happen. Where did you find it?'

'It's stuck up all over the last damn station I visited. Your drawing is being used as a wanted poster. It looks like your Foundation is offering a hefty bounty for me. Why the hell didn't you mention this when you contacted me?'

'I should have. I didn't know how to.'

'Don't give me that. What about: "Gryffin, they have a picture of your face"? If I were you, I'd be running.'

Not knowing what else to do, she takes hold of Gryffin's hand. 'I didn't have a choice but to give my captain the drawing. Someone I considered a friend forced me to hand it over. I'm so sorry this happened.'

His eyes narrow as he looks down at her hand. 'If you want to keep your hand attached to your arm, you'll let go now.'

She quickly removes her hand and he turns to walk away from her. 'Please don't go like this.' He turns to stare at her again. She knows this is her last chance to convince him. It's important he doesn't take off thinking she betrayed him. She locks onto his eyes and puts every bit of sincerity she can muster into her voice. 'I swear to you Gryffin, I drew it for myself. I honestly had no idea this would happen. You have to believe me. Stanner found it and threatened to go to the captain if I didn't. I had no choice. I never meant to betray you like this. Please believe me.'

Confusion clouds his features. 'Drew it for yourself? Why?'

She shrugs. 'I wanted to remember … you. I know I should have been more careful with it, but I can't change that now.'

Instead of leaving, he quickly steps up in front of Terra and pushes her back against the wall. He rests his hands on the wood at either side of her head and leans in without touching her. Terra's heart beats loudly in her chest as she relishes his scent of leather and musk.

She feels like his dark blue eyes are drilling into her brain. His hair tickles her cheek as he moves his face closer to hers. His warm breath against her neck sends shivers through her body. Terra closes her eyes and swallows deeply when her throat suddenly goes dry. 'Terra?' She feels his breath on her ear as he whispers to her.

'Yes?'

'It doesn't make a difference to me if you gave it out on purpose or not. You betrayed me. Now, get the hell out of here before my crew catches and kills you.'

As she's about to respond, he curses loudly and shoves himself away from her. He doubles over and grabs his head. Terra reaches for his shoulders, but withdraws her hands when he snarls at her. 'Back off!'

'What's wrong?'

He pushes her away from him and slides down to the ground. 'Nothing. Just go.'

'I'm not leaving you like this. You got me this far. I'll help you the rest of the way.'

He pushes her hand away and grabs his head again, using his metal arm to support himself. 'My crew is coming.'

The building shudders as another missile strikes. The already unstable stone walls along the corridor start to topple. 'If you stay here much longer your crew will be digging you out.' Terra pulls Gryffin around the corner as rubble lands where he stood a moment ago. She helps him to his feet and practically drags him along the corridor. Terra has to pause every few steps when the pain becomes too much for him. She doesn't know what's wrong with him, but he's in bad shape.

Terra finally drags him outside without bumping into any of his crew. She tries to lay him down gently but catches her foot on a stone. Losing her footing, she falls and lands flat on her back with him on top. Gryffin manages to put his arms out so he doesn't crush her. 'Are you okay?' she asks.

'Yeah,' he replies even though it's clear he's still in pain. 'You?'

She nods. In complete disregard for everything going on around them, they stare at each other for a few minutes. Gunfire sounds in the background, but all she can think about is how nice it feels to have his body pressed tightly against hers. She had imagined being with him like this many times since the station. Of course, they always had fewer items of clothing on in her versions.

Before she knows what's happening, she kisses him. His entire body freezes for a moment, but he doesn't pull away from her. Instead of stopping, as she probably should, she tries to pull him tighter against her. Initially, he resists, but then slowly lowers himself closer to her. She runs her hand through his thick, dark hair, loving the way the silky strands feel.

She moves her knees apart and manoeuvres so one of his legs is between hers. Terra presses tightly against him in a way that drives her insane. His tongue hungrily explores her mouth as she grabs onto his leather-covered thigh. Terra pushes harder against his leg, wishing they are a lot more naked, and she clearly isn't alone. There is no mistaking his body's reaction to what is going on.

She reaches under his shirt and runs her hand up his side, along the hard muscles. Gryffin surprises her by growling as he pushes tighter against her. Terra runs her hand up the ridges of his stomach but stops when she feels the cold outline of the metal. He suddenly pulls away from her, draws his gun, and points it directly at her head. His purple eyes glare accusingly at her.

Terra sits up quickly and struggles to comprehend what he's doing. 'Gryffin, what are you doing?'

'Get the hell out of here now before I shoot you.'

Her heart drops. Coming down brutally fast from the high she had been on, Terra wishes the ground would open up and swallow her. Thoroughly confused and extremely embarrassed, Terra slowly gets to her feet. Seeing nothing but hatred in his cold blue eyes, she straightens her shoulders and walks away.

15

Roman curses to himself. He started the evening with an excellent buffet and is ending it by chasing a group of mercenaries through the forest. With the radios still down, they have no way of tracking Terra, and the locals are worse than useless. He can hardly blame them. Within an hour of signing with the Foundation, their world had been attacked. *Infinity* has broken orbit and is providing assistance where it can. The Nomad have stopped attacking but haven't left, which means Gryffin is still on the surface — possibly with Terra.

'Sir, radios are back on,' Stanner reports.

'Obtain a reading on Terra.'

Stanner spins around with his gun raised. 'According to this, she's coming up behind us.'

As he finishes speaking, she bursts from the trees, gasping for breath.

Roman stops himself from doing something embarrassing like hugging her. Instead, he nods. 'In one piece, Lieutenant?'

'Apologies, sir. I got separated while looking for you.'

Roman looks at her again and instantly knows something is wrong. Instead of hiding the recently shed tears, the torchlight only highlights them. 'Terra, are you all right?' he asks in a low voice.

She puts on one of her worst *I'm fine* faces and smiles. 'Yes, sir.'

Not fooled for one minute, Roman grunts. 'Stanner, contact *Infinity*. Find out where the Nomad ship is and the location of any remaining ground crew. I think they've outstayed their welcome.'

∞

Gryffin uses his night vision to scan the path ahead. *Ares* is around the next corner. He should have been off the surface by now but he had listened to the weaker side of himself again and followed Terra until she met with her people. It's the least he could do after pulling his gun on her.

He curses and thumps the tree beside him, surprising the crew members with him. Threatening to shoot her had to be one of the stupidest things he's done. It's not like she had done anything wrong. She kissed him and he kissed her back. It's what normal people do. They kiss and touch and don't pull guns on each other because of it.

Initially, he didn't mind her touching him. Touching had always been a big no-no for him. In the past, contact had meant pain and to this day it's hard to separate the two. The constant checks Klay has to run on him don't help either. It makes his stomach churn.

But not this time. She'd run her fingers through his hair and he had sort of liked it. The soft and gentle actions felt very different to anything he's experienced before. It didn't hurt, so he wanted more and wanted to give her more.

But then it all went wrong. She had touched the metal on his chest. Something inside him snapped back on. He went from not being close enough to being too close. The incredible feelings and sensations disappeared. It wasn't her fault. He's the one that can't separate the present from the past.

118

That's why he pulled his gun on her. He had to force her to leave before he fell off the slippery slope of his sanity. If she didn't take off straight away, he could have hurt her and made things worse between the Foundation and the Nomad.

Now, thanks to his actions and following her back to her people, he is being tracked by the Foundation back to the ship. To make things worse, five of his crew are also with him. His stupidity has placed them in the firing line.

He instructs his team to move while he covers the rear. They round the corner and he breathes a sigh of relief when he sees *Ares*. Klay put her down in the only open space he could detect: the middle of the lake. Not the easiest escape route. His team burst into the clearing and pause for a moment when they see *Ares*. If it weren't for the metal sails and large engines, you could easily think you were looking at an ocean vessel trapped in a lake.

Getting his mind back on his task, Gryffin turns his attention to the Foundation hot on their heels. The Nomad take cover and hold them back, but there's no way they can return to *Ares* without leaving themselves exposed.

Gryffin scans the darkness and picks up heat signatures for five shooters. The easy option would be to call in more support from *Ares*, but it's not something he wants to consider. Anyone on the loading ramp would be a sitting target and the ground crew could easily get caught in the crossfire. Simplest solution is for him to cover the team.

He shouldn't use the implant again so soon, but he'll deal with the consequences after they're all safely on board. He activates his radio and contacts Klay. 'Open the side lower hatch. We're coming in hot.' Turning back to the team, he reloads his gun. 'I'll keep them busy. Access *Ares* through the port lower hatch. Most of the door will be under water so don't miss it. Be ready to move on my mark.'

He lets his well-practiced control slip and feels himself getting pushed to the back of his mind. Using the small amount of control he has left, he charges his arm. Knowing it's going to hurt like hell afterwards, he steps out of the trees with his weapon raised in front of him. He fires a few rounds and orders his team to break cover while he blocks them from the Foundation bullets.

∞

'What the hell is he doing?'

Stanner shakes his head. 'I don't know. We're hitting him, but he's still standing there as if nothing is happening.'

Roman peeks around the tree, fascinated by what he sees. Gryffin stands blocking the path to his ship. Electricity seems to be coursing all over his body, originating from his arm. It's protecting him from their rounds. Surely the Foundation must have known about this capability. Cursing, he pulls his head back, narrowly missing Gryffin's bullet. Stanner yelps as another bullet punches into his shoulder.

'Stanner?' Roman asks.

Stanner winces and checks his wound. 'It's gone through. Damn it, a bit of warning of this talent would have been nice.'

Roman grunts. 'Couldn't agree more.' Roman moves position and peers out from behind a tree. The glow from the Nomad leader's purple eyes makes him appear all the more threatening. This is only going to end one way, and it doesn't involve his team walking away with Gryffin in custody. It's clear they're way out of their depth. 'We need to evac to *Infinity* and regroup. I'm not jeopardising my crew until we can figure out a safe way of capturing and containing him. Fall back.'

Stanner turns to him. 'You're letting them escape?'

Roman looks back to his son. The more he learns about the Nomad leader, the more questions present themselves. 'He's bought himself a brief reprieve. For now.'

∞

Their escape proves easier than he thought it would be. Gryffin stays in front of his men until the last of the Foundation crew disappear into the forest. They may have made a tactical retreat, but he's not stupid. They'll only redouble their efforts next time.

When he's sure he's alone, he shuts down his arm and steps into the water. He dives under the surface and swims towards the submerged side door of *Ares*. He locks on to the lights surrounding the door and pulls himself through the water.

Gryffin swims through the door and surfaces inside the ship. He breaks the surface to face the rest of the landing party on the platform above him. When they see it's him, they lower their weapons and break formation. Gryffin activates his radio. 'Klay, get us out of here.' Mere seconds later the engines power up and pull *Ares* from the lake.

Once the room is clear of water, he seals the door and tears off his jacket and top. He takes off his mask, looks down and groans to himself. While his arm helped to slow most of the bullets down, it didn't stop them altogether. Seems the Foundation don't care what condition Roman delivers him in.

There must be a dozen holes in his chest and arms along with a through-and-through on his left side. There's no blood yet, but once he takes control of himself again, it'll start. Luckily his team are on the case. Chayse bursts in with a gurney and med kit, but doesn't move further than the edge of the platform. Gryffin needs to take control back from the implant before they'll go anywhere near him.

Gryffin takes a deep breath and fights as hard as he can to push the implant out of his mind. As soon as he attempts to shut it down, the control implant blocks him. The urge to strike out at anyone near him is difficult to ignore. He squeezes his fists tightly and turns to face the wall. It's better for everyone if he can't see any targets.

Gryffin clenches his teeth as a flash of pain sears through his brain. For a minute, he doesn't think he's going to win this battle but he gradually begins to gain the upper hand. He knows he's done it when the familiar pain hits. He wipes away the blood seeping from his nose.

Crimson oozes from the flesh wounds on his chest and arms but flows more freely from the larger hole in his side, pooling at his belt before running down his leathers.

He wants to stay focused and strong, but he can't. The sudden blood loss mixed with the razor sharp withdrawal pain knocks him sideways. He crashes into the bulkhead but manages to grab onto a support beam before he lands flat on his back.

He hears someone shouting for Klay before Chayse slides down the ladder. 'I need a gurney!' Chayse helps him onto the gurney. 'Can you hear me, sir?'

Gryffin nods. 'Of course I can bloody hear you.'

'Did you use the implant or did it force control?'

'I used it.'

Chayse's face grows concerned and he's not the only one. Gryffin is not looking forward to being patched up either. If the implant had forced control, he'd lose consciousness within thirty minutes or so — no one knows why. Any stitching or operations took place before he came to. Easy.

Unfortunately, because he controlled the implant, there'd be no blissful sleep for him. Even if heavily sedated, he'd wake up as soon as he felt any pain. His creator had built in a failsafe so his subject wouldn't miss any of the fun. His pain receptors trigger something that counteracts all drugs. The damn implants keep him conscious and very much aware of every single cut or stitch.

Four minutes later, Gryffin is sitting on the gurney in the med bay with a pair of tweezers in his hand. He adjusts the angle on the mirror arm and sticks the top of the instrument into the first wound. Gritting his teeth, he digs it further into the hole, grabs onto the bullet and pulls it out. 'Any casualties on any team?'

Klay nods at Chayse, who is bandaging a crew member's leg while two more wait patiently for their turn. 'That's it. We were lucky. Well, apart from you. How are you doing?'

Gryffin grunts before bullet number two drops into the metal dish.

'Great.' He had decided to remove as many of the bullets as he could himself. Not only did it give him something to concentrate on but the pain helped keep him grounded. It also meant no one would have to touch him. After what happened with Terra, he didn't want Klay or Chayse working on him yet. 'Did you catch up with the Taldoran leader?'

'Eventually. He got in contact after he noticed some of the supplies were gone.'

Gryffin focuses on the next bullet, takes a deep breath and goes after it. 'I'll bet.' He hisses in pain as he pulls the metal out. The blood continues to drip out of his body and down his trousers from the deeper wound in his side. Klay and Chayse will have to deal with that one due to its location.

'They pleaded with me to leave the weapons and medical supplies,' Klay says. 'But I said you won't change your mind. They'd made their bed with the Foundation and they can damn well lie in it. Let their new friends help them sort out the mess.'

Gryffin doesn't feel sorry about his decision. There's no way he can protect any colony with ties to the Foundation. He rinses off the tweezers and digs the metal prongs back into his flesh.

It's going to be a long night.

16

'Well, did you find anything?'

Milla swings her seat around and sighs dramatically. 'Jeez, Terra, give me a chance. I do have a full-time job.'

Terra pulls up a chair and slides closer to her friend. 'I know you, Milla; you found something, right?'

'Yes, but you're not going to like it.' Milla opens her drawer and pulls out her personal tablet. 'Gryffin's records read like everyone else's: routine vaccinations, health checks, a concussion when he was six from a tumble at school. Did you know he rated top in his class?'

'Really? What career was assigned to him?'

Milla scrolls through the data. 'You probably won't believe me, but your Nomad was in line for a Council position.'

Terra's mouth falls open. 'What? Gryffin would have been one of the Council Twelve?'

'Apparently.'

'Hang on. The identity of the Council members is secret. How did you uncover that information?'

Milla blushes slightly and turns her attention back to the screen. 'That's need-to-know, I'm afraid.' She looks back at her friend and shrugs. 'You want the information or not?'

Terra shakes her head. 'Go on.'

Milla goes back to the original set of records. 'I couldn't unearth anything to explain how he is ... well, the way he is. There is one peculiar entry about two months after his disappearance. It's very well hidden and I almost missed it.' She points to a line of text on her screen: #35.

'Any idea what it means?'

'Nope,' Milla replies. 'I'm at a loss. It doesn't match with anything else in the medical records.'

Terra transfers the data to her unit. 'I'll run it through the system and see what I find. It wouldn't be there unless it meant something.' Milla crosses her arms and quietly watches her friend. 'What?'

'Be careful, okay?'

Terra laughs. 'Relax, Milla, I'll make sure Roman doesn't hear about this.'

'I'm not talking about Roman.' Milla opens the file on the murdered recon officer. She turns her screen around and shows Terra a photo of the mutilated body. 'I know you don't believe he did this, but he did. The bones were broken by hand. No human can do that.'

Terra shakes her head but Milla continues. She leans closer and lowers her voice. 'Terra, Gryffin tortured and killed him. It's conclusive.' Milla gently takes Terra's hand in hers. 'Listen, I know you want to help him and you more than likely have a soft spot for him.'

Terra tries to pull her hand back, but Milla holds it firmly. 'Don't try to talk me out of this, Milla.'

'All I'm asking is for you to examine the evidence and keep it in your mind. The person you're protecting did that,' she says while pointing at the screen. 'I don't want you on my examination table next. There's no record of anything like him in the database. We don't even know exactly what he is, or how the implants affect him. I'm all for taking risks, but this is a step too far.'

Terra can't think of anything to say in his defence. Milla is right but, even though she agrees with what her friends says, Terra still wants to take that risk.

∞

'Are you sure that's what he said?'

'Of course I'm bloody sure,' Balfe shouts. The last thing he needs now is the Scientist questioning him. 'Roman described the incident in great detail. The subject somehow managed to produce an electrical current. I'm getting the impression this is news to you.'

The Scientist takes out a tablet and makes notes, completely ignoring Balfe. It's probably a good thing the conversation is taking place by video instead of face to face. Otherwise, they could very well be looking for a new expert. 'Did you know he could do that?'

He looks up from his work and shakes his head. 'Of course not. It wasn't part of my original design. Perhaps the Nomad added to my work. Did your ship capture him?'

'Have you not been listening? They couldn't possibly prepare for what happened. Do you have any suggestions?'

'Capture him before he uses the additional defence.' The Scientist signs off, leaving Balfe to stare at his reflection in the blank screen. It takes a good six minutes before he's calm enough to think logically.

Damn Scientist doesn't know the difference between reality and fantasy. If he thinks it is as simple as waiting for the Nomad leader to turn off his power, the Scientist is as mad as ... well, as mad as he is. The absence of major details like the subject being able to conduct electricity could shut the project down.

He pours himself a glass of whiskey, savouring the heat as the liquid glides down his throat. He'll push Roman to come up with a solution, but if this is going to happen at all, Balfe himself will have to

126

take charge. He needs to push things along.

He pours another glass as he ponders the problem. The focus seems to be on Gryffin's strengths, but there must be a flip-side. There's no way he's invincible. Everyone has a weakness. All Balfe has to do is know where to search.

∞

Gryffin rubs his sore eyes and stares at the ceiling. The equipment monitoring his vitals beeps and hums in the background.

After a slight disagreement, he had finally relented and allowed Chayse and Klay to stitch him. He has to admit they carried out the task quicker than he could have. With seventeen bullet wounds, it probably would have taken him all night. He'll add that to the list of reasons why he's not keen on the Foundation. While the injuries are far from life threatening, his vitals are a little off. It isn't surprising. He had used the implant twice and been repeatedly shot.

The area around his ocular implant itches, but he doesn't have the energy to raise his arm, let alone scratch. Using the implant mixed with the injuries has left him as weak as a baby. He needs sleep, but he's too wound up to consider it at the moment. His body may have given up for the day, but his mind is wide awake.

He pulls Terra's slightly wet drawing out of his pocket and stares at the blurred pencil lines. He lets the implant to the surface enough to sharpen his vision and watches as the lines solidify to form an image that shocks him. He had known the drawing showed him, but now that he can see the finer details he's stunned. He very rarely looks in the mirror as he hates the metal and scars on the reflection.

The picture shows the real him. Terra managed to capture him as he's never seen himself before. The flesh, scars and metal almost compliment each other. He looks ... well ... like a man instead of a machine. He reaches out, ignoring the way his arm shakes and traces the line of the scar running across the top of his nose on the drawing.

Terra had drawn it in such a way it seems delicate, unlike the jagged tear he sees. Maybe she told the truth about why she drew it.

He curses himself, scrunches the drawing up, and lowers his hand onto the bed with a thump. God, Terra is confusing the hell out of him. Even after he collapsed, she stayed to help instead of saving her neck.

She makes him do stupid things, like forget who he is and letting unfamiliar emotions take control. They were bad news for each other — end of story. Leaving aside what happened between them and how much he wanted to continue, they couldn't go any further. They were enemies. She had reported him to the officials and drawn that picture of him, after all. Time to stop daydreaming and face reality.

He picks up the pad lying beside him on the bed and glares at it. He plays the messages again as he closes his eyes to let the information sink in. A colony has requested his services. They want him to kill a corrupt thieving politician they can't legally remove from office. After that, it's on to a small colony requesting his protection. He's a killer one minute and a protector the next. His life is completely messed up.

Gryffin throws the pad back down on his bed and stares at the ceiling again. His head hurts and his eyes feel like they're full of sand. He hasn't had a decent rest for five days.

Trying not to get tangled in the wires, he turns on his front and buries his head under his arms to block out the noise of the machines and the ship in general. Usually, he can't sleep when it's quiet, but for some reason, the banging, hissing, and clanging is annoying him.

After a few minutes, his shoulder and elbow start to ache from having his mechanical arm at that angle, so he puts his right arm down by his side. Ten minutes later the pressure on his chest implant and wounds gets too much to ignore, so he turns onto his right side.

Again he can't get comfortable. Moving on to his left side doesn't work either as it hurts to lie on his facial implant for too long. Finally, he moves onto his back and ends up staring at the ceiling again. Not only is he completely awake but he also has aching implants, tangled wires, and a big case of pissed off and frustrated added to the mix.

With no other distractions, he picks up the pad again to listen to the data for the third time.

17

'It's already been a month, Roman,' Balfe shouts. 'I don't have to tell you this isn't doing your career any good.'

Roman grinds his teeth. 'Sir, Gryffin isn't your average criminal. Have you not read my report? From what we can make out, he's not only the captain of one of the ships, but also the high commander of the whole fleet. More than likely a much larger fleet than we anticipated. He's protected on all of his colony worlds and by the rest of his fleet. Getting close to him will prove next to impossible.'

'And yet you got close. You stood in front of him and did nothing.'

'With all due respect, sir, he caught us completely unawares. We had no idea he'd be on the planet.'

'Captain Roman. I've had a rather unpleasant meeting with the Council,' Balfe says. 'I managed to buy us four weeks, then they are going to make a more forceful move on the Sector. They want the risk taken out.'

'Sir, Gryffin isn't the only threat out here. Surely it would be best to try and work with the Nomad, gain them as allies rather than enemies.'

'So you would rather we side with a known criminal than arrest him and see he gets the punishment he deserves?'

'I would rather we find a common ground.'

'Common ground with the likes of the Nomad? I'll forget you said that, Captain. You have four weeks to capture him. If not, both you and the Nomad will regret it.'

∞

'Are you sure?' Rayde asks. 'It happened a hell of a long time ago and you weren't quite yourself.'

Gryffin clears his throat and tries to ignore the way his tongue suddenly feels too big for his mouth. 'I'm sure. Chayse hacked the Foundation system and downloaded an image of Balfe. When I was in the lab, a group of people visited one day while they were operating on me. He was one of them.'

Rayde sighs, 'We're talking about twenty-odd years ago.'

'I remember him!' Gryffin shouts louder than he meant to. 'They were the only other people I saw the whole time I was there.'

'Okay, settle down, son. I believe you. You still in control?'

'He's Foundation, Rayde,' Gryffin continues without acknowledging the question. 'Fairly high up, too. You think they're involved?'

Rayde moves back from the screen. 'Bit of a risky affair if they are. It would threaten their whiter-than-white image.'

'Why else would he be there?'

'I honestly don't know, Gryffin.'

'Did you see any sign of the Foundation on the station?'

Rayde chuckles. 'We were kinda focused on you. We weren't expecting to discover anyone, so when I tripped over you in the dark, it surprised me. Then the auto-destruct sounded and we got the hell out of there. I wish I had more answers for you. I really do. I'll ask around. See if I can dig up any information. In the meantime, you need to stay out of it. Keep your head down. Does the crew know about this?'

Gryffin shakes his head.

'Keep it that way. We'll need to gather evidence before we take them on.'

'Rayde, I can't just do nothing.'

'That's exactly what you need to do. At the moment, they've only got a handful of ships here. In a few months, there could be more. It'll make more of an impact having the Nomad go up against the whole Foundation fleet.'

'You saying we should start a war? I meant killing Balfe, not going up against the full Foundation.'

'And what's to say Balfe acted alone? How do you know it wasn't the whole Foundation? That's why you need to wait. Let me look into it for you.'

Gryffin doesn't say anything. He trusts Rayde, but Gryffin's not going to forget about it until he hears back from him. He'll get Chayse to continue what he's doing — but make sure Rayde doesn't hear about it. 'I want retribution.'

'And you will have it. You worried this is why they're looking for you?'

Gryffin barely represses a shiver. 'I can't let them cut me open again.'

Rayde nods solemnly. 'I know, son. Hell, I don't know how you got through it the first time. The Nomad have your back this time. We're not going to let anything happen. You have my word, if the Foundation is behind what happened to you; I will personally not quit until each and every one of them pays.'

∞

'He did what?'

Terra takes another large mouthful of drink and slumps back on the couch in her room. 'He pulled his gun and threatened to shoot me.'

Milla blows out a long breath. 'Talk about a passion killer. Shit, Terra, I'm sorry.'

Terra snorts. 'You don't have to be nice to me. I got carried away with everything. I mean, think about it. What exactly do I know about him apart from rumours?' She rubs a hand over her face, embarrassed by what had happened. 'We were getting all heated while a gunfight took place a stone's throw away. I risked my career for a quick fumble! What the hell came over me?'

Milla shuffles up beside her. 'You weren't exactly using your brains at the time. You got caught up in the moment and there's nothing wrong with that. He had rescued you ... again.'

Terra grimaces. 'I'm a Foundation officer, not a damsel in distress.'

'Listen, while I agree it wasn't the best thing you've ever done, you can't undo it. Anyway, you're leaving out the relevant information. Details, please.'

Her bright red face answers for her as usual. 'Probably the most intense experience I've had. But that doesn't excuse what I did.'

Milla smiles. 'We've moved past that bit. So, you had a great time and you will not be venturing down that path with an outlaw again.'

Terra empties her glass then lays her head back on the cushion. That's exactly what she should be doing. Years of hard work earned her this place on the crew. She couldn't throw it all away for a man, let alone one as wrong for her as Gryffin. 'I don't know what's going through my head at the moment, Milla. I don't do things like this. I don't break the rules. Why is Gryffin having this effect on me? Why am I letting him?' Terra laughs abruptly. 'Seriously, can you imagine if I brought Gryffin home to Roman?' Terra meets her eyes. 'I need you to help me get over whatever this is. Please.'

'Sorry — nothing I can do about that.' Milla leans closer to Terra. 'You like him, Terra. Believe it or not, that's a very healthy reaction. I mean, he's bound to attract your attention. He's well outside the Foundation norm. He's a pirate, Terra. Can't get more different than that.' Milla tucks her legs under her and slouches back in the chair. 'Quit over-thinking everything. Go with the flow. If I'm honest, I'm kind of jealous. Leaving out the gun part, of course.' Milla shrugs. 'But you're right. He's a complete jerk and you should stay away from him.'

Terra places her empty glass back on the table in front of her as she tries to ignore the smirk on Milla's face. They know each other too well. Milla knows even though Gryffin is a 'jerk' as she called him, Terra still wants him. She wishes she knew what had changed with him so suddenly.

∞

Gryffin opens his eyes and looks around the room in horror. This isn't right. He's back in the lab. He fights to keep the contents of his stomach in place. He shouldn't be here. He escaped years ago, didn't he?

Gryffin reaches up and touches the thick metal collar tight against his neck, restricting his air supply. The heavy chain linking him to the wall only increases the pressure on his neck. Panic swells in his chest as he gasps for breath. He falls to his front and screams as the pain shoots through his body.

He looks down and cries out when he sees the dissected remains of his chest. Blood and large ugly surgical wounds cover his chest. Some are crudely sealed and others are open to expose the muscle and metal under his skin. Every precious breath he takes grates his broken ribs against each other and sends waves of agony through his chest.

He slowly reaches down and pulls a shard of metal from his chest with a sickening squelch of blood. It drops to the ground and Gryffin tries to scramble away but is pulled back by the chain attached to his collar. He's trapped.

Through the darkness, a shape emerges. It's the Scientist. He kicks Gryffin onto his back and drags him to the table by his collar. Too weak to resist, he barely puts up a struggle as the metal restraints secure him to the surface. The table rises from the ground and stops at chest level. A blinding bright light turns on directly above him.

Suddenly, a white hot pain erupts on the side of his face as the Scientist cuts into his flesh. The man smiles down at him as he slices into the skin above Gryffin's eye. Gryffin can feel the blood trickle down the side of his face and into his ear. The Scientist picks up some metal, pushes it into the incision and screws it firmly to Gryffin's skull beside his eye.

Gryffin wakes up and barely manages to hold back a scream. His stomach lurches as he stumbles out of bed. He hits the ground hard and lands on his sensitive chest. Gritting his teeth in determination, he puts all his strength into fighting against the remnants of the dream, but it keeps pulling him back. He touches his chest and even though there's no blood, his stomach still churns violently.

Gryffin forces his arms under him, but struggles to heave himself off the ground. He needs to get up off the floor. If he can get up, the dream will go away, but he can't move. It feels like a weight is placed on his back, pressing him tight to the cold floor. The air thickens around him and he begins to gasp in spite of his implant's assistance.

His programming will keep him alive for a few minutes without oxygen, but that doesn't rein in the panic as his throat constricts. He reaches up, fully expecting to feel the metal collar around his neck, cutting off his air supply, but there's nothing there.

His body is telling him it's finally had enough abuse, but he'll be damned if he's going to give up. Gryffin drags himself over to the chair beside his bed. He clutches the metal leg and yanks it over. His radio and implant diagnostic kit crash to the ground out of his reach.

The effort proves to be too much for his body. He can't even lift his head off the damn floor. With no choice but to accept the inevitable, Gryffin stops struggling and lies on the ground. He listens to the sounds of the ship around him. Not quite the way he planned to die — face down on the ground of his room in nothing but his boxers. It's strangely appropriate; he spent what he can remember of his childhood on a cold metal floor, so why not die there too?

∞

'So, you finally decided to talk to me,' says Balfe.

Sayber bites his tongue. As much as he hates the man, he can't walk away from the one hundred thousand credits Balfe promised him. For the moment at least, he had to play the dutiful subordinate. 'I've been pretty busy blowing stuff up for you. I can't come running every time you call. People will start to get suspicious.'

'I thought you'd be further along than you are. What's the delay?'

'The Hunters need to be seen in the Sector in their own right too. If the Nomad think we're taking a step back, Gryffin will destroy us. We're working through your list. That's all I can say.'

'I'm afraid that's not good enough. You'll have to work faster.'

'I don't have to do anything, Admiral,' Sayber replies. 'As I said before, you need me a lot more than I need you. So, unless you're going to put your ass on the firing line and send some ships here to help, you'll have to back off and let me do what I promised I would.'

He stops himself there before he pushes back too hard. He wants to show Balfe he's not a pushover but also doesn't want him to hire someone else to take down Gryffin. Not that there is a list of possible candidates; it pretty much starts and ends with the Hunters.

Balfe quietly examines him before nodding. 'Very well. I'll leave it in your capable hands. I will stress, however, we need to finish as quickly as possible.'

The screen goes blank. Sayber lets out a deep breath. All well and good for Balfe to tell him they're on a deadline. Balfe is sitting thousands of miles away in a luxurious office in some equally luxurious secure building. He isn't here running the risk of a fire fight with the Nomad. Three of Sayber's ships already had close calls with them in the last week. It's only a matter of time before Gryffin gets wind of Sayber's involvement and comes after him.

To try and muddy the waters a bit, he had decommissioned a few of his older ships and given them Nomad makeovers. It won't fool Gryffin for long, but it might buy him enough time to finish this. The sooner this relationship with the Foundation comes to an end, the better for everyone.

Chayse takes a deep breath and eyes the dented, buckled metal door with trepidation. It's only a damn door, but it may as well be an enemy with a weapon.

It's the door to Gryffin's quarters. He can't explain what it is about the captain's quarters, but he hates crossing the threshold. Apart from the less-than-comfortable cold temperature the captain prefers, the blood-stained, warped metal walls also unsettle him. The room doesn't feel like someone lives there. The complete lack of any personality or warmth is obvious.

He straightens his shoulders and knocks on the door. After waiting for a minute, he utters a silent thank-you, places the file Gryffin requested on the floor and turns away. A loud crash echoes from inside the captain's room and stops Chayse in his tracks.

He beats his fist against the door and calls out, but the room is deathly silent again. Chayse rips open the door control panel and overrides the programming. Chayse runs into the room to discover Gryffin on the floor gasping for breath. He activates his radio. 'Klay!

Report to the captain's quarters now! He's in trouble!'

Chayse drops down beside his captain and drags the diagnostic kit over to him. 'Shit, shit, shit. Don't you dare,' Chayse says. 'Stay with me, sir. I don't know what to do.'

Gryffin gestures towards his chest. Chayse hooks the monitors up to Gryffin's chest plate and quickly scans through the information. According to the screen, he has only six minutes before the lack of oxygen kills Gryffin. It's already been three minutes since he took a breath. Chayse doesn't have time to wait for Klay. It looks like he's on his own.

He wipes his sweaty hands on his trousers as he concentrates on the information. Think! His lungs themselves seem fine, no other injuries anywhere, so it must be his implants. He systematically works his way around the schematic of the implants on the small screen, while trying to ignore Gryffin slowly dying beside him.

Chayse cries out in victory when he finally locates the implant assisting the captain's lungs. It has shut down. He pulls the med kit from under Gryffin's bed and takes out a large needle attached to a thick cable. While he's seen the procedure performed, he hasn't carried it out without Klay's supervision. If he gets it wrong, he could seriously damage Gryffin's internal mechanics. The clock continues its countdown beside him. He doesn't have time to hesitate.

He lays Gryffin flat on his back and places an oxygen mask over his face. 'Sir, if you can hear me, I apologise for this.' Chayse takes a deep breath and pushes the needle into his captain. It passes through the external plating and deep into Gryffin's body. The captain arches off the ground but there's no time to worry about the pain he's inflicting. Once the cable has linked to the implant, Chayse furiously taps on the screen, all too aware of the timer counting down in the corner.

Only two minutes left.

He runs the program but curses loudly as it loads and reboots the implant far too slowly. 'C'mon. Go faster.' He holds his breath and stares intently at Gryffin as the program finishes. Just when he thinks he is too late, Gryffin suddenly takes a deep breath.

'Oh, thank God. Easy, sir: try to take slow, even breaths.' He takes his own advice and forces himself to calm down. Chayse glances at the clock; only twelve seconds left. That was far too close.

After giving the captain a few minutes to breathe, he helps Gryffin sit up. Chayse continues to check equipment as Gryffin gets himself together.

'What happened?' Gryffin asks. Chayse turns the screen around so Gryffin can see, but he shakes his head. 'Tell me.'

'Sorry, sir. I don't know why, but the implant on your lungs failed. Because your organs can't function on their own anymore, when the implant stopped working, so did your lungs. You were suffocating.'

'I figured that last bit out for myself.' Gryffin leans back against the side of his bed and frowns at the cable sticking out of the edge of the implant.

'Yeah, sorry. I had to jump start the implant controlling your lungs.'

Gryffin pulls off the mask and tries to drag himself to his feet but only gets as far as his knees. He gestures towards the bathroom as he wraps an arm around his stomach. 'Going to be sick.'

Chayse bends down and pulls Gryffin to his feet. He picks up the pad attached to Gryffin's chest and tucks it under his arm.

Gryffin leans heavily on him as they shuffle towards the bathroom. Once close enough, Gryffin grabs onto the sink and retches.

'Do you need anything, sir?'

Gryffin nods his head tiredly. 'Find out where the hell Klay is.' Chayse turns to exit the room. 'Chayse, thanks.'

Chayse smiles. For the first time since he boarded *Ares*, he finally feels like Gryffin accepts him. 'You're welcome.'

∞

'You can't retire.'

Admiral Grafton leans over Balfe's desk. 'Oh yes I can. This whole thing has gotten way out of hand.'

Balfe pushes back from his desk. 'Everything is not out of hand. *Infinity* has secured another dozen colonies.'

'I'm not talking about that part and you know it. Do you even have any idea of what's going on at the Port?'

'Of course I've heard.' Balfe had seen the reports earlier that day. News got out the Foundation chose to target Gryffin and some people took offence to it. Any ships going through the Port were attacked as soon as they appeared. The inmates on the prison moons were starting to riot, so everyone is being locked down. With no access to fresh subjects, the project could be in jeopardy before they capture the Nomad leader.

As if hearing his thoughts, Grafton addresses that issue. 'They've started cataloguing the prisoners. I've already had two reports on my desk listing seventeen missing. It's only a matter of time before the Council hears about it. How the hell am I supposed to explain seventeen highly dangerous prisoners disappearing off a high-security moon?'

Balfe curses. He had hoped the Council would be so preoccupied with the events in the Outer Sector they wouldn't notice the prison problem. They had been so close when they lost the station. It would have been crazy not to continue.

It had taken a few years to obtain a new location and track down the Scientist, but he'd done it. As Grafton took charge of the area housing most of the prison moons, Balfe had arranged for him to supply the Scientist with subjects to work on. While Balfe wasn't in the slightest bit conflicted sacrificing these criminals for the greater good, the Council would no doubt frown on it.

Unfortunately, most of the inmates hadn't survived for long, but the Scientist had made a few advancements with their help. Balfe hopes this work will speed up the overall process with the Nomad once they have him. 'Escapes happen. It's nothing to worry about.'

'For you, perhaps. Those people disappeared on my command. I've decided to step down, retire, and distance myself from this mess.'

Balfe gets up and walks around his desk. 'And I suppose I'm meant to trust you won't speak of any of this?'

Grafton snorts. 'I made a pact. I'm hardly going to admit to being involved in a project that tortured children.'

'I'm glad to hear that. Before you ... retire, I need you to find the additional men.'

Grafton opens and closes his mouth a few times before he can force the words out. 'No. You agreed they were to remain in a secure location for however much longer they have.'

'Desperate times, Admiral. We can't risk the Council discovering the project. Not until we have results.'

'But those men are completely unpredictable. Hell, they were in prison for a reason. What the Scientist did made them all the more dangerous. Releasing them would have devastating results.'

'Or beneficial results. Having men with similar abilities could speed things up.'

Grafton shakes his head. 'They aren't even in the same league as the Nomad leader. They don't have any implants. The Scientist used them to see if he could manipulate areas of the brain to allow fitting and acceptance of the control implant. In short, they were made more violent with no way of controlling them.'

'Sounds like they'd give the Nomad a run for his money.'

'I said no. It would be suicidal. They couldn't be trusted not to turn on us.'

Balfe sighs. 'You're right, of course. If we don't have trust, what do we have?' He jabs a needle into the side of Grafton's neck and empties the contents into his bloodstream. Grafton stares in shock at Balfe and then grabs his chest. Balfe sits on the edge of his desk and watches Grafton as he gasps for breath. 'I told you at the start no one could back out of this. We're all in it for life, which for you ends in about one minute.'

Grafton struggles for another few seconds before he stops breathing. Balfe pours himself a drink and swallows it in one go. He then walks slowly around his desk and activates his radio. 'This is Admiral Balfe. Medical emergency in my office. Admiral Grafton has had a heart attack.'

∞

Chayse passes Gryffin another sparring stick and quickly steps back to avoid being hit. He stumbles over the five broken sticks on the ground but manages to dodge out of the way in time. Gryffin strikes the drone in front of him and slams it against the metal wall of the training room. 'Sir, do you want me to come back later?'

Gryffin ducks to avoid the drone's attack. His boots squeak on the metal floor as he regains his footing. 'Talk.'

Chayse clears his throat. 'I've checked the system and can't detect anything to back-up or refute what Klay said.'

Gryffin spins around and kicks the drone. It falls to the ground with a bang and black smoke billows out of it. He finally turns to face Chayse. 'So, you don't know if he's lying or not.' Gryffin drops the stick in the rack on the wall. 'You'll need to do better than that. If Klay ignored your call and was going to let me suffocate, I damn well need to know!'

'Sir, the call I made to him does show up on the ship system. But it doesn't show up on his personal unit.'

Gryffin leans against the wall and crosses his ankles. 'So, he's telling the truth. He didn't get the transmission.'

Chayse shakes his head. 'I'm not so sure, sir. There was a glitch in the system but we don't know what caused it.'

Gryffin grips his biceps and looks down at the ground. His arm and face implant glows red. 'Dismissed.'

Chayse opens his mouth to say he'll keep digging, but decides against it. Gryffin is pissed and he doesn't want to aggravate him further by pushing the issue. Chayse's boots echo on the metal steps as he climbs up to the walkway above the training room. As much as he doesn't like Klay, it is hard to believe the commander would try to kill Gryffin. He'd have a fleet of extremely loyal and angry Nomad to deal with if anything happened to their leader.

19

'What the hell is it playing at?'

Gryffin ignores Klay and looks closely at the vessel in front of them. It looks Nomad. The swirling artwork on her hull screams Nomad, but it's not one he recognises. He knows each ship in his fleet and each crew member. They move closer and Gryffin growls. There's a familiar griffin painted on her sail. Whoever this is, they're pretending to be him. Only *Ares* carries his symbol. Gryffin immediately tenses. 'Klay, patch into the defences. I want to know who we're dealing with and how the hell they can fire on the surface.'

They intercepted the distress call from Ultar over an hour ago. In spite of Klay's objections, *Ares* had made the three-hour journey in an hour. They pushed the ship to the brink of her abilities, but she arrived at their destination on schedule. The extra strain had blown one of the main engines, but Gryffin had other issues to worry about at the moment. They can repair the engine after *Ares* destroys this vessel. 'See if you can contact Aleena.'

Aleena is the leader of a small farming colony based on Ultar. They met her and her people five years ago when they landed there to raid the colony. No one was as surprised as him when they left with a new trading partner. Depending on their schedule, he usually tries to land *Ares* there every few months so the crew can relax and catch up with the Ultarans. In all their years as friends, the Ultarans had never once used the distress beacon.

'Sir, I've got Aleena for you.'

Gryffin activates his communicator. 'Aleena, it's Gryffin.'

'Gryffin! Thank goodness you responded.'

'Aleena, have any vessels been able to land?'

'Your defences seem to be preventing that for the moment, but I fear it will not hold them for long. They are firing on us from orbit, but they are getting closer than anyone has before. I have evacuated the main populated areas, but we have still had some casualties.'

'You hurt?'

'I am well.'

'Stay like that. We're on the way.'

Gryffin directs his eyes to the vessel in front of them. He had ordered Klay to keep *Ares* cloaked, but after seeing the ship attacking Ultar, Gryffin decides to alter tactics. 'Raise the colours. When we uncloak, I want that bastard to know who blew his ship out of the sky.' The large flags rise from the top deck, leaving no doubt whose ship it is.

He feels his eyes shift as the anger builds inside him. He clenches his fists tightly and fights to remain in control.

'Sir, should we wait for verification?'

'No need. It's not one of ours. The people down on the surface are having their lives destroyed as part of a game.'

He doesn't take his eyes off the ship as he speaks to the Nomad at the helm. 'Turn us around. Klay, every bit of available power to weapons.' Without waiting for a response, he activates the ship-wide intercom. 'All teams battle stations. Brace for impact.' *Ares* and the other ship spin around to face each other. Before they complete the manoeuvre, Gryffin orders the attack. *Ares* vibrates as her guns bombard the other vessel.

'They've taken a direct hit, sir.'

'They've locked on to us!'

'Keep us moving.' The ship rocks as she's hit. 'Why is that ship still able to fire on us? Take it down.'

'Sir, three transport vessels have landed. The colony is taking more casualties.'

Gryffin ignores Klay. There's not a lot he can do at the moment. Unless they can get rid of this ship, they won't be able to help anyone. *Ares* rocks again and the alarms sound. He puts his fist through the screen to shut it up. He looks at the other ship. It's heavily damaged, listing to the side. Another hit should finish it. Right on schedule, a transmission comes in from the other vessel.

'Sir, they're offering their surrender.'

Gryffin smiles. 'Take it down.'

∞

'Sir, I'm picking up a distress call from a nearby world.'

Roman gets up and goes over to Terra's console. 'How far is it from our location?'

'Two hours, sir.'

'Get Balfe for me.' He wants to help whoever is in distress, but it's not an option. Once they go off course, Balfe will know and he'll be in a hell of a lot of trouble. He settles in for a long wait, but Balfe surprises him by answering immediately. 'Have you got him?'

Roman groans to himself. Of course Balfe thought he captured the Nomad. No wonder he jumped on the transmission. 'Not yet, sir.'

Balfe clenches his jaw 'Then why are you contacting me, Captain?'

'We've received a distress call from a neighbouring world called Ultar. Requesting permission to intercept.'

Balfe grabs his module off his desk and taps the screen a few times.

'It's on your list of settlements to recruit. You're not due to visit there for another few weeks.' He leans back in his leather chair and rubs his jaw. 'Why not? Having the Foundation come to the rescue of a little farming world will earn us some points with the locals. May get us a few colonies too. Keep it short and sweet, Roman. Two days max.'

'Sir.'

He goes to sign off, but Balfe stops him. 'While you're there, see what you can reveal about the Nomad. No doubt someone on the surface will know something. I'll wait for your report.'

The screen goes blank and Roman sits back in his chair. He should have known there'd be a reason for Balfe's willingness. He was hoping for a few days without having to think about capturing his son. 'Get us to Ultar as quick as you can, Stanner. Terra, monitor all frequencies. I want to know the second you detect another ship.'

'You expecting trouble, sir?' Stanner asks.

'Of course. All we seem to be doing at the moment is attracting that very thing.'

∞

Chayse checks his weapon for a fourth time and earns a puzzled look from Gryffin. He forces his hand onto the grab rail running along the side of the cargo deck and turns his attention out the window.

They are three minutes from landing on Ultar and his first venture at leading his own team. Chayse discreetly glances around the rest of the Nomad with him. None of them seem the slightest bit anxious or concerned. He clutches the rail as a wave of dizziness hits him.

'Get ready,' Gryffin shouts as the ship breaks cloud cover. Chayse turns to face the rear loading ramp. The men mount the six vehicles, their weapons primed and faces covered with metal. Feeling someone looking at him, Chayse lifts his head to face Gryffin. The Captain doesn't say a word, but somehow, by looking at him, Gryffin helps him focus.

148

Klay lands *Ares* outside the village and engages the cloaks to keep her hidden. Before she's settled down properly, Gryffin leads the teams down the ramp. Chayse watches the four transports take off in different directions while the two remaining vehicles assigned to him move towards the central town. Luckily they don't meet any resistance, unlike the other team. The sound of gunfire echoes through the trees around them.

Their four-wheel-drive transport bursts through the trees and enters the town. The damage caused by the attackers saddens him. The once quaint well-kept centre has been replaced by smoking ruins. Their vehicles skid to a halt beside what used to be the town hall. Chayse climbs down from the transport and stands for a moment to get his bearings. He points to two of his men. 'Stay here and guard the trucks. We may have to get out of here quickly.' He gestures to another two to his left. 'Secure a building for us to use. Preferably somewhere central.' He looks at the last two crew members. 'You're with me. We need to locate Aleena.'

∞

'Sir, we've reached Ultar but they won't let us land.'

Roman turns to face Terra. 'That's strange. Are you sure they're getting our message?'

'Positive, sir. There seem to be probes surrounding the planet blocking us from getting any closer.'

'Strange. Why send out a distress signal then refuse help? Can you establish direct contact with anyone on the surface?'

After a few minutes, a blonde woman in her early forties appears on the screen. 'Can I help you?'

'I'm Jensen Roman, captain of the Foundation ship, *Infinity*. We intercepted your distress call.'

The surprise is evident on her attractive face. 'I apologise, Captain. I did not realise the Foundation would hear the call. Thank you for responding so fast, but we no longer need assistance.'

Weeks of being brushed off finally gets to Roman. Instead of agreeing and moving on, he stands firm. 'With the greatest respect, we're not here to cause any trouble or take over your colony. We responded to your distress call out of good faith. We're here now. Perhaps we could help in some way.'

She studies his face for a few minutes before she speaks again. 'One moment.' The screen goes blank as she blocks the transmission.

'That was a bit strange,' Stanner says.

'I'm starting to get tired of our welcoming committees. Lieutenant, are there any other ships in the area?'

Terra examines the screen in front of her before shaking her head. 'Nothing is showing up.' She frowns as she looks at the screen in front of her. 'There are residual weapon flares on the surface. Something has attacked them — badly, by the level of damage. There's also debris — looks like the remains of a ship. Captain, we're being contacted again.'

The woman appears on the screen in front of him again. 'Captain, apologies for keeping you waiting. The Foundation's presence here is unexpected and has caused a few concerns among some people on the surface. However, I would be doing my people a disservice by turning away your kind offer of help in this situation. We have sustained a great deal of damage and I would be grateful for any assistance. However, I must apply one condition.'

'Go on.'

'I must have your assurance you will not conduct any official Foundation business on the surface. This planet is independent and we will not tolerate any venture to alter that.'

'Of course. As I said, we're only here to offer assistance. I give you my word.'

'Very well. You may land to the west of the village. I will meet you there.'

'Will you put your gun away and listen to me for a moment?'

Gryffin completely ignores Aleena and keeps his weapon firmly in his hand as he paces her living room. His boots wear a track on the sheepskin rug in front of the fireplace as he marches up and down.

The Nomad crew successfully managed to destroy the attackers' transports and were in the process of tracking down any trespassers left on the surface. She does not agree with his tactics but could not argue with the results.

'Why didn't you tell me as soon as I arrived?' he asks.

'I planned to tell you when I received the communication from the Foundation ship but you were busy protecting us.'

'So, you get what you want from us, then bring the Foundation in to clear up the mess.'

'Gryffin, please calm yourself.' Aleena knew he would be annoyed, but threatening to greet the Foundation by killing them is extreme — even for him. She clasps her hands in front of her on the antique wooden table. Many of her people lost their homes during the attack but Aleena had been extremely lucky. Apart from a broken window, her property and belongings were intact. Most of the furniture had been made by her late father and meant a great deal to her. She only hopes Gryffin doesn't lose his temper and destroy any of the pieces.

Aleena pushes back the pastel green drapes and glances out the window at the two Nomad security guards stationed outside the house.

Gryffin snorts. 'Don't worry, Aleena. They'll come to your rescue if I try to kill you.' He may have said it in anger, but he is speaking the truth. After working with him for years, Aleena is familiar with his temper. Over time, she learnt the warning signs he displays when he is close to losing control. It is always best to have back-up, especially as he is exhibiting some of the warning signs right now. He locks his eyes on to hers. Swirls of purple distort the usual calm blue. 'That is not funny, Gryffin.' She pauses to gather her thoughts. 'What are you so upset about, Captain?'

'The Foundation wants to arrest me.' His voice alters ever so slightly, almost like he is having difficulty forcing the words out. Another sure sign he is struggling for control.

'I would imagine quite a few people want to arrest you. When you operate as a mercenary, you would tend to gather a few enemies.'

He scowls at her as he continues to play with his gun. 'Back to that old argument again.'

She moves to the window to keep the security near her. 'You know how I feel about what you do.'

'You've made it clear over the last few years.'

'So because you attempt to hide that side of you, I should forget it exists?'

He stops walking and turns to face her. Gryffin finally holsters his gun and sits on the arm of her worn leather chair next to the fire. 'You knew everything when you signed up for my protection. If you've got a problem with what I do, I can always let you out of the agreement.'

'That is unfair. You know I have a problem with what you do. How could I not? Gryffin, I care deeply for you, but you are like two sides of a coin. You do everything possible to protect us, but also have no issue killing for money. I may not agree, but that does not mean I am going to refuse your protection.'

He crosses his arms. 'Seems a little hypocritical.'

'Like you, I will do whatever is necessary to protect my people.' Gryffin grunts in response and rises to his feet. The wooden floor creaks under his boots as he paces again. 'Gryffin, are you going to cause problems?'

'They have no right to be here.'

'Why do you say that?'

He tightens his grip on his gun. 'They're Foundation.'

'You say that as if it is a good reason to wipe them all out. You cannot discriminate against them for that reason. As for arresting you, the captain has agreed not to conduct any Foundation business here. If he does try to capture you, I am sure you can take care of yourself.'

'This world has nothing to do with them. They're not welcome here.'

Aleena abruptly stands and knocks the vase of flowers off the table. Gryffin quickly moves from the other side of the room to catch it before it hits the floor. 'How dare you dictate who lands here!' Aleena replies sharply. 'We are an independent colony, Gryffin. As long as I am leader, I can let you, the Foundation, or whoever I want, land here. It is none of your business.'

'Of course it's my business, Aleena! We put a lot of time and effort into protecting this world, and what do you do? You turn off the protection I gave you and invite our enemy to land. What next? You plan on asking the Hunters for afternoon tea?'

'Now you are being ridiculous! Are you forgetting the small fact your protection failed to work? Those men managed to land on the surface. If you cannot respect my decision as leader of this world, then perhaps you should leave.'

He throws the vase against the far wall. It shatters on the stone chimney breast and peppers the wooden floor and rug in glass. Gryffin walks right up to her, but she does not flinch away from his glare, or the electricity dancing over his arm. She stands firm, even though the hairs on her arms tingle from being so close to him. 'You'd tell me to leave? After everything the Nomad have done for you.'

She is on very dangerous ground, and the full attention of the security outside focused on her provides little comfort. 'I am not disputing everything your people have done for us, and you know I am grateful, but you have to realise we do not belong to the Nomad.' She sighs and moves away from him, as she attempts to rein in her anger.

He may be listening to her, but she knows he is not entirely on board with what she is saying. 'Gryffin, I will not accept any trouble from you. Do you understand? You will either work with them or leave.'

Instead of losing his temper, which she expects, he takes a step away from her. 'I won't forget this, Aleena.'

'And I will not forget you acted in the same way as the attacker's ship did when you first landed here. Innocent Ultarans died because you and your crew decided to raid this world. We may have reached an accord, but we built our relationship on blood.'

Her heart beats faster as the power rushes down his arm. Gryffin clenches his jaw, then pulls the electricity back into his body and leaves the room without another word.

∞

Gryffin pushes past his security and grunts an order for them to stay with Aleena. Before they can respond, he has mounted his motorbike and disappeared along the road back to town.

That damn woman knows which of his buttons to press. They've often argued — mainly about her disapproval of some things he does.

He's not proud of all his decisions, but he can't change the past. She needs to get over what happened years ago and let him get on with his job.

He kicks the bike up a gear and accelerates over the brow of the hill. He thought Aleena had more sense. The last thing he wants is the Foundation poking around. He needs to concentrate on making sure the Ultarans are safe, and exposing whoever ordered the attacks. Instead, he'll waste precious time trying to dodge Roman... and Terra.

He isn't looking forward to seeing her again. Pulling a gun on her the last time wasn't the best way to say goodbye. Not a lot he can do about that now. He'll have to make sure to keep his distance.

Gryffin pulls his bike into the central square and parks beside the well. He joins his team clearing the rubble and making some of the houses watertight. He needs to do something physical to help work off some of his tension.

By the time Aleena and her security arrive twenty minutes later, he's on the unpleasant task of collecting the dead. He knows he's in trouble with her again when she storms up to him. 'Are you purposely trying to go against me today?'

'What exactly have I done now?'

'We bury our dead. We do not dishonour people by dumping them unceremoniously in a pile.'

'These people are not yours.'

'It makes no difference. They deserve the same respect.'

Gryffin throws another body on top of the pile before he turns to glare at her. 'I don't get you sometimes. They attack your world, but you still want to bury them. Do you think they'd have done the same for you?'

'That does not matter. We have our ways and I intend to follow them. I expect all visitors to Ultar to abide by our laws and traditions. That includes you.'

He picks up the last two bodies and drops them at her feet. 'Suit yourself,' he replies, wiping his bloody hands on his trousers. 'You always do.'

Aleena glares at him and then calls one of the villagers over. After giving him instructions, she pulls Gryffin aside so her people can attend to the bodies. 'When were you going to tell me about the Foundation seeing your face?'

'Who the hell told you that?'

'I contacted *Ares* to check on my people. Klay filled me in.'

Of course he did. Sounds like he needs to order Klay to keep his damn mouth shut. 'It's nothing to worry about.'

'Of course it is. You of all people know what is at stake.' She lowers her voice as a villager hurries past. 'We have not spent all these years keeping your identity safe for fun. With the truth out, it could be dangerous — not only for you, but also the people who have risked themselves to hide you. Perhaps you should have—'

'Should have what?' he snaps. 'Stayed hidden in a cave somewhere? Only one Foundation member saw me.' He looks down at his boots. 'She decided to draw a picture and give it to station security.'

Aleena places a hand on his shoulder. 'No one believes you should hide away. You of all people deserve a life after what you went through, but maybe having you so visible was too much of a risk, for all of us. Is the drawing accurate?'

'Unfortunately.' He pulls away from her. 'I couldn't stay hidden forever. I'll increase patrols.'

'That may be wise.' She brushes a wisp of hair from her face. 'I do dislike arguing with you, Gryffin.'

'Yeah, well, you're not going to back down and neither am I.'

Aleena nods. 'As usual, we will have to agree to disagree. I do not understand myself; you infuriate me yet I am also very fond of you,' Aleena gestures at the body in front of him. 'In spite of your best efforts to alienate me.'

Gryffin smirks briefly at her. 'Guess I'll have to try harder.' He goes quiet for a minute. 'I found out the Foundation had something to do with my past.'

Aleena's face drops. 'Gryffin, why did you not tell me sooner?'

His communicator sounds in his ear, ending the conversation. 'Gryffin here.' He listens for a few seconds before looking at Aleena again. 'Understood. We're on our way. Your guests have arrived.'

'You had better get out of sight,' Aleena says.

'No point now.' Despite what he says, he still activates his mask; more out of habit than to hide his face. 'If you're going to invite potential enemies here, at least let me do my job and make sure you're safe.'

∞

Terra waits in the transport bay with Roman, Stanner, and Milla as the ship goes through the final landing procedures. Roman has another ten crew members with them in case things turn bad. Terra looks out the window on the way down and admires the rich green fields full of livestock surrounding a large town with a perfectly square area in the centre.

'Everyone be prepared,' Roman says. 'We're getting some strange readings from outside the town centre. There may be a cloaked vessel on the surface.'

Stanner consults his handheld. 'The Ultarans don't have the technology, but that doesn't mean other groups they associate with don't.'

Roman nods. 'That's what I'm afraid of. The extensive collection of beacons and alarms surrounding the world is probably the most sophisticated we've encountered. It's clear this planet is under someone's watchful eye. According to our records, Ultar is a farming community, so something doesn't add up.'

Terra places her hand on the weapon strapped to her belt. After the last few encounters, Roman isn't taking any chances with his crew. Everyone is going in armed.

157

Terra blinks a few times as the daylight bursts into the bay when the doors slowly open. Once her vision adjusts, she looks at their welcoming party. There are two people waiting at the bottom of the ramp. As promised, the leader is there to meet them, but she hasn't come alone.

Excitement twists at Terra's stomach when she sees the other person at the base of the ramp. Even though she can't see his face, she knows it's him. His tall, firm body is poised to attack and electricity courses down his covered right arm. His purple shielded eyes shine in the afternoon sun. Terra's excitement ebbs as Gryffin raises the large black gun in his hand. She reacts quickly but pulls her weapon a few seconds too late. Gryffin already has his gun pointed straight at Roman's head.

21

'What the hell do you mean you lost the signal?'

Sayber stands up and faces his command crew. Usually, he'd take pleasure from their cowering, but not today. Today he has bigger problems.

He absent-mindedly runs a finger along the raised skin on his hand. The large scar spreads from his right thumb up to his shoulder. It was a present given to him by Gryffin. He can't help but smile when he remembers his retaliation.

Sayber had tried to separate Gryffin from his head but only succeeded in severely wounding him. At least he left Gryffin with a large scar, a constant reminder Sayber is hot on his heels. Not close enough, however. Now, to add to his problems, the Nomad had more than likely destroyed one of his ships.

'In the Commander's last transmission he reported a Nomad ship attacking them,' Quinn replies from the comms station. 'The ship was flying Gryffin's colours.'

'Damn it!' Sayber says. 'He wasn't supposed to be in the area. Bray and the ground crews?'

'No response,' Quinn replies.

Sayber closes his eyes and counts to ten. Twenty-three crewmen are missing, including his first officer, and one ship destroyed. The plan was to attack Gryffin's beloved Ultar and withdraw with no Hunter losses.

'Alter course back to Ultar.' He isn't about to write off Bray and the crew yet. They are well trained and Sayber has every confidence, if still alive, he will get himself and any remaining crew members to safety. On the other hand, if Gryffin killed Bray, Sayber is going to take extra pleasure taking him down once and for all.

∞

Time seems to slow down for Roman. Two meetings with Gryffin, and his son threatened to kill him on both occasions. Not the best father/son relationship so far. Perhaps they will laugh about it someday, but for now Roman is tired of being on the defensive.

Roman glances quickly around the field and counts twelve Nomad scattered in front of them. The different scenarios race through his head as he closes his hand around his gun. Aleena shakes her head.

'I would not do anything rash, Captain. I have instructed Gryffin to hold his fire. He will, usually, do as I say, but occasionally he completely ignores me. It would be best to play it safe.'

'We're here to offer our help.'

'To what end?'

'As I said, we're here to offer assistance. It appears we're surplus to requirements.'

'The Nomad have matters under control but we sustained a lot of structural damage. We would be most grateful for any help if you will still provide it.'

Roman can't help but notice the muscles in Gryffin's hand tightening around the gun. He's not grateful they're here. If anything, his posture shows he's ready to take them all down. 'So why the friendly welcome?'

'We have been attacked, Captain. I am also playing it safe. I am aware you are under orders to capture Gryffin. We will not permit it while you are on Ultar. Gryffin is welcome here and I will not allow you to take him. Are we clear?'

'So you're his protector?'

She smiles widely. 'He is more than capable of looking after himself and his crew. Whatever happens off this world is between the two of you. On this world, however, it is a different matter. You can get on your ship and depart voluntarily or, as I'm sure Gryffin would prefer, not so voluntarily. On the other hand, you can keep the promise you made to me and refrain from any Foundation business while on this planet, which includes taking Gryffin. Choose.'

There is no choice. If he leaves, Balfe will want to know why. Staying will also help him bide his time and figure out what to do while still keeping the Nomad within his sights. 'We'll stay and help.'

She smiles again. 'I am glad. My name is Aleena. I am the leader of Ultar. Gryffin, put your weapon down.'

Gryffin doesn't move. Aleena steps in front of him, but he keeps his focus and his gun on Roman. 'Gryffin, put your weapon down.' He still doesn't move, so she steps in front to block his view of Roman. 'Put it down. Now.' After a tense few minutes, he finally looks at her and slowly lowers his arm, but he's clearly not happy about the situation. With one last glance at Aleena, he turns in the opposite direction and walks away.

She smiles at Roman again as if nothing has happened. 'If you will follow me. Please stay close to the Nomad. There are still a few of our attackers wandering around.'

Roman nods but can't find his voice. Before Gryffin stormed off, he noticed something that made his heart drop to his feet. A platinum griffin pendant hangs on a leather strap wrapped around his neck; the same pendant Roman gave to Maggie while he was dating her. Even though the DNA results had been in front of his face in black and white, a small part of him had still refused to accept the truth. Tests can be wrong, after all. But the sight of the pendant around his son's neck instantly squashes any lingering doubt.

With one last glance in the direction Gryffin went, he pushes his shoulders back and follows Aleena to the village.

∞

'How are you doing?'

Terra stands up and stretches out her arms. She's helped Milla by treating the less severe casualties, and there are plenty of them. The queue seems unending. She accepts the bottle of water and smiles. 'Getting there. I need some more antiseptic.'

'That's not what I was asking.'

She smiles with reassurance at her friend. 'I'm all right. Really. I'm over it. How's the captain?'

'Hard to say.' She glances over Terra's shoulder towards the door. 'Well, while you've been trying to dodge your sexy Nomad, I've found one of my own.' She leans in closer to Terra and lowers her voice. 'Luckily for me, he's co-ordinating things between the Ultarans and the Nomad. He can co-ordinate with me all he wants,' she says, winking at Terra.

'Milla, they're all wearing masks.'

'You can tell a lot from someone's body. Oh my God. Don't look now, but he's right outside. I said don't look. Okay, look, but be casual about it.'

Terra glances towards the group of Nomad standing outside the door. The Nomad stand out like a sore thumb among the locals and Foundation crew. Like their captain, they are all wearing black leather, have numerous piercings and a wide variety of tattoos among them. More importantly, they are heavily armed and appear as intimidating as any group can. So far, though, they've held the truce

162

placed on them by Aleena.

There are about ten people in the group Milla is looking at, but she doesn't have to ask which one has caught her friend's attention. The person in question is standing slightly apart from the group and has short, light brown hair sticking up in messy spikes around his mask. Both ears have numerous piercings and she can see the outline of swirling black tattoos covering both arms and peeking out from under his black vest.

'I think I should introduce myself.'

'Can you not control your hormones for one minute?' Terra asks.

Before Terra has finished the sentence, Milla steps up to him and holds out her hand. 'I'm Doctor Milla Collins.'

He looks up at her and seems a little thrown by her apparent interest. 'Chayse.'

'Nice to meet you, Chayse.'

Terra shakes her head and walks away from her friend. The last thing she needs to witness is flirting between Milla and Chayse.

∞

Bray crawls out from behind the water tanks to peer around the door of the barn. Hiding wasn't exactly promoted among his crew but it had helped save his life. The water tanks had come to his rescue at precisely the right time.

He doesn't know how many of his crew died when the attack started. Everything went to plan until the Nomad arrived. The intel they received apparently wasn't worth a damn thing. No Nomad vessels were meant to be anywhere near the colony. Someone had got their information seriously wrong. A Nomad ship didn't show up on any of their initial scans, meaning it got to Ultar a hell of a lot faster than anyone had anticipated. Now he is possibly alone on the surface with a seriously pissed off group of Nomad — not quite fitting in with his well thought out plan.

There'd be time enough to worry about what went wrong later. First things first, he needs to get the hell out of the village and then the planet, without being used as target practice.

Easier said than done with a village full of Nomad in his way. He checks his weapon, counting the three bullets again for the tenth time. Bray securely fastens his knife to his belt. No point putting it off any longer. With a deep breath, he stands up and leaves his hiding place.

∞

'What the hell do you mean you let him get away?'

Klay takes a step back from Gryffin. 'Sir, we went after the intruder seen in the town, but we lost him. I believe he has left the surface, sir.'

Gryffin turns away from the ruins of the town hall to face Klay. 'How'd we miss him?'

'He was spotted near the large storage barn on the outskirts. He must have hidden inside.'

'How did he go if we destroyed all their transports?'

'I can answer that, Captain,' Aleena interrupts. 'I have received word one of our small rescue crafts is missing. We recently equipped it with your cloaking technology.'

Gryffin curses and punches the brick wall beside him. 'What happened to the basic protocol? You should have locked down all transports.'

'Do not take out your bad mood on me.' Aleena steps up to him, barely controlling her temper. 'We may have failed to lock down the ship, but your protection also failed with far more disastrous results. The priority is to repair your probes, so this planet is safe. That is what we are paying you for after all!'

She storms off, leaving a stunned Klay and silently fuming Gryffin. 'Aleena give any idea how long her guests will be here?'

'The Foundation has offered to help Aleena with the clean up so she's agreed to let them stay on the surface overnight.'

'Of course she has,' Gryffin replies. 'All we need now is Sayber and we'll have a full house.'

'I can't believe she let them land. Do you want me to ... convince them to leave?' Klay asks.

Gryffin shakes his head. 'Aleena says no. We behave or leave.'

'And we're doing what she wants?'

'For now. Keep an eye on them. They try anything, all bets are off. Any ideas what happened to the defences?'

Klay shakes his head. 'Not yet. We'll need to get some readings from the ones left in orbit and the one they shot down. Any thoughts?'

'A few. We need to get some information from the probes first. Don't let the Foundation take anything from the crash site.'

'You think a Nomad gave the codes up?' Gryffin doesn't respond. Klay sucks in a breath through his teeth. 'That's a bit of a stretch. Sayber attacking, I get, but one of our own betraying us? Doesn't bear thinking about.'

'That's what we need to figure out. Send another team to repair the orbiting defences — that's the priority. Anyone left can help with the clear-up. You coordinate with the Foundation. Send a team to check the probe crash site and take some readings. How's Chayse getting on?'

'He's on schedule. One of the Foundation crew is helping him.'

'Make sure we have Aleena covered at all times.' Gryffin leaves to patrol the area before Klay can agree. His day is going from bad to worse. In fact, ever since he rescued that irritating woman things have been going slightly off for him. Once alone, he steps behind the nearest building and removes his mask. He lays his head back against the cold stone and lets the breeze blow through his hair. He hates wearing the damn mask. Usually, Ultar is the one place his crew don't have to hide. Thanks to the Foundation, they're all hiding ... again.

It's time to start getting things back on the right track. His first job involves finding out how the attackers managed to destroy an expensive probe. It should take the team an hour to get there and back, plus another thirty minutes to take the readings.

He smiles to himself as he walks back to the centre. He's looking forward to having a one-on-one chat with whoever betrayed him.

∞

'What's going on?'

Roman gestures to the empty seat in front of him. Terra slowly sits and crosses her legs. She doesn't know why Roman called her to this meeting, but she has a feeling Gryffin is somehow involved. 'Can I ask what's going on?' she repeats.

Roman clasps his hands together on his desk. 'Terra, I think it would be best if you stayed on board for the duration of our stay on Ultar.'

'But, sir, you can't do that.'

Roman shakes his head. 'Don't waste your breath, Terra. If any of the Nomad discover you drew the picture of Gryffin, they may come after you. Do you seriously think it would be a good idea to put yourself in danger?'

Terra wants to argue, but it's pointless. Roman is right. Perhaps allowing her to mingle with the Nomad is a step too far. 'No.' She turns from him and clenches her teeth.

'I know you have skills we can utilise on the surface, but the risk is too high. I don't understand why the Foundation released the drawing with your name on the bottom, but it's done. We can't do much about that now. I guess there have been quite a few lapses in judgement made in relation to the Nomad leader.'

Terra glances up at him. She only hopes he is referring to the drawing and not the transmission to *Ares*.

'Nothing to say?' He sits on the edge of his desk and crosses his arms

'Sir, you ordered me to stay away from him. I will follow your orders.'

Roman grunts. 'Make sure you do.'

Terra stands up and straightens her jacket. 'Right, well, thanks for the advice.'

'This isn't a game, Terra.'

'I'm well aware of that, Captain.'

Roman silently scrutinises her for a moment. 'I'm trying to help you, Terra. Please, stay away from him.' He stands up and places his hands on her shoulders. She slowly raises her head to focus on his icy blue eyes. 'We're here to do a job, Terra. Nothing good will come by letting emotions take over. I'm not going to deny my emotions are giving me trouble. However, our first loyalty is to the Foundation. Nothing else matters. Personal feelings have no place here.'

22

Avoca watches Balfe from across the room as he mingles at the drinks reception for Admiral Grafton. The service had been dignified and solemn, with friends and colleagues gathering from all over the Sector to pay their respects.

Avoca quickly glances at Balfe again but turns away before he's caught. He doesn't know why, but he has a horrible feeling Balfe had something to do with Grafton's death. There's something not right about the whole thing. The coroner had examined the body and ruled a heart attack as the cause of death. Grafton always ate well and regularly exercised. He was probably the fittest out of all of them.

Whether Balfe is behind it or not, he is all the more determined to keep his mouth shut. Although it sickens him, he'll have to go along with everything for appearances sake. That doesn't mean he is going to abandon his plans. He'll just have to be extra careful.

Balfe gestures to him across the room. With dread filling him, he puts down his drink and follows Balfe outside. He squints in the bright sunlight, wishing he could enjoy the scenery rather than talk to

Balfe. He finally stops at a seat next to a large lake beside the house. Leeson is already waiting for them. He appears as happy as Avoca is to be there.

'Is this the best time for a private chat, Balfe?'

Balfe leans against a tree and peers out over the water. 'I can't think of a better time. I imagine you both have your suspicions about what happened. I'm not going to confirm or deny my involvement. What I will say is he wanted out. Draw your conclusions from that.'

Avoca turns cold. Balfe indirectly admitted to killing Grafton. Balfe made it clear from the beginning that once in, they were all in for life. He knows Balfe is capable of questionable things, but killing a fellow admiral is too much, even for Balfe.

Swallowing deeply, Leeson looks up at Balfe. 'So, what happens now?'

'I know something that can help us. Unfortunately, Grafton wouldn't give up the location. Leeson, I need you to get Grafton's personal unit. Bring it to me.'

Leeson gapes at him. 'How exactly do you expect me to do that?'

'Use your brain. Say you suspect him of treason if you have to. I don't care — just get that unit. And fast.'

Avoca doesn't want to ask, but curiosity gets the better of him. 'What exactly have you found?'

Balfe looks back over the water and smiles. 'More survivors of our project.'

∞

Gryffin pushes past the Ultarans in his way, knocking some of them to the ground. Once he gets to Aleena's house, he throws open the door and ignores her protests as he pulls a picture off her wall to expose the small screen behind it.

'I'm looking at the screen now. What the hell is going on, Klay?' Gryffin shouts into his communicator.

'Sir, we've spotted the intruder again outside the town near the eastern side of the lake.'

Gryffin traces the path along the lake with his finger. 'Got that. Stay put.' He opens a communication to all of his crew on the surface. 'Teams five and six, report to Klay's location. One intruder seen. I want him taken out. All other units, hold your positions.'

Aleena peers at the screen showing a layout of the surrounding area. 'Is there no other way, Gryffin?'

'No. He's here.' He points to the location on the map. 'Too close to the town for us to take chances. We're intercepting, but best if you get everyone indoors until we clear up.'

'I will sound the alarm and notify Captain Roman.'

He bites his tongue but, judging by the glare Aleena directs at him, he doesn't manage to keep the distaste from his face. He activates his communicator and addresses Klay again. 'I'm moving towards your location.'

'Stay put, sir. We can't risk anything happening to you.'

Gryffin growls and opens his mouth to argue but Aleena cuts in. 'Commander Klay is right. It may be a trap.'

As much as he wants to rip the intruder to shreds, they're right. 'Do not let him out of your sight, Commander. Try not to kill any of the Foundation crew,' he adds before shutting down the communication. Maybe this will work out for the best and the intruder will take out a few of the Foundation team.

∞

Bray calms his breathing and focuses on the track leading to the village. The house should be around the corner. He heard the Nomad calling Gryffin with an update, so knows he will be in this location.

He fully intended on boarding his borrowed craft and getting the hell off the surface, but he couldn't pass up the opportunity handed to him. It is part of his mission after all. He just has to make sure he doesn't get himself on the business end of Gryffin's gun or arm.

Bray crouches down between a woodpile and a clump of bushes to wait. It would take the Nomad about an hour to restore the defences. That means he has thirty minutes to locate Gryffin and get back to the transport. Not a lot of time, especially if Gryffin has a large security detail with him.

Ten minutes later, the door opens. A ghost of a smile crosses his face. Looks like his bet paid off. Even with his mask on, Bray instantly recognises the Nomad leader. The two security personnel with him scan the surrounding area while Gryffin speaks to someone in the house. Gryffin instructs his men to stay with the Ultaran leader while he strides past Bray's hiding place and around to the back of the house.

Although he has studied all available information on the Nomad leader, this is the first time he has physically seen him. He always marvelled at how someone so young could command a group like the Nomad, but after seeing him, Bray understands. Even in the act of walking, Gryffin is an imposing man. The other two Nomad with him must be easily over six feet tall, but Gryffin still towers above them.

Bray licks his dry lips and attempts to steady his breathing. He knows you don't underestimate Gryffin — hell, it had been drilled in to him for months — but the lethal, predatory air flowing from the man gives him reason to doubt his plan.

Bray pushes aside his fears and slowly leaves the safety of his hiding place to follow Gryffin. He only has one shot at this. If he messes up, Gryffin will be on him in seconds and no doubt pull him limb from limb.

Gryffin pauses for a moment at a black motorbike parked behind the house. He opens one of the side panniers and removes a bag. After checking the surrounding area again, Gryffin walks into the large, derelict barn behind the house. Bray rushes nearer to the entrance and ducks down behind a hay-stook. He peers into the barn, but can't see any sign of Gryffin.

Bray takes a step into the barn, then sees Gryffin in the far corner stacking hay bales for some reason. Without trying to figure out what the hell Gryffin is doing, Bray takes another cautious step. Luck seems to be on his side — the Nomad leader is making enough noise to cover his approach.

Bray hides behind some hay, silently releases his breath, then steps out and fires. The Nomad leader spins quickly with his gun aimed at Bray. Luckily, Bray's dart hits home before Gryffin fires. The specially formulated, extra high dose of sedative instantly knocks Gryffin out.

Not wasting any precious time, Bray crouches beside the unconscious Nomad. He quickly rolls him onto his back and pulls open Gryffin's jacket. The drug he gave him would kill the average person within a few minutes, but not Gryffin. There is every chance he'll be up and pissed off in less than two minutes. Bray falters for a moment when he sees the metal embedded in the Nomad's chest. The engineer in him wants to take readings and examine the work more closely, but he doesn't have time. Bray locates the correct spot and pushes the knife deep into the Nomad's body.

∞

'Clear out of the way!' Milla yells. 'What happened?'

Klay wipes his hand over his face. There is a large bruise on his face and a weeping cut on his forehead, but he still stands protectively in front of Gryffin. 'Back away from him.'

Milla stands firm and crosses her arms. Klay is holding a cloth to a large gash along his arm. 'That's a nasty cut, Commander. Let me see to him while the team patches you up.'

Klay remains where he is for another few minutes, then begrudgingly steps aside.

Milla puts on a pair of gloves before slowly cutting Gryffin's blood-soaked t-shirt away from the protruding knife.

172

'This isn't good.' She gently probes the edges of the wound with her fingertips, careful not to dislodge the knife. 'He's losing blood fast. We need to get him into surgery as soon as possible.' She opens her bag and takes out a roll of bandage and some tape. With Chayse's help, she secures the knife and quickly dresses the wound. 'The wound is deep. He needs surgery in a proper operating theatre. The risk of fatal infection is too great. Help us carry him back to *Infinity*.

Klay shakes his head. 'Not happening. We have a med bay set up in the village. I'll see to him there.'

'Let Doctor Collins assist you, Klay,' Aleena suggests. 'Is your pride worth losing the captain over?'

Klay pauses and blows out a deep breath.

'Let me help,' Milla offers. 'The longer we argue about this, the worse he's going to get. We've already wasted too much time.'

Klay sighs deeply and shakes his head. 'He's going to kill me for this.'

∞

Bray bursts through the trees towards the hidden transport. He opens the small back hatch, climbs in, and slams the door shut. Sitting down in the cockpit, he pulls up his top and probes his chest. He has some bruised ribs to go with the various cuts and bruises.

Gryffin had started to wake up a bit quicker than Bray planned. The semi-conscious, clumsy swipe of the Nomad's metal arm had hurt like hell.

He starts the engines and slams the craft into gear. He needs to get off the surface before the Nomad reactivate the defences. The small vessel judders as it slowly lifts from the ground. Its old engines struggle to pull it over the trees. He releases his breath when the ship eventually gains enough height and glides away from the surface.

Now all he can do is hope he had inserted the knife deep enough into his initial wound tract. If not, the chip won't be able to do its job and that means they are all screwed.

23

When they enter the makeshift sick bay, Milla shouts orders to her team as the Nomad lie Gryffin on the large table in the centre of the room. Klay begrudgingly allows the medical team to examine his arm while Milla concentrates on Gryffin. 'I'll need you to remove his mask.'

'No bloody way!'

Milla turns to face Klay. 'How the hell am I expected to help him with that thing on? For God's sake, Klay, we all know what he looks like. Take off the damn mask.'

Klay grumbles to himself for a moment, then slowly removes Gryffin's mask while Milla and her team help to pull the rest of Gryffin's shirt off.

'Bloody hell.' Gryffin's back is facing Milla, giving her a clear view of his scarred skin. Milla walks around the table and sees the horrific injuries continue across his chest around a large W-shaped implant.

'Doctor, you need to start.' Klay prompts, trying to pull her out of her shock.

Milla continues to stare at the patient. 'What the hell happened to him?'

Klay stands in front of Milla to block her view of Gryffin. A fresh bandage covers Klay's arm and the left side of his forehead, but his eyes appear clear and focused. He was lucky to escape a concussion. 'It's got nothing to do with you or this,' Klay says. 'You don't need to know to help him. Now are you going to stand gawping or help Chayse?'

'I'm done gawping, thank you. Any problems with sedatives?'

'Yeah. They don't work.'

She turns to face him quickly. 'Sorry?'

'His implants neutralise any sedatives within a few minutes. There's a high chance he'll wake up once you start.'

'You're kidding right?'

'Why would I joke about something like that? His pain threshold is high. He won't interfere with the surgery.'

Milla stumbles with the tray of instruments she's carrying. 'I'm not worried about him interfering. I'm worried we'll be sticking our hands in him while he's awake.'

'Yeah, well that's the way it is, so either scrub up or get out of the way.'

She turns to address the rest of the team. 'What are you all standing around for? Move.' She turns to Klay as Chayse wheels Gryffin from the room into surgery. 'I'll have to take my lead from Chayse in relation to your captain. If the pain gets too much or he needs a break, I'll need to know.'

Klay's voice softens for a moment. 'No need. He'd want to get it over with as quickly as possible. Saying that, if you do anything to jeopardise his life, I will stop you. Do you understand?'

She never thought she'd say this, but she's glad Klay has an injured arm. The idea of operating with him assisting isn't something that excites her. 'I took an oath. One I take very seriously. I'm here to help.'

He pauses for a moment then nods. 'What are you waiting for?'

'I'm not sure this is the best idea,' Leeson says as he looks out the window of the transport.

Avoca couldn't agree more. With forged papers, a stolen transport, and wearing nondescript outfits, they can't be further from their comfort zones. Leeson had managed to get the unit as ordered. Thankfully, it didn't require tarnishing Grafton's record with a treason charge. To be honest, he doesn't want to know how he got it. He heard something about a break-in and switched off. The less he knows about it, the better. Balfe, as usual, hadn't said much to them. Neither man wants to argue with Balfe. Neither of them wants to have a mysterious heart attack like Grafton.

The prison moon comes into view and Avoca has to suppress a shiver. The lifeless rocks housed the prisons in climate-controlled tunnels deep underground. Avoca had never been to one before and would have preferred to keep it that way. Little is known about the prisons themselves. Usually, once you go in as a prisoner, you stay there. The Foundation doesn't believe in rehabilitation. According to the Council's philosophy, you get one chance. Avoca has to hand it to them — it certainly keeps crime low.

Their transport shudders as it docks with the small station on the surface. The hatch opens and a five-man security team greets them. One of the guards holds out his hand. 'I need your papers.'

Balfe hands them over. According to the documentation, they are scientists acting on behalf of Admiral Grafton. Being so far from the main Foundation, the prison will not have been notified of his death yet. The security team clears them and leads them to a large metal lift.

One guard taps in a twelve number sequence and they start their descent into the main body of the prison. A good five minutes later, the cage stops at the bottom. They follow the security through the maze of stone tunnels. The walls at either side house individual cells, each one with a small window cut into the door. Avoca wishes more than ever he had been allowed to keep his gun on him. He's not a violent man; even in training, he hated having to fire his weapon. Places such as this one changed his mind.

The security finally halts at a large, newer looking door. They enter another code and the door swings open. The area they walk into is like an entirely different place from the upper floors. Instead of carved stone walls, they are met with sterile metal. Six cells line the right side of the corridor. These, too, differ from the primary cells. The doors seem to be much thicker with larger locks. Without a word, the security leaves and shuts the door.

Balfe clears his throat. 'We're looking for Logan.'

Nothing but silence meets them. Balfe glances at his two companions and tries again. 'I guarantee you will want to talk to us.'

The sound of mattress springs creaking comes from behind the third cell. 'Logan doesn't exist anymore. Call me *Forty-Three*.'

∞

Milla watches as the bubbles swirl down the drain. Her hands are well and truly disinfected by now, but she repeats the procedure all the same.

It's not like her to delay. In all her years of training, she has always been the first into the operating theatre. It's why she entered into medicine in the first place. But this time it's different; this time her patient is conscious.

Chayse peeks around the corner and she drops the bar of soap. Piercing, light blue eyes shine out of a ruggedly handsome face. 'Where's your mask?'

He smiles a mischievous, lop-sided grin. 'We're about to operate on the captain. Don't think wearing a metal mask will help much. Anyway, he's ready whenever you are.'

Milla forces a smile on her face and nods. 'I'll be right there.'

178

Chayse doesn't seem convinced, but leaves her alone with her thoughts. Milla takes a deep breath and forces her shoulders back. Time to get into doctor mode. With more confidence than she feels, Milla walks into the room and over to the monitoring equipment. Various wires and cables snake into the computer system. She examines Gryffin's vitals on the screen and frowns. 'There seems to be a computer problem. I'll need a new system.'

Chayse joins her at the screen and, after reading the data, shakes his head. 'It all seems right to me.'

'But his heart rate is steady. According to this information, his body isn't suffering a trauma.'

'His implants are regulating his vitals. They keep his body operating at its peak.'

Milla can't stop her mouth from dropping open. 'That's incredible. But his heart rate was fluctuating when we found him.'

'His programming isn't perfect; it sometimes takes a little time to kick in. It won't be able to keep this up for much longer, so you probably should begin.'

'Of course.' She turns from the screens to the prone body of her patient and gasps when she notices the heavy chains securing Gryffin to the bed. 'What the hell is going on?'

Chayse blushes slightly and looks at the ground. 'Klay insisted and I have to agree. Gryffin will wake up and I guarantee you won't want to be on the receiving end of his metal arm. He swings at you, you'll have a few broken ribs to deal with — if you're lucky.'

She looks in horror at the thick chains wrapped securely around Gryffin's wrists. His arms are over his head and pinned to the underside of the gurney. 'Are there any more restraints I should know about?'

'His ankles are secured too.' Chayse stands in front of her and meets her eyes. 'Trust me. It's not the first time we've taken these precautions. The captain is used to it.'

'Can you not knock him out? Have you tried ... I don't know ...

Getting him extremely drunk?'

Chayse laughs and shakes his head. 'Alcohol is treated the same way as anaesthetic. His implants neutralise it almost immediately.'

Milla nods and tries not to focus on the restraints. What she wouldn't give for a regular appendectomy right now. Klay bursts into the room, pulling a heavy cylinder behind him on a trolley. He parks it beside the monitoring equipment at the head of the gurney and unpacks tubes from the storage tray.

Chayse pushes a rubber gag in between Gryffin's teeth for something to bite down on if the pain gets too much. Klay attaches a tube to the tank then pushes a face mask on the other end. He secures the mask over Gryffin's nose and mouth before opening the valve on the tank.

'I'm almost afraid to ask …' Milla says.

'Anaesthetic,' Klay replies. 'It won't keep him under once you cut into him, but it should make him … Well, less likely to hurt you. Wouldn't want to give you any reason to back out of your agreement with Aleena.'

Chayse stands by Milla, ready to assist. It doesn't appear she can stall any longer. She glances down at her patient. The white sheet preserving his modesty does little to hide the series of horrific scars scattered over his body.

She takes the modified scanner from Chayse and begins examining the area around the knife. Milla would have preferred to use her equipment, but apparently Gryffin's implants distort scanners; a useful trick when trying to evade capture.

Milla slowly moves the scanner over Gryffin's body.

'Enough, Doctor!' Klay interrupts.

'I always take a full body scan before I operate. It's standard procedure.'

Klay slams his hand on the table. 'You're here to get that knife out of his side, not invade his privacy.' He crosses his arms across his chest. 'Knife. Now, Doctor.'

'You know, a bit of faith wouldn't go astray here.'

'You couldn't buy my trust, Doctor,' Klay replies. 'Get a move on.' He looks over at Chayse. 'I'll be back in an hour. I want the captain in recovery by the time I get back.' He storms out of the room, bumping into Aleena as he pushes past her at the door.

Milla grinds her teeth together and tries to hold back her terse reply. 'Cheery fellow.'

Aleena steps closer and smiles apologetically. 'He is an awkward man.' Aleena takes Klay's seat and moves it closer to Gryffin. 'Very protective of Gryffin. I find it is best to avoid him.'

Milla grunts. She nods at Chayse and he grips the handle of the knife in Gryffin's side. He slowly applies pressure and begins pulling the blade out. Gryffin's eyes fly open and he roars in pain through the gag. The chains groan in protest as he fights to get his arms free. Aleena instantly jumps to her feet. 'Gryffin, please calm down. Chayse is trying to help you.' Aleena nods at Chayse, instructing him to continue, so he takes a hold again and pulls.

Gryffin bites down on the gag as he tries to hold back a scream. Chayse extracts the knife and places it on the trolley beside him. Milla tries to focus on the wound, but the pure loathing in Gryffin's eyes distracts her. She has no doubts, if unchained, he would swat her away like a fly. Chayse steps up to her. 'Hey, what's wrong?'

'I can't do this while he's looking at me.'

Chayse glances at Gryffin before turning his attention back to her. 'Concentrate on the wound.'

Milla nods. She turns back to Gryffin and attempts to focus solely on her task instead of his angry purple eyes. To his credit, the Nomad leader remains as still as he can while she repairs the damage caused by the knife. Once completely absorbed by tending to him, she doesn't think about him being awake and staring at her.

She works steadily while continuously keeping a close eye on the scan information. After what seems like a lifetime, she repairs the internal damage and begins suturing the wound. Only then does she allow herself to relax slightly. It seems her patient has the same idea. Although he still winces slightly, his gagged verbal protests have ceased. Milla places the last suture and steps back from Gryffin. Chayse reduces the amount of anaesthetic being pumped into Gryffin's lungs before patting her on the back. 'You did good, Doc. We'll take it from here.'

She looks down at Gryffin, who appears to be unconscious. 'Usually, I'd know the answer to this, but I'm not going to assume anything. Will he recover?'

Chayse pulls his gloves off and throws them onto the instrument trolley. He runs a hand through his spiked hair and blows out a breath. 'After some rest he should be okay. Hopefully, he'll get some sleep now you've finished.' He gently squeezes her shoulder. 'Hey, you okay, Milla?'

'Why wouldn't I be okay? I've operated on a fully conscious cyborg while he was chained to the table and looked like he wanted to kill me for the whole thing. Best day ever!'

He chuckles and shakes his head. 'That wasn't part of Foundation training?'

Milla blows out a breath and smiles. 'I'll make sure they add it to the curriculum. I better go and write my report. After that, I'm going to have a large drink. Care to join me?'

'I'd love to, Milla, but I've got work to do.'

She places a hand on his arm and winks. 'Your loss.'

Milla wanders into the room beside the makeshift operating theatre and slumps back in the chair. She stares at the blank computer screen and tries to sort through her thoughts. This isn't going to be the easiest report to write, but she knows Roman will need it to give to the Foundation.

Even though it is going against her orders, she will be keeping some of the information to herself. The Foundation don't need to know every intimate detail.

Before Klay stopped her, she learnt something about Gryffin the

Nomad leader would no doubt rather keep to himself. Someone had tried to castrate Gryffin at some stage in the past. Luckily, they either changed their mind or were interrupted before they finished. The entire area suffered severe damage and he's incredibly fortunate anything works at all.

She would never admit she saw this scarring. Gryffin deserves some form of privacy and Roman sure as hell doesn't need to know that about his son.

24

Roman pauses at the door to the cottage serving as the medical centre. Milla contacted him to say Gryffin had survived the procedure and should make a full recovery. His first reaction had been relief, which he quickly pushed aside. He has to rein in these emotional slips.

He smiles as Aleena steps up to the door and leans against the frame. 'Loitering, Captain?'

'I'm here to speak with Milla but don't want to interrupt her.'

Aleena nods. 'Are you sure that is the only reason you are here?'

He tilts his head to the side and purses his lips. 'What do you mean?'

'Your wanted criminal escaped death. I am sure your superiors will be glad to hear he has survived.' Before he can respond, she disappears back into the building and leaves him alone.

He shakes his head and follows her into the cottage. Aleena enters a room to the left of the corridor and turns to face him as she closes the door loudly. Clearly the Nomad aren't the only ones protective over Gryffin. With only one other doorway off the corridor, he enters the room to discover Milla frowning at the computer screen. The doctor's usually cheery glow has faded, leaving her looking tired. 'Looks like you could do with some rest, Doctor.'

Milla jumps slightly at the sound of his voice. 'Damn, Captain. Don't sneak up on me.'

He rests a hip against the edge of the desk. 'Bit jumpy?'

She wipes her hands on her trouser legs. 'You bet I am. I'm half expecting Gryffin to come in here. He wasn't entirely happy with me poking around his insides — not that I can blame him.'

'Head back to *Infinity* if you prefer. You're done here.'

'I'll stay until I know he's going to pull through. I've never walked out on a patient and I'm not about to start now, no matter how difficult that patient may be. I've got security personnel with me. I'll be okay.'

Roman quietly examines her and tries to ascertain whether she's telling the truth. Not able to tell either way, he nods. 'Any problems, call for assistance immediately. You understand?'

'I'm not about to take on a Nomad like Gryffin — I'm not that stupid.' She pushes the tablet across the table towards him. 'My report.'

Roman lowers onto the seat opposite her and begins reading. After a few sentences, he takes a long drink of water from a glass on her table to try and wash away the bitter tang in his mouth. He doesn't know what he was expecting from Milla's report, but the detailed description of his son's — the Nomad leader's — injuries is proving to be too much.

According to Milla's report, Gryffin has extensive scarring internally as well as externally. It appears he's undergone dozens of operations over many years, probably to fit the numerous internal devices scattered throughout his body. The level of scarring suggests Gryffin's muscles were tense when the incisions were inflicted to insert the implants. It's not conclusive, but Milla is of the opinion the operations took place without anaesthetic.

Roman pushes the horrific thought aside and concentrates on the report, but it doesn't get any better. Most of Gryffin's bones have old fractures; some clean breaks while others had clearly been shattered. Some of the injuries even date back to his early teens. There is no doubt Gryffin had endured severe torture for some time.

Roman leans back in his chair and looks up at Milla. 'I have to ask: is this report accurate?'

Milla nods solemnly. 'Yes, sir.'

Roman grunts and clasps his hands in front of him on the desk. 'Were you able to retrieve any information on his implants?'

She clears her throat before continuing. 'Not much I'm afraid. He's had his artificial arm for roughly fifteen years. The arm links into his nervous system internally. He can operate it like a flesh and blood limb. It's pretty ingenious, really. All of his implants are.' She reins in her enthusiasm when she sees the less-than-amused expression on Roman's face.

Roman points at the ocular implant. 'What about his vision? Does the metal impair it?'

'From what I can make out, the implant enhances his vision. On the flip side, I'm pretty sure if the implant failed he'd be blind. Whoever did this severed the nerve to fit the implant.'

Roman tries to rein in his emotions. 'Right. Is it Nomad technology?'

'Sir, I doubt it had anything to do with the Nomad. Well, not his crew anyway. It's obvious they're all genuinely concerned for him. Either way, I wouldn't think anyone could identify Nomad technology. From what I can see, they re-use other technologies.'

'You mean they steal other technologies. Is there any way of shutting down the electrical charge to his arm?'

'Not that I know of.'

'So have you learnt anything we can use against him? Any way of containing him?'

'Not at this moment, sir. I need to do more scans, but the Nomad — especially Klay — are being very protective of him. I'll try what I can, but I may not be able to get close to him.'

'Do what you can without drawing attention to yourself. Keep me informed of his progress.' Roman says, calling an end to the meeting.

'Sir, before you go, I've found something else troubling.' She moves to the next image showing a detailed cross-section of the wound site. 'Someone tried to kill Gryffin.'

Roman pushes back his chair and rubs his face. 'Perhaps you need some sleep, Doctor. Your memory is clearly affected.'

'What I mean is someone stabbed him twice in the same place.' Noticing she finally has Roman's full attention, she continues. 'From what I can deduce, the dart he was hit with contained a powerful sedative. When he lost consciousness, someone pushed a knife, or something similar, into the same place twice.'

'I thought sedatives didn't work?'

'They work for a few minutes until his implants neutralise them. Whoever did this knew that. They used something I've never seen before. It did a great job knocking him out.'

This could be the thing they need to capture Gryffin. 'Can you reverse engineer the sedative?'

'I'm not sure yet. Most of it's been neutralised.' Milla leans forward, almost as if she is afraid someone will overhear their conversation. 'Sir, you don't accidentally insert something into the same wound twice.'

Milla is right — it does sound like someone else has Gryffin in their sights. This will only put added pressure on him to bring Gryffin in. He doubts the Foundation will step aside and allow someone else to take down the Nomad. Unless, of course, it's an internal Nomad issue. Perhaps a disgruntled crew member has decided to overthrow Gryffin. Roman is quiet for a moment before he shuts down the screen and stands up. 'This has nothing to do with us. Our main priority is to get him in custody as quickly as we can. We don't have time to worry about conspiracy within the Nomad.'

'But, sir, we can't ignore this.'

'That's an order, Doctor! I don't want to hear another word from you on this subject.'

Roman pushes off the chair and leaves the room. He slams the door behind him with a loud thump. Roman runs a hand through his hair as he hurries from the house. He needs to put some distance between himself and the Nomad leader. If he isn't careful, he could very well do something stupid like interfere. He can't fault Milla for her concern. She had saved Gryffin's life, so it is only natural she wants to keep him alive.

Roman nods at his security detail as he climbs into the transport. So, by ignoring her protests, is he actually saying Gryffin deserves to die? Roman pushes the thought to the back of his mind. No, his orders start and finish with him bringing Gryffin back to Foundation space. All he can do is try to capture Gryffin before the other party kills him.

∞

Stifling a yawn, Milla turns off her screen. After studying the images of Gryffin's implants for the last hour, she is no closer to deciphering what they do. Without the ability to scan him correctly, she's practically blind. She pushes her chair back and takes a sip of her coffee, grimacing as she swallows the now-cold liquid. She turns off the screens and stands up to stretch her stiff muscles.

She doesn't even know why she's spent the last hour looking at the images. Roman told her to leave it, but the doctor in her couldn't. His modifications fascinate her and it is only natural she wants to know more about them. Add that to the fact someone had tried to kill him and it leaves her with a big mystery. Milla loves a good mystery.

She glances at the time and decides she should check on the patient. Technically, she should have done it before now, but had been putting it off as long as possible. The relatively simple task seemed all the more awkward thanks to the intimidating Nomad security.

Intimidated or not, her patient requires her attention. Taking some comfort from the presence of the Foundation security, she picks up her tablet and slowly makes her way out of the bedroom serving as an office. Two of the Foundation security stay close to her while the rest remain at their posts. As she approaches the Nomad security, they stand to attention and block her way. Milla stands tall and folds her arms to try and hide her nervousness.

'Excuse me,' she says. Neither guard moves.

She tries her best stern glare and stands her ground but it's not easy when faced with two large and masked men. 'Right, let's get one thing clear. Your Commander Klay left orders. Gryffin is under my care until he gets back from your ship. Do you really want to be held responsible for something happening to your captain because you stopped me treating him?'

They glance at each other and slowly step to the side.

'Thank you.' She pulls the privacy screen across and takes a moment to read through her notes again. When she's finished, she looks at him properly for the first time. She hadn't looked beyond his injuries and implants until now. With his trademark mask removed, she has a clear view of the face that seems to have hooked her friend.

Even though Terra's picture had let that cat out of the bag weeks before, Milla had presumed she applied some artistic licence to the drawing, but it depicts him perfectly. She has to hand it to Terra — she knows how to pick them. He is breathtaking — even with the harsh metal and ragged scars. She hates to use the cliché tall, dark and handsome, but it fits him perfectly.

She leans over to check his pulse and has barely touched him when he wakes up suddenly. Gryffin locks onto her arm with an iron grip. He sits up and twists it behind her back, so she ends up facing away from him. Holding her tight against his body, he puts his metal knuckles to her neck and forces her chin up. The electricity moves up his arm towards his hand and creeps closer to her face.

25

Forty-Three walks towards the small window cut in the door of his cell. He tilts his head to the side and examines Balfe through the bars. 'Your people put us here. Why would we believe anything you have to say?'

Balfe would much prefer to conduct this conversation face to face instead of through a small window into a dark cell, but until he has their cooperation, he can't afford to let them out. Even one of them could kill them in an instant. He doesn't want to think what six of them would do. 'Logan — apologies — *Forty-Three*, we are here to ask for your assistance. In return, you will be freed.'

Forty-Three remains quiet for a few minutes. Balfe wants to get out of here as quickly as possible but isn't keen on pushing him. Balfe needs the men to at least partially trust him. Once they do what he needs them to, he doesn't care where they end up.

Forty-Three looks up at him again. 'What do you need us to do?'

'We need your help to capture someone. A few attacks here and there will help speed things along and push him into the open. Your unique talents will be useful.'

Unique talents didn't do them justice. While the Nomad leader was the sole survivor of the work on the station, the Scientist had continued his work in other areas. Grafton had tasked him with trying to alleviate the predisposition to violence in some of the Outer Moon prisoners.

According to Grafton's records, the Scientist made modifications to the subject's brain, leaving the prisoners with severe violent tendencies. Whatever the Scientist had attempted, it had made them more dangerous. While they didn't have the main control implant in their brains, it had been attempted, causing brain damage in each of them.

'Very well,' *Forty-Three* says. 'We agree.'

Balfe glances at the other cells. 'You've checked with your colleagues?'

'No need. I speak for them. Now, get us out of here.'

Balfe bangs on the main door. The security guard opens it and steps back to let them out. 'Well? What do you want to do with them?' the guard asks.

'They're coming with us.'

∞

Gryffin tries to work through the hazy feeling in his head. The woman seems familiar, but it takes him a few minutes to place her. When he does, he has to bite back a groan. 'You're Foundation. Where am I?'

'On Ultar. In a house in the village,' she whispers.

In the village? How did he end up here? He squeezes his eyes shut, trying to remember what happened, but nothing comes.

'You were injured,' she gasps, as if reading his mind. It's then he notices the stabbing pain in his side. He looks down and is horrified to see he's wearing a gown of some sort. Judging by the cold feeling on his back, the horrible thing is open-backed too, meaning he's practically naked. And to top it all off, his gun is nowhere to be seen. He lets a little more power travel down his arm towards the woman.

One of his guards slowly moves towards the bed. 'Sir, you're not a prisoner. The Foundation helped save your life.'

Gryffin eases his hold on the woman's arm slightly but keeps the electricity crackling inches from her face.

'Let me go. I need to examine your wound, Captain,' she says.

'You're not touching me,' he growls in her ear.

'Well, that's going to make treating you difficult.'

Gryffin doesn't bother responding. His primary concern at the moment is trying to breathe with lungs full of cement. The implant working with his lungs must be malfunctioning. He tries to steady his breathing as Chayse enters the room.

'Oh damn.' Chayse's face drops when he sees Gryffin awake. 'Sir, please let her go. She helped save your life,' he says, trying to calm the situation.

'Chayse? What the hell is going on? Where's your damn mask?'

'I'll explain. Firstly, though, Doctor Collins helped you. You can let her go. Please.'

Gryffin stares at Chayse in silence for a moment and then slowly releases his hold on Milla. As soon as she's free, she backs away from him.

Chayse steps closer to him. 'What's the last thing you remember?' he asks.

Gryffin looks down at his legs and scrunches his brow. 'I remember sending Klay after the intruder. I went outside to the barn... nothing after that.' Gryffin concentrates, but the memories seem to be disjointed. A face suddenly pops into his head. It's the face of a man. He tries to ignore the noises around him and focus on the face, but he can't hold on to the image.

It's not the fact the man had stabbed him that's bothering him. It's the fact he got close enough to do it. Gryffin's hearing and reflexes are far superior. No one has ever been able to sneak up on him. 'I don't remember anything after that.' He slowly sits up in the bed and his flesh wrist throbs when he puts pressure on it. The angry red imprint of a heavy chain probably has a lot to do with that. 'The Foundation wants to arrest me, so Klay chains me to the bed and hands me over to their doctor. If he wanted me off the ship, couldn't he have come up with something less obvious?'

Chayse looks down as he tries to avoid his captain's icy glare. 'You were hurt pretty badly, sir.'

'Look me in the eye when you're talking to me,' Gryffin growls.

Chayse glances quickly at Milla before focusing on Gryffin. 'Yes, sir. Doctor Collins did help to save your life, sir.'

'And you trust her. Trust her enough to show her your face?'

'You needed her help. We couldn't risk anything happening to you.'

'I asked if you trust her.'

Chayse doesn't even hesitate. 'I do.'

Gryffin looks from Milla to Chayse and back to Milla again. He fights against the unreasonable urge to tell Chayse to get him the hell out of here, but he feels lousy. He's no good to anyone with a hole in his side. 'Quick check.'

Chayse motions for Milla to come over. She stands in front of him and crosses her arms. 'Now, I'd appreciate it if you didn't try to kill me while I check your wound.' Milla peels the bandage away and examines the incision. 'By the way, I'm open to accepting apologies.'

Gryffin stays silent.

'You missed your cue to apologise.'

'For what?'

She shakes her head as she replaces the bandage, pressing a little too firmly on the wound. Gryffin hisses in pain. 'You're having difficulty breathing. I don't know enough about your implants to give you anything.'

'Give the information to Chayse.'

'I can't just leave it at that.'

'Yes you can.'

Milla opens her mouth to argue, but decides against it. 'Right, well it's your decision I guess.'

Gryffin ignores her, lies back and closes his eyes. Even though there's a Foundation doctor standing beside him and he should stay alert, his body has different ideas. Putting his trust in his well-chosen security team and Chayse, he leaves them all to it and falls asleep.

∞

Chayse looks at the screen and reads the information again. 'Are you sure about this?'

Milla nods. 'I went through the data several times.'

Chayse runs a hand over his spiked hair and stands up to pace the small bedroom. 'You know what you're saying, right? You know what this means?'

'It means that someone is trying to kill Gryffin.'

'Damn it.' Chayse slumps back into the chair. 'Who else knows?'

'Roman, Terra, and you.' She watches a variety of emotions race across his face, but surprise isn't one of them. 'This isn't news to you.'

'Can I see a breakdown of the sedative?' he asks, ignoring her comment.

Milla brings up the information for Chayse. She knows she's disobeying a direct order and Roman could have her job for it, but she made an oath to save people. How is keeping what she discovered to herself helping anyone? By keeping her mouth shut, she is effectively helping the person attempting to kill Gryffin.

Once she made the decision to discuss her findings, Chayse was the obvious confidant. In the very short time she's known him, he has come across as a trustworthy person. Then again, the Nomad are a group of thieving mercenaries. Surely lying and deceiving people comes as part of that.

She glances over at him. His icy blue eyes meet hers as he smiles.

'Why me?' Chayse asks, echoing her thoughts.

'Here's where I come across as naïve. You're his aide. I figure it's your job to keep him safe. I don't know if I trust anyone else with the information.'

Chayse looks at her strangely. 'You didn't suspect me? As his aide, I can get closer to him than most.'

Milla looks closely at him for a minute before shrugging. 'I've seen you with him. You have too much respect, too much admiration for him.'

He shakes his head. 'That means nothing. It's part of the job.'

Milla sits down beside him and puts her hand on his arm. 'We both know it's more than that. While I have you here, I want to thank you for earlier. I thought Gryffin was going to kill me.'

He looks at her for a moment before shaking his head. 'He wouldn't have killed you.'

'You're a lousy liar.'

He blushes slightly. 'I'm glad I got there when I did. Better?'

'Sounds more like the truth. I'm glad you arrived too.'

They gaze stupidly at each other before Chayse finally clears his throat and turns his attention back to the screen. 'I know this compound: it's used mainly to kill. You inject it into the target and they suffocate in their sleep. Looks like a natural death.'

'Target?'

'Yeah, like in a contract kill.'

'Oh.'

'I haven't ever used it. I know about it from Gryffin.'

She holds up her hands and shakes her head. 'Hey, it's none of my business.'

'I know. I wanted you to know that … You know … I haven't used anything like that on anyone.' He clears his throat before getting back to business. 'Using that drug doesn't make sense though.'

Milla frowns. 'How so? If they wanted to kill him and not have anyone get suspicious, surely it's the best way.'

'For a regular person, yes, but not Gryffin. His implants can usually neutralise any foreign toxins, but even if some gets into his blood stream he'd still be okay. His implants back up his major organs. If his lungs shut down, the implant linked to them would keep breathing for him. He'd be short of breath for a bit, but it wouldn't kill him.'

'Maybe they didn't know. Klay made it clear his implants are *need to know*.'

Chayse looks like he's about to say something else, but shakes his head.

'What?'

'Nothing. I probably told you more than Klay would want you to know.'

'My lips are sealed.' She emphasises her point by pretending to zip her lips and throw the key over her shoulder. 'So, assuming they knew it would only knock him out for a few minutes, why go to all that trouble? Why risk getting caught by Gryffin to stab him? It doesn't make sense.'

Chayse scratches his jaw and grunts. 'Couldn't agree more. Did anything show up in the wound?'

'No foreign bodies, no toxins. Nothing at all. So, who'd do this? Someone after his command?'

Chayse shakes his head. 'It doesn't work that way. It's not only this command they'd be after but also his other role.'

'Other role?'

Chayse shakes his head again and smiles apologetically. 'Sorry. Forget I said anything. Again.'

Milla smiles. 'You Nomad are very fond of your "need to know" aren't you?'

Chayse leans back in the chair and returns her smile. 'Comes with the territory. We all have secrets. Makes us more interesting.'

'Care to share any of yours?'

Chayse smirks. 'Don't think we're at that stage in our relationship...yet. Besides, you've seen my face. That's probably my biggest secret.'

Milla smiles widely. 'Thank you for trusting me enough to take off your mask.'

Chayse shrugs. 'I doubt it will cause any problems for me. Gryffin is the one we're all trying to protect by wearing them.'

'So what now? Are you going to tell Gryffin about the attempt on his life?'

'It's not the first time and it won't be the last. I need to do a bit of digging before I broach the subject with him. Not that I don't trust your results. I just need to be sure before I start making accusations.'

'Well, if you need someone to run things by, I'm always here.'

'Yeah, well if we're wrong about this, I'll definitely be doing some running.'

26

Despite Terra's better judgement and everyone's warning to keep away, her curiosity gets the better of her and she finds herself at the door to the cottage housing Gryffin. Up until two minutes ago she had decided not to do this. She still isn't sure it's the right thing to do, but she has no choice. It doesn't matter what she does: he is always at the back of her mind.

Terra creeps up to his bed. He is asleep, so she silently sits down and looks at him closely for the first time since that initial night. Gryffin is lying on his side with the sheet covering him up to his waist. Gryffin has abandoned the open-backed gown in favour of a pair of black boxers, which shows off his tattoo in all its glory.

His breathing quickens and he throws his arm over his face. When he moves, something catches her attention. He has the number thirty-five branded in figures on the back of his left shoulder. She can just about make it out through the griffin's wing.

Terra's breath suddenly catches in her throat. The report Milla found mentioned the number thirty-five. A horrible thought crosses her mind as she examines the brand burnt into his flesh. It looks like an identifying mark. Why would the Foundation have a note of that number in his file? She seriously doubts he would have had the brand before he disappeared. The medical records from his childhood detailed every bump and scratch. Surely two digits burnt into his skin would have been highlighted.

But that raises more questions. If the Foundation knows about the mark, they must know what happened to him after he disappeared. She shakes her head and scolds herself. There must be some other explanation.

Her thoughts are interrupted as Gryffin mumbles in his sleep and turns over to face her. His metal hand twitches and hangs over the side of the bed. She leans back in the chair and can't help but smile to herself as she watches him slowly breathe in and out. Some locks of hair have fallen across his face to hide his implant and again she has to stop herself from reaching out to brush them out of the way.

Her hand reaches for the pencil in her pocket before she stops herself. Drawing him has landed her in enough trouble without doing it in clear view of his imposing security personnel.

He surprises her by quickly opening his eyes, blinking a few times to clear his vision. Feeling like a cat caught in the headlights, she blushes slightly. 'Hi. How are you feeling, Captain?'

He licks his dry lips and slowly sits up. 'What do you want?' he asks abruptly.

Taken aback by his tone, she smiles, trying not to let it show. 'I wanted to see if you were okay.'

Gryffin slowly leans back in the bed. He rests his metal arm on his stomach and knocks the sheet away from him to expose a well-toned leg. He tries to lean over to pull the sheet across, but fails to reach entirely, hissing as his wound protests.

Terra instantly stretches over to help, but he pulls away from her. 'Don't touch me,' he growls.

'Stop being stubborn and accept help.' She attempts to grasp the corner of the sheet again, but he jerks away aggressively and curses as the movement pulls on his wound. Terra leaves him to his struggles with the covers and sits on the chair beside his bed. 'Gryffin, I couldn't help but notice you have two digits on your shoulder.'

His unsettling purple eyes lock on to her like they're locking onto a target. 'Gryffin, your eyes ...' Her words fizzle away and her hand reaches towards his face.

'Get your damn hand away from me.' He eases onto his side and presses his metal hand against the bandage. It takes her a few seconds to realise he's pressing on the surgery site. Blood begins seeping through the bandage as he continues to apply pressure.

'Stop it, Gryffin! What the hell are you doing?'

He grinds out a curse and opens his eyes. 'So, you were examining me when I was sleeping?'

'I couldn't help but notice the brand.' Terra's relief at seeing his dark blue eyes again is short-lived as the blood-stained bandage on his side draws her attention. 'Are you okay?'

He grunts at her. 'Of course I'm not okay,' he says. 'I should be back on *Ares*, far away from here, instead of being stuck in bed on this world with a security detail watching me.' He turns to face her and she takes a step back at the hard anger in his eyes. 'You've caused me enough trouble. Now get the hell away from me.'

'I'm sorry you feel like that.' Terra turns away from him and leaves the room.

∞

Don't cry. Don't cry. Don't cry.

Terra continues her inner chant as she walks quickly back to the transport. The inside of her cheek is raw from biting back the threatening tears. The image of Gryffin deliberately hurting himself will stay with her for a long time. The pain had somehow affected his eyes, changing them from blue to purple, but that's as much as she knows.

She climbs back into her commandeered transport and starts the engine. Roman had been right. What did she honestly think she would achieve by seeing Gryffin again? Apart from being left with disturbing images of what he did to himself, the incident had been embarrassing and upsetting.

The engine roars as she tears along the dirt track back to *Infinity*. She knows Gryffin blames her for his injury. None of this would be happening to him if that first meeting hadn't taken place. Of course he's angry and regrets helping her.

She stops suddenly in the centre of the town. Why did she run away instead of attempting to explain herself and her actions?

Spurred on by anger at her stupidity, she spins the vehicle around. Terra leaves the engine running, jumps out, and bursts in the door. Terra ignores his security and storms straight up to his bed, clearly surprising him. His blue eyes turn towards her.

'Yes, I am to blame for some of what happened, but it doesn't give you the right to speak to me like that.' He opens his mouth to reply, but she continues before he can talk. 'What happened is not entirely my fault. You need to take at least some responsibility.'

'Really? How'd you figure that out?'

'If you hadn't gotten in my way on the station, you wouldn't be in this mess now.'

'I got in your way? I'm pretty sure you were the one who ran into me. And if I hadn't stopped, they would have got you.'

'I was perfectly capable of handling the situation myself. I didn't need you to come in all guns blazing and save me.'

He furrows his brow. 'I didn't fire one shot.'

'I didn't mean literally. It's a saying.' He tilts his head to the side and quietly looks at her. 'Oh just forget it. What I mean is that I didn't need your help.'

'You were running towards a dead end. What was your big plan to get away with only one round?' He lies back on the bed while keeping one hand on the blood-soaked bandage. 'Well?'

Okay. So maybe he has a point there and he knows it judging by the smug look on his face. 'My plan is none of your business.' She inwardly cringes at how pathetic that sounds. 'Anyway, it was you who met with us on Taldor to threaten us. It was your choice to be there.'

'Taldor was a Nomad colony until your Foundation arrived. There was no way in hell I was just going to do nothing while you took it.'

'So attacking the colony was your answer?'

'Yes.'

She struggles to find a response to his calmly spoken reply. 'You could have killed the colonists. You nearly killed me.'

'You're going to complain about *nearly* dying? Nearly dying means you're still alive. Nothing to complain about.'

Her mouth drops open. 'This is all normal for you — isn't it? You genuinely can't see anything wrong with attacking colonies and near-death experiences.'

'There's a lot worse that can happen — believe me. Your ship arriving here kicked all this off. If you and your Foundation hadn't been in the Sector in the first place, none of this would have happened. You keep sticking your nose in and people are getting hurt as a result.'

'You think I wanted any of this? I sure as hell didn't want to be running for my life through a dark station with three men after me. I didn't mean to bump into you. I didn't mean for you to get involved and I certainly didn't want you to get hurt. Up until about ten minutes ago, I was glad I did bump into you.'

'That makes one of us.'

That one comment turns her skin cold. There is so much venom in his voice. 'You know, I was worried about you today. Hearing you were hurt... I was so scared you might die.' She takes a step back and wraps her arms around herself. 'I should have kept my concern for someone who deserves it.' Without another word, Terra turns around and leaves him by himself again.

∞

Gryffin lies back on the bed and closes his eyes. Another fantastic display of his people skills. His destructive side doesn't seem to be satisfied unless he's pushing people away. Of course it wasn't her fault. He does have one regret about helping her on the station: he should have stepped in sooner than he did.

He hits his head against the pillow and puts his hand over his face, annoyed with himself. He didn't mean any of that the way it sounded. Why can't he think before he speaks?

'Good one, Captain!'

He opens his eyes as he hears someone clapping slowly. Sitting up again, he sees Milla coming out of the next bedroom. Great. That means Chayse also heard everything.

'Well done. I've been trying to find a way of telling her you're not worth bothering with and you've just saved me the job. Cheers.'

Gryffin glares at Milla before he stares up at the ceiling again.

'Oh, and for the record, she really does ... well, did like you. Hearing her picture had been used devastated her. She felt so guilty for putting you at risk. The silly fool wants to protect you. You've just managed to alienate the only person in the Foundation on your side, willing to fight for you. The only one who gave the slightest damn about you.'

She turns back around and leaves the house. Taking the not-too-subtle hint, he decides he's outstayed his welcome. Whether *Ares* is ready or not, that's where he's going. It's a small cut in his side. He's had worse.

He slowly slides his legs off the bed and sits on the edge with his arm pressed tightly to his side. Okay, maybe it's slightly worse than a small cut. Pushing against the wound will have done nothing to improve it, but at least the pain helped him keep control. He squeezes his eyes shut until a wave of dizziness passes. Leaving may not be as easy as he thought. He takes a few deep breaths and then calls Chayse out of his hiding spot in the room next door.

Chayse pauses for a moment before sticking his head around the corner. 'Sir?'

Gryffin notices his hesitation. 'How about we both forget you were in there. Get my uniform.'

'Sir, I don't think that's a good decision.'

'I'm not asking you to think. I ordered you to get my uniform.'

Chayse has the good sense not to disobey and comes back a minute later with his uniform. 'Captain, Klay wants me to keep you here until *Ares* is ready. And you've just had surgery. You're not well enough to leave yet.'

'I don't give a damn what you think. Now unless you want me to do something stupid, you'll get out of the way. Now.'

Chayse finally lowers his head and turns his back to Gryffin, giving him privacy so he can get dressed. Gryffin doesn't even glance at him as he slowly walks towards the door and leaves.

∞

Chayse brings the transport around the back of *Ares* as gently as he can. Gryffin doesn't look too well and the last thing he wants to do is cause more problems by bumping him around. The ten-minute trip from the village passed in complete silence. The captain isn't happy and there is no way Chayse is going to say anything to set him off.

The cargo bay doors open and Chayse can't help but eye the large purple griffin painted on the hull. It keeps watch over the transport as it enters the bay in total darkness. Landing lights lead him to his allocated spot at the far end of the bay. He glances over his shoulder to check on his captain. Gryffin is leaning against the side wall of the transport with his eyes squeezed shut. He's pale, breathing strangely and has his arm pressed tightly to his side.

205

Chayse turns the small craft around and hovers over his landing spot as the crew clear the area. Chayse can't quit thinking about how someone got close enough to stab the captain twice. It doesn't make sense. He can usually hear an insect approaching; an enemy with a knife shouldn't have been able to get within twenty feet of him.

It doesn't help that Gryffin ordered his security team to stay with Aleena before the attack. Unfortunately, the two Nomad didn't hear or see anything. One thing was going to change though: Gryffin would not be going anywhere without at least two bodyguards. The captain may not want to accept it, but even he needs someone to watch his back. He's too vital to the Nomad and their survival.

Chayse can only hope Gryffin will remember more about what happened once he recovers from the surgery. Maybe he'll be allowed to work with Milla to try and figure out what happened. Chayse silently chastises himself. There's no way that's going to happen. In fact, he'll be very surprised if he ever sees Milla again.

His mind is pulled back onto his job as he is directed to land. The transport lowers into its allocated spot and Chayse shuts down the engine. Before he can even unbuckle his harness, Klay storms into the bay. The commander stops in front of the carrier with his arms folded across his chest. Chayse curses loudly and slowly stands up. Luckily, Gryffin either doesn't hear or chooses to ignore him.

Klay glares at Chayse as he gets down from the transport. He plainly blames him for bringing Gryffin back sooner than recommended. He's not bothered. At the end of the day, he answers to Gryffin, not Klay.

'How are the repairs coming along, Commander?' Gryffin asks.

'Forget the repairs. What exactly are you doing, sir?'

Gryffin steps off the ramp. All signs of pain vanished as soon as the transport landed. Joys of being the captain, Chayse guesses. 'Trying to get onto my ship.'

Gryffin tries to move past Klay, but the commander blocks him. 'Sir, you should be resting. I thought we agreed you'd stay in the village for a bit longer. We're on limited power. We've only got emergency lighting in most areas until tomorrow.'

'I didn't realise I had to explain myself to you.'

'You don't, sir.'

'Can you get out of my way then? Chayse, bring the repair reports to my quarters in ten minutes.' He pushes past Klay and slowly leaves the bay. Not wanting to get into it with Klay, Chayse hurries out the door after Gryffin.

27

'The rogue group has attacked another colony while flying your colours. Sayber also attacked one of your ships — *Enyo*,' Klay reports.

Gryffin curses to himself. This group is quickly becoming a bigger thorn in his side than Sayber. Add this to the growing Foundation threat and it makes his headache worse. He leans forward on his desk and discretely pulls his shirt away from his wounded side. Even the pressure of the material is uncomfortable. 'When?'

'Yesterday. Fourteen people are dead on the surface. *Enyo* sustained substantial damage but no casualties. It'll take a few weeks to repair her. Until then, she's going to need protection.'

'Yesterday! Why am I only hearing about this now?'

'I just got word,' Klay replies. 'All messages were delayed with the ship powered down for repairs.'

'Is there enough power to send a communication now?'

'If we piggyback off the main tower on Ultar.'

Gryffin sits back in the hard chair and tries to get more comfortable. 'Send *Hermes*. She should only be a few hours away.'

'I'll tell them. What about this other group?'

'Contact the rest of the fleet. I need to know if it's only our colonies being targeted. As for Sayber, do some digging. Try to uncover what the hell he's doing. It's not like him to start ramping up the attacks for no reason. Where are the reports on the repairs I requested?'

Gryffin takes the report from the engineer accompanying Klay and picks out the numbers from the rest of the indecipherable letters. Aleena had attempted to teach him how to read once, but he didn't have the patience for it. Not being able to read hadn't held him back so far. Luckily for him, numbers are easily recognisable, but everything else is gibberish. The crew keeps the basic layout of the reports the same, so he knows what the numbers relate to. Klay and Chayse verbally record any other reports for him.

'When can we take off?' he asks without looking up from the screen. The engineer doesn't respond, so he looks up. 'I asked you a question.'

'In a few days, sir.' The engineer quickly ducks to avoid being hit by the tablet, as Gryffin throws it across the room and against the metal wall.

Gryffin erupts. 'A few days! What the hell has everyone been doing?' He sits up quickly and immediately regrets it when his wound complains. They can't stay here for a few more days. They have to get away now. 'I leave you by yourself for a few hours and things grind to a halt. What the hell happened?'

The engineer knows better than to argue with him when he's in a mood like this. 'I have no excuse, sir.'

'The engines should have been repaired first. Everything else can wait. If we're dead in the water, we're vulnerable. What the hell are we supposed to do if Sayber shows up again? Open the hatch and let him come in and help himself?' he shouts.

'We'll put in extra shifts to catch up, sir,' Klay says, trying to calm the situation before it escalates.

Gryffin turns to face Klay as his eyes begin to shift colour. He can

209

feel the buzzing at the back of his head. To try and keep control, Gryffin presses his fist against his wound and focuses on the stab of pain shooting through his side. 'You need to sort out your damn priorities, Klay.' Gryffin pushes himself to his feet and leans heavily on his desk. 'We need to shut Sayber down for good and fix the Foundation issue. We can't do that without a damn ship. We're leaving tomorrow morning, fully battle ready. I'll hold you responsible if that doesn't happen, Commander,' Gryffin growls.

'Yes, sir.'

Gryffin lowers himself into his seat and closes his eyes briefly when the room spins. When he doesn't hear anyone leaving, he opens his eyes again. 'What are you still doing here? Move!'

∞

Aleena takes a seat on one of the benches overlooking the training room. A loud and explicit curse from the room below draws her attention. She quietly peers through the railings in time to witness Gryffin kick the training drone.

He angrily shakes his head and takes a step forward to restart the program. He tries to block the initial assault but hesitates for a moment when his wound protests. Gryffin curses as the blow hits him on the shoulder and knocks him off balance.

Aleena can barely watch as the drone continues to strike him for the next few minutes. Gryffin finally stops the program and throws the stick to the floor. After glaring down at the weapon for a few moments he bends down to pick it up again.

He suddenly doubles over and grabs a fistful of hair. He cries out in pain and falls to his knees. Even though it goes against her very nature, Aleena remains where she is. Gryffin would not accept comfort of any form. All she can do is wipe away a tear as his anguished screams echo around the open space.

Gryffin made it clear numerous times that nothing helps the pain.

It lasts for a few minutes then eases. No amount of alterations by Klay has helped the situation. Gryffin has no choice but to endure it and that does not sit well with Aleena. There has been enough pain in his life without these additional episodes.

After a minute, the pain seems to ease. Gryffin slowly straightens and leans against the wall for support. Once he's upright and steady, he restarts the program. This time he effortlessly blocks and swiftly takes his opponent down.

She loves to watch him train; his movements mesmerise her. There is a grace and fluidity to his steps that she has never seen replicated by anyone else. Not for the first time, she intently watches his body move. The tight cords of muscle shift under his skin as he savagely attacks the drone, fiercely and brutally pushing it back.

She could watch him for hours. If they had met under different circumstances, they might have become more than friends, but she has seen the ruthless side of him firsthand and seen him kill without remorse. It is not something she can easily forgive or forget.

As a result, she is content to remain close friends, although she has to remind herself of that often, especially in situations like this.

'Aleena?'

She stands up and smiles down at him. 'Apologies, Captain. I did not wish to disturb you.'

He pushes damp hair off his face and frowns at her. 'Yeah, well you have. What do you want?'

She climbs down the spiral metal stairs. 'You have just undergone serious surgery. Should you really be training so soon?'

'What I do is none of your damn business. Thanks for understanding.'

She clasps her hands in front of her and nods. 'I see you have been working on your manners.'

'I allow you on my ship. That not enough manners for you?'

She smirks as she performs a mock curtsy. 'For that I am forever grateful.'

Gryffin turns to face her fully but says nothing.

'So, not in the mood for humour today.' He looks at her through his damp hair. 'This is a conversation. What usually happens is I say something and you say something.'

'Sounds more like an interrogation. What do you want?' he says again.

Aleena ignores his harsh tone. She is well used to dealing with his moods. 'I am here to invite you to the party tonight. You have yet to attend and if you keep avoiding these events, I am going to get offended.'

'Then you're going to get offended.'

'Would you like to offer an excuse, or leave it at that?'

'Are the Foundation going?'

'I have invited them, so I presume so.'

He curses and shakes his head. 'You make it damn hard for me to protect you when you keep pulling stunts like that.'

She decides to ignore his comment. It is not a surprise he refused the invitation. If she is honest, she asked him as a courtesy. Gryffin does not socialise.

He tilts his head slightly to the side and narrows his eyes. 'What?'

'Excuse me?'

'You didn't come here for that. What is it?'

Aleena sits on the bottom step of the stairs and clasps her hands on her knees. This is not a conversation she is looking forward to and his mood does not bode well for success. 'Lieutenant Rush.'

She did not know two words would have such an instant effect on him. His entire body tenses. 'What about her?'

'Forgive me, but I overheard your conversation last night.'

A faint red glow emanates from his implants. 'What the hell does a private conversation have to do with you?'

'You removed your mask for this woman, yes?'

'Aleena,' Gryffin warns.

'Gryffin, I am worried about you. The position of high commander is yours because you are the most dedicated, unwavering man in the group. The fact you broke one of your own rules and placed the group in such danger concerns me. Why her? What made you take that action?'

Gryffin hurls the stick against the wall, raining splinters over the rusted metal floor. He stalks right up to Aleena and forces her back against the metal stairs. His purple eyes drill into hers as he looms over her. 'I will continue to do my job and protect your colony. That's all you need to know.'

He turns away from her to get control of himself. Perhaps she should not have attempted this without a security team. As she is about to reach for the panic button on the wall, he faces her again. His implants have ceased glowing and his blue eyes appear calmer. She takes a step closer to him, but he shakes his head. 'Don't, Aleena.'

Aleena completely ignores him and closes the distance between them. She stops in front of him and waits until he meets her eyes. Her intended words catch in her throat at the sight of such overwhelming sadness in his blue eyes. Gryffin shakes his head and looks at the ground for a moment. 'I'd never hurt you, Aleena. Not you.'

Aleena nods, even though a small part of her still doubts his words. 'I apologise for questioning you on such a private matter, Captain.'

'I don't know why I took my mask off. I ... Damn it, I can't explain it.'

'You needed her to see you.'

Gryffin scrunches his eyebrow as he considers her statement. He nods once, then turns his back to her. He pulls another stick out of the rack on the wall and gestures towards the door. 'Goodbye.'

28

Terra stands back and looks at her two dress options. After her shift on the bridge, she had gone back to her quarters to get ready for the party. It has been some time since the crew of *Infinity* have had the opportunity to dress up and 'go out' for the night, meaning this evening has been the subject of conversations all day.

After a hell of a lot of badgering from Milla, Terra had finally given in and promised to wear one of her dresses. It had taken her a long time to convince Roman to let her attend and he had only relented after Aleena assured him Gryffin wouldn't be there himself. Apparently, the Ultaran leader didn't even know if he still remained on the surface. His whereabouts were unconfirmed and many locals assumed he had left Ultar hours ago.

She tries not to let this news upset her. Although she had hoped to see him again, she couldn't let Roman see her disappointment. Her career and position on *Infinity* are important to her, but Gryffin... Well, he affects her in an inexplicable way. Knowing the attraction and resulting feelings are foolish, didn't help to quash them. The last time they spoke, he had been vile and rude, but it did nothing to deter her. She's angry at him for what he said, but has no control over the fluttering feeling in her stomach at the thought of the stubborn and bad-mannered Nomad.

After staring at the choices for another few minutes, she finally chooses a floor length, deep purple halter-neck silk dress over the shorter black one and leaves her dark hair falling in curls down her back. She applies slightly more make-up than usual followed by a spritz of her favourite perfume. Her mother's pearl necklace and earrings complete the outfit.

While she had laughed at Milla's suggestion to pack some fancy dresses, now she is grateful she insisted. She examines herself in the mirror and smiles in approval. It's a shame Gryffin won't be around to impress. She shrugs at her reflection, slips her feet into a pair of nude heels and pulls her shawl off the chair.

Terra steps off the transport with the rest of the bridge crew and can't help but gaze in wonder as she clears the trees surrounding the village. The villagers have gone to quite a bit of trouble to decorate the town for the party. Fresh flowers line the path from *Infinity* to the venue with tall, brightly lit lanterns scattered along the way. A large fire in the village centre illuminates the tables set up in a square surrounding it. Hundreds of lanterns hanging from the surrounding trees amplify the overall atmosphere.

She slowly turns and casually searches the crowd, but there's no sign of the Nomad captain. Perhaps the rumours of his departure are accurate. She hears her name being called and smiles when she sees Milla walk towards her with a noticeably unmasked Nomad crew member. Terra silently thanks Milla and her companion for the distraction. 'Terra, this is Chayse. You remember him, right?'

He smiles at her as he holds out his hand and his pale blue eyes immediately get her attention. What is it with the Nomad? Both Gryffin and Chayse have the most unusual blue eyes. Gryffin's are the darkest blue she's seen and Chayse's are the lightest — so light the iris is almost white. Even without his mask he looks quite a bit different from the last time she saw him. He suits his black combat trousers, black boots and white shirt. Milla has had her eye on him since she first saw him and Terra can fully understand why. Trust her to hunt him out.

'Good to see you again, Terra.'

'You too, Chayse.'

'First time at a party here?'

'Yes. Any advice you can offer?' Milla asks.

Terra smiles to herself. Milla is standing very close to Chayse and keeps touching his arm: classic Milla flirting.

'Well, stay away from the ale. Unless you fancy spending the next week in bed with a hangover, limit yourself to one small glass. It's powerful stuff.'

'Is everyone here?' Terra asks, trying to make the enquiry sound offhand. The sly smirk on Milla's face tells her she is less than successful.

To add to her embarrassment, Chayse clearly knows who she is asking about. 'I'm sorry, Terra. The captain's gone.'

She tries to keep the disappointment out of her voice. 'Gone where?'

Chayse grimaces. 'Sorry. I can't say. It was too risky having him on the surface with your captain so hell-bent on capturing him. We'll rendezvous with him after we leave.'

'When we depart, you mean.'

Chayse scratches the back of his neck. 'I was trying to be nice, but yes.' He glances over his shoulder at Klay, who is beckoning him. 'I'm sorry. Duty calls.'

'Are you okay?' Milla asks her after Chayse is out of earshot.

She shrugs. 'No choice really. It's probably for the best anyway.'

Milla nudges her arm and gestures towards the drinks table. Pushing her shoulders back, Terra lifts her head and links arms with her friend.

'Are you sure?'

Gryffin nods. 'No other explanation.'

Aleena gently picks up the hem of her dress and paces her office. He may try to keep a professional distance from her, but even he has to admit she looks striking tonight in a floor-length emerald green dress with her long blonde hair pinned on top of her head. Very different to the everyday Aleena he's used to. Then again, this is the first time he's seen her on a party night. He didn't see the purpose of the event so had spent every other one alone on *Ares*.

For everyone's safety, he decided to go into hiding while the Foundation remained on the surface. With him gone, they should leave his crew alone. Usually, he doesn't mind being on Ultar, but this time he wants to be away from it as soon as possible. He glances out the window at the brightly lit town square. The rest of his crew is there right now with the Foundation team. It did cross his mind to ban his crew from going, but Aleena had convinced him otherwise.

'So what now?' she asks, breaking him out of his thoughts.

'I need to head back to the ship. We found something that could help. Need to persuade him to open up though. Hopefully, we can uncover who ordered the hit, who hired them, then kill both parties.'

Aleena stops pacing. 'Found something? You mean a prisoner. Gryffin, there has been enough death today. Please let me accompany you. Perhaps I can extract answers without resorting to violence.'

'We don't have time.'

'Gryffin, I have seen you interrogate before. Does this man really deserve to die at your hands? Surely there must be another way.'

'There isn't,' he replies, ignoring the flash of anger that crosses her face. 'Just because I take your advice on some things doesn't mean you get to question everything I do. It's my way on this.'

'Please do not do this.'

'No arguments. The probes were deactivated using Nomad codes. That means one of my people gave those codes out. It's my problem. Once I discover who it was, I'm damn well going to make sure mine is the last face they see.'

∞

After a stern reprimand from Klay for talking to Milla, Chayse walks to the edge of the square and locates a seat beside some crew members from *Ares*. They don't acknowledge him and he's not surprised. On the plus side at least they didn't get up and walk away, so he must be making progress. In any case, he'd prefer to be alone than with the Nomad at the moment — especially Klay.

He glares over at the commander, who's deep in conversation with a group of Ultaran women. Chayse turns away before he carries out his urge to get up and hit the man. It doesn't help his cause that Klay has a point. He'll have to make sure Klay doesn't see him talking to Milla again.

Klay glances up at him almost as if checking he's still behaving. Chayse has no doubt in his mind he's enjoying every minute of showing him who is boss.

Chayse sits back and quietly watches the people around him. Masked Nomad mill around the central square where the Foundation gather. The masks are only removed when alone with the Ultarans. It isn't the most relaxed event, but needs must.

Chayse looks over at Terra and Milla again. He'll be searching out Milla in a few hours — in private. Hopefully, Klay will be so drunk he won't see Chayse slipping away.

Apart from the fact Milla is beautiful, her bubbly personality is infectious. Even now, she and Terra are laughing hysterically at something. Terra's attention doesn't seem to be fully on Milla, however. She may be laughing, but he can't help notice she also looks a bit disappointed. It is obvious she wanted to see Gryffin again. He understands the reason for the deception. It's in everyone's best interests to at least appear like Gryffin left the area.

'You're needed back on the ship.'

Chayse stands up and looks down at Klay. 'Sir?'

'I presume that is a "yes, sir" as opposed to a question.'

'Yes, sir.' Chayse turns away from Klay and slowly makes his way back along the forest path to *Ares*. Before he disappears into the darkness, he looks towards Milla, hoping he'll be allowed to come back.

∞

Chayse wants to focus anywhere but at the scene in front of him, but he can't. Apart from the fact the rest of the crew would never let him live it down, he physically can't tear his eyes from the cell.

One of the scouting teams had found an injured crew member from the other ship and brought him back so Gryffin could talk to him. Chayse wishes Gryffin hadn't called him in, but he had. Unlike most of the rest of the crew, Chayse hadn't been privy to his questioning tactics.

The man chained to the wall is roughly the same age as Chayse, but after an hour with Gryffin, he looks older. His bruised, battered face turns towards Chayse briefly before looking at Gryffin again. The prisoner tries to ease the pressure from the thick chains cutting into his wrists.

Expertly hiding the fact he's still recovering from major surgery, Gryffin crouches down in front of the prisoner and looks at him for a few minutes. The fact that none of the men in the room are wearing masks speaks volumes.

Gryffin addresses Chayse without breaking eye contact with the prisoner. 'Was my beacon orbiting the planet before the raid?'

'Yes, sir.'

'Was it working?'

'The planet was and is still clearly marked as being under your protection.'

Gryffin nods and lets the implant gain a little control over him, turning his eyes purple. 'Then why were you here?' he asks. The prisoner remains silent as he glares at Gryffin through bruised eyes. 'You landed on a planet under my protection and attacked it, which means you're an idiot and so are the rest of your crew and commanding officer.'

The prisoner looks away from Gryffin and remains silent.

Gryffin's response is to punch him in the leg with his right hand. The man's bone breaks with a loud crack. He screams in pain and Chayse has to twist away for a moment. After the anguished screams have died down a little, Gryffin takes a hold of the prisoner's neck. The red glow from his arm highlights the pain on the man's face. 'I get a little tetchy when I'm ignored. Try again.'

The prisoner struggles to breathe past Gryffin's tightening hand. 'I don't ... know ... anything!'

Gryffin's applies a little extra pressure. 'Who do you work for?'

'Go to hell,' the man gasps.

Gryffin looks away briefly then breaks the other leg. The prisoner screams in pain again. Chayse discretely leans against the pillar beside him as the room spins. He tries to focus on the captain's back instead of the bloody bones sticking out of the prisoner's legs. Why the hell isn't the man telling Gryffin what he wants to know? Chayse has no doubts the captain will kill the prisoner no matter what, but surely a quick death is better than a drawn out, painful one.

'I was... just part... of the... ground... crew,' he says through clenched teeth.

'Who hired you?'

The man curses and squeezes his eyes shut. 'Don't... know.'

Gryffin stands up and lets the electricity crawl down his arm. 'You expect me to believe you joined a crew but don't know anything about your captain?'

Gryffin increases the power to his arm and makes a fist which he levels at the man. 'Wait!' the prisoner shouts. 'He had... a scar!'

'Where?' Gryffin demands.

'His... arm.'

The captain falters for a split second. It is barely noticeable but, after working with him for a few months, Chayse sees it. There's only one person Chayse can think of with a scar like that.

'Sayber,' Gryffin growls as he crouches down beside the man again. Electricity jumps from Gryffin's arm to the prisoner and kills him instantly. Before he leaves the room, the captain gestures at the Nomad next to Chayse. 'Get rid of the body.'

Chayse hurries after his captain, trying to keep up with him in the cramped corridors. All he wants to do is throw up in a corner somewhere. He can't believe Gryffin killed that man for no real reason. Lost in thought, he doesn't notice Gryffin has stopped in front of him. Walking straight into his back is like walking into a wall. Gryffin turns suddenly and looks down at Chayse.

'I'm so sorry, sir. I wasn't paying attention.'

'I got that bit.' He opens the door to his quarters and turns on the light in his small bathroom. Not sure what to do, Chayse follows him into his room and waits as he washes the blood off his hands. He pulls off his shirt and throws it in the corner before he turns off the light. 'Chayse, find out who he was.'

'But I don't have any information on him. I can't even run a search for his face anymore.' Any chance of using the prisoner's image to unearth his identity disappeared during the interrogation.

Gryffin gestures at the tablet on his bed. Confused, Chayse activates it and can't help but be impressed. Gryffin has recorded the man's fingerprints and a full set of stats along with a before picture. 'That enough for you to go on?'

'Yes, sir. It'll take me a few days.'

'This is your priority. Anyone asks you to do anything else, send them to me. I want to know who the hell's screwing with us and at the moment he's our only lead.'

'Do you think someone gave them the codes?'

Gryffin sits down on his bed and massages the back of his neck. 'Probably. Have you found out anything else about what happened to me on the surface?'

'Aleena's stolen craft left the surface before we reinstated the defences. I can only presume your attacker took it.'

'How the hell did he get so close?'

'I'm still looking into that, sir.'

'So you don't know anything?'

Chayse opens and closes his mouth a few times before he finally finds his voice. 'No, sir.'

Gryffin sighs and leans back against his pillow. 'Head back to the party.'

'Do you need anything before I go?'

Gryffin shakes his head and closes his eyes, marking the end of the conversation.

29

Avoca wanders through the freighter, too wrapped up in his thoughts to give any attention to where he's going. They got back from the prison moon five days ago with their new 'friends' as Balfe likes to call them.

The six men had been barely recognisable as human when they left their cells. After a much needed shower and shave, they look better, but still far from human. Years locked in the cells had left them pale and thin. Avoca doesn't know whether it was the prison or the Scientist that left a disturbing deadness in their eyes.

Something about them gives Avoca a cold feeling in his core. Balfe must be mad to let the men out. Surely he can see there is no way to trust them. Once the men find out it was Balfe himself who had ordered the experiments, they will kill him and everyone else involved. He just has to make sure he is nowhere near when that happens.

He enters the central laboratory and forces himself not to look at the Scientist. Even sitting at his computer, he manages to send chills up Avoca's spine. Avoca glances over at the six ex-prisoners as they lean against the far wall in silence, each one looking at the Scientist with hatred filled eyes. As with all his *creations* they are unable to hurt him in any way. It is a failsafe the man had built into each of them.

Forty-Three makes eye contact with Avoca; his robotic left eye locks onto him as he walks across the room. Each of the men has an artificial eye — something the Scientist changed from his original design. Instead of the eyeball being replaced, he fitted a metal plate over each eye socket. It left the men with what looked like a large eye patch surrounding the eye.

Balfe gestures for the six men to join himself and Avoca at the table. As one, they cross the room, *Forty-Three* in the lead as always. None of the men want to be called by their original name. For some reason, they have all adopted the case number given to them by the Scientist. Avoca can't remember any of the other figures, but he does know one of them is sixty-something. He thought that the Nomad leader being number thirty-five was bad enough. Knowing that there were at least another twenty-five subjects makes him want to throw up.

'We've got three weeks left before the Council come to the Sector in force,' Balfe explains. 'Once they do that, it's over for us. We'll be entering the Port tomorrow to meet up with Sayber and his Hunters. *Forty-Three*, your men will be put onto some of his ships. I want you to take orders from me alone. Do you understand?'

'Yes.'

'Good. Once on the surface, please feel free to express yourselves any way you see fit. The sooner we force the Nomad out of hiding, the quicker we can get him back to Foundation space.'

'What about the ships patrolling the other side of the Port?'

'Sayber will keep them occupied so we can come through. The main priority is to get the freighter out of the way and hidden near the Port. It's equipped with state-of-the-art shielding, which will help, but it has to be deactivated for us to pass through.'

'And Leeson?' Avoca asks.

'Leeson is staying here. I need him to stay close to the Council. Be my eyes and ears.' He turns to the Scientist. 'Is everything ready to go here?'

'All I am missing is the subject.'

'How long will it take to get the information you need?'

The Scientist checks some figures on his unit. 'It depends on how cooperative he is.'

'I think we can assume he'll be as uncooperative as he can be.'

'He must be weak for the implant to take a firm hold. I would estimate a few days to weaken him, then another few days to recover from the surgery.'

'Weaken him how?' Avoca asks.

The Scientist smiles. 'Beating, torture, sleep and food deprivation. Whatever it takes.'

Avoca nods. From what he's learned about the Nomad, it will not be a simple task to break him. According to the reports from the prison Gryffin was in years ago, the Nomad leader managed to escape with a broken leg, ribs, and hand, after being tortured.

Balfe stands up, which calls an end to the meeting. 'Avoca, stick with the freighter for now. I'm going back to *Omega*.' He points at the Scientist as he walks away. 'Make sure he has everything he needs before we depart tomorrow.'

As soon as Balfe leaves, the Scientist goes back to his computers. Left alone with him and the six men, Avoca has never felt more uncomfortable in his life. He needs to get as far away from them as possible, so he exits the room to go back to his ship. He has a lot of work to do before he leaves tomorrow.

∞

Gryffin stands at the edge of the town centre and watches the party. He shouldn't be here. After Chayse left, he tried to keep busy by training, but his mind wasn't on it. It's here.

So instead of sitting by himself on the ship, he's skulking in the shadows like an idiot.

He tries to tell himself he's here to make sure the Foundation doesn't try anything with his crew, but in truth he's here to try and catch a glimpse of Terra. He shouldn't have taken out his frustration on her when she came to see him.

Over the years, as his reputation grew, so did colonist's fear of him. Perceptions didn't bother him. He spent so long alone, he preferred his own company anyway. It was just easier to keep his defences up and not let anyone get close — not that he wanted someone close to him. The wall he put up around himself protects him from the looks and the whispers, but it also helps push people away. People like Terra.

Then he sees her. However appealing he thought Aleena looked earlier, she is nothing compared to Terra. She easily outshines every other woman, with her dark hair cascading down her bare back. He can't tear his eyes away from her long, lean body highlighted by her figure-hugging dress. His enhanced vision picks up on the torchlight reflecting off each strand of hair to highlight the liquid gold through the chocolate brown. He would give anything to run his fingers through her hair.

He digs his fingers into the palm of his left hand. Even if he speaks to her, "*Hi Terra, sorry I was an ass. I actually do like you*" won't wipe the slate clean with her. The modifications made him a fighter, not a romantic. Cursing his unfamiliar human side, he turns away and disappears into the shadows.

∞

Terra drains the last of her water and looks around the square. She should have called it a night hours ago. Apart from a few slightly tipsy locals, she's the last one left. Everyone else has either gone back to their houses or ships. Milla has even abandoned her to spend some time with Chayse. The two seem a good match and spent most of the evening dodging Klay so they could talk.

She stands up and straightens her dress as she takes one final glance around. Her heart races as a flash of light reflects off metal in the darkness. She moves forward a few steps but stops when a man comes out of the shadows carrying some extinguished lanterns. Terra curses her stupidity and wanders back towards the ship alone.

All of a sudden someone grabs her by the arm and quickly pulls her into the shadows. The scream stops in her throat when she sees Gryffin in front of her. Before he can do or say anything, Terra's emotions get the better of her. She pulls her arm back and swings at him, catching him on his jaw with her fist.

His head jolts to the side, but other than that he doesn't move a muscle. She reaches back and strikes him again. He stops her fun before strike three by catching her hand in his before she makes contact. He spits out some blood and licks his split lip. 'Two you get. Three is pushing your luck.'

'That's your opinion. You pulled a gun on me, Gryffin. You humiliated and embarrassed me. Then you blame me for all your problems. Did you really think I'd be happy to see you?'

'No.'

She crosses her arms and glares at him. 'That's it? No? That's the best you can do?'

'Who were you looking for?'

'Excuse me?'

He moves closer to her. 'You spent most of the evening looking for someone.'

'You've been watching me? Do you have any idea how creepy that sounds?'

'You didn't answer my question.'

She pushes away from him. 'I don't have to answer your damn

questions, and I'm not in the mood for another argument. I have to get back to my ship.'

He takes a step back. 'Come with me.'

'You can't be serious. You think I'd go anywhere with you?'

Gryffin shrugs 'You can come with me voluntarily, or I can carry you.'

Terra's mouth drops open. 'You wouldn't dare.'

He tilts his head to the side slightly before he quickly throws her over his shoulder in a fireman's lift. Terra's angry protests fall on deaf ears as Gryffin moves briskly through the undergrowth. She repeatedly beats her fists against his back to no avail. Even threatening to shoot him does nothing to deter him.

After walking through the forest for about three minutes, Gryffin steps up onto a porch and pauses to unlock a door. He steps inside, lowers Terra to the ground and locks the door behind them.

'Where are we?'

'In a house outside the village. Aleena has assigned it to my crew to use when we're here.' Terra looks around the room and takes in their surroundings. Aleena is certainly spoiling the Nomad crew.

The cottage is immaculate. They're in a large open-plan room with a tall stone fireplace against one wall housing a roaring fire. A vase of fresh flowers sits on the table by chair, and a snowy white sheepskin rug covers the worn wooden floor. Against the far wall is a wooden-framed bed covered in a thick blanket.

Aleena must have prepared the cottage for his arrival. She doubts Gryffin would give much thought to flowers or lighting the fire. 'Chayse said you'd left the surface.'

He leans against the side of the chimney breast and crosses his arms. 'I know.'

'What if my captain sees you here?'

'That doesn't matter.'

She raises her eyebrows at his flippant response. 'Well? What do you want?'

He looks down and rubs the side of his ocular implant. 'I shouldn't have... Damn it. You didn't deserve that.'

Terra hides her surprise and somehow also manages to hide the big smile that wants to spread across her face. She remains composed and nods. 'Which bit? The humiliation, the gun, or what you said?'

He looks up and meets her eyes. 'All of it.'

Terra nods and runs her hand over the flowers sitting on the table. 'I'm sorry too. I've done nothing but cause you trouble.'

He shrugs. 'I haven't helped.'

'Care to tell me why you suddenly changed your mind about ... Well, what we were doing?'

Gryffin looks away from her. 'It's my problem, not yours.'

Terra sits on the wooden chair and crosses her legs. 'Yeah, well it may be your problem, but it affected me too.'

'It was a reaction — one I couldn't help.'

The way his voice drops for the last part of the sentence instantly gets her attention. The pain in his voice is a physical thing. He's telling the truth.

Terra admits defeat. She slaps her hands on her knees. 'Fine. Apology accepted, Captain, if that was an apology.'

'Just Gryffin.'

'Okay ... Gryffin.' He smiles slightly when she says his name which makes her heart skip a beat. She didn't think it was possible, but he looks even more attractive when he smiles.

'So,' she says, clearing her suddenly dry throat. 'Why the ruse about leaving?'

'Thought it would be a good idea to be out of the way.'

'You missed a great party.' He doesn't say anything as he looks at her with a strange expression on his face. She can't blame him. With everything going on, a great party is probably far from the top of his to-do list.

The sound of nocturnal wildlife from the forest surrounding them drifts from the village through the open window to fill the slightly awkward silence. For someone who wanted to speak to her, he's doing a great job of staying silent.

She turns towards the door, calling an end to whatever is going on. 'I should go. We'll both get into a lot of trouble if they find us together.'

He crosses the room in an instant and presses her back against the table. 'You're not leaving.'

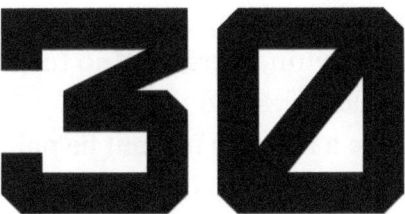

Gryffin wants her, but the thought of touching her terrifies him. Ever since she kissed him, all he's wanted to do is try it again. No amount of telling himself they need to stay away from each other has helped. They're enemies and nothing good will come of seeing her again, but he's not having much luck. His feelings are roaring to the surface and refusing to be silenced again.

He can't remember ever having felt this way about anyone before. She's somehow managed to get to him in a way he never expected. Her reaction to him certainly isn't what he expected either. She shows no fear; no sign he intimidates her. Even his implants and scars don't seem to put her off. This is the third time she's been alone with him and she still doesn't appear to be worried.

Before he can move closer to her, she pushes him away. 'What the hell do you think you're doing?'

'You need a diagram?'

'Do you really think this is a good idea?'

He leans closer to her and places a hand on the wall at either side of her head. 'You tell me to leave and I'll walk away.'

∞

Terra blows out a breath and looks at the ground. Of course she doesn't want him to leave. It still doesn't mean this is a good idea. Apart from the minor detail of disobeying orders, she knows once she takes that step with Gryffin, there'll be no turning back for her. She looks into his deep blue eyes and the decision is made for her. Terra reaches up and places a hand on his, but he pulls away.

Her immediate reaction is to feel offended, but something about his body language screams uncomfortable. Maybe he doesn't like or want to be touched. That could explain what happened the last time. 'You know we're going to have to get a bit closer to do this. You okay with that?'

Gryffin looks into her eyes and moves his hand from the wall. He slowly runs the back of his gloved finger down her cheek. His usual air of confidence seems to have wavered slightly. She may be wrong, but she gets the impression this is unfamiliar territory for him.

∞

Terra runs her hand across his shoulders to stroke up and down over the leather. She moves her head to his chest and he tenses when he feels her breath against his skin.

Gryffin glances down to see she's manoeuvred her face so it's against the patch of skin visible at the neck of his shirt. Her skin feels soft against his. God, she's turning him into a nervous and excited wreck. Even the smell of her hair is driving him crazy. The delicious fruity scent of her shampoo intoxicates him.

Gryffin wants her. His entire body wants her. Unfortunately, his brain is still holding him back. He's rarely indecisive. In his day-to-day life, he never has to think about what to say, or how to act. For some reason, Terra completely shuts down the part of his brain needed for thinking — or not thinking, in this case. And he's letting her affect him.

He decides to take back control of this entire situation, so he leans in to meet her mouth. To his delight, she doesn't back away. Terra tightly wraps her arms around his neck and runs her fingers through his hair. He kisses her gently, ignoring the sting from his split lip. His gloved hand moves down her bare back as he kisses her more deeply and hungrily. Any uncertainty disappeared as soon as he kissed her. He's not in the lab and Terra is not going to hurt him the way the Scientist did.

She pulls off his gloves and pushes his jacket off his shoulders. It drops to the ground and is joined by his shirt shortly after. Then it all comes crashing to an abrupt end. Even though he is expecting it, the gasp from Terra cuts him more than he would have liked.

'Terra?'

∞

Transfixed on his chest, she doesn't respond immediately. She had forgotten about the patchwork of angry scars scattered over his torso. There must be at least a dozen or more cuts in various places over his chest. It's only now, when she sees the scars clearly, that she realises they're all surgical cuts. Initially she assumed they were the result of fights but the cuts are too neat, too precise.

Her throat goes dry when she sees two scars disappear under his waistband at either side of his groin area. Who could do this to him? She assumes he didn't do it to himself. Terra breaks out of her daze and makes eye contact with him again. 'Sorry, I— '

A cold tone enters his voice. 'What?'

She looks up at him and cringes when she sees the anger on his face. 'Never mind.'

He takes a step back from her and crosses his arms over his chest.

'Say it!'

'Gryffin...'

'Just go, Terra.' He turns his back to her and stands by the fire.

Terra stares at his slightly less scarred back and feels like screaming. She can't believe he's pushing her away again. She runs her hands through her hair and decides to resurrect some of her pride. Terra grabs her shawl off the chair but holds back her verbal attack when she looks at him again. His arms are wrapped tightly around his chest as he stares at the fire. The realisation hits her. He's ashamed, and staring at him like she did wouldn't have helped.

Feeling like a prize idiot, she drops her shawl back on the chair and moves closer to him. 'I'm sorry. I was surprised. The scars... I apologise.' She walks up to him and places her hand gently on the centre of the implant. His whole body seems to freeze under her hand. Terra senses the need to take it slowly, so carefully runs her fingers along the lines of his chest. 'Would it hurt you if I touched them?'

'Touched what?'

'Your implants.'

He eyes her suspiciously and takes a step back. 'You want to touch them?'

Her heart breaks. In those few words and actions, he tells her more than he probably wants to. It upsets her that he doesn't understand why someone would want to touch him. Terra smiles at him. 'By the look of things, they're a pretty big part of you, so it would help if I could. If you're not happy about this at any stage, I'll stop.'

He pauses for a moment as if deciding whether she's serious or not, then nods his head. 'I don't ... It doesn't feel ... Just go gently.'

'Of course.' Terra smiles and steps back to look at him. He stands in front of her with the firelight reflecting off his implants and highlighting the hard muscles of his chest. Mixed with the large tattoo, he looks gorgeous; sexy and dangerous at the same time. Leaving aside the sinister nature of the scars, they make him seem all the more intriguing.

She slowly steps behind him and gently kisses along the griffin's wing inked across his back. Even though his muscles tense under her touch as she moves down his arm, she doesn't stop. She wants to earn his trust. Gradually, he relaxes as her lips move back up his arm before proceeding to his chest. Terra gently runs her hands over him to familiarise herself with the hard angles and lines of his body. She gingerly brushes her fingers along the raised, scarred skin at the edge of his chest implant.

As soon as she touches the metal, his entire body tenses and he seems to stop breathing. To try and put him at ease, she leaves her hands on the outside edges of the 'W' on his chest and reaches up to kiss him. Once he begins breathing normally again, she slowly traces her fingers along the edge of the implant.

He suddenly gasps as her fingers move down the line where metal and flesh fuse. Terra immediately stops and quickly pulls her hand away. 'Sorry, did that hurt?'

He looks at her with slightly glazed eyes and shakes his head. 'No.'

'Should I continue?'

He nods, so she bends down slightly and decides to take a gamble. She moves her tongue slowly along the apparently sensitive skin and makes Gryffin cry out in pleasure.

∞

He can't think straight. Gryffin steadies himself against the fireplace as his legs wobble. He never thought anyone touching him could feel good. He's only ever experienced pain when anything comes in contact with his chest.

Terra straightens and smiles at him as she slowly unfastens her dress and pushes the silky material down her lean body. She kicks off her shoes and steps out of the dress. Gryffin can't help but just look at her. Her sheer black underwear barely covers her perfectly flawless skin. Lean muscles tone her legs and stomach to help give her an athletic build. Her dark hair falls over one shoulder to touch her breast as she smiles shyly at him.

Gryffin swears his heart stops for a moment. He's never felt anything like this before and hopes his implants aren't failing. He cautiously runs his hand over her perfectly smooth skin but takes care to keep his metal hand away from her. It's too cold and crude to be anywhere near her.

She steps up to him again and traces her fingers along the edge of his chest implant and down to the front of his leathers. Terra bites her bottom lip as she runs a finger along his length. She glances up at him with her bottom lip still caught between her teeth and a wicked twinkle in her eyes.

Gryffin quickly kicks off his boots and lifts her up. She wraps her long legs around him tightly while he lowers them effortlessly onto the rug in front of the fire. He puts his arms to either side of her head to keep his body from touching her. His dark hair mingles with hers as he lowers his head.

∞

Terra reaches down to unfasten his holster. She pulls it from around his waist and throws it onto the couch. He raises his hips slightly to give her the room she needs to undo his belt and the zipper on his leathers.

Once free of his trousers, Gryffin slips his leg in between hers again. With only the thin lace of her underwear as a barrier, she groans as he increases the pressure, all the while assaulting her mouth with his tongue.

Through the haze of pleasure, she's aware his metal hand is as far from her as it can be. He breaks away from her mouth as he works his way down her neck. 'Use your other hand.'

He pauses and looks at her from under his tousled hair. 'What?'

She moves against his leg and bites her bottom lip as a wave of pleasure hits. 'I want you to use your other hand.'

He hesitates slightly but shifts his weight and gingerly places his metal hand on her stomach. As soon as it touches her she loses control. She takes his metal hand and pushes it down her body to where she wants it. Terra groans into his mouth and bites his bottom lip as his hand presses against her where his knee was. He hisses in pain as she pulls on his lip and retaliates by ripping her underwear along the seam.

She gasps as his fingers start to explore. 'Please, Gryffin.' She doesn't know what she's asking for; all she knows is that she wants more. She raises her hips and draws a growl from him as she presses hard against him. She runs a nail along the edge of his chest implant and scratches the already sensitive flesh. Gryffin curses and pushes his fingers deep inside her. Sensation explodes in Terra as his tongue and fingers drive her over the edge again and again. When she thinks she can't take anymore, he removes his hand. He grabs both her wrists in his flesh hand and holds them firmly above her head.

She wants him so badly and he knows it. Terra can do nothing except lie helplessly under him. Gryffin ignores her pleas as he holds his hips away from her. He lavishes attention on her breasts and gently bites at her nipples with his teeth. When she thinks she's going to lose her mind, he suddenly pushes inside her. He doesn't move for a minute as she gets used to his size. Even the sensation of him inside her is enough to have her moan in pure bliss. Before she recovers, he moves.

She wraps her legs around him, hanging on as he continuously sends her over wave after wave of pleasure. She looks up at the sheer size of him above her. The way his stomach muscles roll as he moves, the light reflecting off his metal chest plate, the slight sheen of sweat on his skin, the sheer dominance in his dark blue eyes — it's all too much for her. She throws her head back and screams.

Terra glances up from the piece of paper to look at her companion lying next to her in the bed. Gryffin is sound asleep; his breathing soft and steady. He appears younger and a lot less tortured and brooding in his sleep. She gingerly reaches out to stroke the side of his face, tracing the line of the implant down his forehead and around his eye.

After the floor, he'd taken her to the bed and what she thought couldn't get better, did. Even though she's exhausted, aching, and more satisfied than ever before, she can't sleep. How can she with Gryffin lying naked beside her?

The pencil in her hand takes on a life of its own as it rushes to draw every contour of his magnificent body, the location of every scar, every ridge and hollow of his stomach, the griffin tattoo hugging his powerful biceps and stretching across the expanse of his chest. She could draw him every day and not run out of inspiration.

Her pencil lifts from the paper as her eyes move to the angry scars on either side of his groin, disappearing under the sheet. She's no doctor, but she's seen enough knife wounds to know his missing testicle had been cut off. And they didn't want to stop there. The scarring stretches across his groin and extends up the base of his shaft.

He didn't comment on the injury and she didn't ask. She didn't notice it while they were together, but it does help to explain his initial uncertainty at the start of the evening. Tonight must be the first time he's been with anyone. He hadn't said as much, but it all adds up. His injury and aversion to touch probably kept him away from any intimacy.

Possibly being his first brings a smile to her lips. She can't believe he trusts her enough to take such a big step with her.

While it breaks her heart to imagine what happened to him, all his scars and injuries do nothing to lessen her attraction to him. He's clearly been through hell and come out the other end as a strong and powerful man. He deserves her respect for that, not her pity.

She carefully folds the page and slips it into her purse. Once the drawing is safely hidden, she lies back down beside him and presses tight to his warm skin, gently tracing her fingers around his ocular implant.

∞

Someone touches his face, tracing along the length of the metal. He opens his eyes to his past. The stark white lights of the lab momentarily blind him. He tries to move, but can't. The leather straps dig painfully into his ankles, wrists and neck to hold him firmly onto the metal table.

Gryffin struggles against the restraints but it does no good. He's too small and weak to get out. He cries out for help, but the only response he gets is a soft chuckle. The Scientist steps into the light beside the table and Gryffin's stomach churns. It hurts whenever he's around.

The Scientist presses a surgical knife against Gryffin's wrist as he watches the expression on his test subject's face. With a serene smile, he digs the blade into Gryffin's flesh. Red, hot pain erupts from his wrist and Gryffin roars. The Scientist ignores his screams and continues to pull the blade back and forward through his flesh, slowly sawing into the bone to separate Gryffin's hand from his arm. The Scientist picks up the severed hand and throws it onto Gryffin's chest, the bloody stump facing him. He opens his mouth and screams again.

'Gryffin, wake up!'

He suddenly jerks awake and opens his eyes. Still stuck between dream and reality he sees a figure looming over him. He scrambles away from whoever it is, falling off the bed onto the floor.

'Gryffin, look at me.'

He forces himself into the present and is horrified to see Terra sitting naked on the bed, staring at him. The dream was incredibly realistic. He could feel every slice the blade made as it cut into him. He glances down at his mechanical arm but can only see a bloody severed stump. He cries out and tries to stand but falls heavily against the wall. Terra reaches out for him, but he pulls away again. He somehow makes it into the bathroom and slams the door shut.

Gryffin slumps to the floor by the shower, pulls his legs up to his chest, and rests his head on his knees. His body shakes and a cold sweat runs down his bare back. He takes deep breaths to try and clear his head.

Hopefully, Terra will leave while he's getting himself together. He can't bring himself to go anywhere near her, especially not after she saw him freak out like he did.

∞

Terra sits on the edge of the bed and stares at the closed door. She doesn't have a clue what to do.

Her first instinct is to go to him and offer whatever comfort she can, but she knows he won't accept that from her. On the other hand, she can't sit back and leave him to it. Terra slowly opens the bathroom door and gasps when she sees him slumped on the floor, shaking.

'Did I hurt you?' Gryffin asks.

'No, of course not. Are you okay? Can I get you anything?' He slowly shakes his head and pulls himself to his feet. 'Why don't you come back to bed? Get a few more hours sleep.'

'I need a shower.' He closes the door in her face. Terra stares at the knots in the wood for a moment, not quite sure what to do. She eventually pulls herself away from the door and keeps busy by straightening the bedclothes and making them both a drink.

Gryffin emerges from the bathroom ten minutes later. Instead of offering an explanation for what happened, he completely ignores her and searches for his clothes.

'I've made you a hot chocolate. Why don't you come back to bed and drink it?' She knows it's a stupid thing to say, but has to say something to break the horrible silence.

'I can't.'

'Yes, you can. Just take two steps and sit. It's not difficult.'

'That's not what I mean.' He gathers his clothes and stuffs his feet into his trousers.

Terra does her best to keep her emotions under control. She can't let him leave like this, especially after everything they shared tonight. 'What are you doing?'

'I can't go back to the ship naked.'

'That's not what I mean,' she says, echoing his previous statement. 'Stay and sleep. You don't have to go. Everyone has nightmares from time to time. Do you want to talk about it?'

'It's not that simple.'

'Then tell me.'

He turns his back to her as he pulls up his trousers. The muscles shift under his skin, making it seem like the large griffin tattoo is moving.

She feels a bit embarrassed staring at him, so clears her throat.

'Not talking to me now?'

He pulls on his shirt and then sits on the end of the bed to put on his boots. 'There's nothing to talk about. It's done. You got what you wanted and I got what I wanted.'

His statement completely destroys her. He's reduced everything they shared tonight to sex — nothing more. 'It meant nothing to you?'

He stands up and pulls on his jacket. 'What else would it be? I'm going back to *Ares*. You can stay here until the morning.'

'Hang on a minute.'

'It's over, Terra.'

He turns to face her and she forgets any reply she was planning. 'Gryffin, your eyes are purple!'

∞

Even as she's saying the words, Gryffin can feel the familiar buzzing build at the back of his head. *Please, not now. Not with her here.*

He clenches his fists and takes a few deep breaths, trying to settle himself, but it doesn't work. He's going to lose control and Terra is going to get hurt. 'Get out of here. Now!'

'Gryffin? What is it?'

He puts his head in his hands. This shouldn't be happening. 'Leave! Now!'

He doesn't need to tell her again. She quickly puts on her underwear and pulls on her dress as Gryffin forces himself to stay where he is. Terra rushes to the door and stops.

He charges her and pushes her out of the house. 'Go!' he roars before he slams the door in her face.

∞

'Would you like another cup of tea, Captain?'

Roman smiles at Aleena. 'Yes, and please call me Jensen. This will be the last cup though. I should get back to *Infinity* soon.'

'I am sure they can survive without you for a while longer.' She takes a seat opposite him and tucks her feet underneath her.

Roman follows her example and stretches out his legs in front of the fire. Between the warmth and the tea, he feels completely at ease for the first time in years. The company might have something to do with it too. He looks across at Aleena and tries not to stare. She is beautiful. Over the years he's met hundreds, maybe even thousands of people, but apart from Maggie none have interested him for more than a few minutes. Aleena, however, is entirely different. He's not bored of her. In fact, he'd be quite happy to sit on her couch in front of the fire forever.

The conversation has flowed between them for the last few hours. He discovered they have quite a bit in common, which makes for a pleasant change. Being stuck on *Infinity* most of the year, he's grown used to his own company. While he enjoys spending time with individual crew members, no one has similar interests to him. Although he'd never admit it, loneliness and his life go hand-in-hand. He has accepted he will never have a companion to share things with. After all, he is not exactly a great prospect.

His life is the Foundation and *Infinity*. He has to depart Earth for years at a time, which rules relationships out. What woman would wait years to see their husband, only to have him back for a week before leaving for another few years? It wouldn't be fair to her.

However, he would retire if he found the right person. He thought Maggie was the one for him. Clearly, though, she didn't feel the same way about him. If she did, she would have told him he was a father. She would have contacted him as soon as Daegan was born so he could meet his son. They had lost touch over the years, but she managed to track him down when Daegan went missing. If she had wanted him to know he's a father, she would have told him.

All the secrets just proved she never felt the same way about him.

But he did get a son — a son he never thought he would have. True, Gryffin is not exactly the poster image of a child he had in mind, but he is a part of him, whether he likes it or not.

'What are you thinking about, Jensen?'

'Life.'

'Quite a large subject. Would you like to narrow it down?'

'I'm not sure I can.'

Aleena gazes into her cup for a minute before she speaks. 'Why are the Foundation so intent on Gryffin's capture?'

Roman can't believe Aleena even has to ask. 'For obvious reasons. They don't agree with what Gryffin does.'

'And what is your opinion, Jensen?'

'I agree. Being a captain in the Foundation means Gryffin goes against everything I believe in.'

'What about the work Gryffin did here today? Does that go against what you believe in?'

'I believe today was the exception rather than the rule.'

Aleena lets the silence hang for a moment as she puts more wood on the fire. 'Do you believe in your role in the Foundation, or is it merely a job?'

That's the one question he's asked himself over the last few months and he's no closer to an answer. 'Aleena, that doesn't matter. The Foundation are coming to the Sector, so outlaw protectors like Gryffin will be obsolete. It's only a matter of time before none of this will matter.'

'What are the Foundation planning?'

'I'm too far down the chain of command, but your people and other worlds like Ultar shouldn't worry. The protection the Foundation offers will far surpass what Gryffin provides.'

Aleena gets up and paces the rug in front of the fire. 'Whether the Foundation arrives in the Sector or not makes no difference to me or my people. We will never join the Foundation. Besides the fact Gryffin would be less than happy about it, we have no interest in becoming part of the group.'

Roman puts down his cup. 'It'll be much better for you to align with the Foundation going forward than a rogue group like the Nomad.'

'Jensen, you should be careful what you say about the Nomad. In this Sector, Gryffin's group is not thought of as rogue. Outside the Foundation, his is the largest, most powerful group we can be associated with. Gryffin answers to no one. There is no board to confer with, no group of superiors to debate the issue with. If something needs to be done, he does it. Can the Foundation offer that?'

'We can offer protection without breaking the law.'

'Whose laws do you refer to?'

'It's only the Foundation laws that matter to me.'

Aleena stops pacing and crosses her arms. 'Precisely the problem. The Foundation thinks nothing else matters except what they believe is important. That is why they take over when they "protect" a world. Tell me, if they decide they want Ultar, where would that leave me? You and I both know I will be obsolete. The Foundation will never allow me to remain the leader. All our laws and traditions will be overthrown and replaced by those of the Foundation. Our identity, who we are, will disappear. They will transform us into another Foundation planet with no independent voice. You may not like Gryffin or what he does, but he has given us more freedom over the last few years than ever before. He does not care who runs the colony, what laws we put in place, what political groups we have. All he cares about is keeping us safe. What makes the Foundation think they can do a better job?'

Roman's response is cut off as someone thumps loudly on the door.

32

The fact Roman comes to the door of Aleena's house doesn't surprise Terra as much as it probably should. Roman's eyebrows shoot up as he takes in her dishevelled appearance. In her rush to locate help, she had forgotten she probably looks like someone just out of bed. Not the best way to prove her obedience to Roman.

'What the hell happened to you?' Roman asks.

'I got lost in the forest and fell.' *Great, why not come up with a different excuse than getting lost again.* 'Sir, I think Gryffin is in trouble.'

Aleena pushes past Roman. 'Where is he?'

'In a cottage about half a mile up the path. He seemed to ...'

'Did you happen to see his eyes?' Aleena asks.

Terra nods. 'They changed colour.'

Aleena takes a radio from the table by the door and calls for Klay's assistance. She pulls her coat off the peg and shrugs into it. 'Jensen, it would be best if you and Terra go back to *Infinity*.'

'But—' Terra begins.

'No, Terra. Please go.'

Roman stands beside Terra. 'I think it would be safer if we go with you, Aleena. I insist.'

Aleena opens her mouth to argue but relents. Roman, Terra, and Aleena race back towards the house. As they near the location, the sound of crashing from inside stops them in their tracks.

'What the hell is going on in there?' Roman asks.

Klay steps out of the shadows with a team of Nomad. 'Should have guessed you'd try to get him.'

'That's not why we're here,' Roman says. 'We're here to support Aleena.'

Klay takes out his gun and points it at Roman. 'You and your little lady need to withdraw now.'

Roman holds Terra's arm to keep her away from Klay.

'How dare you speak to me like that!' she replies.

'Enough, Terra!' Roman commands.

Klay closes the distance between them and presses his gun against Roman's forehead. 'Last chance, Captain.'

Another loud crash comes from inside and Roman pushes Klay to the ground as a chair flies out the window. Klay pushes Roman aside and rises to his feet.

'Stop this pathetic bickering!' Aleena shouts. 'I do not care who stays or who goes, but someone needs to get in the house and aid Gryffin. Now!'

Klay pushes his shoulders back and squares his jaw. He gestures to a Nomad to his right. 'They are leaving now. If they come anywhere near the house, shoot them.' Aleena takes a step towards him but Klay holds up his hand. 'Not now, Aleena.' He pulls a tranq gun from his belt and walks towards the house.

∞

Terra stands in the shadows behind the house. She can't let them

247

tranq Gryffin like some wild animal. He's the captain of their ship and his second-in-command wants to treat him like that?

Not if she can help it. She'll face the full wrath of Roman once she gets back to *Infinity*, but it will be worth it. While Roman watched the commotion from the cover of the surrounding trees, Terra had slipped away and circled around the back of the house.

She quietly opens the window into the small kitchen area and peeks over the sill. The house is silent and she can't see any movement inside. Terra rolls her dress up above her knees and ties a knot in the fabric. It's far from ideal, but it will have to do. Next time she'll make sure to pack a pair of trousers.

Terra kicks off her shoes and carefully pulls herself up onto the ledge. She drops down onto the wooden floor and holds her breath as the sound of her bare feet hitting the ground echoes in the dark. Terra steadies her breathing and she slowly stands. She searches the shadows using the fading light from embers in the fire, but she still can't see him. Her mind wanders back to a few hours ago. The warm glow from the fire had set a much different scene then. Now, the shadows are sinister, hiding the unknown.

A floorboard creaks behind her from the direction of the bed. Her breath catches in her throat when Gryffin steps out of the gloom. He stops beside the bed and looks down at his hands as he clenches and unclenches his fists. She can see his large chest move up and down as he takes deep breaths. He doesn't seem to realise she's there. Before she can chicken out, she takes another step forward. 'Gryffin. It's me, Terra.'

He continues to clench his fists and breathe slowly. She ignores the loud pounding of her heart and forces herself to take a step closer to him. He suddenly raises his head and she gasps when she sees his glowing purple irises.

Terra pushes aside the thought that maybe this is her worst idea ever and reaches out her hand towards him. 'It's okay, Gryffin. I won't hurt you.' What the hell is she saying? He's the threat to her at the moment.

Before she can react, he crosses the space between them and knocks her to the ground. He crouches over her as Klay and the rest of the team burst into the house. They pause for a moment, then start to shoot at him. Gryffin lowers his body closer to her and shields her completely from his crew and their darts. She can hear him grunt as shot after shot hits his body. A few seconds later, Gryffin slowly moves to the side and collapses on the floor.

∞

Chayse quietly watches his captain's slow painful battle to get back in control. Gryffin is unsettled, mumbling and thrashing around on the floor of the cell. Chayse looks away from his captain's face as it contorts in pain.

Chayse grinds his teeth as he recalls bringing Gryffin back to *Ares*. The usual careful handling of the unconscious captain was replaced by rough treatment. Klay treated Gryffin as he would a prisoner. Chayse even had to go into the cell and roll Gryffin onto his side so he wouldn't choke. Klay had just dumped him and walked away.

He wipes a hand over his face a few times and tries to wake himself up. The cold cup of coffee in his hand does nothing to help him, but there's no way he's going anywhere until Gryffin wakes up. Someone should stay with him until he finally comes around.

Thirty minutes later, the violent movements finally cease. Gryffin slowly opens his eyes, sits up and leans back against the metal cot.

'How are you feeling, sir?'

Gryffin stares at his bandaged hand. 'Did I hurt her?'

'Unfortunately, yes,' Klay says as he enters the room. 'She bruised her ribs when you pushed her to the ground. Luckily we got to you before you could do anything worse. What the hell happened, Captain? You didn't exactly stay hidden. You attacked a Foundation member with her crew and ship on the surface. Great move.'

Gryffin lowers his head into his arms, either unwilling or unable to say anything. Chayse bites the inside of his mouth. All he wants to do is defend his captain. Surely Klay can see he's not going to get anywhere with Gryffin right now. He's too exhausted to talk to him.

'Sir, we need to figure out what happened,' Klay says. 'None of the alarms went off. Your readings stayed at a safe level. I'll run some tests and see if I can detect a problem. Do you need anything?' When Klay gets no response from Gryffin, he shrugs and turns to exit the room. Chayse wants to stay with Gryffin but knows he won't want any spectators. With one last glance at his captain, he quietly follows Klay from the room

∞

Terra stares at the small lights on the ceiling of the sick bay on *Infinity*. Her chest hurts from where Gryffin threw himself against her, so Milla insisted on keeping her in. She thought maybe Terra was in shock after what happened. She is in shock, but not the way Milla thinks. She's shocked at the treatment of Gryffin by his crew. In fact, it infuriated her.

They had been taken back to *Infinity* as Gryffin's crew secured him to a gurney and took him back to his ship. Before he left, Klay had glared at her, like he blamed her for what happened. He was the one that burst in and shot at Gryffin, not her.

Tears come to her eyes when she thinks of what they might be doing to him on the ship. What if his crew have been hurting him all along and that's why he's the way he is? She tries to tell herself that's stupid. He's big and bold enough to stand up for himself. There's no doubt in her mind if someone was hurting him he'd end it pretty quickly. And he is the captain, after all. He'd hardly keep a crew that mistreated him.

She lies back on the bed and pulls the covers around her. How did such an incredible night end so disastrously? In spite of all her doubts, she had broken through his wall and he relaxed with her — well, after a while. What surprises her more is his well-hidden softer side. He was so gentle and took extra care that he didn't hurt her.

There is no doubt in her mind he wasn't trying to hurt her when they burst in. He pushed her to the ground, but it was to protect her. He must have known his crew was going to come in to get him, so he pushed her down and covered her with his body, taking the shots that could have hit her.

Milla assured her his implants will neutralise most of the drug on the darts, but that doesn't make Terra feel any better. Then again, she doubts anything would.

She's falling for him. Fast.

It was one night and she hardly knows him. Her feelings are completely irrational, especially after what happened tonight, but that doesn't turn her off. Initially, the attraction for him grew from his reputation — and his looks, of course — but now it's much more. He had suffered in his life and by the looks of things, he still is. She squeezes her eyes shut and tries to hold back the tears. It's starting to look as though Milla may have been right. Someone had tortured him.

Maybe Gryffin acts the way he does because of what happened to him. Being treated that way would certainly leave its mark on a person. It would certainly explain why he doesn't like physical contact.

The message light flashes on her tablet lying on the bedside table. She doesn't need to read it. Roman told her to expect written confirmation of her first ever official warning. To say he is furious at her is an understatement.

She seriously doubts he'll let her go anywhere alone ever again.

∞

Gryffin squeezes his eyes shut and beats his metal fist against the cell floor. If he thought he was a risk, there's no way he would have gone anywhere near her. He's losing control of himself. The implant has never affected him like that before. There was hardly any build up.

The few hours he had with Terra were fantastic. She made him feel like a real person for the first time. She didn't shy away from him or his implants. He remembers falling asleep with her in his arms. She had pressed her face tightly to his chest as he ran his metal hand through her hair. He had never experienced anything as close to normal before.

He fought against the implant and didn't let it fully take control as everyone thought. If he had, the villagers would have suffered and so would Terra. No question. He put every ounce of energy he had into staying in control. The pain from fighting the implant so hard was like nothing he's experienced before. Together with the effort used to stay in the house, it's left him weak, nauseous and exhausted. He's made it worse for himself by fighting against it. The after-effects will stay with him for days instead of hours, but he doesn't regret fighting. It helped keep him grounded and gave his crew time to get to him.

Then Terra walked in. She had come back to try and help him. Placed herself in danger to check on him. Terra had broken through the fog in his brain. Her being there had helped him keep focused. She gave him something to fight for in a way. In all the years he's been living with the implant, he's never stayed as focused as he did with her in the room.

But then his team had broken in. Instincts took over and he pushed Terra to the floor. He was trying to protect her. If she'd been caught in the crossfire because of him, he wouldn't have been able to live with himself.

He slowly pulls himself off the floor and lands unceremoniously on the small cot. Maybe Rayde was right. He shouldn't have let himself get carried away. He is a machine after all.

∞

Roman sits in his command chair and stares out the window in front of him. The report in his hand does nothing to distract him. He's worried about Gryffin and no amount of reading reports will alter that.

Over the last few hours, he'd made attempts to contact *Ares* but the Nomad ignored all requests. He didn't even know if the ship was still on the planet. For all he knows, they could have snuck away when they got Gryffin back. He looks at his watch and sighs. The Foundation expects him at his next location in three days. Another ten minutes, then they'll leave.

Fifteen minutes later, he finally calls it a day. 'Sir, we have an incoming message from Aleena.'

Roman hides his surprise as much as he can as he sends the transmission to his personal unit in his office. 'Aleena, I didn't think I would see you again.'

She smiles at him and moves closer to the screen. 'I had to say a proper goodbye. The evening did not end as I would have liked. I hope our discussion did not offend you or your people.'

'Of course not. To be honest, I enjoyed the debate. Being captain, you rarely get the chance to have a healthy debate like that. How are you after last night?'

She looks down at her hands and sighs. 'Well enough. It was unfortunate things ended the way they did, for everyone. How is Lieutenant Rush?'

'She has a slight bruising to her ribs but otherwise is fine. And Gryffin?' He curses himself as the sentence pops out before he can halt it.

'He is well.' She pauses and looks down at her hands again. 'Captain, I must ask you to leave Ultar now. I am not choosing sides, but we need to get the defences active again. For this to happen, you must depart.' She meets his eyes again and smiles. 'I do hope our paths cross again. I enjoyed our time together a great deal.'

'As did I.'

Her face grows serious again. 'Gryffin is not to be underestimated. If you go after him, he will retaliate with force. His reputation is well founded.' She ends the transmission. He stares in silence at the screen for a moment, then orders the crew to get *Infinity* out of the area.

33

Bray hisses as Quinn examines his ribs.

'Think one might be broken.'

'You don't say,' Bray replies. 'Gryffin's arm packs one hell of a punch. Surprised it didn't go right through.'

Sayber clasps his hands in front of him as he quietly watches proceedings. Bray knows the captain is itching to debrief him, but he will wait. He is a firm believer in the idea a ship is only as good as its crew and their health. He won't ask anything until Quinn is finished checking his injuries.

While he waits for the prodding and poking to come to an end, he rests his head back against the pillow. He spent two days stuck in that geriatric shuttle. Two days of waiting for *Perses* to pick up his distress call. Two days of dodging the high Nomad presence in the area. Now all he wants is a shower, food, and his bed. Fingers crossed Sayber would keep the debrief short.

Quinn finishes seeing to his injuries and leaves him alone with Sayber. The captain leans back against the wall and crosses his legs at the ankle. 'You doing okay?'

'Glad to be off that shuttle, sir.'

Sayber nods. 'I'll bet. So, what happened?'

Bray runs through his verbal report. As he speaks, he watches the stony expression of his captain alter depending on what he hears. Once finished, Sayber looks down at his feet and says nothing. 'Sir, how many got off the ship?'

Sayber meets his eyes and shakes his head. 'You're it, Bray. The Nomad wiped out the ship and the crew. You're damn lucky to be here.'

Bray lets his head drop and rubs the back of his neck. He knew there would be casualties once the Nomad arrived but never thought he would be the only survivor. A lot of good Hunters had lost their lives. They couldn't even offer them the dignity of an official Hunter send off. 'How the hell did *Ares* get there so fast? Was our intel off?'

'Nothing wrong with the intel. *Ares* was in another area when you started the assault on Ultar. Probably should have taken Gryffin and his death wish into account.'

'Sir?'

'He blew his main engine to get to Ultar faster.'

Bray hears the words, but can't quite get them to make sense in his head. 'Are you saying Gryffin intentionally put his ship and crew in danger to protect a farming colony?'

'That's pretty much it in a nutshell. I know he's unpredictable, but that's pushing it. If I had any ships in the area, I would have taken great pleasure showing him how stupid a move it actually was.'

'It's going to put the rest of our plans at risk. If he's willing to go to extremes for a group of farmers, what will he do for one of the more advanced ones?'

'Did you notice anything different about the colony? Anything that could explain his extreme reaction?'

Bray pauses as he thinks, but nothing comes to mind. 'I spent most of the time dodging Nomad crew but the colony appeared to be like every other colony. A few farms, no significant technology apart from what the Nomad installed, and outdated transports. Nothing unusual. Unless it has something to do with the fact the Foundation wants the colony. It probably made him a bit nervous.'

Sayber shakes his head. 'I'm not buying that. Gryffin doesn't get nervous. Besides, the Foundation got there after he did. No, there's something not quite right about all of this, but I'm damned if I can figure it out.' He gets up and grips Bray's shoulder. 'Get some rest.' Sayber turns to leave the room. 'I have a feeling we'll be pretty busy over the next few weeks.'

Once alone, Bray allows the grief out. He lies back on the cot, closes his eyes, and covers his face with his hands.

∞

Chayse stands with his back pressed tight against the closed door, his arms down by his side. He's desperately trying not to fidget, but he's not quite successful. Unfortunately, the other occupant also notices.

'If you don't quit twitching, I'll break all your fingers,' Gryffin says.

Chayse stands to attention. 'Sorry, sir.'

Gryffin shuts down his screen, pushes away from the desk, and gestures for Chayse to sit. 'So, what did you find?'

Chayse pulls up the other chair and puts his computer on the desk. 'It took quite a bit of digging but I found out the guy you dispatched is a Hunter. Or was.' He pauses as Gryffin growls and clenches his metal fist on the table. Chayse clears his throat before he continues. 'I also did some checking on the ship. Up until a few weeks ago, it had been a Hunter ship. Sayber decommissioned it, then sold it to an unknown buyer. In truth, he just moved the ownership.'

'So Sayber is involved.'

Chayse nods. He feels slightly uncomfortable at the vibes coming off his captain. Sayber and Gryffin's relationship is as bad as it gets.

It's no secret the captain would happily kill Sayber if he had the chance and Sayber would do the same to Gryffin. 'Why would he hide?'

Gryffin stares down at his desk for a moment before answering. 'I don't know. His ground crew are impersonating us. There's only one reason to do that: to get closer to *Ares* and me. Dismissed.' He looks around at Chayse before he leaves. 'Oh, and Chayse? Arrange some more work for me.'

'Sir? You've taken enough contracts recently to do us for the next six months at least.'

'You're not here to question me.'

Chayse shuffles from one foot to the other. He hates arranging contracts for the captain. Gryffin shouldn't have to work as an assassin to keep the Nomad financially sound. It was lonely and degrading work, but the captain insisted on carrying out the hits himself. Unfortunately, the implants helped make him the best one for the task. 'I'm not questioning you, sir. I'm confused as to where all the money is going. Is there something I can do to aid with income?'

Gryffin's purple eyes cut him off. 'Nomad income has damn all to do with you. I put a roof over your head and food on your plate. All I need in return is your obedience and loyalty.'

'Understood, sir.'

Gryffin glances up at him again. 'Then why are you still here?'

'Sir, about what happened on the surface ... with Lieutenant Rush.'

Gryffin pushes away from the desk. 'Stop right there. You intentionally trying to piss me off?' Gryffin stands up and looks down at Chayse. With nowhere to go, Chayse remains rooted to the spot. 'The last thing I need or want is to talk about it. And I don't need your advice.'

'I'm not offering you my advice, sir, but you do need to address this.' Chayse knows he's heading in a dangerous direction, but it's his job to support Gryffin, so that's exactly what he's going to do. Even so, the stony, emotionless look on his captain's face gives him reason to doubt this conversation. 'Sir, have you ever lost control after ... I mean when you've been with ... someone ... like that?' Gryffin crosses his arms and silently looks down at Chayse. He raises his eyebrow as he waits for Chayse to continue or stop the conversation. Chayse blushes and clears his throat. 'Right ... Well. What I'm getting at is that I think it was all wrong. Not what happened between ...'

'Get to the point before I'm forced to kill you to end this conversation.'

'What I mean is the attack seemed, well, wrong. Nothing about it adds up. It doesn't match any other attacks you've had. The events leading to it, the severity and the after-effects were a lot worse than they should have been.'

'I fought for control. That usually makes the after-effects worse.'

'Not as bad as they were. It doesn't feel right.'

Gryffin backs away and sits on the edge of his desk. 'Check my scan results. Let me know if you uncover anything. Make a copy of the data for me.'

Chayse blushes again. 'Do you want me to get a message to her discreetly?'

'Why would I want to do that?'

'I thought maybe you wanted to see her again.'

'I could have killed her. Don't think she'd be interested in a rematch.'

'Are you sure?' Gryffin sits back behind his desk and concentrates on the paperwork in front of him. He's clearly reached his limit with regards to this topic, as has Chayse. 'Permission to be excused.' Gryffin nods and allows Chayse to escape.

∞

Gryffin tries to get back to his reports, but it doesn't go well. He's even less interested than usual. Instead, he's thinking about a certain dark-haired Foundation officer.

He could kill Chayse for bringing it up. All it does is put ideas in his head. He gives up on the reports and pushes away from his desk. Maybe he could see her again. His contact should be able to track down the Foundation ship. All he needs to do is plan to be there at the same time.

He curses himself and stands up to pace the room. He is considering pulling *Ares* off course so he can meet up with a woman. He must be losing his mind. That's the problem, however. It seems he is losing it. If things kept going downhill like they have been recently, he doesn't have much time before he loses full control.

Another thought enters his mind. One he doesn't want to consider. If the Foundation were involved with his implants did that mean Terra knows about it too? She's younger than him, so she wouldn't have had direct involvement, but she might know about the project.

He runs a hand along the edge of his ocular implant and tries to massage the headache away. If she knew anything, she would have said. He may not be sure of many things, but he was sure of that. There's no way she could have been intimate with him if she knew what had happened to him.

∞

Chayse pushes back from his desk and frowns at the screen. He takes a bottle of water from his fridge and sits down on his bed. Chayse takes a swig as he looks around his small metal box of a room.

Until his conversation with Gryffin, he had no idea the Nomad were in financial trouble. But, on his way back to his room, he started to notice things. While they take care of *Ares*, she does need repair work carried out. The transports could do with an overhaul and the food preparation units need to be replaced. There's only so long rations could satisfy hunger.

Chayse lies back on the thin mattress and stares at the various rust spots on the ceiling. The Nomad work relentlessly to protect colonies and trade for supplies they need. It makes no sense Gryffin would have to take on more work. Chayse has searched the system, but there's no record of any income. Gryffin takes care of all that, so naturally there will be no record on the system. Chayse knows Gryffin isn't spending the money on himself. The captain's quarters house a bed and a desk. Hardly lavish by anyone's standards.

The curious part of him wants nothing more than to dig into the matter more, but he knows if Gryffin finds out, he'd probably kill him. He's just going to have to trust Gryffin knows what he's doing.

34

Gryffin slows his bike and pulls to a stop before the path splits. He turns off the engine and sits listening to the sounds of the forest around him. Nothing out of the ordinary. No one following him.

He starts the engine again and takes the road into the town. After ten minutes, he gets nearer to civilisation and passes more vehicles, carts and pedestrians. Breaking his own rules, he isn't wearing his mask. A lone masked Nomad would attract more attention. Instead, he is wearing a jacket with the hood pulled up to keep the top half of his face hidden. He blends in with the locals in his brown leather trousers and white shirt. Even his bike more or less fits in, as long as no one looks more closely at it.

For a brief moment, he lets himself enjoy the freedom. He doesn't get out like this often, just him and his bike. The wind in his hair would have topped the day off perfectly. Maybe on the way back to the ship he'll risk it for a bit.

He pulls up outside the thatched pub and parks his bike in a stable around the back. He knows the owners well and trusts no one will discover it. Gryffin lifts the seat up and takes out his knife and gun. The first gets pushed down the side of his brown boot and the latter into his waistband under his shirt. If his information is correct, the person he came to see should be inside in the next few minutes. The timing had better be right. He doesn't have long before Klay notices his absence and sends a team to look for him.

Gryffin brushes dust off his trousers. He pulls his hood further over his face and makes sure his gloves cover his hands before he leaves the stable. The bar is full to the rafters, so he can wander through the room unnoticed. He locates a relatively empty corner and leans against the wall with his arms crossed and one foot against the stone. An unfamiliar feeling settles over him. He's nervous. Before he can think about it too much he sees the person he's here to meet.

∞

Terra pauses at the doorway to the bar and smiles. It's one of the nicest places she's been to since *Infinity* left Ultar. The old wooden beams tower above her to line the high ceiling and walls. Fires burn at each end and take the chill out of the air. Old style wooden benches line the walls.

Pushing through the crowds, Terra smiles at anyone she squeezes past. The locals seem friendly and don't appear to have an issue with the Foundation presence. The meeting they had today went well. Although the leader wasn't keen on joining the Foundation, he had no qualms with *Infinity* staying for a few days. While Roman and Stanner dined with him, the rest of the crew had been excused for the night.

Terra finally reaches the bar and orders drinks for herself and Milla, but the bartender refuses her money. 'The drinks are on the house.' He nods his head, indicating someone behind her. Turning to look around the room, she can't see anyone obvious. Everyone seems engrossed in their own conversations. Even Milla is occupied and doesn't notice her confusion.

Then she sees him.

There are too many people blocking her view to see him clearly, but she'd know that body anywhere. Even in a crowded room, she can feel his hidden eyes boring into her. Muttering something about the restroom to Milla, she weaves through the crowd towards him. She stops in front of him and her stomach lurches as familiar scents of leather and musk hit her. Without a word he holds out his gloved hand and she takes it.

Gryffin leads her out a back door and down a passageway. He opens the door of a shed and she steps into the dark space. Once he turns the light on she finds herself in a stable. Instead of horses, the only thing in this stable is a large black motorbike.

'You knew I'd be here. How?' she asks turning to face him. To her delight, he lowers his hood. It doesn't matter how many times she sees him, he still manages to take her breath completely away. His piercing blue eyes look at her through locks of hair.

He leans against his bike and folds his arms. 'I have my ways.'

She smiles. 'Let me guess: this is one of your colonies, isn't it?'

He doesn't answer her question. 'I'm surprised you want anything to do with me after the last time.'

Terra takes a few steps closer to him. 'What happened with you?'

He crosses his ankles and looks down at the ground. 'There's something in my head. It's malfunctioning. Makes me lose control like I did. I wouldn't have hurt you.'

'Oh Gryffin! Can it not be removed?' He shakes his head. Terra doesn't know what to say. She can't imagine what it must be like for him to live with that. 'Thank you. For keeping me safe when your crew came to get you.'

'Didn't do a great job.'

'On the contrary; you did fine.' She holds out her arms and turns in a circle. 'See. In one piece. I was more worried about you.'

He lifts his head and rubs along his ocular implant. 'Me? Why?'

'The way your crew acted with you. They were so rough when they restrained you. I was worried you'd get hurt. I'm glad to see you're okay. You are okay, right?'

He shakes his head. 'I don't understand you. I was rude to you. Then I lose control. I could have killed you, but you were still worried about me.' He closes the distance between them and stops in front of her.

She shrugs and tilts her head back to meet his eyes. 'What can I say? I'm a nice person. So, why did you want to see me?'

He hesitates before speaking. 'I needed to be sure.'

'Of?' she prompts when he doesn't expand further.

He gently moves his gloved hand up to her face to trace the line of her jaw with his thumb. 'That I didn't hurt you. They told me you hurt your ribs when I pushed you down.'

'I blame the floor, not you.' He nods, drops his hand to his side again, and takes a step back to lean against his bike.

All she wants to do is be with him again. Having him so close is driving her mad. 'So, I guess you're a fan of meetings in private. Is this standard practice for you? Meeting with women in dark places?'

'No. I wanted to be alone with you.'

The way he says the last part of the sentence sends a shiver up her spine. There's no mistaking his intentions. 'You're not doing a great job of keeping away from me.'

He shrugs and smiles briefly. 'You were warned to stay away from me too. Guess we're both bad at taking direction.'

'I know the captain has my best interests at heart, but I can make my own mind up about people.'

Gryffin crosses his arms. 'Why is it so difficult for you to stay away? I am a murderer and a thief. You can do a hell of a lot better than me.' He focuses on his boots again. 'Isn't there some well-bred Foundation man for you instead of me?' He looks up at her again.

'I don't want a well-bred Foundation man.'

'Yeah, well, then you must be an idiot. Why else would you even look twice at a criminal? Especially one like me,' he says while waving his metal arm. 'I've done a lot of things that would shock you. What happened on Ultar between us — it shouldn't have happened. I need to keep away from you.'

He turns to mount his bike, but Terra grabs his arm. 'What if I don't want you to?'

'You don't have a choice!' He pushes away from his bike and steps up to her. 'This can't happen, Terra. And, as much as I like the intel, you have to stop contacting me too. You shouldn't be risking your career to help me. Hell, risking your life!'

'Some things are worth the risk. Like the truth. Like you.' Terra reaches out to him, fully expecting him to back away, but he doesn't. Instead, he curses before wrapping his arm around her. He pulls her tightly against him and tilts her head up to press his lips to hers. Before she can react, he lifts her off the ground and places her on the worn leather seat of his bike, never breaking contact with her mouth. Gryffin is not gentle with her; his mouth and hands seem to be touching her everywhere at once, letting her know in no uncertain terms he wants her.

He stops kissing her long enough to tear off her shirt, scattering most of the buttons over the straw floor. His shirt lands on the ground beside hers seconds later. Faced with his massive chest, she is again rendered speechless. She traces her fingers along the edge of his chest implant, marvelling at the way the metal defines his muscles. He lifts her up briefly to rip her trousers off, growling when they don't come off quick enough for him.

Gryffin takes a breast in his mouth and grazes his teeth across her nipple. Terra gasps and grabs a handful of his hair. She pulls his head closer to her as he moves to the other breast. Terra wraps her legs around his waist and drags her fingernails down his scarred back, leaving tracks in his flesh. Gryffin curses and retaliates by gently biting her breast.

'Wait, Gryffin, we can't do this here. What if someone comes in?'

266

He nibbles along her collar bone as he slips a finger inside her. 'I'll kill them.' Gryffin pushes deeper into Terra. 'You want me to stop?'

Whatever he does with his fingers as he's asking the question makes her moan. He has no intention of stopping any more than she does. 'Never.'

'Look at me.'

Terra opens her eyes and smiles when she sees him. His tousled hair frames his flushed face, his parted lips are slightly swollen, and the scratch marks from her nails stand out on his shoulders. But it's the look in his eyes that affects her the most. She has no doubts he would actually kill anyone foolish enough to interrupt them.

She reaches out and trails her finger along the metal on his face as she locks onto his eyes. He holds her gaze as he unfastens his trousers. He pulls her closer to him, using his metal arm to support her back as he slips inside and starts moving. Terra throws her head back as he increases his pace.

'Look at me,' he commands as he pushes deeper into her. She does as she's told and focuses on his purple eyes. The intensity of his gaze only adds to the pleasure. His bike groans under her but Gryffin's metal arm keeps her firmly in place. Unable to escape from his powerful gaze, her release rips through her faster and harder than she has ever experienced before. She closes her eyes as the waves course through her. Gryffin grips her chin firmly.

'Open your eyes.'

He keeps his pace up as another orgasm hits her. His now fully purple eyes seem almost to glow as his release shudders through him.

Afterwards, they lie in a mess of limbs on the straw covered ground. She is breathless, aching and euphoric. Terra rests her chin on his chest and looks up at him, smiling. 'I like your meetings. Better than any I've ever been to.'

He smiles, but it's one filled with sadness. 'Better than any I've been at too. I usually have more clothes on.'

Terra traces her finger along the wing tattooed on his chest. Even after what they've done, he still tenses under her touch. He isn't comfortable with it, but she has to touch him. If she lets go of him, he will disappear. She holds on to him tighter, ignoring the way his chest goes rigid under her. If this is to be the final time she sees him, she is going to make it last as long as possible.

His flesh arm tightens around her shoulders. The increase in pressure is barely noticeable, but it's enough. It confirms her fears. Whether she likes it or not, he intends on cutting all contact with her. This is his way of saying goodbye. He is going to erase her from his life as if she doesn't exist. It hurts like hell and all she wants to do is curl up and cry, but there's no point.

He's right, but she doesn't want to admit it — not yet. If either side finds out they had met, they'd both be in a lot of trouble. Roman may decide to put her in the brig indefinitely. She can't imagine what the Nomad would do to Gryffin, but losing his command would be top of the list. After seeing the way the Nomad operate, they could very well kill him. If she has to stay away to keep him safe, that's what she'll do, no matter how painful or difficult.

If only the Foundation weren't so intent on capturing him. If they could all work together, come to a compromise over the colonies, maybe they would have a chance. But as long as they see him as a threat, that will never happen. 'We're not going to see each other again, right?' She doesn't know why she asks when she already knows the answer.

He absently runs his flesh hand over her arm as he focuses on the ceiling. 'No.'

Terra sits up and looks at him closely. She can't help but notice the dark ring under his right eye. He looks exhausted. 'Is everything okay with you?'

He shakes his head and snorts. 'I don't know.' He stands up and helps Terra to her feet. 'Time to go. They'll send a search party for me soon.'

Terra slowly gets dressed, tucking her torn shirt into her trousers to keep it closed. She doesn't want to have to say goodbye to him. This situation is unfair. He's being blamed for something he has no control over. If the Foundation knew... 'I have an idea. Come back to *Infinity* with me.'

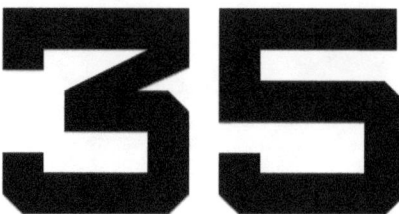

Gryffin freezes and stares at her. 'Did you bump your head?'

She shakes her head. 'I'm serious. We can explain the situation to them.'

He pulls the shirt over his mechanical arm and makes sure the glove and shirt sleeve meet. 'What situation?'

'You know, with your ... head thing.'

'My head thing? I'm pretty sure they already know.' Noticing the blank look on her face, he sighs. 'I have to get back.'

'Wait. Hear me out. When you lost control on Ultar, it wasn't your fault. Presumably it was the same with the recon officer on the supply station and the first ambush on the planet. If you can provide us with some scans to back it up, I'm sure they can help you. Possibly even get the thing in your head out.'

He crashes back down to reality with a bump. She thinks everything has been down to the damn implant. She probably wouldn't even have been with him again if she'd known the truth. He's a fool to have thought otherwise. Time to put an end to it.

He grabs his jacket and puts it on while trying to ignore the sinking feeling in his stomach. He opens his mouth to reply but stops, and puts a finger to his mouth to silence her. He cracks open the stable door and peers outside. A team of Foundation security have landed in front of the bar. From the look of their weapons, they didn't come for a friendly drink. He curses and quietly closes the door again. 'They know I'm here. Foundation security. I have to go.' He pulls out his gun and moves towards his bike.

'Come with me. Please. The Foundation can help you.'

He turns on her so fast she doesn't have time to react. He holds her up against the wall, his metal arm pushing her back against the wood. 'The Foundation did this to me,' he growls.

Terra's brows scrunch together for a moment. 'The Foundation couldn't, wouldn't, do something like that.' Terra shakes her head. 'You must be mistaken. I mean ... you have to be wrong.'

'I'm not.' The shouting and banging from the main building increases. 'I don't expect you to believe me, but it's fact. I won't let them get their hands on me again.'

'*Thirty-Five*,' she mutters under her breath.

Gryffin's deadly purple gaze locks on her. 'What did you say?'

'Your brand. What does the number mean? Is it to do with—' He slams her back against the wall and her face loses all colour. 'I can't breathe. Let go, please.' She drops to her knees when he releases his hold on her.

'Don't ever say that number to me again.' The main door of the barn rattles as someone tries to get in. He unlocks the back door and realises he's in trouble. They have the stable surrounded.

'Gryffin!' Roman shouts from outside. 'We know you're in there. Let Terra go.'

He scans the stable looking for something, anything he can use to help get him out of this mess he's stupidly walked into. When his eyes land on Terra, he stops. He doesn't like the guilty look on her face. For the second time in ten minutes, he slams back to reality. 'You did

271

this, didn't you?' He wants her to say no. He needs her to say no. He needs her to say she hasn't betrayed him.

She gets up and holds her hands out. 'I'm sorry, Gryffin. I thought I was doing the right thing. I didn't know ...' Terra looks away from him to the straw covered floor.

He wants to scream at her. Wants to hit anything and everything in the building, but he doesn't. He stands beside his bike and looks at the ground.

'Gryffin! Is Terra unharmed?'

Great. Roman thinks he's holding her hostage. What would he think if he knew they were naked on the back of his bike earlier?

Terra comes a bit closer to him. 'Please, Gryffin. Let me help you get out of here.'

He can't even look at her. His only concern is to get himself out of here and back to his transport. There's only one way he knows. Terra got him into this mess with her people. She can damn well get him out of it. 'Get on the bike.'

She glances at the motorcycle, then back at him and opens her mouth to speak, but he cuts her off by pulling his gun on her. 'I don't want to hear it. Get on the damn bike.' Needing its help, he lets the implant take over. His eyes transform and apparently convince Terra to cooperate. She quietly climbs on to the saddle. Gryffin quickly frisks her and removes her two guns and radio. 'Now tell your captain you're all right.' She hesitates until he presses the gun to her head.

'I'm all right, Captain!'

'It's over, Gryffin,' Roman replies. 'Come out unarmed. You don't want any of the locals to get caught in the crossfire.'

Threatening one of his colonies doesn't help. It just fuels the fire in his implant. 'What are you going to do?' Terra asks.

Gryffin ignores her and swings his leg over the seat. He settles in the worn leather saddle. 'Put your arms around my waist.'

'Please, Gryffin.'

'Do it!'

She slowly does as he ordered. Gryffin pulls some baler twine off the pillar beside him and ties her wrists together to secure her to him. He doesn't want her to jump off and escape. It also helps placate the emotional human side of him that wants to keep her safe. 'Now move around so you're straddling me.' It takes a bit of manoeuvring but she manages to do as he says.

'Last chance to come out,' Roman shouts.

Last chance all right, but not for him. He checks the magazine in his gun, then looks down at Terra. The hurt on her face cuts him more than he thought it would. He lets his mechanical side take over. Any feelings get pushed aside as he starts the engine. He turns the bike around to face the opposite wall, then places his metal hand on the wood. Concentrating on his arm, he focuses all his energy into it. 'You'd better hang on, Terra.'

∞

Roman doesn't like this. It's taking too long. God knows what he is doing to Terra in there. Once they all get safely back to the ship, he is going to have to have a chat with her. What the hell did she think she was doing approaching him without backup? Not even Milla knew she had met with him. He could have killed her and left the surface before anyone had even noticed she was missing.

He checks his gun again before glancing around at the rest of the team. Twenty crew members have the stable surrounded, each one armed with powerful stun guns. They can't risk killing him. Pity Gryffin won't be showing them the same consideration. Even behind the barriers they are like sitting ducks. Without knowing anything useful about his mechanical arm, they couldn't prepare for it or protect against it. Roman's plan is to take Gryffin down before he has a chance to use it.

The silence around the barn shatters with the sound of a powerful engine from inside. Before he can react, the left wall of the barn explodes. He drops to the ground and covers his head as burning shards of wood rain down on him and his team. Flames engulf the barn and thick black smoke clouds the area. Through the smoke, a large black motorbike charges out. Gryffin opens fire on them and takes down five of his crew before Roman even realises what's happening. The Foundation team start shooting back. A few manage to get close, but Gryffin expertly manoeuvres the bike to avoid most of the rounds. Three Foundation crew jump to the side as Gryffin aims straight for them. One of them releases a round and hits Gryffin in the leg, but it doesn't even slow him down.

Roman zeroes in on Gryffin's chest but pauses when he sees Terra straddling the main body of the bike. If they don't stop him soon, he will escape with her. Seeing that stun guns are having no effect, Roman grabs his sidearm. He aims at his chest and prays Gryffin will shield her if he crashes. Roman squeezes the trigger and hits Gryffin in the side. Gryffin returns fire and hits Roman on the shoulder before he disappears with Terra. 'He's got Lieutenant Rush. Get in the transports. Follow him.'

Stanner runs up to join him. 'We've taken a severe hit. Only three crew and us two are uninjured.' He notices the blood spreading across the front of Roman's uniform. 'Better make that three crew and me uninjured. Get back to the ship. I'll get her back.'

Roman shakes his head and jumps on the transport that lands beside him. 'I'm going to put an end to this personally.'

∞

She's done it again. No matter what Terra tries, she somehow ends up betraying Gryffin. She clings to his chest and wishes she could turn back time. There's no point trying to convince him she only has his best interests at heart.

Up until he told her the Foundation was responsible for turning him into a cyborg, she had honestly believed contacting Roman was the right thing. What life could Gryffin have while being constantly chased by the Foundation?

And now he is on the run again, because of her.

She doesn't know where they're going, or even if he'll let her go once they get there. She destroyed any hope of reaching a compromise back in the stable. He'd never let her help him now and she can't blame him.

She holds on tighter as he skids around a corner, barely slowing down as the bike changes direction. The Foundation transport above them continues on straight. Without her radio, they'll be having a hard time tracking her through the forest.

Terra tries to keep track of where they're going, but he takes so many turns and twists she gets lost. Instead, she keeps her head down and prays they don't crash. Even with her weight, Gryffin effortlessly winds through the trees at breakneck speeds without even a minor wobble. His reflexes are astonishing.

The bike eventually slows down and comes to a stop. He lowers the kickstand and takes a large knife from his boot. He reaches behind him and cuts the twine before he pushes away from her and dismounts. 'Off,' he commands. Terra climbs off and stretches her stiff, cramped muscles. She looks around expecting to see a ship or transport or something. Instead, she sees four paths snaking through the forest around them. He gestures at a large tree stump to his left. 'Sit.'

She looks back at him in horror. 'You expect me to sit in a forest with no gun or radio?'

'I'm the scariest thing in the forest.'

'That's comforting. They'll come after you. The Foundation won't forget and move on.'

His bright purple eyes focus on her. 'You made sure of that.'

She visibly winces at his reply. 'I made a mistake, Gryffin.'

'Damn right you did! You tried to hand me over to your people.'

'You have to believe I was only trying to help you. That thing in

275

your head is in control now. It's the reason your eyes have changed, isn't it?' He doesn't reply. 'I know it is. You look tense and your voice is different.' That at least earns a reaction from him. 'No one has told you? You take a small pause after each word. It's almost like you are trying to force each word out. Like it's a struggle to speak.' She takes a step towards him, taking advantage of his momentary lack of concentration. 'I contacted them because I care about you. You shouldn't have to live like this.'

He gets back on his bike and starts the engine. 'Stay here. Your people will locate you.' Before she can say anything else, his bike is gone.

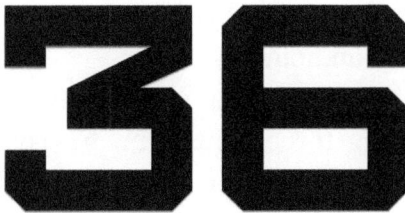

36

'Are you sure you're uninjured?'

Terra pushes Milla's arm away for the fifth time. 'How many times? I'm all right. He didn't do anything to me.'

Roman sits on the ramp of the transport and examines her. She knows he's trying to figure out if she's telling the truth. Putting all her effort into not blushing, she checks her jacket zip is still done up. The last thing she wants is for anyone to see all the buttons on her shirt are ripped off. She is not ready for that conversation.

Roman sighs and nods but clearly doesn't believe her for one minute. 'So, want to tell me what the hell went on in there?'

Not for the first time, she can't help but notice how similar Roman and his son are. Their posture and mannerisms are identical. 'He approached me in the bar.'

'Did you know he was going to be there?'

'Of course not.'

Roman makes a non-committal sound before he gestures for her to continue.

'He brought me into the barn and apologised for how things ended on Ultar. He wanted to make sure he hadn't hurt me.' She stops at that point and blushes. Milla catches her eye and she knows her friend can see right through her. Milla winks and shakes her head before she continues packing away her kit.

'And...' Roman prompts.

'And that's when I contacted you.'

'So you talked for an hour?'

'Yes, sir.' She clears her throat and tries to stop blushing like a tomato. 'I was trying to convince him to hand himself over. I thought it would be better for him if he came willingly.'

Roman glances at his bandaged shoulder. 'Looks like you need to work on your negotiating skills.' He gets up and helps Terra to her feet. 'It was worth a go. Don't suppose you got a good look at his transport?'

She shakes her head, glad the topic of conversation has moved away from what happened in the barn. 'He dumped me off his bike and took off.'

Roman nods. 'I'm not surprised. He's running out of places to hide. The leader of this colony has joined with the Foundation.'

'But I thought he wasn't interested?'

'After what happened I didn't give him much choice. He's closed his doors to the Nomad. If Gryffin or any of his people come back, they'll be refused permission to land. Another few meetings and the Nomad will be shut out of the Sector.'

Terra stands at the bottom of the ramp and looks around the clearing. The tracks left by Gryffin's bike still scar the forest floor. She's never felt so confused and lost before. She knew there was something off about the Foundation's interest in Gryffin, and his childhood file only solidified this. Never did she think her people were the ones that tortured him.

While she doesn't doubt what Gryffin told her, it's hard to believe the Foundation would do that. The contradicting beliefs are driving her crazy. If things were different, she could discuss this with Roman, but she's not sure she can now. Especially after she lied about what happened in the barn. Roman would never trust her again if she told him the truth.

Even if she did tell him, she sincerely doubts he would even believe Gryffin's allegations. Her captain seems to be on board with the Foundation's plans. He is even helping to move the colonisation forward faster than expected. Within a few weeks, they have managed to drive the Nomad from this area and turned an entire group into fugitives. Terra slowly follows her captain up the ramp and into the transport. She may not be sure about many things, but she does know one thing: it's not in Gryffin's best interest to go anywhere near the Foundation.

∞

Gryffin wakes from his nightmare and sits up quickly in bed. The beeping that woke him up continues to drone in the background. It takes him another few seconds to realise it's his radio. He wipes the damp hair off his face then leans over to grab the unit off the chair beside his bed. 'What?'

Klay hesitates for a moment. 'You okay, sir?'

'Yeah. What is it?'

'We've reached the coordinates, sir.'

'On my way.' He gets out of bed and fills the sink with water, ignoring the way his flesh hand shakes. Gryffin stands in front of the mirror and grimaces at his reflection. He looks exactly how he feels — lousy. He runs a hand over his t-shirt to smooth the creases. His hair is sticking up at strange angles and his bloodshot eyes show how badly he needs some decent sleep.

He's had countless dreams about being operated on, but lately they're getting more vivid. He looks at his reflection, not surprised when purple eyes greet him. Even though it was a dream, he's still angry as hell. He needs to calm down fast. With no time for a shower, he sticks his head under the cold tap. It does the trick, helping to clear his head. Not bothering to dry his hair, he leaves his room and climbs the steps to the command deck.

Gryffin moves towards the window at the front. 'Does he know we're here?'

'Not yet, sir,' Klay replies.

Gryffin nods. The unknown ship in front of them is orbiting another Nomad colony. The large purple griffin on its sail taunts him and he is already well and truly pissed off.

It had taken the full effort of all his ships, but after a week of reported sightings of different vessels in various locations, he was able to narrow down a list of possible targets. His ships were in place and ready. It's just his good luck that *Ares* is successful. Might also give him an outlet for his anger.

'Contact them.'

Klay shakes his head. 'Nothing.'

'Open a line.' Klay signals that it's open. 'This is Gryffin of the Nomad ship *Ares*. You've got two minutes to power down and surrender before I blow you out of the sky.'

'Sir, they're breaking orbit and moving towards the surface.'

'Follow them. Fire everything you have on that ship.'

∞

Sayber curses as *Ares* opens fire. There's no time to dwell on how the hell Gryffin found them. Sayber orders evasive measures. He grabs on to the arms of the command chair as the ship ducks and dives to avoid being hit.

He shouldn't even be here. The man supposed to captain the vessel had had second thoughts. Sayber had no choice but to kill him. With little time to locate a replacement, he was forced to step in himself, or risk putting the schedule back. Bray had pushed to take his place, but he needed him on *Perses*. His second-in-command may be acting as though he's recovered from what happened on Ultar, but Sayber doesn't want to push him yet.

'*Ares* is contacting us again. Just a voice message.'

'Let me hear it.'

Gryffin's voice comes over the speakers. 'Sayber, I hope you're on that ship. I've got a missile with your name on it.'

No time to worry about how Gryffin figured out he is involved. The alarms on the ship screech to life as the promised missile makes its way towards them. All hell breaks loose as the counter measures fail and the missile hits.

Sayber orders the thirty crew members to abandon ship while he stays to try and delay their crash. The ship free-falls towards the surface. He powers the reverse engines, attempting to slow the dive. The engines scream in protest as they struggle to have any effect. Sayber can do nothing but watch as the surface rushes up to meet him.

∞

Gryffin waits until the last minute before he orders his crew to release the tethers. The steel ropes fire out of the hull towards the falling vessel. *Ares* jolts as they lock on to their target, the engines groaning loudly as they wrestle to hold the two ships. 'Boarding team one to the transport bay. Klay, keep that ship off the ground until I say.'

Gryffin lets the implant out to play. He's going to need it for this next bit. The bay doors open and the wind rushes through the space. Gryffin holds on to the edge and looks down at the heavily damaged ship dangling from *Ares*. 'Klay, reel her in.' The ship rises up towards them as the ropes retract. 'Hold it there.' Unfortunately, due to the fires spreading through the ship, he isn't going to risk bringing it any closer. That still leaves a twenty-foot drop. He turns to the five men in front of him. 'I'll take the lead. I want survivors. Any sign of Sayber, I need to know.' After getting a nod from each, Gryffin steps off the edge.

∞

Sayber is well and truly screwed. There's no way he can hide from a boarding party from *Ares*, especially if Gryffin leads it. Sayber scrambles over the ruins of the command deck and curses Balfe for landing him in this mess.

While grateful *Ares* stopped the plummet, the ship had caught the back of his vessel, leaving the ship dangling with the front towards the ground. He manages to get out of the room and pulls himself along the floor using the metal wall girders as hand holds. If he is going to survive, he needs to locate the last escape pod before Gryffin or any of the *Ares* crew do.

Sayber looks up through the gathering smoke and freezes for a moment. He could have sworn he saw a purple glow through the smoke up ahead. He holds his breath and listens as the ship groans and creaks around him. Apart from the vessel, all he hears is his own racing heart.

He takes a gamble and climbs again. He makes it to the top of the corridor without seeing anything else suspicious. Sayber reaches up to search for a handhold, but his hand slips. He loses his footing and falls, but someone grabs his arm and stops his descent. Sayber fears the worst as he looks up and meets Gryffin's purple eyes.

37

Aleena keeps close to her trusted security, Lucan, as he pushes through the forest. He pauses to check the coordinates on his handheld. 'Not far.'

She nods and wraps her coat tighter around her to protect her from the night chill. She received the encrypted message a week ago. Even though she had attempted to trace the origin, she had been unsuccessful. The message had been short — *I can help repair him* — and a set of coordinates.

The *him* from the message could only refer to Gryffin. It is clear to her that whatever had been done to him all those years ago is starting to take its toll on her friend. His moods are becoming more intense and unpredictable. Gryffin may be content to let himself fall apart, but she is not. If this mysterious messenger can help, as his friend she must at least see what they can offer.

Lucan stops and holds up his hand. He puts a finger to his lips and motions for Aleena to stay where she is. Doing as instructed, she waits while Lucan checks the area. A few minutes later, he calls for her to come out.

He hands her a small metal box the size of her palm. 'Found this under some leaves at the coordinates. It's scanning as being safe.'

She opens it and holds up a small computer chip. She slides it into Lucan's handheld and loads the information. She examines the data for a moment before smiling. It appears to be a design for an implant modification.

'Good news?' Lucan asks.

Aleena nods and looks up at the sky. 'It appears we have a very well-connected friend out there.' She hands it to Lucan and turns back towards the village. 'I want that tested inside and out. Find out who sent it to us. We cannot afford to take any chances at this stage.'

'You sure it's wise to take it back to the village? The fact someone knew to send this to you is a worry.'

Aleena nods. 'I agree, Lucan, but we cannot ignore the possible implications of this program. If it can somehow aid us, we would be foolish to ignore it.'

∞

'So, what now?' Sayber asks. 'I'm having a shitty day, so if you're going to kill me get it over with.'

Gryffin pulls him up into the adjoining corridor, then drops him down onto the wall. 'I'm not going to do you any favours.' He pushes his gun against Sayber's forehead. 'Want to explain what the hell you're up to?'

'Not really.'

Gryffin applies more pressure. 'Wasn't a request.'

'Still no. This is to do with a contract. You of all people know you never discuss contracts. It's not great business.'

'How good will it be for business if I shoot you?' When Sayber stays quiet, Gryffin sighs and gets to his feet. 'Your choice. Stand up.' He pushes him along the corridor and activates his radio. 'I have Sayber.

Get back to the hatch.'

Gryffin walks behind Sayber while he scans the corridors for any other survivors. Now that he has him, he's not sure what to do. It's not like he can torture the information out of him. Sayber is as stubborn as he is when it comes to pain. Sayber would fight Gryffin till his last breath and a dead prisoner can't say much. The only hope is the ship. If *Ares* can hook up and extract any information, it might shed some light on Sayber's plans. For now, Sayber will just have to stay on *Ares*.

They reach the floor below the access hatch. Gryffin practically throws Sayber up the vertical corridor with his metal arm, then reaches to pull himself, up when a flare of hot white pain explodes in his chest.

Sayber doesn't seem to notice and continues to ascend, oblivious to what is happening. The pain subsides, so he takes a breath and reaches for the corridor wall again. Instead of taking hold of the metal, his artificial arm bangs uselessly against it. He tries to open his hand, but the mechanics jam.

Before he can think about what's wrong, an even bigger wave of pain attacks him. Every breath feels like liquid fire filling his lungs. He doubles over and gasps for breath. The pain begins to travel up his body and settles behind his ocular implant. Blood seeps out of his nose as his vision goes blurry.

Another volley of knives launches itself at his chest and head. He loses his footing and falls hard against the far wall, landing on his already damaged chest. His vision swims again, before his ocular implant shuts down and turns everything black.

∞

'So, fancy telling me what happened in the barn?'

Terra puts on her best innocent face and leans against the door frame. Milla smirks and waves the bottle of drink in front of her, hoping to tempt her. 'I already told you.'

Milla shakes her head and pushes past Terra. She puts the bottle down on the table and takes two glasses from the cupboard. 'You forget who you're talking to. Apart from the fact you turned the colour of a tomato when the captain questioned you, my detective skills have picked up on two vital clues.'

Terra closes the door and takes one of the glasses. 'I'm all ears.'

Milla sits down on the couch, tucking her legs under her. She takes a sip of the drink and blows out a breath. 'Whoa, this Ultaran ale is strong stuff! Right, the first clue: it was pretty warm on the surface, but your jacket was zipped up. I would deduce that means you were hiding something, maybe some scuffs on your shirt, or a mark on your neck.' Milla smirks and wiggles her eyebrows.

In spite of her best efforts, Terra can feel her face turning red. She tries to hide it by working on the drawing on the table in front of her.

Milla claps her hands. 'I knew it. Which one?'

'Neither.' Terra glances up briefly before focusing on her drawing again. 'He didn't want to waste time undoing my buttons.'

'Destruction of Foundation property — you really are living on the edge, Terra,' Milla teases. 'Well, clue two is obsolete now, but you did have a large piece of straw sticking out of your hair. So, details please.'

'No way.'

Milla pouts. 'I deserve something for figuring out the trail of impossible-to-decipher clues you left.'

Terra throws her pencil down, leans back, and crosses her legs. She stares into her drink as the events of the last few hours come back to her. 'Up until I made the stupid decision to call in the Foundation, everything was kind of perfect. I've never experienced anything like it before, Milla. The raw passion — it completely took over.'

A big smile covers Milla's face. 'Go on.'

'He took me on the back of his bike.'

'I know. Most of the crew did see you, remember.'

'No, Milla. I mean he ripped my shirt off and *took* me on his bike.'

Milla's eyebrows shoot up. 'Well, well, well. Terra Rush, I never had you down as a biker fan.' She leans back against the cushion. 'You did a damn good job keeping this side of you under wraps in the academy.'

'This isn't a side of me. I don't know what the hell I'm doing.'

'Sounds to me like you're having a very good time. Stop over analysing. What's the problem?'

Terra's happiness quickly disappears. 'I betrayed him, Milla. We had an incredible time and I ruined it.' She throws her head back and closes her eyes. 'What's wrong with me?'

Milla moves closer to her and puts a hand on her knee. 'Hey, don't be so hard on yourself. You thought it was the right thing to do — for the Foundation and him. He'll see it that way.'

Terra snorts and takes a big mouthful of ale, wincing as it burns her throat on the way down. 'You didn't see him. He was furious. He even used me as a shield to break out.'

'I didn't see that. I saw you pressed tightly to him and well protected. If he'd put you on the back, you probably would've been hit.'

Terra stares into her drink. Maybe Milla is right. She has to admit, in spite of the situation, she did feel safe. 'I never thought of it like that. Thanks.'

Milla smiles and refills her glass. 'That's what I'm here for. You really care about him, don't you?'

'Why'd you say that?'

Milla nods at Terra's drawing. Terra looks down and is surprised to see Gryffin's face on the paper. She didn't even realise what she was drawing. 'Yeah. I guess I do.'

'Well, just don't let anyone get their hands on that drawing — you're in enough trouble as it is. So, don't suppose you're going to give me any more details… '

Terra throws a cushion at her. 'You have a one-track mind. Get your own man and make your own details.'

'Alas, if only it were that simple. It's easier for you. You're having it off with the captain. I'm after his aide. Doubt he can pop off to the nearest barn whenever the urge takes him. More's the pity. Until then, I guess I'll have to live in my head.'

Terra looks at Milla strangely. 'That reminds me. Gryffin said something strange in the barn.'

She wiggles her eyebrows. 'Oh, really?'

'Mind out of the gutter for a moment. He said there's something in his head which makes him lose control.'

Milla hesitates before speaking. 'That makes sense. From what I could tell, he's undergone a lot of modifications.' She shivers. 'Gives me the creeps thinking about it.'

'He also said the Foundation did it to him.'

'The thing in his head or everything?'

Terra shakes her head. 'I'm not sure. He was adamant he didn't want the Foundation getting their hands on him again. Milla, he looked scared at the thought.'

'You believe him?'

Terra pauses. She honestly doesn't know what to say. His reactions were real, but does she really believe the Foundation could have done those horrific things to him? 'I think *he* believes it. Does that make sense?'

'Sure. Why would he believe it though? I mean, I haven't spent any time with him really, but he seems to be a pretty together guy, apart from all his issues. He must believe it for a reason.'

'You think it's true?'

'All I'm saying is that people's beliefs are pretty powerful. If that's what he believes, you're going to have a hard time convincing him otherwise.'

Terra nods but doesn't say anything. How can she possibly tell Milla she thinks there may be something to Gryffin's claims?

∞

He should run. No question.

Then why isn't he?

Sayber looks down the corridor at his enemy writhing in pain on the floor. He doesn't know what the hell is wrong with him but it's the miracle he needs. Except …

He curses himself, drops down the ladder, then climbs along the corridor to Gryffin. As soon as he gets near, Gryffin raises his gun and points it at him. Typical. Stubborn fool still thinks he can fight. He ignores the weapon and assesses the Nomad. Blood is seeping from his nose and ears, his artificial arm lies uselessly on the ground beside him, and his eyes don't seem able to focus on him.

'What the hell is going on with you?'

Gryffin tries to talk, but it results in a lot of coughing followed by blood pouring out of his mouth.

'Don't try talking again.' Sayber is torn. He should take Gryffin down, but he can't. This isn't a fair fight; he might as well strike him down in his sleep. If he's to be the one to kill Gryffin, he wants to be able to hold his head up high afterwards.

That leaves him one option. He pulls Gryffin fully onto his back and curses when he sees the blue tinge around his mouth. He's suffocating. There's nothing he can do to help but, Gryffin's team should be waiting for him.

Sayber reaches over, but as soon as he brushes off Gryffin's chest, the Nomad arches his back and screams in pain. 'Where the hell is your radio?' Moving as quickly as he can, Sayber searches Gryffin's uniform and finally locates it in the back pocket of his trousers. '*Ares*, do you copy?'

'Who is this?'

'Gryffin is down. He's having difficulty breathing. Bleeding from his nose, ears, and mouth.'

'We're on the way.'

Sayber turns Gryffin on his side so he doesn't choke, then moves away. He needs to go now; use the commotion to his advantage. With one last look over his shoulder, he drops to the level below and races towards the final escape pod.

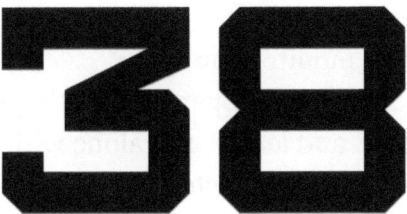

'Welcome back, sir.'

Gryffin squeezes his eyes shut and takes a shaky breath. He feels terrible; weak and aching. He slowly opens his eyes and winces as the light hits his sensitive eyes. 'I thought that was it.'

'It was bloody close,' Klay says. 'Okay, I've turned the lights down now.'

On the third try, he finally forces his eyes open and sees an anxious Klay and Chayse beside him. He tries to sit up but reconsiders when the muscles in his chest protest. While the pain has dulled to a more bearable throb, the attack has left him physically drained. He glances down at his chest and fully expects to see something, anything to explain the pain, but it's exactly the same. 'How long was I out for?' he whispers, his throat raw and sore.

'Nine hours. You had us all worried. How do you feel?'

'Sore.' He lifts his metal arm and flexes his fingers. 'What happened to my arm?'

'I'm still doing some tests, but it looks like you suffered from a system overload of sorts,' Klay explains. 'All your implants went into overdrive.'

'Overdrive and overload doesn't explain why my arm shut down or my vision went.'

'The programming to those areas must have been rerouted to your chest and head. As I said, I need more time to know for sure.'

'Why are you here then?'

'But, sir, I need to monitor you.'

'I need to know what happened. That's your priority. You're dismissed.' Klay nods and leaves him alone with Chayse. 'Sayber?'

'He escaped after he contacted us, sir,' Chayse reports. 'Klay searched for the pod, but it looks like it's long gone.'

Gryffin sits up suddenly. 'Sayber contacted *Ares*?'

Chayse nods. 'He's the reason you're still alive. Your monitoring device didn't work. Sayber made the call and told us you were suffocating. The team came back for you with Klay. You were stabilised and brought back here.'

Sayber helped save him? That doesn't make sense. His enemy was down. He would have expected him to take advantage, not stay and help. It's not that he's not grateful — just confused. 'Did we get anything from the ship?'

'We're having trouble gaining access to the system.'

Gryffin swings his legs over the edge of the bed. 'Hook me up. I'll see if I can get in.'

'Sir?' Chayse looks at him in confusion. 'You can't do that. Can you?'

Gryffin nods once and squeezes his eyes shut when the room continues to dance. 'It's not common knowledge, so keep it to yourself. Aleena is the only other person who knows.'

'But ... how?'

'It happened when I was being scanned by Klay a few years ago. He didn't notice, so I kept quiet. Hooking directly with the system means I can search without leaving any trace.'

Chayse drops down onto the chair in front of Gryffin. 'That's amazing! I would never have even guessed it was possible. So why not do things that way all the time?'

'I can't use it too often. It puts stress on my ocular implant. Messes with my vision afterwards.'

'And you want to hook up now?' Chayse stands in front of him. 'That's not a good idea. You died, sir. Well, the non-implant side of you died. Whatever happened, it caused your heart to stop. The last thing you need to do is put more strain on your body by linking with a ship.'

He died. Well, that finishes the lousy day off perfectly. Klay had conveniently left out that little detail.

'Klay wants me to run some tests on you,' Chayse says while he opens a set of drawers beside the bed.

'Leave it, Chayse.' He's had enough testing to last him a lifetime.

Chayse throws the cable on the floor at his feet. 'Klay insisted, sir. You can't give him any more reasons to doubt you. He's already pissed that because of what happened to you, Sayber got away. We're hiding on the surface now because the locals blame *Ares* for the strike. Add that to all the attacks on innocent villagers and crew, losing control frequently, disappearing to meet Foundation women, and all these problems with your implants, and he has enough ammunition against you.

'You need to do these tests so it doesn't look like you're hiding anything. It's vital the crew see you doing what you can to put this right. If you don't, Klay won't have any choice but to relieve you, sir. You can't leave this room. I won't let you.'

∞

'You can't ask me to kill more people for the fun of it. I don't describe twenty-six dead people as collateral damage, Balfe.'

Sayber paces the main room in the centre of the freighter, while he tries to ignore the creepy little Scientist in the corner. It seems Balfe wasn't being entirely honest when he said the trials had stopped until they had captured Gryffin again. He only hopes the poor soul in pieces on the main table is dead.

Sayber massages a knot in the back of his shoulder. He had been cramped in the blasted escape pod for six hours before *Perses* finally picked him up. He had never considered himself claustrophobic until he spent time in that metal bubble.

Balfe shrugs. 'It is what it is, Sayber.'

'Well, it has to end. We kill Nomad, not innocent colonists. Those extra men you put on my ships are loose cannons. I want them all gone.'

Balfe looks away from the Scientist for the first time since Sayber walked into the room. 'That sounded like a demand, Captain. You're not getting too big for your boots are you? I would hate to have to replace you.'

Sayber pulls out his knife and presses it to Balfe's throat. The fact Balfe doesn't even flinch worries him. If he doesn't fear death, it will make him a difficult adversary. 'I'm still on board with this, but not with those men. You agreed I could do this my way. The raid today was a shambles. Gryffin could have killed everyone on board. And now he has another ship. What happens if he accesses the information on it?'

Balfe shrugs. 'That's not a concern. Everything is encrypted and safeguarded. If he tries to get into the system without the proper codes, the data will be corrupted. Besides, I thought you would be more than capable of handling an altercation with the Nomad. In truth, your performance disappointed me.'

'Maybe if there weren't complete strangers mixed in with my crew, my performance would be better. I don't trust them. My crew don't trust them. This stops until you remove them.'

Balfe smiles. 'Look over your shoulder.'

Sayber lowers his knife when he sees one of those very men behind him with a gun pointed at his head.

Balfe straightens his uniform and pushes his chair back from Sayber. 'Those men are my eyes and ears. They stay. As for halting proceedings, feel free to do what you have to. I must point out if you do choose that route, I will have no choice but to instruct those men to kill the crew on each ship they are aboard.'

Sayber sheaths his knife and takes a step back from Balfe. Balfe nods once and turns back to the screen in front of him. 'Good decision. Now, from what my people report, the plan is progressing well. Colonies are eagerly signing treaties with the Foundation. With your help, we've even managed to outlaw the Nomad in quite a large portion of the Sector. It also seems Gryffin himself is helping our cause.'

Sayber frowns. 'How? He'd rather die than hurt any of his colonies.'

'Negotiations to keep colonies are not going well for him. He lost his temper with a settlement last week. They had signed up with us. In retaliation, he kidnapped a member of the Foundation crew, blew up a barn, and then engaged in a fire fight from the back of his motorcycle right through the centre of the town. Caused quite a bit of damage.

'All in all, it seems the work our dear Scientist did is starting to take over. The machine is winning over the man. However, as much as I'd like to settle back and let him do our work for us, it's not happening as fast as I'd hoped.'

'Hang on,' Sayber says. 'Are you doing something to him to cause this?'

Balfe slowly shakes his head and tuts. 'Come now, Sayber. Can you really see me getting anywhere near him? If that were possible, I would have taken him in myself long ago. Perhaps it is merely normal wear and tear? You should be happy about it. From what I've heard, if not for these glitches, you might be dead right now. I'll keep the freighter near the Port for another few days so we can stock up. Can I presume you'll look after her while she's in Hunter space?'

'Of course.'

'Good.' He waves his hand at Sayber to dismiss him. Sayber turns away from Balfe, dodges around the other man, and makes his way back to the relative safety of *Perses*. Normal wear and tear? Not likely. The look on Balfe's face spoke volumes. He doesn't know how, but the admiral is responsible for the problems with Gryffin's implants.

Six hours alone in the pod gave him time to think about a few things. He doesn't regret his decision to help Gryffin. It would have been a less than honourable victory if he had acted while Gryffin was down. Especially after what he just heard. What happened to Gryffin on the ship unsettles him. Gryffin is one tough Nomad. For him to show that much pain it must have been pretty excruciating.

If they had found a way to harm the Nomad captain from a nice comfy chair thousands of miles away, they wouldn't be doing all of this. No, there has to be someone closer to Gryffin working with Balfe. He shakes his head. Gryffin's reputation is well known. While some may have thought it exaggerated, Sayber knows without a doubt, it is all fact. Only someone with a death wish would consider betraying him like that.

He can't help but feel a slight twinge of pity for Gryffin. He knows first-hand what it's like to have unwanted personnel on his ship. He quickens his pace. Sayber wants to get back to his quarters as soon as possible. Maybe it's time to run a full check on his crew, just to be on the safe side.

∞

As soon as the words leave his mouth, Chayse regrets them. He's crossed a line he can't go back over. You don't order Gryffin to do anything, especially if you're an aide. Chayse holds his breath and resists the urge to run for the door, as he waits for Gryffin to retaliate.

Instead of shouting at him, Gryffin crosses his arms and leans back against the bed. 'You think he'd take my command?'

Caught off guard, Chayse hesitates for a moment. 'Erm, yes. I'm convinced he's prepared to try. I don't think you should give him any excuse. I can run the test if you'd prefer, sir.'

Gryffin smirks quickly. 'After a promotion?'

Chayse freezes again, completely thrown by Gryffin's out-of-character smile. He decides to push his luck. 'Now that you mention it, yes. I would like to be trained with the rest of the crew so I can help on missions. I think I can contribute more to the Nomad, sir.'

'So babysitting the high commander isn't contributing enough?'

'That's not what I mean, sir. I want to do something more important for the Nomad. Not that being your aide isn't important. It is. I meant ... '

'At ease, Chayse,' Gryffin interrupts. He gets up and steadies himself against the wall for a moment. 'I'm going to the other ship. You said it yourself; I need to show I'm doing what I can. Hooking myself up to the vessel and uncovering who hired Sayber is the best way of doing that.' He pulls on his t-shirt and walks towards the door. 'I don't hear you following me.'

'I'm coming too?'

Gryffin looks over his shoulder. 'Of course. It's your job to make sure I don't die again.'

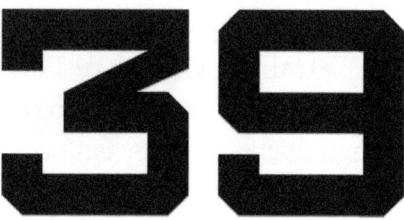

How the hell did you get yourself into this mess? Chayse follows behind Gryffin and repeats that question to himself over and over, but as of yet, no answer has appeared.

The captain has taken him over to the damaged Hunter vessel to — as far as Klay and everyone else is concerned — see if they can salvage anything. Instead, he has to watch Gryffin hook up to an entire ship. He wishes he didn't have the delightful responsibility of making sure the ship doesn't fry the captain's brain. Not part of his job role when he signed up. Although, he has to admit, deceiving Klay did give him a small kick.

Chayse follows his superior through the heavily damaged ship. He ducks under metal girders and hanging wires, then clambers over a fallen wall panel. The torn metal slices through his trousers and narrowly misses tearing the side of his leg.

As they get closer to the command deck, a large patch of blood on the wall catches his attention. He realises it must be Gryffin's blood from earlier. The captain glances at it for a moment as he passes, which confirms his suspicions.

They reach the command deck and Gryffin halts suddenly. It takes Chayse another few seconds to figure out what's attracted his attention. A large piece of the ceiling has fallen down and blocked off the entrance. It must have happened when *Ares* lowered the ship. 'Is there another way in?'

Gryffin ignores his question and pushes the panel aside like he would a piece of paper. The captain clears more rubble out of the way, while Chayse stands in the corridor with his mouth open. 'Find the central system access point.'

Chayse stumbles into the room and after a few minutes, he locates the access point. Gryffin rips the front off the unit and attaches wires to it, while Chayse stares at him in amazement. 'Do you really think this will work, sir?'

Gryffin glances at Chayse and raises his eyebrow.

'Klay said all the systems are locked down and password protected. He tried a few bypasses, but they didn't work. Apparently if he kept trying it would have wiped the data.'

'Thanks for the recap.'

'Will you get any warning before that happens, sir?'

Gryffin shakes his head. 'Ready for your bit?'

He nods with more conviction than he feels. Gryffin sits on the ground and removes his shirt so Chayse can attach his monitoring pads. 'I still can't quite believe you can do this, sir. The thing I don't get is why you don't tell Klay.'

The captain continues to attach the cables. Chayse accepts he's not going to get an answer, so returns to double-checking the pads are firmly stuck to Gryffin's chest.

'I wanted to keep something to myself.'

Chayse looks up at him, but the captain is focused on the cables beside him.

'I've spent most of my life hooked up to a computer. Getting studied like a piece of machinery. Klay and Rayde know every intimate detail of my body. They know every implant, every connector. Every piece of me has been displayed on a screen and examined. Hell, thanks to my heart rate being monitored by the damn device behind my ear, everyone on the ship even knows when I'm angry... or excited.'

Chayse looks away quickly and blushes. He never thought of it like that. He can't imagine what it would be like to have everything monitored the way the captain does — especially intimate things.

Gryffin looks up at him. The pain he sees on his captain's face really knocks Chayse back. In all the time he's helped Klay with the testing, he never once thought about how Gryffin felt. He knew the captain hated it, but he always put that down to his aversion to being touched. He's his aide. Of all people on the ship, he should have figured it out. Should have done something, anything, to help. 'Sir, I didn't know.'

'Don't,' Gryffin orders. 'As I said, only you and Aleena know about this. I'd appreciate if you keep it that way. I'd hate to kill you when you're starting to get useful.' Gryffin stretches his long legs out in front of him. 'Ready to start?'

'Yes, sir. Permission to pull the plug if your vitals drop.'

'As long as you're pulling the plug on the hook-up and not me.' Gryffin opens the connector on the side of his ocular implant and plugs in the cable. He attaches the other end to the side of the central computer. Once finished, Chayse sits down opposite him so he can reach him quickly if something goes wrong. 'Right, sir. You're ready to go.'

Gryffin closes his eyes and jolts back against the wall as the information races into his mind. Chayse keeps his eyes glued to his monitors. So far, all the readings remain within normal levels, but he isn't going to relax until the captain is unhooked. About three minutes into the link, Gryffin's heart rate begins to increase and his brain activity spikes. 'Sir, your vitals are fluctuating.'

'Don't touch anything.'

Chayse looks down at the results again. Gryffin will kill him if he pulls him out too soon, but he's pretty sure he'll be in more trouble if something happens to the captain.

'Sir ... '

'I said don't touch anything.'

All of a sudden the alarms on his monitors sound as Gryffin's levels soar.

∞

Bray jumps at the sound of gunfire from within Sayber's room. He bursts in the door with his weapon raised to see Sayber sitting at his desk with a satisfied look on his face. Unfortunately, it appears to be at the expense of his communications centre.

Bray lowers his gun and shakes his head. 'Feel better, sir?'

'I would have preferred to shoot Balfe, but I guess that will have to wait.'

Bray openly stares at him. 'He contacted you again? That's the third time this week.'

Sayber rubs his forehead. 'He wants quicker results. Appears that by *taking my time* I'm delaying him.'

Bray closes the door behind him and leans against the wall. 'Sir, between you and me, this relationship doesn't feel right.'

Sayber drops his head back onto the headrest of his chair and frowns at the ceiling. 'You're not alone there. Have you found any information on our extra crew members?'

Bray nods and pushes the ruined communication centre aside so he can perch on the corner of Sayber's desk. 'They're well protected, sir. I haven't been able to uncover anything useful except for one small detail. One of my contacts seems to think the one with Balfe on the freighter recently *holidayed* on a Foundation prison moon.'

As expected, that gets his captain's attention. Sayber puts his feet on the ground and spins his chair around. 'That's one pretty big detail.

How long ago are we talking?'

'Weeks. The interesting point is, as far as my contact knows, he can't locate a record of a release. They housed him in a separate area of the facility with the other five men.' Bray waits patiently while Sayber digests the information. He can't blame him. Nothing about the men — or Balfe for that matter — makes sense. He does know one thing: once on a Foundation prison moon, you stayed there. Unless, of course, you somehow got released by the Foundation. It did happen, but it was rare. 'What charge?' Sayber asks.

Bray checks the pad briefly and frowns. 'No record of any charge.'

'Strange. An ex-inmate working with the Foundation. Now why does that fill me with dread?'

'I'd prefer not think about it,' Bray replies. 'Whatever their plan, it won't end well for us.' He pauses and clears his throat. 'I don't want to question you, sir, but are you sure the future of the Hunters is secure?'

Sayber leans on his desk and clasps his hands in front of him. 'A few weeks ago I would have said yes, but now ... We hang on in there. We pull the plug now, that's it for us, but keep eyes on our guests, on the other ships too. I want to know everything they do. Don't leave them alone for a second.'

Bray nods but is not in the least bit reassured by Sayber's words. Sayber will do everything in his power to protect the Hunters, but with these extra men involved, the scales have tipped and not in their favour. He turns to leave, but Sayber stops him as he gets to the door.

'Oh, and Bray? Dig me out a new unit. Wouldn't want to miss our dear friend Balfe if he needs to talk again.'

∞

'Sir, you need to break the link!'

Gryffin hears the urgency of Chayse's voice and concentrates on separating himself from the ship. It doesn't work. He should have paid better attention to how deep he was going. Getting into the system proved hard enough in the first place, but now he's done it, he's trapped.

His stomach jolts violently as his head spins. One minute he's locked in the system, the next he's sitting against the console looking at Chayse. He takes a few deep breaths while his head recovers from the assault of information. Before he can ask how he got out, Chayse holds up the end of the cable linking him to the system. 'I pulled the plug. Your vitals hit dangerous levels.'

Gryffin grimaces as he squeezes his eyes shut. 'Bit of warning next time.'

'Sorry, sir. Did you get anything?'

'No. System thought I was a virus. Threw up a damn firewall.' Before Chayse can ask any more questions or pick him up on the blatant lie, he stands up. Gryffin lets the implant out so he won't lose his sight. 'Go down to engineering. See if you can repair the engines. I'm going to check the armoury.' Gryffin stops at the door and holds on to the frame as his vision blurs slightly. 'We don't have much time. Klay is due at a weapons buy in an hour, so move.'

Gryffin follows the downloaded map to the armoury. He barely notices where he's going. All he can do is think about what he found on the system.

Buried deep in the mission files, he uncovered a list of coordinates. He doesn't need to check — he knows they match all the colonies under his protection. If that isn't enough of a reason to destroy every Hunter ship out there, he found something else.

The list had come from Balfe. His vision clouds as the anger builds in his body. He needs to take Balfe down; painfully. He pushes what he found on the system aside. For now, he needs to see if they can use the ship or anything on it.

He discovers the armoury locked, so punches a hole in the door and rips the locking mechanism out. He smiles to himself. Looks like Sayber planned to arm a small battalion. If he had known about this in advance, he could have done without Klay arranging the weapons buy. He pulls the door closed and goes to find Chayse. They need to get off the ship and lock it down. He'll send someone to collect it later.

He drops down a floor and follows the sound of crashing machinery to the engine room. Chayse pulls himself out from under the engine and wipes his hands on the front of his trousers. 'Probably some parts we can salvage, but that's about it. Afraid all it's good for is scrap.'

'Time to go then.' He throws a portable drive to Chayse. 'Hook that up. I want the ship cloaked.'

Chayse studies the portable cloak. 'Why waste one of these on scrap?'

Gryffin takes two steps towards him to close the distance between them and crosses his arms. 'You're cloaking it because I ordered you to.'

Chayse hooks it up and ten minutes later they climb back on the transport. Gryffin takes the helm as Chayse straps down the two containers of weapons they had brought back. Once on *Ares*, Gryffin orders Chayse to pack the guns away and makes his way to his quarters.

He locks the door, turns on his private unit, and sends a message with the coordinates to the ship. To keep Klay quiet he had taken two crates, but that still left a hell of a lot of guns and ammunition. Lucky for him, he knows the perfect home for the rest of the boxes.

∞

Chayse enters the meeting room and hovers by the door, unsure where to sit. Gryffin nods at the seat to his right, which surprises Chayse. He ignores the dirty look from Klay and takes his place.

Chayse had just finished packing the last of the guns away, when he had been summoned by the captain. Chayse never expected that Gryffin would include him in the gun buy. He'd pinched himself all the way to the meeting, but it's real all right. He is in the meeting room beside the captain at his first official briefing.

As the rest of the team take their seats, Gryffin leans over to Chayse, speaking in his ear. 'You're going in with Klay to buy some guns and ammunition. Your job is to watch Klay without letting on you're watching him. If things go bad, don't hesitate to act, or wait for instructions. Use your training and keep your head.'

'Yes, sir. I won't let you or the team down.'

Gryffin nods and turns to face the group. 'Let's get this started.'

Gryffin tries to concentrate on Klay's report for the weapons buy, but he can't stop thinking about what he found on the ship's computer.

He's known Sayber for years — thought he knew him. Not for one minute did he ever think Sayber would work with the Foundation. Like the Nomad, the Hunters tend to stick to their own and avoid alliances. If Sayber is working with them, he mustn't have a choice. He dreads to think what the Foundation have on the Hunter leader.

'Sir? Gryffin, does that work for you?'

Gryffin looks blankly at Klay. Luckily the layout of the bar is still displayed on the wall with the Nomad crew locations clearly marked. He quickly and discreetly examines it before he shakes his head. 'Spread out more. I don't want you concentrated in the same area. How many locals should we expect?' he asks. He hopes Klay didn't already cover that while he wasn't paying attention.

He hides his relief as Klay scans through the reports in front of him to look for the information. 'Three or four dozen in the central bar area. Possibly a dozen more outside.'

'A three-man team outside. Cover the two exits and the path back to the docking bay. Keep the access to the transport clear. Another three-man team with Klay. If it gets messy, I don't want anyone to hold back. The weapons are the priority. Klay, you know what you're doing?'

Klay scrunches his brows. 'But, sir, I thought you were going to meet the Melda brothers yourself?'

Gryffin leans back and shakes his head. 'You have your orders, Klay.'

'With all due respect, sir, the Melda brothers have been talking about raising our prices. You were going to convince them otherwise.'

Gryffin lets a small amount of electricity travel down his arm. 'You have your orders! Now, clear the room!'

The teams file out. Klay is last to get to his feet. He rubs his hands on his trousers, smooths his shirt, nods once, then leaves the room.

Gryffin shuts off his electricity and massages the skin along his ocular implant. He hates watching his men leave *Ares* without him. At times, being captain has its drawbacks. He gets up and watches the transport vessel clear *Ares*'s bay. If all goes to plan, they should be back on board within the hour.

∞

It may be Chayse's first meeting, but he knows one thing: it's not going to plan. What should have taken about ten minutes is heading towards forty. From what he heard on the way here, usually the Melda brothers don't argue about pricing but, for some reason, Klay seems to be getting nowhere.

Chayse leans against the wall outside the small room and adopts a casual stance. Like the rest of the team, he has to appear he is one of the crowd, but also be ready to move if he needs to. He glances around the dark, cramped space, but he can't tell if anyone poses a threat or

307

not. He discreetly turns up the volume on his earpiece. He doubts he'd be able to hear anything over the screeching music. Screens line the wall behind the bar displaying the drink and food menu. Women dressed in skimpy luminous outfits weave through the crowd balancing trays full of drinks, while the mainly male occupants leer at them.

Chayse jumps suddenly as a man lands on the ground in front of him. He looks up to see another man leaning over the railing from the floor above. Another member of Chayse's team gives the all clear from the upper level. It is just a bar brawl.

Chayse looks down at the still unmoving body on the dirt floor in front of him. Maybe just being Gryffin's aide isn't such a bad thing after all.

As he relaxes slightly, one of the alarms goes off outside, at the same time as his communicator in his ear. The team outside has been ambushed. His earpiece buzzes with reports from the different units. It seems all hell has broken out at the station. His heart beats faster with each report of hostile contact.

Klay suddenly bursts out of the room with his weapon raised. He shouts into his radio. 'Fall back!' He turns to Chayse. 'You and your team provide cover until we get the guns out of here.'

Without another word, Klay races up the stairs and disappears out the door. Chayse follows his other team members' example and fires at anyone with a gun pointed at him.

Chayse moves back towards the meeting room as he tries to find cover. He peers around the corner and sees the three brothers lying in blood on the floor. Seems like Klay's negotiations didn't go to plan. Chayse pulls another magazine out of his pocket and tries to reload, but looks up to see one of the Melda security team in front of him. The man smiles as he points his gun at Chayse's head.

∞

'Sir! Captain, don't jump!'

Gryffin ignores his security detail and opens the back hatch on the transport. He leaps from the ramp and lands on the ground about thirty feet below. Gryffin's boots splash through the puddles as he races along the dock. He kicks open the doors to the bar to discover his men embroiled in the middle of a bloody bar fight. Gryffin fights his way through the crowd and locates one of his men being attacked by three of the bar's security personnel. He electrocutes two of the men and shoots the third. Gryffin hauls his man up and pushes him towards the door. 'Fall back now! Get on the transport.'

He doesn't know what the hell went wrong but his people are being targeted and that pisses him off. His earpiece bursts to life again. 'Sir! Where the hell are you?'

'Secure the guns and get out of here.'

'Not without you, sir.'

Gryffin may hate having a security detail, but he can't fault their loyalty. 'I'll be right behind you. I just need to find Chayse.' Protests continue to buzz in his ear, but he ignores them. He scans the moving crowd and finally locates his target.

∞

Chayse is well and truly screwed. He stands up straight and waits for the shot, but it never comes. The man in front of him convulses as electricity ripples over his body. A few seconds later, he falls to the dusty ground in a heap. Chayse looks up from the body and releases the breath he was holding as Gryffin steps out of the crowd with electricity running down his arm.

Before Chayse can thank him, Gryffin gestures to the stairs. 'Stick close and shoot to kill.' Gryffin clears most of the path using his arm while Chayse tries to stay alive and not get in the way. Chayse jumps over various bodies and follows Gryffin up the stairs to the upper floor. He reaches the top of the stairs behind his captain and leans over the railings to survey the carnage below. Gryffin throws a man over the railing and pulls open the door to the transport bays. As soon as the door opens, Gryffin takes out the man on the other side while Chayse holds back the team coming up the stairs behind them.

Chayse follows Gryffin into the large warehouse behind the bar and reaches the rest of the Nomad team as they secure the last crate.

'Where the hell is Klay?' Gryffin shouts.

'He took the first shipment of guns in the Melda brothers' transport.'

Chayse glances sideways at his captain and feels a pang of sympathy for Klay. Gryffin's nostrils flare and he bares his teeth at the news, which doesn't bode well for Klay. If there's one thing Gryffin believes in more than anything else, it's that you never leave anyone behind.

'Let's get the hell out of here,' Gryffin replies through clenched teeth.

Chayse manages to hold back a sigh of relief. He might just survive his first trade. The sound of gunfire quashes his short-lived relief. Gryffin stands at the entrance of the passageway to hold back the approaching attackers. 'Get those guns out of here.'

'Not without you, sir,' one of his security team shouts.

'Get the guns out of here. Go!'

Chayse watches in despair as the transports take-off to leave them stranded. 'What, now, sir?'

'Hold them back long enough for the transports to get away.'

Gryffin continues to fire as Chayse reloads his gun. It suddenly becomes apparent to Chayse why the captain comes back battered and bruised. If all trades went like this, he's surprised anyone survives.

The rotten wooden walls of the building vibrate. Chayse looks at Gryffin, but he also appears to be at a loss. 'What is that?'

Gryffin shakes his head. 'I don't know. It's not one of ours. Don't think we should stick around to find out.' He pushes Chayse down the corridor in front of him while he continues to fire behind them. The building shakes again as a transport flies overhead. Gryffin grabs Chayse by the back of his jacket and launches the two of them out of the window. They crash through the glass as a massive explosion destroys the warehouse.

∞

Gryffin opens his eyes and blinks a few times. White fluffy clouds drift across his field of vision. Strange. He can't remember being outside. Gryffin decides to enjoy the peace instead of worrying about how he got there. He frowns as plumes of black smoke obscure his view. He turns his head to face a smoking ruin and it all comes back to him with a painful thump.

He was blown up.

Gryffin does a quick mental assessment but feels pretty good for someone who flew out the window.

He tries to sit up but something heavy presses down on him and pins him to the ground. Dirty blonde spikes of hair greet him when he finally raises his head. Chayse is lying on top of him. At least he broke Chayse's fall. He checks for a pulse and breathes a sigh of relief when he feels the steady beat under his fingers. 'Chayse, can you hear me?'

Chayse slowly opens his eyes. The confusion on his face melts to embarrassment when he realises where he is. 'Sir? You okay?'

Gryffin can't help but smile. Chayse gets thrown from a building and his first concern is his captain. 'I'm okay. You?'

Chayse groans and closes his eyes again. 'I have a feeling it's going to hurt tomorrow, sir.'

'Can you get off me now?'

'Sorry, sir.' Chayse gets to his feet and Gryffin pulls himself up. He turns around and studies the wreckage. 'Go to the secondary rendezvous point. Whoever did this could come back.'

Gryffin climbs over the smouldering pieces of timber and makes his way back towards the site. He needs to find out who attacked them. He tries his earpiece but it crackles with static. Hopefully, the transports got back to *Ares* in one piece. He scans the debris and something catches his eye. He digs it out from under the mud and gets a better look. The explosion tore the metal, but there's no mistaking it as part of the outer casing of a missile. Some rubble dislodges behind him. 'We'll have to work on the whole obeying orders part, Chayse.'

Chayse falters for a moment. 'As the captain, you're meant to have at least one, if not two, security personnel with you when off the ship. I'm all you've got ... sir.'

Not much he can say. Chayse is right; that's what Nomad rules state. Gryffin scans the trees and climbs higher over the rubble. 'Smoke about a mile to the east. Could be one of ours.' Gryffin holds a hand up to silence any reply. 'They're coming back. Move! Get under cover.'

Chayse follows him into the thick trees but struggles to keep up. A high pitched shriek cuts through the undergrowth, moving towards them. Gryffin grabs him and pushes him to the ground. The captain crouches over him as the missile flies overhead and hits the warehouse again. 'Sir, you need to get out of here.'

'Shut up. They're scanning the area. Don't move.' Chayse freezes. Gryffin looks up through the tree canopy and hopes his implants will hide them both.

It works. The ship passes overhead and flies in the opposite direction. Gryffin holds out his metal hand to help Chayse up. 'What now, sir?'

'Check out the smoke. If I order you to leave, you going to go or disobey me again?'

'I'm not leaving, sir.'

Gryffin curses and turns away. After a few steps, he stops and looks over his shoulder. 'What the hell are you waiting for? Move!'

41

'They're all dead.'

Chayse looks down at the three bodies in front of Gryffin. Bodies of crew he had been on the transport with only an hour ago. From the burnt remains of the ship, it is clear that they were the victims of a missile — the same type that destroyed the warehouse. He only hopes they had a quick death.

Gryffin straightens from his crouching position next to the remains of the crew. He had dragged each one out of the wreckage, but he couldn't save them. Gryffin suddenly curses and slams his fist into the bulkhead again and again. Chayse turns away to give him privacy.

Chayse is all too aware the attackers could come back any minute, so quickly searches the site for the guns. He crawls inside and shoves debris out of the way in his search. Finally, he locates them under a piece of the transport side. He crawls back out to report to Gryffin, but freezes when something moves in the bushes to his left. Chayse pulls his gun out and directs it towards the area. Gryffin silently joins him with his weapon pointed in the same direction.

The captain's purple eyes scan their surroundings. 'I count at least four.'

As he finishes speaking, the silence erupts in gunfire. Chayse and Gryffin throw themselves behind the charred remains of the transport and return fire. Chayse's heart beats in time to the guns. He can't believe this is happening to them again. Their attackers clearly want them dead. They're not pausing for even a moment. Chayse unclips another magazine from his belt and reloads while the captain continues to hold the attackers back.

'Can you get the radio working?' Gryffin asks.

Chayse ducks as a round whizzes over his head. He looks through the remains of the window. 'The unit seems more or less intact. I should be able to, sir.'

'I'll draw their fire. Think we need a rescue.'

'Can you not blast them all?'

Gryffin looks at him over his shoulder and snorts before he turns his attention back to the forest around them. 'I blast them, I blast you too. Besides, if it doesn't work, you'll have to fight them off and carry your unconscious captain back to the ship. Send the message.'

Chayse takes his lead from Gryffin. He waits until Gryffin draws their fire, then runs around the back of the ship. He tries to keep his mind on the task and ignore the fire fight going on outside. He climbs over the seats and pulls himself into the cockpit. On closer inspection, the unit has taken a bigger knock than he thought. He won't be able to receive any transmissions. Hopefully, that won't matter. They only need *Ares* to hear the message. He hits the send button and glances up in time to see a man enter the back of the transport.

∞

Gryffin ducks behind the transport and loads another magazine into his gun. Through the gunfire, he hears Chayse send the distress call. They just need to stay alive long enough for *Ares* to get here.

He empties another clip and takes out one of the men but, with them hiding in the trees, even his heightened vision can't help much. If they're to have any chance, he needs to get the attackers out in the open.

He glances in at Chayse and curses when he sees a man about to shoot him. Gryffin jumps out and fires towards the trees as he targets the other man with his arm. His aim is true and the man falls to the ground as electricity courses through his dying body. 'Chayse?'

'Sir, behind you!'

Gryffin turns and faces twelve men. Looks like he walked into that one. A man from the back pushes through the others and stops in front of him. The artificial eye in the centre of the metal plate on his face shines a dark red colour.

'I see by your face you've noticed the similarities, *Thirty-Five*.'

Gryffin falters for a moment and a sudden coldness snakes through his body. He hasn't been called that for nineteen years. 'Who the hell are you?'

The man gestures at one of his colleagues, who drags Chayse out of the transport. Gryffin curses himself. He took his eye off the ball again and now Chayse is involved. 'I'm *Forty-Three*. From my designation, you can tell I'm a newer model.' Two men join him, each one with an artificial eye. 'These are two of my brothers.'

Gryffin can't make sense of any of this. He should focus on trying to get Chayse and the guns to safety, but his brain won't work. Flashes of his past invade his head to pull him away from the here and now. His mind drags him back to the lab and locks him in chains again. *Forty-Three* saunters closer to him with a satisfied smile on his face. 'Reminiscing, brother?'

For some reason, *Forty-Three* calling him brother pulls him back into the present. 'I'm not your brother.'

'In a sense you are. We all have the same creator — same father if you will — so, we are brothers.'

In that instant, Gryffin knows the man in front of him hasn't been sane for a long time. Anyone who can label the Scientist as a father figure is as messed up as anyone can get. 'You killed my men?'

'We fired a missile at their ship. That may have resulted in their deaths when the ship crashed.'

'You expect me not to retaliate?'

Forty-Three smiles. 'We're counting on it.' He moves closer to Chayse along with his two "brothers." 'He dies unless you duel.'

He pushes Chayse towards the rest of the group. The nine men stand in a circle around them with Gryffin and the three modified men in the centre.

A thousand questions fly through his head, but he doubts any of the men will give him a straight answer. 'So, I have to win to get my crew back?'

'You will not win.' One of the brothers removes his jacket and steps up to him. With no other choice, Gryffin pulls off his coat and throws it to the ground. He could use his arm to take them all out, but it looks like the brothers have planned for that. All nine of the remaining men have their guns pointed at or pressed against Chayse's head. If one of them manages to pull the trigger before getting completely knocked out, Chayse will die.

The man in front of Gryffin swings out and strikes him square in the jaw before he can react. A second blow quickly follows the first, which drives the air from his lungs. It seems he has more in common with them than he hoped. The other man's reflexes match his own. He needs to get the upper hand, so returns the favour. Instead of knocking him to the ground, the man remains on his feet with a stupid smile on his face. Gryffin growls and stops playing nice. He puts all his strength behind his next blow and aims for the man's artificial eye. His mechanical fist clashes with the metal plating over the man's eye. The other man screams in pain and falls back with his hand pressed to his face. Without waiting for him to recover, Gryffin grabs his head, pulls him over, and drives his knee into the other man's chest. When he hears the satisfying sound of a rib or two breaking, he lifts him up and throws him against the side of the transport.

He turns to face *Forty-Three*, who looks at his fallen comrade with a blank expression on his face. 'You next or your friend?'

'You have an interesting technique, if you could call it that. I believe you can also conduct electricity along your arm.' He gestures to his other brother. 'Use that during the next duel.'

Gryffin has been through enough tests to know what this is. They want to see exactly what he can do. 'I'm not playing this game anymore. Let my man go.'

'Outnumbered and away from any assistance, yet you still make demands.'

'Bad habit I guess.'

It's then he hears her. *Ares* is moving in their direction, fast. Caught unawares, the men surrounding Chayse fall to the ground as covering fire hits them from the ridge behind. *Ares'* powerful engines carry her over the hill as the crew try to take out the other men. Chayse uses the distraction to relieve one of them of his gun and takes down a few more in the process.

'Get the bodies on board.' Gryffin shouts to Chayse over the engines. He leaves Chayse to secure the remains and he targets the modified men again but the cowards use the accompanying humans as shields. Under *Forty-Three*'s orders, the human shield runs towards him. With little choice, he fights back. He breaks the first man's neck then grabs the second by the shirt and throws him against the side of the transport. He kicks the third in the chest and slams him and his freshly broken ribs against the craft. The man lands on the ground next to his companion. Gryffin hopes the rest of them will get the message and back off, but the idiots keep coming. Instead of one at a time, they rush at him. He curses their stupidity as he charges his arm and tries to get a shot off, but they're too close. All too quickly he is crowded while they hit, punch, and kick him.

Gryffin is getting irritated. 'Is everyone clear?' he shouts into his radio. Over the shouting, he hears an affirmative response. He closes his eyes and ignores the attacking crowd. He pulls the power back into his body and sends it all out his arm in one blast. The crowd flies off the ground and lands about twenty feet away from Gryffin.

He rises to his feet and picks up his gun. He has about five minutes to get back to *Ares* before the exertion from releasing so much power catches up with him. He puts a bullet in anyone still alive, then looks up at *Ares* above him. Chayse is leaning over the edge with a shocked expression on his face, but Gryffin ignores him. He takes hold of the bottom rung of the metal rope ladder and signals for the ship to leave.

As *Ares* turns around, her thrusters part the trees when she passes. Before she accelerates, he catches a glimpse of three men smiling up at him through the trees. Something cold settles in the pit of his stomach. He has a horrible feeling he just played right into their hands with his little display.

42

'Didn't go well then, sir.'

Gryffin winces as Klay digs around in the wound. The last ten minutes were spent trying to locate and remove dozens of splinters. He had been unconscious for an hour, which was a hell of a lot shorter than usual. The downside is Klay hadn't finished patching him up before he came to. 'What happened during the buy?'

Klay rinses the tweezers in a bowl of water. 'They wanted more money. I had no choice but to kill them to get the weapons.'

'You left crew behind to save yourself.'

Klay drops the tweezers. 'You ordered me to get the weapons — they were my priority. I removed them from the warehouse in the Melda's transport. I purposely didn't take ours so everyone would be able to get out.' Klay pulls a suture pack from the drawer next to him and tears it open. 'If we didn't get the guns, we'd be screwed, sir.'

Gryffin teases the last large splinter from his arm. Klay has a point. Technically, he did nothing wrong. He winces as Klay begins to stitch one of the more extensive wounds. Chayse had been seen to first and received five stitches where a piece of wood had cut into his side. Gryffin ignores the pull of the thread through his skin and focuses on the rest of the shrapnel. Being thrown from the building was bad enough without the addition of the dozens of wooden splinters to the mix. For once he'd like to come back from a job, take a long hot shower, and go to bed. No questions. No tests. And no stitches.

'Sir,' Klay says, interrupting his thoughts. 'I didn't know this would happen. I knew we couldn't trust the Melda brothers but I never thought they'd betray us.'

Gryffin sits up in bed and pushes Klay aside. He's had enough of being stuck with a needle. The fact he's acting like a spoilt child doesn't escape his attention. With everything going on, he deserves at least one lapse. 'It's your job to know. If you weren't sure, you should never have arranged the meet.'

Klay looks down at the bowl of bloody water. 'Yes, sir.'

Gryffin's eyes narrow. 'And you knew nothing about the ambush when it was taking place?'

'I didn't know anything until I got back with the weapons.'

So much for the monitoring device behind his ear. His heart rate would have undoubtedly gone up during the explosion, especially after he flew out of the window. 'Any sign of the other ship?'

'Gone.'

'Three of them had implants.'

Klay frowns. 'What do you mean they had implants?'

'What bit didn't you get? They had implants. The one I fought matched my strength.'

Klay puts a dressing over the stitches. 'But you beat him — literally.'

Gryffin shakes his head. 'He let me win.'

'You sure?'

'He winded me. That took a fair bit of strength. There's no way I should have been able to take him down so fast. The whole thing was a test.'

Klay leans back on the table and crosses his arms. 'Test for what?'

'I don't know. I want the bodies of our men prepared for burial once we get away from this planet. We give them a proper send-off later today.'

'Sir.' Klay glances at Chayse before he leaves the room.

Gryffin gets back to the smaller splinters but can't concentrate. Chayse should be writing his report, but every minute or so Chayse stops and looks at him. After another few minutes, Gryffin can't ignore it any longer. 'What?'

'Sir?'

'You keep looking strangely at me. You either want to say something or you're interested in me. I sure as hell hope it's the first one.'

'Sir, about what that man said on the surface... When he called you *Thirty-Five*?'

Gryffin freezes with the tweezers in a wound before he forces himself to continue in silence. There's no way he's going to go there with Chayse. But, as usual, his aide doesn't know when to shut up.

'I mean, I've seen the brand on the back of your shoulder.'

Gryffin slams the tweezers down on the table and locks on to Chayse with purple eyes. 'You don't ask me about that again. Do you understand?'

'Yes, sir. I was just—'

'Just what? You're my aide, not my friend or counsellor. If you can't stick to your damn role, there's no place for you on my ship. Now get the hell out of here!'

He doesn't need Gryffin to tell him twice. Chayse quickly gathers his things and leaves Gryffin alone to curse his actions. Chayse didn't deserve that. This whole situation has completely thrown him off. He always assumed he was the only survivor of the project. The rest of the children taken with him are dead. He remembers each and every death like it was only yesterday. The guilt at being the only survivor eats away at him daily.

These new men must have been at another location. He's pretty much been all over the Sector and he's never seen or heard of anyone else like him. Had many more survived? He rubs his bruised ribs and grimaces. He sure as hell hopes not.

∞

'You confronted him?' Balfe roars at the modified men in front of him. 'What the hell did you do that for? I gave you specific instructions to destroy his transports from the air, not get up close and personal.'

'I wanted to see how his development had progressed,' the Scientist replies from behind him.

Balfe spins quickly, stunned the Scientist was able to sneak up on him. 'You told them to do this?'

The Scientist sits down at his terminal and places his hands on his knees. 'I'm a little surprised you did not instruct them to do it. The man you seem so eager to capture bears no comparison to the prototype I designed.'

'Hang on a second. I thought you knew him inside out.'

'Perhaps literally, yes. Consider this.' The Scientist sits back in his chair and pushes his glasses up with his middle finger. 'The prototype has been continuously using the modifications I made for twenty years. We already know he can conduct electricity along his arm — something I did not design. What else can he do? Unless we know now, we can't hope to contain him successfully.'

Balfe has to concede. They would waste years of work and a substantial quantity of money if they captured him only for him to escape again. 'Very well. What did you learn?'

The Scientist gets up and walks towards the main operating table. One of the men from the prison lies unconscious on top of it. From the looks of it, he suffered quite a beating. Even his artificial eye looks damaged. '*Thirty-Five* did this without much exertion and without

322

using his electricity.' The Scientist smiles and clasps his hands together. 'It's quite impressive. It appears the machine and the man have learned to work in complete symbiosis. Each part enhances the other, which makes him quite a formidable opponent. I cannot wait to study him.'

Balfe grimaces. He knows full well what the man means by *study*. 'Yes, well, once his task is completed, feel free to do as you please. As long as you can duplicate the work, I don't really care how you study him. Are you confident you can hold him?'

'Yes.' He nods towards the screen in front of him. 'We will have to use a stronger metal in the chains. It may also take a bit more effort to weaken his body. We may have to get creative.'

∞

'I hear the gun buy went well.'

Gryffin does a double take. He must have misheard Rayde. 'You're joking, right?' *Well* doesn't even show up on the list of words he'd use. It was a complete balls-up.

'Well, no. You got most of the weapons. I'd call that going well.'

'We lost three crew,' Gryffin replies. 'Then I get blown up. I'd call that a bloody disaster.'

Rayde shrugs. 'It's unfortunate we sustained losses, but they knew the risk when they joined *Ares*. They died with honour.'

'Honour? They died at a weapons buy. We weren't saving a colony or fighting a war.'

Rayde leans back in his chair and places his hands behind his head. 'This is war, Gryffin. You need to accept what's going on — in this Sector, and with you. Things are getting worse for us, surely you must see that. When you took over command things improved — I'm not denying that — but you have to admit it's not working anymore. With Sayber's group, the arrival of the Foundation and the mysterious attacks, we're under more pressure. As a group, we're not powerful enough to stay independent.'

Rayde has never spoken of joining the Nomad with anyone. The Nomad operate independently of everyone else. As long as he holds the high commander role, it will stay that way. 'Not happening.'

'Then we should think about doing things like we used to.'

Gryffin drops his hands to his sides. 'You mean randomly steal and kill again?'

'I know it's a bit severe, but at least it would show that the Nomad mean business.'

Gryffin stands up and walks up to the screen. 'With all due respect, sir, I think you're out of your mind.'

Rayde's eyes turn cold and harsh. 'Watch your tone, Gryffin. I'm trying to help you. I'm attempting to save you before someone kills you. People aren't afraid to come after you anymore. What happened today proves this. That wouldn't have happened a few years ago. You wouldn't have let it happen.'

'So you're saying I've gone soft. That I should have ordered Klay to blow the place up. Kill everyone for the sake of it?'

Rayde runs his hands through his hair and snorts. 'No, of course I don't think that. I'm saying the trading has helped us prosper, but it's killing our reputation. It's killing *your* reputation. People feared you, Gryffin. No one would even chance crossing you because they knew you'd come after and kill them. No longer, though.'

Gryffin steps back from the screen as the electricity crackles along his arm. 'There's more to us than having people fear us — fear me. We deserve better than to always watch our backs. Our people didn't work this hard to get out of the gutter, just to put ourselves back there again. You fought alongside me for this. What's changed?'

Rayde shrugs. 'Your priorities, for one. I'm offering an alternative to the group I spent years building up, being wiped out without a fight. It's you who needs to sort out your priorities.' Gryffin stands his ground as Rayde rises from his seat to look down at his screen. 'Nomad or the colonies. You can't have both.'

'We will not turn back into petty thieves and thugs.' He moves up close to the screen, almost touching it with his nose. 'Final decision.'

Rayde nods and ends the transmission without another word. As soon as Rayde disappears from the screen, Gryffin curses loudly and propels his fist towards the wall. He doesn't need to add fighting with his mentor to his list of problems. It isn't even Rayde questioning his decisions that annoys him the most. It's the fact he may have a point.

Years ago they did have a reputation among the Nomad group and he knows it developed due to the way Rayde did things. While he didn't regret anything he'd done under his captain's command, the idea of starting it all up again left him more than a little conflicted.

He reaches into his pocket and pulls out the piece of shrapnel. He turns it over in his hand, rubbing his thumb along the faint numbers carved into the side. It's only four digits, but it tells him the weapon that blew them up belonged to the Nomad at some stage. It's not from *Ares*, but that gives him little comfort. Before he jumps to conclusions, he'll get Chayse to check if any ships have lost a missile. He doesn't want to think about the alternative.

43

Aleena sips her water as she looks around the room of delegates. The leaders from the six worlds neighbouring Ultar have gathered at the request of Nera, the leader of Maylar, the smallest of the six worlds. She has a fair idea why Nera called this meeting.

Things have reached a critical point in the Sector and colonists feared for their safety — with good reason. While she would have preferred the meeting to take place from the comfort of her office, some of the other leaders thought the Foundation may intercept any communications. Aleena doubts the Foundation would be interested in small talk about trades and long range weather, but had agreed to this in-person meeting nonetheless.

A young woman places a glass of wine on the table in front of Aleena and moves to the delegate next to her. Nera is certainly pulling out all the stops for this meeting. The large conference room fills the upper floor of the town hall. Ornately carved wooden beams support the walls and soar into the double height ceiling. Various animal busts hang over the enormous stone fireplace and thick pelts line the floor.

It is a beautiful, if not somewhat intimidating room. She has no doubt that is exactly Nera's intention.

Nera interrupts her train of thought when he clears his throat and stands up to address the room. 'Thank you for meeting with us, Aleena.'

She immediately feels uneasy. 'Us?' She makes eye contact with the other four people around the table. 'It appears I am somewhat at a disadvantage. I presumed you wanted to discuss something with the five of us.'

'I apologise for bringing you here under false pretences but I had little choice.' He gestures towards the other delegates. 'I have met with the others numerous times over the recent weeks about how best to proceed, and we now feel it is time to speak to you.'

The looks that pass between the occupants of the room do not go unnoticed by Aleena. They appear almost afraid. The strange part is the fear appears directed at her. 'I do not appreciate being deceived. Explain yourself, Nera.'

'We have called you here today to tell you we have decided to pull out of our agreements with the Nomad and would like you to do the same.'

She tries to keep the anger and shock from her face and voice. 'So you have all reached this understanding?' One by one the other leaders nod in agreement.

'It is the right thing to do, Aleena,' another delegate, Aron, replies.

Aleena takes a breath to steady her growing irritation. 'I must ask why you would make such a decision.'

'Surely it cannot surprise you,' Nera says. 'You must have heard of all the trouble lately. Gryffin's men are attacking their colonies. It is only a matter of time before they do the same to us.'

'Oh, come now, Nera. You do not believe these attacks have anything to do with Gryffin?'

'Of course I do. We all do,' Nera says.

The delegate opposite her, Reba, clasps her hands on the table in front of her. 'Aleena, I have spoken to people who have witnessed the attacks first hand. The men wear his symbol on their arm. They fight like his Nomad. I am as shocked as you are, but it is him.'

Aleena stands up and slowly walks around the room. She looks at each of the occupants in turn, but takes no pleasure from the way they all shrink away when she passes them. 'So you plan to pull out of the agreement? Very well. What do you intend to do after that? What plan have you devised? How do you expect to look after yourself without any weapons or ships? I do not think you have thought this through.'

'As a matter of fact, we have,' Aron argues. 'We have had talks recently with the Foundation. They offer a more secure alternative.'

Aleena shakes her head and stares openly at each of the other leaders. 'You cannot be serious! How can you even consider joining with them? They will take your independence along with their fee.'

'At least we will not be living in fear of being attacked by the very person we are paying to protect us.'

Things appear worse than she thought. She doubts she will be able to change their minds. 'Have you actually seen him lead any of these attacks? Has anyone else seen him?' The room falls silent, which only serves to confirm her suspicions. 'As I thought. Does that not strike you as strange? Have you ever known Gryffin to stay away from a fight — any fight? We are all aware how he operates. If something needs to be done, he will usually do it personally. He would never send a team anywhere without leading them himself.'

Nera remains quiet as he gets up to stand in front of Aleena. 'That may be true, but we cannot take any chances. Surely you cannot be blind to the shift in the balance of power. We must do everything we can to survive however we can. With the Foundation, we will receive protection against the Nomad and any other groups that could threaten us.'

'Look at what all of you have gained by being partnered with Gryffin. You have grown wealthy with his help. Your trading partners stretch throughout the Sector.' She gestures out the window at the bustling town centre, filled with stalls selling a broad range of items from cloth to food to furniture. 'You would have none of this if not for the Nomad.'

'So we remain in his debt forever? Allow him to kill us one by one if he chooses? He has gained too much power, is too feared. We need someone in the Sector with enough power to stand up to him. Surely you know of the other side to the Nomad? They line their pockets by hiring themselves — more usually Gryffin — out as hired killers. Perhaps it is time he answered to someone.'

She turns to face Nera quickly and a cold chill runs up her spine at his calm demeanour. 'What do you mean?'

'There is a condition to our agreement. We must arrest Gryffin the next time he steps onto the surface of any of our colonies.'

The cold chill quickly turns to a firm feeling of dread. Nera, Aron, Reba, Ward, and Cal honestly think they can survive trying to arrest Gryffin. She wants to laugh out loud at the suggestion, but their faces tell her they are entirely serious. She turns to address the whole room.

'Friends, please tell me you are not going to do that. You know he will kill you if you try to capture him. Have no doubts about that. And even if you do manage to arrest him, his crew will get him back. Many of your people will suffer as a result. For what? To sign an alliance with a group so rigid in its structure they assign jobs to people they cannot alter? They dictate how many children they can have and where they may live. Surely you must see, as soon as you sign the contract, they will do the same to your people.'

'The decision is already made,' Ward announces. 'We are due to sign within the coming days.'

Cal leans back in his chair and crosses his arms. 'Are you sure it is wise to exclude Ultar from this?'

'Is that a threat, Cal?'

Nera knocks on the table to draw her attention from Cal. 'Aleena, please. We are not here to threaten you. Do not let your personal feelings get in the way of you making the correct decision. You will not help your people by staying, out of a misguided sense of loyalty to him. You're the leader of the colony, Aleena, not a Nomad. Perhaps it is you who needs to think carefully about the future of your colony. Do you really believe he will come to your rescue? From what I hear, he is the very person you need protection from. Do not let your people suffer because of your inappropriate feelings for Gryffin.'

She bites back a sharp retort and takes a breath to calm herself. It would do her no favours to show emotion after such a statement. It would play into Nera's hands. It is no surprise he brought up her having feelings for Gryffin. They found it hard to understand why *Ares* spent so much time on Ultar compared to the other colonies.

Their tiny minds could not come up with any explanation other than a sordid relationship with her and the Nomad captain. Quite pathetic, really. 'My reasons for staying with Gryffin have not changed. He offers the best protection and trading terms of any of the groups. I believe you are making a mistake getting into bed with the Foundation, but it is your decision. I can assure you Ultar will stay independent.' She turns on her heel and leaves the room.

∞

Gryffin locks his office door and unscrews a panel from the wall behind his desk. He removes the small console from the space and powers it up. After making sure to engage the guards so no one can see or hear what he's doing, he opens the channel and waits for Aleena to respond.

After a tense few minutes, her face appears on the screen. 'I heard about the explosion. Is everything all right?'

'I lost three men. Bad few days.'

'I am afraid I have to add to the bad news. I have returned from a meeting about you.'

'Should I be flattered or worried?'

'I am afraid it is not good. Colonies are losing faith in your abilities.

They fear you may pose a bigger threat than the Foundation or even Sayber.'

He doesn't know what to say. If people are willing to side with the Foundation or Sayber as opposed to him, it isn't good. Not that he can fully blame them. No doubt word of what happened with the buy is already out. No leader in their right mind will trust the safety of their colony to someone who attracts that much trouble. It's too much of a risk. 'How many?'

'After today's meeting, a total of twelve colonies will back out.'

'Great.' He tries to massage the building headache away without success. 'Did you salvage the ship?'

'Yes. Thank you. We will utilise what we can. The weapons were an unexpected but welcome gift.'

'You can thank the late Melda brothers for that.'

Aleena shakes her head. 'No honour among criminals. Can I presume you repaid them for their good deed?'

'Things coming along?' The last thing he wants to do is get into another moral debate with her over how he does things.

She pauses for a moment but moves on instead of pushing her point. 'Slow, but we are making progress. We do need more funds, however. What you have given has been used for the last shipment. I hate to ask, but we will struggle over the coming week if we do not have anything to spend.'

'Damn it.' He paces in front of the screen. 'What did you spend the last lot on?'

'As agreed, I will not discuss it with you. You have promised your full support and that is what I am asking for.'

Gryffin grits his teeth before he finally nods his head. 'Salvage the ship and sell what you can.'

'That will not be sufficient.'

'Fine. I'll line up a few contracts.'

'Can you not earn money by other means?'

'You can't have it both ways, Aleena. You need money; I need to

331

work to get it.' He changes the subject before an argument breaks out. 'I hooked up to the Hunter ship. I found a message from Balfe to Sayber.'

'Balfe?'

'He's the admiral I remember from the experiment.'

Aleena nods slowly. 'So you found proof the Foundation are behind the attacks. Are you going to approach them?'

'No. I lied about what I found. I told Chayse I couldn't access the information before the system corrupted it.'

'That is not like you. Why did you feel it necessary to deceive him?'

The very question he doesn't want to answer. He has spent all the life he remembers with the Nomad. For two decades, he's trusted them, no question. But since all this started, he's not sure anymore. 'I don't know who to trust, apart from you.'

'Chayse would not betray you.'

'Yeah, well I can't risk Klay finding out. He lives in Rayde's back pocket. If Klay gets wind of this, he'll go straight to Rayde. Rayde will want me to act. If other Nomad hear I did nothing, they'll lose faith in me.'

Aleena nods. 'You did what you felt necessary. This new information will put increased pressure on us.'

'I know.' He leans against the wall, suddenly feeling weary. 'I also met three men with similar eye implants.'

Aleena leans closer to the screen. 'Did you recognise them?'

He shakes his head. 'The leader had a higher number designation than I had. I have the horrible feeling they modified him after the station blew up.'

'So the project continued. Quite unsettling.'

'How long until you're ready?'

'Weeks at the earliest. You fear they will capture you?'

He shrugs. 'Either way, you need to finish. I could turn into a pretty big threat soon.'

'What about reproducing what they did to you? Is that possible quickly?'

Gryffin leans heavily against the wall. 'I doubt it. They tried after I survived the surgery. It didn't work. They wouldn't go to all this trouble if they sorted out the problem in the meantime. Once they capture me, it'll take them some time to figure out what to do.'

'What will they have to do to figure it out, as you say?'

'All we need to focus on is what to do after they have me.' The last distraction he needs right now is to think about being pulled apart again.

The fact he evades the question does not escape Aleena's attention, but she has the sense not to push him. 'That means you have to do your bit as soon as possible.'

'There's time enough yet.'

'Cease stalling, Gryffin. If the Foundation get to you before you do what you need to, everything we have worked so hard for will be for nothing. It will take you three days to get to Ultar. You will not get a better time. Why must you delay?'

He scratches the raised skin on his cheek next to his implant. 'I don't want to mess up another life.'

'I understand, but you do not have a choice. How will you do it?'

'I'll plant incriminating data on the system. It'll speed up the process.'

'Are you sure it is wise to link to another ship so soon?'

'Quit worrying. Focus on what you have to do.'

'This is getting serious, Gryffin. Someone has to go from your crew. Time is running out.'

'Don't you think I already know that?' he snaps. 'You'll have your money in a week or so.' He ends the conversation by slamming his fist against the panel to shut down the screen.

Looks like this week is going from bad to worse.

44

'Sir, I need Lieutenant Rush on board. I can't send her off on a holiday.'

Balfe moves closer to the screen. 'This is a crucial time for us, Roman. By acquiring Ultar, we can tip the balance in the Sector. The task of convincing that farming colony to align is proving harder than we thought. The leader believes she is above Foundation assistance.'

Roman resists the urge to defend Aleena. 'I don't see how sending Terra to Ultar can help sway her in our direction.'

'She's been trained in negotiations like everyone else.'

'But why her? There are other people.' He could hardly tell Balfe that Terra had been less than successful while trying to negotiate with Gryffin previously.

'She's young and enthusiastic. If you're so worried about her, send someone with her. To be honest, I don't care. Make sure she's on the surface by the end of the week. She's to do whatever she needs to. Just make sure Ultar signs up to Foundation control.'

Roman signs off and pours himself a strong cup of coffee. He remembers the conversation with Aleena while on the surface. She made it more than clear the planet is independent. Convincing her otherwise will be a hard, if not impossible, task. Also, if the Nomad find out about Terra touting for business, she'll be in trouble. What if Gryffin himself showed up? He knows without a doubt that she will easily forget her task if his son turns up.

Roman curses his slip up and empties his cup. He has to stop thinking of Gryffin as his son if he is going to get through this. With no other choice, he calls Terra and Stanner to his office. If she has to go, she will be going with back-up.

∞

'What's this?' Gryffin asks when Klay hands him a computer pad.

Klay shuts the door to Gryffin's office. 'Sir, I've been analysing the data from the series of tests Rayde requested.'

Gryffin forces himself not to look at Klay. He doesn't want to show how much he resents being discussed like any other piece of machinery on the ship. The fact Rayde felt he had to request these tests doesn't help ease the feeling.

Klay continues when he realises Gryffin isn't going to acknowledge him. 'Sir, I hate doing this, but I have no choice.'

'Sounds ominous.'

'I've compared the results of the tests I've been running with the latest series and something has shown up.'

Gryffin manages to keep his poker face firmly in place as he gestures for him to continue. 'Drawing it out isn't helping my mood.'

'What I'm having difficulty saying is someone has been altering the programming for your implants.'

Gryffin finally turns away from his screen to face Klay. 'You got a name?'

'Sir, it's Chayse.'

Gryffin fakes a surprised look. He looks up at Klay and notices a faint smile before he composes himself. Seems the commander is enjoying this a bit too much. 'You'd better be sure before you make allegations.'

Klay points to the information. 'From what I can see he's made adjustments without my knowledge. Sir, it may have caused some of the issues you've been suffering from.'

'I need to check this first. You're dismissed.'

'What do you want to do, sir?'

Gryffin stands up and walks around his desk. 'I'm going to check your data and if it's true, I'll deal with him.'

'There's no need, sir. I'll see to it if necessary.'

'No. I'm the one he's screwed with. I'll sort him out — if what you say is true.' Gryffin ignores the smile on Klay's face. 'How are we doing for supplies?'

Klay shakes his head. 'Not good. We urgently need to restock. We've probably only got a week left. Ultar is the only colony near our location where we're still welcome. Thanks to all the attacks, we've been blacklisted everywhere else.'

With his part done, Gryffin nods. 'Contact Aleena to make sure.'

Gryffin waits for Klay to leave the room before he slowly goes back to his seat and drops down heavily onto it. He can't believe he's kicking Chayse off the ship. Being charged with trying to harm the captain isn't the career path he expected for Chayse. He doesn't have a choice, however. Aleena needs Chayse on Ultar and that is more important at the moment.

Since Chayse joined the Nomad, he's been nothing but loyal to him, eager to integrate into the crew and serve the Nomad the best he can. Gryffin knows life hasn't been easy for the young aide aboard *Ares*. Klay went out of his way to make things difficult for him and the rest of the crew don't trust him. They think Chayse will run back to him and report if he hears anything negative about him.

Gryffin could have ordered Klay and the crew to back off but it is part of ship life. That reaction went hand in hand with his role.

Helped make Chayse a stronger person; a better Nomad. Gryffin has seen the difference in him over the last few weeks.

Resigned to the fact it's not going to end well for Chayse, he takes out a cable from his desk and hooks it into the module. He attaches the lead to the edge of his ocular implant. The data from the pad flies through his vision and makes his stomach roll. After a bit of concentration, he slows the connection down to give himself a chance to decipher it. Knowing Klay, he'll run and tell Rayde. The least he could do was check Klay hadn't pinned anything else on Chayse.

A few minutes later, he detaches himself from the module. Everything in the report reads exactly as he had left it. Klay probably couldn't believe his luck. The data Gryffin had added was all he needed. He lowers himself to the ground and places his head in his hands. Dark patches leak into the edges of his vision as the ocular implant recovers from the assault of data. He can only slouch against the wall as the inky blackness settles to block out his vision.

Gryffin puts a hand on the rough metal floor at either side of him to ground himself. He slows his breathing down and concentrates on the familiar sounds of *Ares*; the groan of the metal, the sound of footsteps on the gantry, the hum of the engines.

With nothing to do but wait, he closes his eyes and focuses on the sounds while trying not to think about what he's doing to Chayse.

∞

Chayse stares at his dinner but can't eat. Something is seriously wrong. Gryffin has completely pulled away from him in the last few days. He lay awake at night trying to figure out what he's done, but he can't think of anything apart from him questioning the captain about the brand on his back. That still doesn't explain the severe reaction.

Something else must have happened three days ago — almost like he flicked a switch. Gryffin put up a sturdy wall in front of him and refused to let him past. It was worse than when he first started on

337

Ares.

He rubs a hand over his face and stabs a piece of meat on his plate. What adds to his worry is that Klay seems almost happy around him. Like he knows something Chayse doesn't. He has a bad feeling. Unfortunately, there's no escaping it. He's off the ship. It's only a matter of time.

'Hey, you going to eat your food or continue stabbing it?'

Chayse glances up at his friend Tret and drops his fork. 'Sorry. Not hungry.' He pushes the plate of food across the table knowing all too well Tret will empty his plate for him.

As expected, Tret happily accepts it and stuffs a forkful of meat into his mouth. 'So,' he says with his mouth full, 'what's up with you?'

'Just seen my career flash before my eyes.'

'Hey, don't be too hard on yourself. It's not like the captain is warm and fuzzy with anyone. Maybe he's having a bad week. He won't kick you off the ship.'

Chayse laughs harshly. 'You know as well as I do he would. I'm his aide and I've somehow managed to piss him off. He's jettisoned people from *Ares* for less before.' He puts his head down on the table and closes his eyes. 'I'm finished. Any second now he'll— '

He's cut off by the last voice he wanted to hear. 'Chayse.' The entire room falls silent as their captain enters. Chayse takes a deep breath. He glances briefly at Tret, who is discretely eating the rest of his dinner. Tret shrugs and motions towards Gryffin with his fork. Chayse stands up and walks towards the door. He can feel the eyes of everyone in the room on him. They're not stupid. They all know why their leader wants to see him. He stops in front of Gryffin and salutes.

He hands Chayse a tablet. 'Want to explain this?'

Chayse frowns and looks at the information. 'I ran tests to try and figure out why you were in pain. Is there a problem, sir?'

'You could say that.' He crosses his arms over his chest. 'Klay found your tests made things worse, not better. In fact, it looks like you're the reason I've been in so much damn pain lately.'

Chayse can feel every set of eyes in the room on him as he struggles to make sense of what he's being accused of. 'I double checked everything before I did it. I don't see how I could have made things worse.'

'So Klay is lying?'

'No. I'm not saying that.'

'With me. Now.'

Gryffin leaves the room and Chayse follows. He runs through the scan information in his head, trying to figure out what went wrong. The information Gryffin showed him came from his personal computer. It wasn't anywhere near the primary system, so how the hell had Klay found it? Could he have accidentally uploaded the information while connected to his work station? He's sure he wouldn't have done anything that stupid. If it was common knowledge he'd examined Gryffin's implants in any detail, he would have been in serious trouble. Pretty much like now.

Maybe he should have eaten his meal after all. It could have been his last one. Hell, if he'd known, he would have eaten Tret's dinner too.

Cold water hits him in the face and brings him out of his daydream. He finds himself at the bottom of the ramp leading from *Ares* to the surface of Ultar. The black sky hints there's more than just rain to come. Not the right time for a walk, but Gryffin keeps heading away from the ship into the rain, so he follows. A clap of thunder sounds in the distance followed a few minutes later by the bright flash of lightning. Chayse looks longingly back at the ship as they continue to move further away from it. At least he won't meet his end by being jettisoned out of the airlock. If this is it for him, he'll die on solid ground. Not much consolation.

Chayse tries to compose his thoughts. He looks at Gryffin's back and realises something. It's the first time he's seen the captain off the ship with his face and arm uncovered. He's left his gloves and jacket on the ship and the black sleeveless t-shirt he's wearing shows his entire metal arm. He can see the large wing of the griffin across his back peeking out around the shirt. He's also carrying no weapons. Then again, they're on Ultar. Hardly in the middle of enemy territory. It's probably the one place he can show himself and go unarmed. Maybe he plans on killing him with his bare hands.

Gryffin finally stops in a small clearing about ten minutes from the ship. He turns to face Chayse, who puts all his concentration into not fidgeting. Gryffin's stare is unnerving him but then again that's probably what his captain wants.

'Who are you working for?'

'I'm loyal to you — always have been.' He has to shout over the rain and thunder.

'Prove it.'

'How?'

'Fight me for your place on my ship.'

'I ... I don't understand.'

Gryffin takes a few steps closer but stops out of arm's reach. He brushes his wet hair off his face and looks Chayse directly in the eyes. 'I need to know I can rely on you to do what I need.'

'Of course you can.'

'Then prove it.'

Chayse must have misheard him, but after a quick glance up at Gryffin he realises his captain is serious. Gryffin takes a few steps back and stands in front of Chayse with his feet apart and arms down by his side. Although he looks relaxed, Chayse knows he is far from it. He's seen him train enough to know Gryffin is ready to attack. His clenched fists make the muscles in his arms bulge under his bare skin.

'I can't, sir.'

Gryffin steps closer and lowers his voice. 'I need you to show me you're loyal.'

'How can I prove that by fighting you? You'll kill me.'

'Sometimes we need to fight people we don't want to. We do it for the good of the group. It's part of our life. If you can't do that, there's no place for you on my ship.'

This is one hell of a punishment. Maybe it's all a joke. While the idea Gryffin would tell a joke — let alone play — borders on the absurd, he wants to hang on to that idea. Anything is better than having to battle him.

He doesn't want to fight him, but it is something he has to do. He's being accused of trying to harm the captain. Might as well go out fighting.

He looks over his shoulder at the ship and tries to delay things so he can discreetly adjust his stance.

The right side of Gryffin's mouth turns up slightly. 'About time you acted like a proper Nomad.'

'So what do I do?' Gryffin takes a step back and stands with the rain pouring off him to gather in puddles around his boots. 'Are you going to kill me?'

'Probably.'

Gryffin's statement does nothing to put him at ease.

'What weapons can I use?'

'Whatever you have.'

'Right. What are you going to use?'

'Nothing.'

'Right,' he says again. There's no way he can delay any longer. Before he can talk himself out of it, he lunges at Gryffin.

45

Terra spends three hours staring at the ceiling above her bed before she finally gives up on sleep. Her occupied mind refuses to consider shutting down for the night. Instead, she throws on a pair of sweats and makes her way to the gym.

After an hour in the gym, she decides to settle in the Rec Room before she tries to sleep again. With only a few occupants, she quickly settles into an empty seat in the corner, beside the large window that takes up one wall. She nods at the two crew members engrossed in a card game at the other side of the bar. Terra slouches down in the comfortable brown leather seat and stares out the window.

Every night has played the same way for the last few weeks. It doesn't matter what she does, her mind won't switch off. Every time she closes her eyes, she sees him. Every time she dreams, it's of him. He won't leave her alone. While the dreams are anything but bad, when she wakes up she feels empty and alone. The more she thinks about what happened the last time they met, the worse she feels. How could she have betrayed him?

'There you are. I've been searching for you everywhere.' Milla sits down next to Terra and puts her feet up on the seat opposite her.

Terra shrugs. 'Just thinking about a few things.'

'More dreams?'

She runs a hand through her tousled hair and sighs. 'I feel like I'm losing my mind. On one hand, I know what the Foundation is doing has to be done, but on the flip side, I don't want them — us — to get him. I feel like I'm betraying my people and also betraying him.'

Milla leans back in her chair and crosses her arms. 'You want my professional opinion? Sounds like you're well and truly screwed.'

'Thanks,' Terra replies sarcastically. 'Fantastic help.'

'Okay, serious time. When we first came across the Nomad, I was fully behind the Foundation plans. I mean, a group of space pirates — not a great thing. But after I worked with them on Ultar and saw everything they've done for the colonists, I'm kind of at odds too. Things don't seem as desolate out here as the Foundation led us to believe.'

'So what can we do?'

Milla moves over to huddle beside her friend. 'Nothing we can do. Orders are orders.'

'Even if it means something bad happens to Gryffin — to Chayse — because of what we do?'

'You know how I feel about Chayse. I'd do anything to keep him safe, but our hands are tied. It's us against the Foundation. Not a lot we can do.'

'Have you been able to dig up anything else on the digits in his file?'

Milla makes a face. 'Yes and no. I found one file containing that designation. "Project Conscript." I hit a wall every time I tried to gain access. Whatever Project Conscript is, it's highly classified.'

'Hang on, you could reveal who the Council members are but you can't get into this?'

Milla huffs. 'Hey, I'm good but I'm not perfect.'

Terra wraps her arms around herself. 'He was telling the truth. The Foundation does have something to do with this.'

Milla sits up straight. 'I didn't say that.'

'Think about it, Milla.' Terra pauses as a crew member walks past them. 'The number thirty-five entered in his file after he went missing, the same number branded on his back, and now this Project Conscript entry. Something feels all wrong about this.'

Milla shuffles closer to Terra. 'I'm with you, but there's nothing else we can do. If I push too hard, we could both be targeted.'

Terra looks at Milla as if she's crazy. 'Targeted?'

'Think about it. Whoever is behind this Conscript project has gone to extreme lengths to hide their tracks. If they were somehow involved or responsible for changing Gryffin, there is going to be a hell of a lot of money invested. The technology on and in him has to be worth close to a million credits, maybe more.'

'My God,' Terra gasps.

'Exactly. You don't mess around with people who have that much invested in the project. We could find ourselves with metal implants or dead. Can't say I'm overly keen on either option.' Milla stands and straightens her hair. 'I have to get some sleep. I'm on the early shift tomorrow. Listen, Gryffin and Chayse are big boys. They've been out here a long time and have done pretty well without us so far. We have to trust they have each other's backs.'

∞

Chayse can't go on much longer. Every time he thinks he's close to victory, Gryffin shows him it's not going to happen. Gryffin is utterly ruthless when he fights, even when holding back as he is now.

Chayse wipes his mouth and looks up at his opponent through the rain. Gryffin stands firm and waits patiently for Chayse to make his next move. The only sign of movement is his broad chest, which rises and falls as he breathes. 'Are you holding back, sir?'

'You're still breathing, aren't you?'

Chayse can't argue with that fact. He has been fighting with Gryffin for what seems like hours. If he is honest with himself, it is more like he's gently play fighting with Gryffin. Real fighting means actually hitting the other person and Chayse is doing very little of that. In fact, the captain is making more contact just defending himself. Exhausted, bruised, and bleeding, Chayse grits his teeth against the pain as he picks himself off the ground again and spits out a mouthful of blood.

Chayse silently curses himself. What the hell is he doing? He should give up and stop letting Gryffin play with him. If he had any sense, he'd admit defeat and walk away. There's no shame in it. He's survived fifteen minutes. Surely that's something to be proud of. Then why isn't he going to back down?

Simple answer.

He wants to show Gryffin he's serious and he will do anything necessary for the well-being of the group. Chayse collects his thoughts and plans his next and probably final charge. He clenches his fist on the muddy ground. He ignores the pain, cold, and rain, takes a few deep breaths, and thinks about the battle so far. Thinks about how Gryffin moves, how he reacts.

He leaps forward and anticipates Gryffin's next move before he makes it. Chayse pulls out his knife and screams in victory as it sinks into Gryffin's shoulder.

Gryffin responds by throwing Chayse over his injured shoulder, then drops him on the ground. Gryffin crouches over Chayse and kneels on his chest to pin him down. Chayse's body sinks into the sodden ground as Gryffin leans heavily on him. The combined weight of the captain and his heavy metal implants drives the air from his body. Chayse braces himself for the death blow as he watches Gryffin pull the knife out of his shoulder. With a roar, Gryffin drives the knife towards Chayse's head. Chayse screams as he feels a sharp pain and everything goes black.

∞

Gryffin wipes the blood from his knife and activates his communicator. 'I've dealt with Chayse. Officially remove him from the crew.'

'What charge, sir?'

'I'll leave that up to you, Klay. Endangering the high commander or something similar.'

Gryffin ends the communication and looks down at Chayse's body one last time before he turns away. He contacts Aleena and tells her where to locate Chayse and then takes his time walking back to *Ares*. For some reason, he doesn't want to go back. It's dark, dreary, and although surrounded with his crew, painfully lonely on board.

He delays the inevitable and sits on a rock to look out over the lake. He uses his ocular implant to peer through the mist and rain, but sees no one else around. Then again, you'd have to be mad to venture out in weather like this. The usually mirror-like lake is being stirred up by the wind.

Waves crash against the shore and wash over his boots. The howling wind whips his sodden hair against his face, mud covers every inch of his body, and his boots are full of water, but he doesn't care. The cold has never affected him. There are worse things than being cold and wet.

His mind drifts back to Chayse. In a strange way, he'll miss him on the crew. Chayse had his back in a way no one else ever did. That's why it had to be Chayse and why he had to go now. He needed to get Chayse off the ship before Klay relieves him as captain and he loses the ability to make any decisions.

He lets his vision blur again and closes his eyes. Klay would go mad if he knew he's sitting on a rock, unarmed and alone, but he needs some time to himself. Needs time away from the constant reminders his world is slowly falling apart. He can see the threads of his life unravelling before his eyes, but he can't be bothered fighting. He's slowly losing control of his crew and ship, relying more and more on Klay to step in for him. The Nomad deserve a strong leader; someone who can fight for them. If he can't even control his body, what chance does he have of fighting for them?

He's always known he's on borrowed time. Everyone dies at some stage. Whether by natural causes or not, it happens to everyone. Death played such a big part in his life so far. He wished for it every day for five years as a prisoner. Every time he lost consciousness he hoped it would be the last time. But, somehow, he stayed alive until the Nomad found him.

He fully accepted he wouldn't die an old man. His occupation alone guaranteed that. Add that to his less than reliable implants and any thoughts of a long and happy future disappeared. He didn't have a problem with that.

Until now.

For the first time in years, something is stirring inside him. A tiny part of him wants a long, happy life. The stubborn thought is firmly in his mind and no amount of ignoring it helps. He's no longer content to carry on like this until he dies. Up until a few weeks ago, he'd have had no problem sacrificing himself to save the Nomad or his colonies. He'd still do that without hesitation, but a small part of him would regret not living. Regret not having a shot at a happy life, like so many other people have. Possibly a life with Terra.

She's the reason he's starting to think like this. The sums add up. One minute he knew what he was doing, and then she ran into him and left behind this doubt. It doesn't matter that there's no way anything long term could occur between them. Sense dictates a Nomad captain and a Foundation officer can't live happily ever after. She could be used to get to him. Possibly hurt because of him. There's no way in hell that's going to happen.

All his well-thought-out plans could ultimately go to shit because of his irrational and dangerous feelings for Terra.

Terra opens the curtains and smiles. The sun's rays stream in the window to fill the room with its warmth. Very different to the thunderstorm that kept her awake last night. If she weren't accustomed to the luxuries of life, she could stay on Ultar forever. It's relaxing and peaceful but it's not going to last. Her week-long stay is quickly coming to an end.

As expected, Aleena isn't the slightest bit interested in aligning with the Foundation, but Balfe ordered Roman, in no uncertain terms, to keep trying. Feeling slightly frustrated, herself and Stanner continued meeting with the neighbouring worlds and each one had signed up without hesitation. In fact, they'd even agreed to try and arrest Gryffin and any of his Nomad if they show up.

Staying here may be a waste of Foundation time, but she plans on enjoying every minute of it — especially today. Stanner will be tied up all day, so she can spend her time doing whatever she wants, starting with breakfast in Aleena's house.

She starts by having a leisurely shower before dressing in a pair of red loose trousers and a white t-shirt. After securing her hair in a messy bun, she leaves the house to join Aleena. She makes her way along the tree-lined path from her appointed cottage into the town square. The scars from the battle all those months ago still show in the square, but not as obviously as before. The town hall even sports a new roof.

She stops at a stall selling bread and cakes and chooses a freshly baked cinnamon loaf and two sticky iced buns for later. Terra thanks the stall holder, then climbs onto the back of a passenger cart and sits back to enjoy the scenery. The driver guides the horse along the road and cheerily waves at anyone he passes.

Terra can't imagine a more perfect scene. Foundation Earth is nothing like this. Perhaps years ago it was, but with the rise of the Foundation comes order. Things had to be just so. Every tree in a well-planned line, every flower the right colour and the right place. Random doesn't exist anymore. Not for the first time, she questions the Foundation's presence here. After a week on Ultar, she understands why Gryffin and his Nomad battle as hard as they do for the colonies.

The horse and cart rounds the corner into the small clearing surrounding Aleena's house and she has to hold on to the side of the cart to stop herself toppling off. Gryffin is leaning against the door frame.

She mutters a quick thank you to the driver and climbs down. Aleena pushes past Gryffin to come out of her house and greet her. 'Terra, I am so glad you could come.'

'Yeah. Erm, Gryffin's here.'

Aleena clears her throat and glances over her shoulder at him. Without a word, he turns and goes back into the house. 'I believe your excitement is a little premature. I am afraid he is less than happy about your reasons for being here.'

Terra isn't the least bit surprised. Roman spoke to her about Gryffin before she left, and ordered them both to leave immediately if he arrived. Technically she should call Stanner — he is only ten minutes away — but she can't bring herself to do it. 'I can handle him. You kept his visit quiet.'

'I was not sure how long he would stay. He arrived last night. Perhaps we should reschedule. He is in a particularly bad mood.'

'That's his problem.'

'I could not agree more.' She points towards the bags in her hands. 'Do I smell cinnamon loaf by any chance?'

Terra smiles. 'Couldn't resist. What about Gryffin?' she asks as Aleena walks towards her house.

'He does not like cinnamon loaf. More for the two of us, it would seem.'

Terra slowly follows Aleena into the house. Sharing cinnamon loaf is the last of her concerns when it comes to Gryffin.

Terra closes the door and turns to face Gryffin. He leans against the sink and Terra can't help but notice his size makes the room seem so much smaller. His arms are crossed over his chest and his dark eyes drill into her head. He clenches his jaw and visibly digs his metal fingers into his bicep. Clearly sensing the tension, Aleena puts herself in between them. 'I will not have any trouble.'

He crosses his arms and looks over at Terra. 'You think you're going to sign this colony?'

'Of course not. The Foundation ordered Roman to send me. He didn't have a choice. That's the only reason I'm here.' She shrugs. 'I don't know what else to say to you.'

'You want to talk about handing myself over again?'

She deserves that. 'I owe you an apology for what happened the last time.' She takes a step closer to him. 'Listen, I'm not putting any pressure on Aleena. She's perfectly capable of making her own decisions.'

Aleena moves to stand beside Terra. 'She is right. Having the Foundation here changes nothing.'

He slams his metal hand against the work surface. 'It changes everything! It doesn't help when colonies make things worse by inviting them in.'

Terra doesn't like where this is going. Gryffin seems to grow more agitated as the conversation continues. Terra tries to draw his attention back to her while she keeps the table between them. 'This isn't Aleena's fault. You're angry at me, not her. I admit I made a huge mistake the last time, okay? If I could turn back time, I'd do things differently.'

He takes a step forward, his movements slow and almost predatory. Terra feels like a rabbit in front of a lion. 'I've spent my life protecting the colonies. It is Aleena's fault if she turns her back on that.' He lashes out with his metal arm and smashes it down on the table to split the wood straight down the centre. Terra jumps back as the table crashes to the ground. When he looks up, his cold, purple eyes startle the two women.

Gryffin pulls out his gun and charges his arm but instead of aiming at them, he suddenly turns and fires at Lucan, who bursts in the back door. Lucan narrowly avoids being shot and jumps behind a cupboard. In the confusion, Terra pulls out her weapon, but Gryffin moves faster than she thought possible.

He throws his knife, knocking the gun from her hand. Lucan fires at Gryffin again, giving Terra a chance to dive for her gun, but Gryffin is ahead of her. Her gun is kicked across the room before she reaches it. Terra rolls behind the table remains while Lucan provides covering fire without actually hitting Gryffin.

Aleena peeks around the kitchen door and signals to Terra. She puts a stun gun on the floor and pushes it towards the table. Terra grabs the weapon and waits for Lucan to fire again. As soon as he distracts Gryffin, Terra rises and fires at Gryffin over the edge of the table. Three shots later, he finally falls to the floor.

The three of them slowly come out of their respective hiding places and cautiously approach Gryffin. 'Everyone all right?' Terra asks.

Lucan wipes his arm across his forehead. 'What brought that on?'

Aleena steps over a splintered table leg. 'I do not know. It was entirely unexpected.'

Terra crouches down beside Gryffin. 'What now?'

Aleena gestures to Lucan who opens the door to the basement. 'We must get him to safety before he wakes up.'

Aleena and Terra takes a leg each while Lucan lifts his upper body. The three of them manage to carry him down the stairs and lay him on the floor next to the back wall.

Lucan rolls him onto his front while Aleena attaches a set of chains to two anchor points on the wall and the floor. Lucan snaps cuffs around Gryffin's wrists and ankles before he secures them to Aleena's chains.

'Is that necessary?'

'I am afraid so. He is a danger to himself and others while like this.' Aleena pulls a confused Terra up the stairs, turns the light off, and locks the door.

Lucan clears away the remains of Aleena's table while Terra stands in the middle of the room unsure what to do. 'How long will he stay like that?'

Aleena shakes her head. 'A few hours. You should go. Commander Stanner will be looking for you.'

'I'll stay with him.'

Lucan throws another piece of wood on the pile that used to be the table. 'Aleena, you need to check on one of the colonists, remember.'

'With all the commotion, I completely forgot.' She needs to go but is not happy about leaving Terra alone with an out of control Gryffin. Even now, the banging and thumping from downstairs is getting louder.

'Go, Aleena,' Lucan prompts. 'I'll stay with Terra.'

Feeling a little more at ease, she concedes. After all, she did have a crucial colonist to see.

∞

Chayse opens his eyes and looks up at Aleena's worried face. He tries to sit up, but a sharp pain in his head forces him back to the bed.

'Do not move. Gryffin gave you a nasty bump.'

'I'm not dead.'

Aleena laughs and shakes her head. 'No. You are very much alive. Damaged but alive.'

'What happened? Where's Gryffin and *Ares*?'

Aleena speaks to another woman behind her before turning back to him. 'Gaela was kind enough to watch you so I could attend to some business. Gryffin is still here, but you will not see him. Now, please lie still. He severely injured you.' She rummages in the basket of bandages at her feet. 'I hoped he would be gentler.'

Chayse remains silent as Aleena checks his wounds. His body goes numb as he remembers the events that brought him here. It seems the test, whatever it was, meant nothing. Gryffin made Chayse think he had a chance of returning to *Ares*. In truth, all Gryffin did was beat him, then leave him for dead.

He glances over at the corner of the room and sees Gryffin has left all of his stuff. Seems his fate was sealed before the captain took him out of the mess.

The one small consolation is that he's still alive. And it's as much of a surprise as anything. When Gryffin went to stab him, Chayse was convinced he would die. Why go to the trouble of pretending to kill him? As far as he knows, anyone removed from the ship for punishment doesn't survive. Maybe Gryffin's going soft in his old age. He licks his dry lips. 'What's the damage?'

'Two cracked ribs, a sprained wrist, concussion, and too many cuts and bruises to count.'

No, Gryffin's not going soft. He just left him alive for some reason.

Aleena stands up and wipes her hands on a towel. 'That is all I can do for you for now. How do you feel?'

Chayse pauses as he thinks about how to answer her question.

'Terrible. How are you supposed to feel when your home leaves without you?'

'Perhaps you should look on the bright side.'

Chayse laughs harshly but winces when his ribs protest. 'Which is what, exactly? My captain — sorry, ex-captain — beat me up and dumped me here. I have no money, no job, and no home. I can't even go to another Nomad ship. I'm blacklisted.'

'But you are alive.'

He shakes his head but immediately regrets it when the pain shoots through his skull. Maybe he shouldn't move. 'I don't get it, Aleena. I thought he was going to kill me. Why did he change his mind?'

'He did not change his mind. He never had any intention of killing you. Everything that happened was for show. It had to appear to anyone watching that he killed you.'

'No offence, Aleena, but I'm not in the mood for games.'

'I completely agree. It is not the time. We will talk later. For now, you need to concentrate on getting better. Get some sleep. It will all become clear.' She gets up and leaves him alone. Instead of trying to assimilate what Aleena said, his body decides it's had enough. He closes his eyes and gives his body the rest it so badly needs.

47

Gryffin wakes up with his head on Terra's knee and her fingers running through his hair. That's the only positive thing as far as he can tell. The chains he can feel around his wrists tell a story he's not sure he wants to hear. Flashes of images come to him — images that churn his stomach.

He knows he should get up, get as far from her as possible, but he can't get himself to move. Even lying on the floor, he's more comfortable than he can remember ever being. Her fingers gently run through his hair, helping to soothe him.

He doesn't know what's different about her, why her touch doesn't make his skin crawl and his stomach twist. Unlike every other person he's met, he's drawn to her touch. Wants the warmth and safety it brings. Strange that someone programmed as a warrior feels safe in the arms of a woman. The feelings should make him ashamed and weak, but instead they have the opposite effect. He'd be proud to stand by her side. Feel stronger with her in his life. Every part of his human side aches for her. The more he sees her, the more he wants her. He thought the feeling would go, but after sleeping with her, that plan went out the window. If anything, it made things worse.

And it's killing him.

He quickly opens his eyes and shuffles away from her.

Her green eyes are full of concern when they meet his. 'Hey, how are you feeling?'

He licks his dry lips. 'How much time?'

'Two hours. Are you going to answer my question?'

He can't because he doesn't trust himself to talk again without being sick. The withdrawal creeps up on him. He swallows deeply, trying hard to control the queasiness. 'Why are you still here?'

Terra opens the small window above his head to allow the last of the sunlight into the dreary room. 'I was worried about you. Would you like some water?'

Without waiting for an answer, she gets to her feet and goes to the kitchen. He glances out the window and groans when he notices the sun is starting to set. He leans back against the damp stone and closes his eyes. If he doesn't report back to the ship soon, Klay will come looking for him. The last thing he wants is for Klay to discover them together. He'd never hear the end of it.

'Gryffin?'

He quickly opens his eyes, surprised she was able to catch him unawares.

'Give yourself a minute. Here.' She hands him a cup of water and sits on a box opposite him. The worry on her face makes him feel worse.

'You should go.'

Terra shakes her head. 'I'm not leaving — not yet. Do you need anything else? Should I contact *Ares*?'

Her pity and concern seems to flick a switch in him. The helplessness, regret, and anger spill to the surface. 'Leave! I could have killed you. Damn it, when are you going to start taking that seriously?'

357

'Do you like me?'

His mouth drops open to continue the argument and then closes again. 'What?'

She shuffles the box closer to him. 'Answer the question, Gryffin.'

'That doesn't have anything to do with this.'

Terra pauses as she clearly struggles to keep her temper under control. 'So you can't even admit it. Why would you be worried about me staying if you don't care?'

'I care about myself. I don't want or need the hassle you bring.'

She closes the distance between them. 'I can't believe I'm going to say this to you, but if I don't, I'll regret it.' She meets his eyes as she takes a deep breath. 'I'm falling in love with you and I have to figure out how to let that go.'

∞

'Better?'

Chayse walks around the room and stretches his legs. 'Bit stiff but yeah, a lot better. Thank you, Aleena.'

'You are very welcome.' She gets up and clasps her hands in front of her. 'I am sorry to push you, but are you ready to have some of your questions answered?'

He takes a deep breath and winces as his ribs protest. 'I don't have anything else to lose.'

Chayse barely pays attention to where he's going as Aleena leads him through the house to a large barn outside. He'd spent the last few hours in bed and feels a bit better. Although Gryffin apparently held back, he still caused a fair amount of damage. Every breath sends knives through his chest and his head throbs where Gryffin hit him. Emotionally he's no better.

He bumps into Aleena when she suddenly stops to type a long code into a panel hidden in the support post. A heavy metal hatch opens in the floor to expose a flight of stairs disappearing into the ground.

'What is this place?'

'Please follow me and I will show you.'

Chayse follows her through a maze of tunnels and through a large steel door into an open cavern. When he sees what's in the cavern, his jaw drops in awe. The ship is enormous — much bigger than *Ares*, but she clearly shares the same design. But this is no normal Nomad ship. Usually, their ships are old and battle-worn by the time the Nomad steal them, but not this one. This one is practically shrink-wrapped; her dull grey hull is flawless.

Aleena puts her arm around his shoulders and smiles proudly. 'This is why Gryffin pretended to kill you. He needed to get you off *Ares* as he has other plans for you. Captain, may I introduce you to your new ship, *Nemesis*.'

∞

Gryffin laughs harshly. 'You're serious? You really are stupid if you think you love me.'

Terra shakes her head. 'Believe me, I'd like to say this is a big joke, but it's not.'

Gryffin drags himself to his feet, using the chain's anchors as leverage and leans heavily against the wall. 'Then that's your problem.'

She knew he'd push her away again, but it still hurts. Terra pauses for a moment. She tucks a lock of hair behind her ear and takes a deep breath. 'As I said, I'll get over it. And you.'

He lifts his arm and rattles the chain securing him to the wall. 'I'm chained to the damn wall so I can't hurt you. That should help you get over me.'

She wants to say more to him but fears she's already said too much. It's painfully clear he's not the slightest bit interested in anything she has to say. Terra gets to her feet and forces herself to stand strong in front of him. 'Do you know what your problem is?'

He tilts his head down to look at her.

'Your problem is you're scared. Afraid of feeling. Scared to let someone close to you. So instead you use people. Take what you want when you want it and stuff the consequences. Anytime someone wants to get close, you shut yourself off and push them away under the guise of trying to protect them. You hide behind your implants, behind the fact you're part machine. You use that as a reason not to let anyone get close. You seem to forget you're also human. You need to stop being angry at everything long enough to realise that.'

The electricity runs down his arm and he clenches his fists.

She steps closer to him, ignoring his power. 'Look at you now. You can barely stand, but you're still trying to intimidate me. That's all you know. That's your answer to everything, isn't it? Violence. Things get uncomfortable, so you threaten people.'

She breaks eye contact and slowly shakes her head. 'Well, guess what, Gryffin? You win. You're not worth the hassle.'

Without another word, she turns around and walks away from him.

∞

Chayse leans against the sink and slowly opens one eye. He breathes a sigh of relief. His surroundings have finally stopped spinning.

He looks into the small mirror over the sink but doesn't fully recognise his reflection. Apart from the large bruises and cuts on his face, he looks pale and tired. Not surprising he feels dizzy. How can Gryffin possibly expect him to captain *Nemesis*? He's never commanded anything in his life, let alone a ship.

He groans as Aleena knocks on the door. 'Chayse. Are you all right?'

He forces himself to stand straight and opens the door. 'Yeah. Never better.'

She smiles kindly at him. 'Gryffin said you would be surprised, but I did not expect you to react in this way.'

He sits on the ground beside the toilet. 'How exactly did you expect me to react?'

'Chayse, Gryffin needs you to step up and take control of *Nemesis*. You have become closer to him over the last months. You know how difficult it is for him to place that much trust and faith in anyone. Especially trust them to command this new vessel.' She walks to the door and looks out at *Nemesis*. 'Everything he owns has been put into the ship. He has saved every fee he has ever received and put it towards this. It is the reason he barely eats and works himself to exhaustion. It is his legacy. A legacy he would not trust to just anyone.'

She turns back to face him. 'I believed he had made the correct decision choosing you, but if you are going to throw it back in his face because you are angry he took you off *Ares*, he may have been mistaken.'

Chayse walks to the door and examines his new ship. 'That explains it.' Aleena raises her brows in a silent question. 'A few months ago, Gryffin asked me to arrange more work for him. He had run out of credits. It didn't make sense, but he shot me down when I asked.'

'Gryffin has been funding the project from its birth. I have assisted where I could but, primarily, it has been Gryffin.'

Chayse steps into the large hangar and slowly walks up to *Nemesis*. 'Why me? Gryffin has access to hundreds of highly trained Nomad. I'm probably the least experienced person he could have picked.'

Aleena joins him at the rear loading ramp. 'You have always acted in the Nomad's best interest. Gryffin let you close to him over the last few weeks for this very reason. He involved you more with his implants, let you accompany him during interrogations, and brought you off the ship. You know him now; have a greater understanding of why he does what he does. He wants you to use that knowledge to help lead your crew to success.'

She steps closer to him and holds his gaze. 'He did not want to do what he did to you, but he had no choice. Gryffin fabricated the information because he needed to get you off the ship quickly. We were running out of time.'

Gryffin planted the data? Now Aleena spells it all out for him, things start to fall into place. He hadn't noticed Gryffin suddenly began involving him in more important duties. He can't believe the captain has that much faith in him. 'What about the crew?'

'Gryffin has sorted out the crew already. There are people on the surface trained to operate the ship. They are loyal to Gryffin and will follow your orders without question.'

'What orders? What the hell does he expect me to do?'

'*Nemesis* has one objective, and he trusts no one else to complete it. You have proven to him that you are the right one.'

'How?'

'By fighting him. By putting aside your personal feelings for the benefit of the group as a whole.'

Chayse opens his mouth to ask her to explain, but it suddenly hits him. It must show on his face that he knows as Aleena nods and smiles sadly. 'Yes, Chayse. The objective is as you fear. We built *Nemesis* to protect and defend the colonies from the weapon Gryffin will be turned into.'

48

Cold water hits Gryffin's face and drags him back to consciousness. He opens his eyes and hisses in pain when they protest. When he finally forces his eyes to focus, he finds himself flat out on the forest floor. Thunder rumbles overhead and the rain soaks into his clothes.

He tries to get up, but that doesn't work either. His arms and legs don't seem to want to cooperate. His stomach rolls violently and he just manages to keep the contents where they should be. He must have lost control. That's twice in the space of a few hours. Something is seriously wrong with him.

He manages to push himself up onto his elbows and looks around, but has no idea how he ended up in the forest. The last thing he remembers is chasing after Terra.

Terra.

She could still be out here, alone. He grits his teeth and pushes himself to his knees but freezes when he sees blood covering his metal hand.

He immediately reaches for his gun, but the holster on his hip is empty. His knife is missing too. Gryffin slumps back to the ground and stares at his hands. The blood's not his, so what the hell has he done? An unfamiliar feeling settles in his stomach — he's worried. Gryffin finally gets to his feet and scans the area. Something is lying on the forest floor to his left. The feeling of dread only intensifies as he slowly makes his way towards it. The indistinguishable lump turns into a body; the sodden pile of material changes into a white shirt and red trousers. The long brown hair is saturated and matted with blood, but he'd know her anywhere. He rushes to Terra's side and checks for a pulse. It's there — faint, but there.

Blood stains her skin and clothes — it's everywhere. Gryffin holds his hands up in front of him and it all sinks into place: the blood belongs to Terra.

∞

'What happened?'

Gryffin pushes past Aleena and carefully lays Terra on the bed.

'Gryffin, what happened?' When he continues to ignore her, she grabs him by the arm and turns him around. 'Gryffin, you are scaring me.' Aleena looks down at his hands and the colour drains from her face. 'What did you do?'

He shakes his head. 'I don't know. You have to help her.'

Aleena pauses for a moment and then pushes him aside. 'Get my med kit from the kitchen. I will also need some warm water.'

Gryffin races downstairs and pulls apart each cupboard until he locates what he needs. After filling a bowl with water, he goes back upstairs where Aleena is pulling wet, bloody clothes off Terra.

'Put them on the ground.'

He does as instructed then stands, silently watching Aleena work. Terra is too still. Too pale. 'What can I do?'

Aleena stays focused on what she's doing. 'You've done enough. Leave. Now.'

364

He wants to stay, he needs to stay, but Aleena is right.

He looks down at his hands. He's done enough.

∞

On the third try, Terra finally manages to get her eyes to stay open. Everything hurts but she doesn't know why. She slowly turns her head towards the sunlight shining in through the window and meets Aleena's worried face. 'Hi.'

Aleena smiles. 'Hello, Terra. How are you feeling?'

'Sore. What happened?'

Aleena's face drops and she looks away. 'Gryffin found you in the woods yesterday. You have numerous cuts and bruises and a large gash on your forehead. We do not know what happened to you but ...'

It takes Terra a moment to understand what Aleena is trying to say. Flashes of memories come back to her: Gryffin's metal hand around her throat, their argument, and her running away from him. 'Gryffin wouldn't do this.'

Aleena takes her hand in hers. 'Terra, Gryffin is not in full control of himself anymore. It has been getting worse over the last few months. Do not forget he tried to strangle you yesterday. Is it really so hard to believe he may have done this?'

Terra looks up at the ceiling. She can't believe Gryffin did this to her. She won't believe it. 'Where is he now?'

'Terra, I do not think that is wise.'

'Aleena, I need to see him. Please.'

Aleena opens and closes her mouth, then leaves the room. Terra slowly sits up in bed, taking a few deep breaths as her head throbs. She pulls the soft blanket around her and lays her head back against the feather pillow. This isn't going to be an easy conversation.

∞

Gryffin stops at the door to Terra's room, turns around, and leans against the far wall. He can't go in there — not after what he did. Aleena stands opposite him with her arms folded across her chest. She is still angry he refused to go back to his ship, but he doesn't care.

He called Klay and gave him some excuse to buy himself more time. There is no way in hell he is leaving before he knows Terra is all right. Unfortunately, that means actually opening the door. He's faced multiple enemies single-handed — he can walk into her room.

Gryffin closes his eyes and knocks on the door. As soon as he steps into the room and sees her sitting up in the bed, the relief washes over him, but it only lasts for a second. All he can see are the dark bruises and harsh white bandages covering the wounds. He freezes in the doorway, unable to make himself move further into the room. Terra shuffles over in the bed and pats the space beside her. 'Can you please sit for a moment?'

He slowly lowers himself onto the bed, keeping as far from her as possible. 'Did you mean what you said, Gryffin? That you don't care about me? I want the truth. You owe me that much at least.'

He drops his head, his hair hiding his face. 'No.'

She pulls the blanket over her stomach and hugs it to her. 'Why would you say all of that?'

That is the question he didn't want her to ask. He can't answer it without telling her things he never intends to talk about. 'It doesn't change anything. I can't be with you the way you want me to. I need you to accept that.'

Terra pushes her shoulders back. 'Look at me.' He raises his head and meets her green eyes. 'I have a proposition for you, Gryffin, and I need you to stay put until I've finished.' She turns to face him and sucks in a sharp breath in pain.

'Do you want me to get Aleena?'

She shakes her head. 'I want you to shut up and listen to me.' Terra reaches out and places her hand on his arm. 'It doesn't matter how this happened, Gryffin. What matters is what we do now. I want you to talk to Roman.'

'Terra ... I made my feelings pretty clear.'

'You could say that. Things are different now. Roman is starting to question what the Foundation is doing in the Sector. If I'm honest, he's not alone. This Sector doesn't need our help. While I don't agree with some of what you do, I know you're not the person they claim you are. I wouldn't be in love with you if I believed that.' She looks down at her hands. 'I also believe what you said the Foundation did.' She raises her head again, the tears threatening to spill. 'What they did to you.'

Gryffin doesn't know what to say. Hearing her say she believes him means more than he'd like to admit. 'Why do you still want anything to do with me? After what I did to you ... I wouldn't blame you if you want to hand me over.'

She squeezes his arm. 'We're not talking about what happened to me. But you need to trust me so we can figure out what's going on — with you and with the Foundation's interest in you. I'm asking for five minutes, Gryffin. You've asked me to trust you in the past and I have. Now I need you to do the same. Talk to Roman. Tell him what they did.'

He can't believe he's considering this, but he is. 'Five minutes, Terra.'

∞

'Are you sure this is a wise decision, Gryffin?'

He looks over at Terra. She fell asleep on his chest ten minutes ago. Even though he would give anything to stay with her, he made her a promise. 'I have to.'

Aleena steps in front of him. 'I disagree. You feel guilty for what happened to Terra. I understand that, but that does not mean you hand yourself over to her people. There is no redemption to be gained by sacrificing yourself.'

367

Gryffin stands and lifts his jacket from the chair beside the bed. 'I'm way beyond redemption, Aleena. We both know the Foundation will capture me again. It's only a matter of time. Terra's right. This has to stop. I've lost control twice in the space of a few hours. If I hurt Terra, I'm not safe to be around anymore. Isn't it worth seeing what Roman has to say?'

Aleena stays quiet for a moment before finally nodding. 'Promise me you will be careful.'

He nods and pulls on his jacket. 'Make sure Terra's safe.'

With one last glance at Terra, he leaves the house to do something he never thought he would — meet with the Foundation.

∞

Roman gazes up at the stars. With no light pollution, the Ultaran sky offers him a sight he rarely sees on Earth. Unfortunately, he doesn't have much opportunity to enjoy the view. Gryffin should be on his way.

It took Terra an hour to convince him to have this meeting and he's still not sure why he agreed. Every tactic had been used, ending with a bit of emotional blackmail. Roman shakes his head. He's agreed to have a chat with the person responsible for attacking a crew member — he must be going soft. If the Foundation find out, he'll lose *Infinity*, no question.

A small rodent scurries across the path and races towards the safety of the trees. He actually envies its uncomplicated life. A life without orders, politics, and uncertainty sounds like heaven. When he came to the Sector, he never expected things would become so complex.

His priority at the moment is Terra. As soon as this meeting is over, he'll take her back to the safety of *Infinity*. Until then, Stanner won't leave her side. It's not that he doesn't trust Aleena; it's the vessel load of Nomad that worries him

The cold muzzle of a gun pushes against the back of his head. 'Great way to start our little chat,' Roman says.

'I have trust issues.' Gryffin slowly circles around Roman and stops in front of him. He takes a few steps back and lowers his gun but doesn't holster it.

Roman puts his hand on his weapon. 'I wasn't sure you'd show up.'

'I told Terra I would.'

At the mention of her name, Roman can't help the tension that travels through his body. 'Terra is the only reason I'm here too. If she hadn't convinced me otherwise, you'd be in chains on your way back to the Foundation.'

Gryffin's eyes seem to glow for a moment before returning to normal. 'We can both agree neither of us wants to be here, so can we get on with this?'

Roman nods. 'Very well. Terra said you didn't intentionally hurt her. Is that right?'

'Yes.'

'But apparently you don't remember what happened.'

'No.'

'You're not making this easy. If you want me to plead your case to the Foundation, I'll need more than yes and no. Give me something to work with.' Gryffin doesn't move a muscle or say a word. 'Forget it. I don't know why the hell you agreed to this meeting.' He raises his gun and points it at Gryffin. The Nomad doesn't try to defend himself.

'The Foundation did this to me.'

Roman raises his eyebrows. 'What?'

Gryffin finally looks back at Roman and his purple eyes glow in the gloom. 'The Foundation modified me when I was a child. Put something in my head I can't control.'

Roman feels like his head is spinning. Snippets of the report Milla gave him pop into his head. She said Gryffin's body showed evidence of torture, horrendous surgeries, and years of abuse and neglect. If he is to believe Gryffin, which he's not sure he does, that was done at the

369

request of his people. 'Why do they want you back?'

'I don't know. I presume they want to finish the modifications or kill me. Either way I'm not too keen on going back.'

'Do you have any proof?'

Gryffin takes a step closer and throws a small tablet at Roman's feet. 'I'm the proof. My implants are Foundation-grade metal.'

Curious, Roman picks up the tablet and examines the information. His heart sinks when he reads the screen. Gryffin is right; it is Foundation metal. 'Come back to *Infinity* with me. Let Milla do a compositional analysis of the metal. If the readings match what you have here, that changes everything.'

'You expect me to walk with you to your ship?'

'If you want my help, then yes.' Roman holsters his gun and steps closer to Gryffin. 'For reasons beyond my comprehension, Terra trusts you. She wouldn't have suggested this meeting otherwise. Now, I'm going to go back to my transport and trust you don't shoot me in the back.'

Roman turns around and slowly walks through the trees. He can't force Gryffin to come with him but this is his perfect chance to get Gryffin into custody. He's not going to ignore it.

Gryffin sits back on the bed and tries to ignore the Foundation security. The four personnel are standing to attention, and while their weapons remain in their holsters, they are very much ready to act. Milla turns from the desk next to him and clasps her hands on her knees.

'Right, you sure you're happy for me to do this?'

Gryffin nods. He's here now — no point putting it off.

'Okay then. I'm going to take a few readings from your implants, both internal and external. It should only take a few minutes.' She takes out a probe similar to the one Klay and Chayse use on him. He pulls off his top and lies back on the bed. Milla turns to face him, pauses for a moment, and then pushes the probe into one of the connectors on his chest.

Five minutes later, he's dressed and alone with the security while Milla runs the data. Even though he knows the results will prove the Foundation modified him, he still can't help but be anxious. He's not stupid — Roman will try to keep him on board. He wouldn't be doing his job unless he tried.

He slides off the bed when his radio sounds. Gryffin walks to the far end of the room for privacy. 'What is it?'

'Sir, I'm reporting in as requested,' Klay says.

'Report on what?'

'The hit you ordered.'

He casually leans back against the wall so the Foundation security doesn't pick up on his tension. 'Break it down for me, Klay,' he forces out through his tightening throat.

'The two Foundation crew members with Aleena. We took them both out as you ordered.'

Gryffin's head spins. Ordered? Are they dead? Survival mode instantly kicks in. 'Klay, you need to get *Ares* off the surface. Now!'

'But sir, what about you?'

'Forget me. *Infinity* is on the surface. Leave now. That's an order, Commander.' He cuts the connection and checks his previous calls. It must be a mistake. He didn't — he wouldn't — order a hit on Terra. But it's there, clear as day. He made a call to Klay before he met with Roman. Gryffin squeezes his eyes shut. His heart races as the realisation hits him like a kick right in the chest.

He killed her.

He should get the hell out of here before Roman hears the news, but he can't find the energy to move. Instead, he slides down the wall and sits on the ground. He pulls his legs up to his chest and tugs at his hair with his flesh hand as his metal one crushes the radio.

The Foundation security surrounds him, but he couldn't care less. 'Hey, are you all right?'

He doesn't answer. It's not a question he can answer.

Right on cue, Roman enters the room with his gun raised and directed at Gryffin's head. The look on Roman's face confirms his worst fears.

'I got a disturbing call from Aleena.' Roman takes a step closer to him. 'I was hoping you wouldn't know what I am talking about, but your face says differently. Lock him up. If he fights back, kill him.'

∞

Roman steps off the transport outside Aleena's house. He doesn't want to go in. Milla checked in about ten minutes ago and confirmed Stanner is dead and Terra missing. She put her trust in Gryffin and has potentially paid with her life.

He forces his emotion deep down, takes a breath and walks into the house. Aleena is sitting in a chair by the door holding an ice pack to the back of her head. 'Are you all right?'

She nods briefly. 'Just a bit shaken up.'

'Let's get you out of here while we examine the house. I'll need to question you when I'm done here, okay?' Without waiting for a response, he gestures to one of Milla's assistants. 'Would you take Aleena back to *Infinity* please.'

He watches as Aleena is guided from the room before he turns back to look at the scene. The once welcoming and homely cottage looks very different. The cosy couch is upturned and the table and chairs lie in splinters over the floor. Terra's sketchbook is in tatters, the pages ripped out and trampled into the floor. He leans down and picks up one of the drawings. He glares at the Nomad leader's face and scrunches the page in his fist.

Roman picks his way through the debris to Stanner. He lies in the centre of the room, his blood soiling the white rug by the fire. Roman crouches down beside him and closes his first officer's eyes. He pushes to his feet and addresses Milla. 'Preliminary report.'

'Gunshot wound to the heart. He died quickly, not that it's much consolation. I'd estimate he's been dead for less than an hour.'

Right when the Nomad leader was with them on *Infinity*. Roman moves around the body and his heart sinks. A large patch of blood covers the floor behind Stanner. 'Is it Stanner's?'

'No.' She pauses and takes a shaky breath. 'I've taken a sample for testing. This is a substantial blood pool, sir. If it is Terra's ...'

Roman doesn't need her to finish the sentence. He addresses two of the security team. 'Two teams. I want this house and the surrounding area locked down. Search every inch, inside and out. Find Lieutenant Rush. Now! Doctor, bring Stanner back to the ship. That testing is a priority as soon as you get back. Confirm who it belongs to.' It's a task that is not necessary. They all know it belongs to Terra.

∞

Chayse curses as he cuts his finger on the edge of the metal sheet. His head isn't on the job. Knowing they're working against the clock is putting extra pressure on him. Gryffin trusted him with this task and he'll do whatever he has to in order to complete it. Even if it means working day and night to oversee the final touches to the ship.

He wraps a bandage around his finger to match the other two from earlier and decides to focus on another job before he does any more damage to himself. After speaking to some of his colleagues, he moves to the bank of computers against the far wall and runs some simulations. In theory, the ship performs as it should. The big test will be when they have it up and running. The problem is, none of them know when they're going to need it.

It's only a matter of time before the Foundation arrives in the Sector in force. He's already heard rumours they've called in all their ships from other Sectors to join with them along the boundary. Without a vessel near the area, Chayse and his crew have no way to verify or to know how big a fleet they will face.

Rubbing his eyes, he leans back in his chair and looks over at the large black motorcycle sitting against the far wall. Another present from Gryffin. Not only did he get *Nemesis* but also Gryffin's beloved bike. While he is over the moon about the motorcycle, he isn't a fool. Gryffin would have given up his artificial arm before he let go of his bike. By leaving it with Chayse, he's clearly saying he doesn't need it himself anymore. He'd give anything to take it out for a proper spin, but that would have to wait. There's a ship to build first.

Lucan enters the room followed closely by Aleena. She slumps into the nearest chair and brushes dust from her clothes.

'What the hell happened?'

Lucan takes a bottle of water from the fridge and hands it to Aleena. 'The Foundation arrested Gryffin, then took control of Ultar. Roman tried to take Aleena back to his ship but I intercepted.'

Chayse pushes away from the console and looks at Lucan like he's lost his mind. He shakes his head and laughs but stops when he sees Lucan's serious. 'You're not kidding.'

Lucan shakes his head. 'Everything's gone to hell up there. Klay knocked Aleena out. When she came to, she found Stanner's body along with a substantial blood pool on the floor from another donor. Terra's missing.'

'Thanks to Lucan helping me to escape, the Foundation will no doubt presume I conspired with Gryffin — not that I am ungrateful, Lucan,' Aleena adds.

'Shit.' Chayse looks apologetically at Aleena. 'Sorry. Didn't mean to curse.'

She smiles at him. 'That is mild compared to some of what I have heard from Gryffin in the past. Lucan has arranged for some more of my trusted people to assist you. We must finish *Nemesis* as quickly as possible.'

'Gryffin suspected Klay wasn't entirely on the level but I couldn't find any evidence.' Chayse kicks the table viciously. 'The double crossing, lying, son of a—'

'We have bigger issues than Klay to address,' Aleena interrupts.

Lucan nods. 'My biggest concern is you, Aleena. This is your new home for the foreseeable future. No arguments.'

Aleena closes her mouth and nods slowly. 'Very well. I trust Roman will not harm any of my people. I feel terrible abandoning them, but I am more use down here. As for the tunnels, Gryffin made sure they are well shielded, but nothing is completely safe. We must not delay.'

Chayse, Lucan, and Aleena look out into the main cavern at the unfinished ship, all thinking the same thing.

They're in serious trouble.

∞

Roman stands outside the cell door, unable to make himself go in. He spent the last half hour with Stanner. It is such a waste of an excellent and loyal officer.

He straightens his shoulders, then opens the door. He nods at the four security personnel as he enters the room. 'Dismissed.' One by one they exit, leaving Roman alone with the prisoner. Gryffin looks up at Roman but his dark hair hides his eyes. Both captains remain silent, neither one giving any emotions away until Roman finally breaks the stand-off. 'We've searched Aleena's house and the surrounding area. Where's Terra?'

Gryffin rises from the metal bench and steps closer to Roman. The chains securing his ankles to the floor force him to stop in the centre of the cell. 'I don't know where she is.'

'Well, I don't believe you. Apart from the fact your radio shows the call to your ship, Aleena also recognised your first officer as one of the attackers.' Roman steps closer to the bars. 'I suppose you're also going to tell me you had nothing to do with Aleena's disappearance?'

'Aleena's missing?'

Roman shakes his head. 'You can drop the act, Captain. We found the officer tasked with taking her back to *Infinity*, unconscious about half a mile from the ship.' Roman paces back and forth in front of the cell. 'You know what I don't understand about all of this? Why meet with me? Why come back to the ship and then not fight back when we seized you? Why did you surrender?'

'I came here because Terra asked me to.'

'So that's why you had her killed? Payback?'

Gryffin shakes his head. 'I don't know what happened.'

Roman stops pacing and spins to face the cell. 'You don't know! Evan Stanner is dead, Terra and Aleena are missing, and the best you have to offer is *I don't know*? You're going to have to do a hell of a lot better than that!'

'What the hell do you want me to say? I'm cooperating.' He gestures to the large metal band circling his right bicep. 'I even let you put this damn thing on me.' Gryffin sits down and stretches his legs in front of him. 'How'd you figure out how to block the current to my arm anyway?'

Roman doesn't reply.

Gryffin shakes his head. 'You still don't see what's right in front of you. Aleena seems to think you have an independent brain, Captain. Can't see it myself. All I see is someone brainwashed by the Foundation.'

'What the hell are you talking about?'

'My arm, Captain. How did the Foundation figure out a way to disrupt the power if they know nothing about me — about my implants? I know your doctor tried but couldn't scan me properly. You shouldn't have any records of my implants on file. Yet your people managed to make this.' He raises his metal arm as much as the restraints will allow.

'We have teams of engineers and scientists on our payroll.'

Gryffin snorts. 'Teams of engineers at your disposal and the best you can come up with is to stick metal pins into my arm?'

'You killed one — possibly two of my crew. Your well-being isn't top of my list.'

'That the Foundation tagline?'

'I'm wasting my time here. You'll be formally charged. My commanding officer is on his way to take you back to Foundation space for trial.'

Gryffin stands up and takes two steps forward before being hindered by the chains. 'Balfe is coming?'

Roman narrows his eyes as he looks at Gryffin. 'How do you know about Balfe?'

'Did your doctor get the analysis of my implants back yet?'

Roman pauses for a moment, thrown off by Gryffin's change of subject. 'No. Do you honestly think I give a damn about analysis after you killed two of my crew?'

'What about Ultar?'

'It's under Foundation control. Aleena's loyalties to the Nomad make her a risk to the Foundation. As soon as we track her down, I'll have no choice but to hold her for aiding and abetting a criminal.'

Gryffin lunges at the bars, making the chains creak in protest. 'Leave Aleena the hell alone! Are you really that pissed with me you'd destroy everything she has?'

'It's a little too late for you to grow a conscience. You're the one that dragged her into this. What happens to her is on you. Just like Stanner and Terra.'

Instead of a rebuttal, Gryffin's shoulders slump. He sits back on the bench and lowers his head. Roman quickly squashes the guilt that hits him. He leaves the room, and locks the cell behind him.

Roman walks along the corridor ahead of the security team. *Omega* had just docked and Balfe ordered him to deliver the prisoner immediately. Roman expected a visit or a debriefing at the least, but Balfe isn't interested. He wants the handover to go ahead as soon as possible so he can get back to Foundation space.

In the two days since Gryffin's capture, Roman avoided visiting him again. An unpleasant feeling of doubt has settled and Balfe's imminent arrival doesn't help.

Admirals don't personally collect prisoners. In all his years with the fleet, he's never heard of it before. He can't think of one logical reason for Balfe to come all the way to the Sector. It just doesn't make any sense.

There's also been no news about Terra. Two days tearing the surface apart and still nothing. It's like she's vanished. Any colonies they've gathered are on the lookout for *Ares*, just in case she is on board, but they haven't managed to track the ship down yet.

He glances back at his son and freezes as Gryffin's navy eyes lock onto his; the same colour as Maggie's eyes. He owes it to her to at least listen to Gryffin. 'Give me a minute.' The security team pauses for a moment, then move down the corridor. Roman waits until the personnel have rounded the corner before he speaks. 'Tell me about the Foundation involvement.'

'You pick your moments.'

'We don't have much time. Please. I need to know.'

Gryffin takes a deep breath. 'Two decades ago, Balfe visited the lab where I was modified.'

'Why?'

'I was the first to survive the initial procedure. There were other Foundation people with him too.'

Roman curses himself. Two days spent hiding from the truth when he should have been doing his job by questioning Gryffin. Now he's left it too late.

'I can hear Balfe coming.' Gryffin takes a step closer to him. 'You can trust Aleena. She's not the enemy. Convince her to tell you the truth.'

Before Roman can comment, Balfe rounds the corner with the security team. 'Problem, Roman?'

Gryffin drives his shoulder against Roman and shoves him against the wall. Balfe signals for the security to break them up. The security personnel force Gryffin to the ground and two of them press their knees into his back to hold him down. Roman can only watch as a thick set of shackles are locked around Gryffin's ankles and wrists. Balfe crouches down to address Gryffin. 'You should have done the right thing weeks ago.'

Gryffin smirks. 'Desperate to see me again, Balfe?'

Balfe's entire body seems to stiffen at Gryffin's comment. He recovers quickly and lifts his chin. 'Gag him.' One of the men comes forward with a metal muzzle-type gag that covers from under Gryffin's jaw to below his nose. The muzzle is firmly locked behind Gryffin's head before he is finally dragged to his feet again.

Balfe turns away from his prisoner and straightens his jacket. 'Well, Roman. It took you long enough, but you got him in the end. Congratulations.'

'Thank you, sir.' Roman's eyes keep drifting to his son. Gryffin's nostrils flare as he struggles to breathe through the muzzle, but it's his eyes that hold Roman's attention. His purple eyes are focused solely on him, almost like he's trying to communicate with Roman.

'I want *Infinity* back in Foundation space ASAP,' Balfe orders. 'We have some support vessels undergoing preparations. I need you to escort them through the Port once they're ready.'

'Sir,' Roman replies. 'And what about my people?'

'Jensen, I assure you Gryffin will pay for killing Lieutenant Rush and Commander Stanner.'

'I'd like to attend his trial, sir.'

Balfe pauses for a moment. 'Well, that is down to the Council to decide. Whatever happens, he will regret his actions.'

'Yes, sir.'

Without another word, Balfe walks away back to *Omega* with Gryffin in chains. Roman stands in silence as they disappear through the porthole and the door hisses shut behind them. He has new orders. He should be on his way to the command deck to follow them, but he can't move. As much as he tries to block it out, the image of his son gagged and in chains is frozen firmly in his mind. There is something seriously wrong taking place and he's assisted by allowing Balfe to take Gryffin. Why didn't he intervene when Gryffin was being mistreated? He only faked the fight to throw any suspicion off Roman. His chest tightens as guilt settles in.

He shakes his head and forces one foot in front of the other. His place is on the command deck. It's only after he has taken a few steps that he realises something. He hasn't made his official report on what happened on Ultar. No names were mentioned at any stage.

How the hell did Balfe know Stanner and Terra were the crew in question?

∞

Terra opens her eyes and winces in pain. It feels like she's been hit on the head with a sledgehammer after a night of drinking. She licks her dry lips, but there's no moisture in her mouth to offer any relief.

She struggles to make sense of what happened. She remembers Stanner coming to her cottage to have a meeting about the negotiations with Aleena but, after that, nothing. After a few more failed attempts, she finally convinces her eyes to stay open. She searches the room, but she's alone. She hopes Stanner is all right.

Judging by the sound of engines, she's on a ship. The decor in the room is simple, but it appears to be clean. The small cot she's on is comfortable, there's a round table in the centre with a set of chairs, and a few shelves on the wall carrying a handful of books. She gingerly gets to her feet and tries one of the two doors. It opens into a small bathroom equipped with a toilet, sink, and a shower. While she'd give anything for a hot shower, until she knows where she is and who has her, all clothes will remain firmly on her body.

She quickly uses the facilities and faces her reflection in the small mirror. She looks pretty much how she feels. Terra splashes cold water on her face to help wash away some more of the drugged feeling. She pries her tongue off the roof of her mouth and, in the absence of a longed for toothbrush, swills some water around her mouth.

Terra wanders around the room and tries the door. It's locked. So, she's a prisoner. She runs a hand down the door. The ship feels old; scars cover the metal walls from various repairs over the years. Her heart beats rapidly in her chest. This could be *Ares*.

Even though she's been drugged and locked in a room, she still can't help but get a little excited. Maybe Gryffin took her to keep her safe. She stops herself before she gets too carried away. If this is his ship, why wouldn't he show himself? Unless this is part of a game. His

382

way of putting her back in her place after she told him to speak to Roman. He made it clear a number of times that he wants nothing to do with the Foundation. She shouldn't have pushed him into the meeting.

She thumps loudly on the door. 'Gryffin! If this is your idea of payback, it's not funny! Open the hatch! Now!'

Footsteps sound outside the door and the key rattles in the lock. A tall man enters the room and leans against the door jamb with one foot against the wall. Whoever he is, he deserves a second look. She'd place his age at between thirty and forty. His dark hair is tied back into a short tail with some locks escaping to frame his face. Dark eyes examine her as he strokes his neat goatee. He looks over his shoulder and nods at someone outside. Another man enters the room and places a tray of food on the table. 'Thought you might be a bit peckish.'

'Who are you and where am I?'

'My name is Sayber and this is my ship, *Perses*.'

Her throat goes dry. 'I've heard of you. You're the leader of the Hunters.'

He nods and smiles. 'I see my old friend Gryffin has been filling you in.'

'What do you want with me? Surely you don't expect him to come and rescue me, do you?'

He pushes away from the wall and laughs loudly. 'No, we just need you where we can keep an eye on you for a bit.' He nods towards the food. 'You should eat. We had to take some of your blood, so you might feel a little weak'

Terra looks down at the small bandage on her arm. 'Why do you need my blood?'

'Nothing sinister, I promise. Is there anything else you want — apart from me releasing you, of course.'

Terra is about to decline but changes her mind. 'I suppose art supplies are a bit beyond your reach.'

He frowns. 'You've lost me.'

'Paper, pencils; anything to draw on and with. You wouldn't want your prisoner to die of boredom, would you?'

He nods. 'I'll see what I can find.' He pauses just outside the door. 'By the way, I haven't installed cameras in the bathroom, so make yourself at home.' He winks and locks the door behind him, leaving her alone and very confused.

Sayber doesn't match the image she had in her head. She had envisaged a big, burly, rough-looking man, not the attractive young man she met. Exhaustion suddenly hits her. She needs to eat, have a shower and get some sleep. If the Foundation thinks she is dead, she's on her own. She's not going to figure a way out of this if she can't even think straight.

∞

'It must be a mistake. I mean, it's a mistake. Right?'

Aleena shakes her head and wipes a tear from the corner of her eye. 'Roman sent me a message to tell me that he handed Gryffin over to the Foundation. I am to immediately report to the town hall for questioning.'

'Hang on. *Ares* left hours ago. Are you saying they just abandoned Gryffin and took off with his ship?'

'That appears to be the case.'

Chayse shouts and throws the spanner against the wall, narrowly missing the hull of the ship. 'This is complete bullshit. There's no way the crew would leave without him. Klay must have fed them a pack of lies about Gryffin.'

'Chayse, please. We must remain focused.'

'I am focused — on killing Klay.' He runs a hand through his spiked hair. 'How the hell did I miss what he was up to? Gryffin's malfunctions must be down to him. He was so protective over the schematics and results. He convinced me he was protecting the captain and I just accepted his story and did damn all about it.'

Aleena takes his hands in hers and squeezes gently. 'Look at me, Chayse.' She waits as he slowly lifts his head. 'Gryffin told me once that he does not regret the past. Today is all the matters. Today we have a ship to complete. *Nemesis* is his dream and he trusts us with it. The absolute least we can do for him is to carry this out. We owe it to him to protect everything he worked so hard to achieve.'

Chayse is quiet for a long time before he finally speaks. 'You're right. Klay can wait.' He nods at the screen in front of him. 'The new implant's operating to the specifications. First round of simulations should be done in an hour or so.'

Aleena squeezes his shoulder. 'That is encouraging. Have you been able to trace where the schematics came from?'

Chayse sighs loudly and rubs his forehead. 'No, whoever sent them was careful about hiding their tracks. Bad news is that we won't be able to remove the control implant from Gryffin's brain. It's been there too long to safely remove it.'

'And the good news?'

'The mod will permanently block any attempt to change his programming. No one will be able to use him again. Unfortunately, we need to physically insert it into Gryffin's head for it to have any effect.'

Aleena frowns. 'Ah. That will be difficult. When word of Gryffin's capture reaches the fleet, they may disband. We will have little, if no, back-up to assist us.'

'Okay — so maybe that's two pretty big problems.'

∞

Terra opens her eyes when she hears the door to her room being unlocked. She barely glances at her waiter; he's another in a long line of crew who leave food for her, then lock her up again.

So far, Sayber is keeping his word. She is regularly fed, has hot water, fresh clothes and a warm bed. The thing she takes offence at is the locked door.

She glances up at the crew member and freezes. Like his captain, this man is very attractive. His wavy brown hair is flecked with blonde highlights and reaches his eyes to frame his handsome face. He sits down on one of the chairs and stretches his long legs out in front of him. 'So, you're Gryffin's woman, huh?'

'Excuse me?'

He takes a piece of bread from her plate and chews thoughtfully on it. 'Funny, you're not quite what I expected.'

'Who the hell are you?'

The man pops another chunk of bread in his mouth and pulls a hand through his hair to brush it off his face. 'I'm Bray, Sayber's second-in-command.' He pushes the plate of food towards the other side of the table. 'That's for you.' He leans forward and rests his arms on his legs while silently examining her.

Terra crosses her arms over her chest and scowls at him. 'Did you come here just to insult and stare at me?'

He chuckles and shakes his head. 'Can't blame me for being curious. Gryffin is known for being ruthless and heartless, but you seem to have wormed your way in. I'm just trying to figure out what's so special about you.'

Terra sees red. 'Get the hell out of here!'

He laughs and holds up his hands in a mock surrender. 'Stand down, Lieutenant.' He gestures at the tray of food in front of her. 'You're not eating much. You need to keep your strength up.' When she doesn't move, he clears his throat and crosses his arms. 'You okay? You're looking at me very strangely.'

'Yeah.' She forces herself to stop staring but something about his mannerisms is familiar. 'So,' Terra says, 'Sayber attacked Ultar.'

'I can't talk about ship business. Now, why don't you start eating?'

'Why should I eat? You're just going to kill me.'

He shakes his head again and sighs. 'You're not going to be killed.' He takes a piece of meat from the plate and shoves it in his mouth. 'I made it myself. It's not too bad.' He smiles at her and pushes the food closer. 'Go on.'

He's right. She's hurting no one but herself by not eating. Terra reaches out and takes the tray.

'See. Not too bad.' He stands up and stretches. A sheet of paper on her bed catches his attention. He picks it up and whistles. 'Wow, this is great. I wasn't expecting you to be able to do something like this with some scraps of paper and a broken pencil. I'm impressed.' He drops the page back on her bed. 'I still can't let you go.'

'Excuse me?'

'Don't get me wrong. I'm flattered you're drawing me, but it's not going to change a thing. You're here until Sayber says otherwise.' He winks at her as he leaves, then locks the door behind him.

Her plate crashes to the floor as she quickly gets to her feet. She grabs the drawing of Gryffin from her bed and stares at it. The image blurs and suddenly, instead of Gryffin's face, it changes to Bray.

She paces the small room for a few minutes, then slumps down onto the cot. The mannerisms, the feeling of familiarity, those dark blue eyes; it suddenly all makes sense.

Bray must be Brayden Sawyer — Gryffin's half-brother.

There is no other explanation. The two men may not look exactly alike, but Bray and Gryffin are so similar — too similar — in other ways. He even sees it himself — that's why he thinks the drawing is of him.

How the hell did Brayden end up on a Hunter ship? Whatever the reason, she's sure it's no coincidence.

Gryffin slowly forces his eyes open and waits while his implant adjusts his vision.

His cell is approximately ten feet square and made of recycled, welded metal with a door cut into the wall opposite him. Wherever he is, it's not a shiny, new Foundation ship. Something warm and wet trickles down his arm. He follows the trail of blood up his arm to his wrists, tightly secured by heavy chains to the ceiling. The skin on his flesh arm has torn from his dead weight hanging on the chains.

He clenches his fists but it just makes the irritating pins and needles worse. He mustn't have been here for too long if he still has some sensation. He tries to move his legs to take pressure off his sensitive arm connections, but there isn't enough give in the chains around his ankles.

He grits his teeth and pulls on his arm restraints, but apart from messing his wrist up even more, the ceiling bolt doesn't budge. Ignoring the pain in his wrist, he tries his leg chains next but there's no way out. He can break out of most restraints so whoever has him knows what he's capable of.

The locks on the door release and it screeches open. A harsh yellow light switches on, temporarily blinding Gryffin's sensitive eyes. When the spots clear from his vision, he comes face to face with the Foundation admiral from his past 'How are you feeling today, High Commander?' Balfe asks.

Gryffin's attention switches to Sayber when he sees him leaning against the door frame behind Balfe. 'You're dead, Sayber. I promise I will kill you for this!'

Balfe walks up to Gryffin. 'You focus on me when I'm talking to you.' The way Balfe looks at him makes Gryffin feel like a specimen. 'So, you're the troublesome Gryffin.' Balfe walks around him and comes to a stop in front of him again. 'Well, I'm usually a difficult man to impress, but I must say, I am actually a little impressed.' Balfe runs his hand down Gryffin's metal arm. Gryffin growls and tries to pull away. 'Get your damn hand off me.'

Balfe laughs. 'You don't seem to understand what's going on here. You see, I paid for your arm – for all your modifications. There's been a lot of money invested in you over the years. We own you — every little piece of metal in you, and on you, and it's high time we got what we paid for.'

∞

Roman sits back in his chair and stares at the blank computer screen. He put out a secured message to Aleena about an hour ago. Whether she believes he's not going to arrest her remains to be seen.

As soon as Balfe left, he turned back to Ultar as fast as *Infinity* could go, his mind racing as fast as the ship. He needs to talk to Aleena — quickly. Unfortunately, he wouldn't be surprised if Aleena never speaks to him again.

His unit sounds and he knocks his chair over in his rush to sit down. Roman activates the screen and breathes a sigh of relief when

Aleena's face appears. 'Thank goodness. I was beginning to give up.'

'What do you want, Captain?'

He doesn't blame her for being angry. 'Is your line secure?'

She looks a bit confused by his question, but checks her system and nods.

'A mutual friend said I can trust you. I need to talk to you.'

Aleena says nothing for a tense minute. 'You and Doctor Collins be outside my house in ten minutes. If I suspect you are anything but sincere, I will not meet.'

'Of course. Thank you, Aleena.' He ends the transmission and leans back in his chair. He's still not sure what he will achieve by meeting Aleena, but if it brings him one step closer to uncovering what the hell is going on, it is worth it.

∞

'How are you doing, son?'

Great, so now he's hallucinating. Gryffin raises his head and looks at Rayde. He's been without food and water before, but never seen things that weren't there. The vision walks further into the room and slaps him on the back. 'You're real?'

'Oh, I'm very real.' Rayde looks up at him. 'Bit of a mess you're in, son.'

'I don't... How are you here?' As much as he'd like to hope, he knows Rayde isn't here for a heroic rescue. There's no urgency. If anything, he looks relaxed, and that worries and confuses the hell out of him.

Rayde runs a hand through his hair and examines the restraints. 'I have a lot of eyes focused on me now. I brought you into the Nomad. I ignored the fair bit of resistance from the rest of the group, but I put my neck on the line for you. After the hellhole we found you in, I thought you deserved a shot. A chance to be the best Nomad you could be. You had your fair share of shaky moments and I can honestly say, on a few occasions, I wondered if I'd made the biggest mistake by putting you on the crew. But you did me proud, son. You know you did. Hell, I've told you often enough.' He pauses and looks up at Gryffin. 'So how do you think I felt when you betrayed me?'

'I what?'

'I give you back your life, assimilated you into my crew, and you thank me by destroying everything I worked so hard for.'

Gryffin is struggling to keep up. 'I didn't,' he stammers.

Rayde turns on him fast and presses his hand tight against Gryffin's throat. 'Yes, you bloody well did! I thought I had found the perfect heir when I literally stumbled across you. Tough, lethal, and more importantly, obedient. Everything I thought the Nomad needed in a leader. All along, I told you to keep your human side under wraps; said no good would come of it, but you thought you knew better. Protecting the colonies? Really? Your trades and protection deals screwed us.'

'But you backed my decision.'

Rayde sneers. 'What other choice did I have? I thought once it backfired you'd see sense and revert. I wasn't expecting it to succeed, or for the rest of the group to support it.'

'We're thriving because of the deals.'

'Well, that's not good enough!' Rayde shouts. 'We don't deal. With someone like you at the helm, we should own the Sector.' He paces in front of Gryffin. 'I mean, look at you. You weren't created to trade in food and medicine. They built you to be an unstoppable warrior, not a damn farmer.'

The anger pushes past Gryffin's confusion. 'They didn't build me!' he growls.

Rayde shrugs. 'Modified then. Either way, you failed to use what they gave you to its full potential. You focused on the human side and got too close to certain people. I told you to stay away from her, that it would never work. What the hell were you thinking?' He suddenly clicks his fingers. 'I know. You wanted to sleep with her. Right?'

'Don't talk about her.'

Rayde grabs Gryffin's hair and pulls his head back. 'You put our people at risk because you couldn't control your damn hormones. Just because you missed out on your adolescence the first time doesn't mean you get a rerun.' Rayde sighs and steps back. 'How could I honestly let you carry on malfunctioning? I had no choice but to take back the Nomad I created.'

'You betrayed me?'

'After you mentioned you remembered this Balfe, I contacted him and agreed to help him on two conditions: he leaves me all the Nomad ships, and he had to help discredit you. I can't overthrow you. You've got too much backing within the group. At least this way, I won't face any opposition when I try to correct this bloody awful mess you've made.'

'You made a deal with the Foundation?'

'That's what your version of the Nomad do, right? Make deals. I don't really care who I have to deal with as long as the end result is me in the high commander role again.'

'Why did you step down if you didn't want to?'

'I didn't have a choice! Loyalty started to shift from me to you. I thought with you as second-in-command, my position would only grow stronger. It had the opposite effect. The crew wanted you as captain.'

'I didn't know.'

'I don't care what you did or didn't know! I've been around long enough, son. I'm aware what happens when crew lose faith in their captain. It was only a matter of time before you were forced to overthrow me. By stepping aside, I got to keep control — through you.'

'So I was nothing but your damn puppet!' Gryffin growls.

Rayde looks at him and smiles. 'That's a good way of putting it.'

'The Foundation officers on Ultar. Did you kill them?'

Rayde laughs. 'You've got no one but yourself to blame for their deaths. You shouldn't be too hard on yourself, though. It is what you were *modified* to do. You're only being true to yourself.'

'So this is what you wanted me for all along. What you said about having my back. You lied?'

Rayde crosses his arms. 'Not quite. When I found you, I told you I'd do everything I could to help you fulfil your potential. Finishing the surgery will do that. And I will be right by your side through the whole procedure.'

∞

Terra lies back on her small cot and stares at the blank metal ceiling. It must be time for her meal. Bray's visits turned into a regular occurrence and in spite of her situation, she can't help but look forward to seeing him. Company is company, and anything to break up the otherwise monotonous day is good. Unlike his brother, Bray is relatively easy to talk to and seems to enjoy speaking to her.

He's no fool, however. All attempts to pry information from him failed. She's still no closer to discovering why she's here. It probably has something to do with Gryffin, but she doesn't know for sure. Right on schedule she hears footsteps approaching. Bray opens the door and sits opposite her as she eats.

'Thought you should know we have him.'

She freezes with a piece of bread halfway to her mouth. The food churns in her stomach and threatens to make an appearance again. 'Who?'

He gives her an exasperated look. 'You know full well who.'

'When?' He shrugs, not giving her any details. 'How is he?'

Bray shrugs again. 'Alive for now.'

'You're okay with all of this?' She stands up and paces the metal floor. 'You can look me in the eye and tell me you're fine with all this?'

'It's a war, Terra. He's my enemy — plain and simple.'

'Have you been to see him?'

He shakes his head. 'No need. It's up to the captain what he wants to do with him.'

She takes a deep breath and takes the plunge. 'Your full name is Brayden Sawyer, right?'

He looks at her quickly; his dark brows scrunched in confusion. 'I haven't told anyone my full name.'

'I know your brother, Daegan.'

He looks as if he's seen a ghost. 'How do you know about him? He died years ago.'

'He didn't, Brayden. I've met him — quite a few times.'

He thumps his fist on the table. 'My name is Bray.' He stands up. 'Listen, I don't know what sort of sick game this is but I'm not playing. My brother is dead.'

She doesn't let his outburst stop her. Terra pushes a sheet of paper across the table. 'This is the drawing I was working on yesterday. The one you thought was of you.'

'What the hell does a drawing of me have to do with anything?'

'Just look at it.'

Brayden sits down and grabs the page. After looking at it for a few seconds, he frowns. 'I don't understand. This is Gryffin.'

Terra sits down beside him. 'That's exactly what I'm trying to tell you. The drawing was never of you. You thought it was, because you and Gryffin are so similar in certain ways. I didn't realise until you pointed it out.'

Bray drops the page and stands up quickly. 'Gryffin ... that cyborg is not my brother. My brother is dead.'

'No. Not yet anyway.'

'What do you mean?'

She shoves the drawing against his chest. 'Maybe you should go and visit your prisoner before it's too late.'

52

Milla doesn't know why Aleena asked her to come too, but she welcomes the distraction. She's worried about Terra and being cooped up on the ship staring at metal walls is driving her crazy.

Their transport comes to a stop outside Aleena's house. Lucan steps around from the driver's side and without a word, opens the back. With no alternative, they step inside and Lucan shuts the door, leaving them sitting in the dark. They drive in circles for what seems like half an hour before the transport lowers in a lift and the back door finally opens.

She follows Roman out and blinks as her eyes adjust to the artificial lighting. Milla looks around in wonder at the vast cave. A network of tunnels leads away in three different directions. Before she can fully take in their surroundings, Lucan pushes them through a small door to their left, down a flight of stairs, through another few sets of doors, and along more winding passageways. After a few minutes, she has completely lost her sense of direction. She suspects that is the idea: take them on the scenic route to make sure they can't find their way again.

Finally, he stops at a large set of metal doors and gestures for them to go through. They enter a vast room with an enormous wooden desk holding a bank of communication units. Tapestries cover the walls and a thick ornate rug sits under the desk. Aleena rises from her chair and gestures for Roman and Milla to sit.

'What do you want to talk to me about?' she asks Roman.

'What is this place?'

'That is not your concern. I have little time and even less patience.'

Aleena's tone shocks Milla. The woman sitting in front of them is completely different from the softer leader they had met initially. By the look on Roman's face, he's just as surprised. 'Gryffin told me the Foundation may be behind the death of Stanner and Terra. He also said the Foundation have been in the Sector before. I've handed Gryffin over to Balfe and, for reasons I can't fully explain, I think it may be one of the worst decisions I've ever made.'

'You got that right.'

Milla turns towards the voice and smiles when she sees Chayse standing by the door.

'You've returned a highly dangerous weapon to its creators.'

∞

Rayde is working with Sayber and the Foundation.

Gryffin curses his naivety. Why the hell didn't he see that coming? He took his eye off the ball by chasing after Terra. The betrayal hurts more than he could ever imagine. His life's just been one big lie.

When the Nomad — specifically Rayde — took him in, it was a second chance. Rayde supported him through every step of his recovery. He sat with him during countless surgeries to put right what the Scientist had done. Rayde taught him how to walk again, how to talk again. He trusted Rayde. For what? So he could end up here again. A part of him wishes Rayde never found him. Knowing what he's lost just makes everything worse.

Blood drips down his forehead and trickles into his eye. If the boredom of hanging in the dark cell doesn't kill him, the beatings might. Apart from the long line of masked guards sent to beat him, he's ignored.

The cell door swings open and Rayde enters holding something that makes Gryffin's stomach churn: a thick metal collar with a long chain attached to each side of it. 'Look familiar?'

Of course it looks familiar. It's the same design as the one he wore for five years of his childhood. Rayde had personally cut it off him.

'Present from me. Should fit you like a glove. We measured you for it when you were unconscious.' Rayde signals behind him and a guard enters the room. He roughly pulls Gryffin's head back by his hair, while Rayde slowly puts the collar around his neck.

Gryffin's throat closes as Rayde locks the collar tightly against his skin. It digs painfully into his neck, making it difficult to breathe and swallow. Rayde pulls on the chain attached to the front of the collar, forcing his neck and head forward while the rest of his body is held in place where it is.

Gryffin tries to concentrate on breathing, but even with his implants, his lungs struggle to keep oxygen moving around his body. The last thing he wants to do is pass out. Determined not to give his mentor the satisfaction, he forces himself to look at him. 'Shouldn't the collar be on you? You're the Foundation's pet.'

The smile on Rayde's face falters slightly. A small victory, but it makes him feel a little better. Rayde picks up a metal bar and hits Gryffin across his upper chest. Gryffin bites back a scream as Rayde slowly walks around the cell. 'I'm no one's pet,' Rayde spits out. 'I answer to no one.'

'Keep telling yourself that.'

He kicks Gryffin in the side and laughs as a rib breaks with a sickening crack. 'The Nomad were better under my command. I put you on the leader's seat so you could continue to run the group the way I did. I mean, seriously, did you really think you were fit to lead? You're a machine and I am your operator.'

Gryffin has no response.

'Struck a nerve, did I?' He hits Gryffin in the chest, driving the air from his lungs, then strikes again across his shoulders, tearing the already bruised skin. Gryffin squeezes his eyes shut and grunts as the pipe makes contact with the backs of his legs. Rayde grabs a fistful of hair and roughly forces Gryffin's head up. 'You know what? I'm going to enjoy watching them cut you open.'

He smiles and pats Gryffin on the back like he's done so many times before. But instead of the reassurance he used to take from the gesture, now it makes his skin crawl. 'Get your damn hand off me,' Gryffin grinds out through clenched teeth.

Rayde laughs. 'Son, you're going to have to get past your "I don't like anyone touching me" issue pretty quickly. From what I've heard, there's going to be a hell of a lot of that going on when they cut you up.'

Gryffin doesn't know why Rayde using that personal bit of information against him pisses him off as much as it does, but something snaps inside him. After years of keeping it to himself, he finally told Rayde how he feels when anyone touches him. Rayde helped him deal with it, only to shove it back in his face now.

His eyes shift as his control slips. The smile on Rayde's face disappears for a moment. 'Losing it won't help you. You're not getting out of here.' He leans against the door frame and examines his fingernails. He may look relaxed, but Gryffin knows different. He's been around Rayde long enough to see the tension in his arms and a slight increase in his breathing.

Gryffin locks his knees and looks down at Rayde. 'Whatever they do to me, I will get control of myself again. I've fought the implant every single time and always won in the end. It might take me a month or a year, but I will get control and then I will kill you. I'm going to enjoy cutting *you* open.'

Without another word, Rayde turns and storms from the room. Alone again, Gryffin lets his head drop. He's not going to be alone for long. Through the open door, he can hear Rayde talking to someone in the corridor. Whoever it is, they're being ordered not to hold back. If everyone else has been holding back, he's in for one hell of a good time with this next visitor.

He locks his struggling emotions away and forces his head up. His purple eyes focus on the guard as he enters the cell. The man pauses at the door and Gryffin smiles. 'What you waiting for?'

∞

'A weapon?' Roman says. 'I don't understand.'

'That's a given,' Chayse replies.

'Chayse,' Aleena scolds.

'I'm sorry, Aleena, but it's too late. He had these second thoughts, but still handed Gryffin over.'

'They were my orders,' Roman argues. 'I couldn't do anything about it at the time. If, and I mean *if*, the Foundation is behind any of this deception, I want to help.'

'Problem is, I don't trust you enough to explain,' Chayse says.

Roman stands up and waves his arms in the air. 'What do you want me to say? I'm trying to make sense of all of this. Stanner was murdered, Terra is probably dead too, and a war is about to break out. I've spent most of my adult life serving the Foundation. According to our tests, Gryffin's implants are made of Foundation-grade metal.'

Roman rubs the back of his neck as he paces the room. 'I've dedicated my life to the Foundation. Fully believed every line they fed me. If they're involved in this, and did something to my people to get Gryffin back so they can torture him again, I need to know. Have I wasted my life fighting for the real enemy?'

Aleena looks over at Chayse and shakes her head. 'I'm sorry, Captain, but too much is at stake. I cannot trust you not to betray us as you have Gryffin.'

Roman runs a hand through his hair. 'I know I've done nothing to prove you can trust me, but I want to help. I need to help. To somehow make amends for whatever wrongs the Foundation committed to this Sector and Gryffin.'

'You can't make amends for what you did to Gryffin,' Chayse argues.

'I know that!' Roman slams his hands on the table top. 'I betrayed my own son by turning my back on him and there's not a damn thing I can do about it!'

Both Aleena and Chayse freeze at his outburst and admission. Aleena stands up and approaches Roman. 'Gryffin is ... your son?'

Roman nods. There's no point denying the truth any longer. 'Milla matched our DNA months ago. Until now, I didn't want to ...' He sighs and shakes his head. 'I refused to accept him.'

Aleena places her hand on his arm. 'This changes things. Please come with me.' She gestures for them to follow her out of the room and along the corridor. When they reach the main cavern, Roman stares in shock at the vast underground space. It's the last thing he's expecting. So is the large, fierce-looking ship occupying it. Teams of people mill around the ship and fill the metal gantry laced up the cavern walls.

Roman walks into the cave, dodging cables, gantry, computers and people as he goes. 'What is this place? Who are all these people? What the hell do you need a ship like that for?'

'I will answer all your questions on one condition. You must be willing to listen and accept what I tell you as the truth. Your son's life isn't the only one at risk.'

∞

Bray paces outside the cell unable to make himself enter. He shouldn't be here. There's no reason for him to be here. If Sayber finds out, he'll be in serious shit, but curiosity is getting the better of him. He has to prove Terra wrong, prove how ridiculous her statement is.

Daegan is dead. End of story. There's no way in hell he's alive, let alone on the same ship as him. He pulls the drawing from his pocket and looks at it again. Yesterday he saw his own face. Today, he doesn't know what he can see. The face still looks like him but, with all the metal and scarring, it's also clearly Gryffin.

He takes a deep breath and pushes the door open. The silence in the room unnerves him as he waits for the light to turn on. Once he sees Gryffin, he is shocked. He's witnessed Sayber's interrogation tactics before, seen the brutality of his captain as he beat information out of prisoners. It went with the job — not particularly pleasant, but necessary nonetheless. What he sees in front of him goes beyond questioning. It's clear Sayber isn't responsible for the injuries. It must have been Rayde.

The Nomad leader hangs limply in his chains with too many cuts and bruises on his body to count, some so deep the blood still runs down his skin to collect in pools on the ground. It looks like Rayde has stuck to beating Gryffin instead of some of the easier methods of extracting information. Whatever is going on with Rayde and Gryffin, it's more than information gathering. He wants Gryffin to suffer.

Bray slowly steps closer, hoping for some movement but gets nothing. 'Are you awake?'

He cringes as his voice echoes loudly in the cell. It works though, and Gryffin lifts his head to look at him. Bray carefully reaches out to move the dirty, lank hair hanging over Gryffin's face. Beneath the blood and bruises, he sees similarities to his features. He quickly steps away and trips over his own feet. 'What the hell is going on?'

'Who are you?' Gryffin's voice is hoarse but still firm.

'He's your brother.'

Bray spins around to face his captain and Rayde. 'You knew?'

Rayde laughs and shakes his head slowly. 'Of course I knew.'

'We're part of a select group Gryffin put together,' Chayse explains. 'He selected us from his ships and sent us here to work with Aleena on his plan.'

Roman leans back in the chair and looks over at the large ship towering in the background. 'What plan is that?'

Chayse gestures over his shoulder at the ship behind him. 'That's *Nemesis* — our secret weapon. Over the last few years, Gryffin secretly gathered another crew, a group of people he unquestionably trusts. He's handpicked forty-three people from across the fleet and they're on the surface ready to crew *Nemesis*. Sayber, the Foundation, and the Nomad know all about our ships. Except this one. Even Gryffin himself hasn't seen it.'

'I thought you said he arranged this.'

'He wanted us to build a ship but, after putting the primary team together, he stepped back. He knows nothing about the vessel, no idea of her size, capabilities, design. Nothing.'

Roman stares over at the ship again. 'You mean you've done all this without him?'

'Yes,' Aleena says. 'Not involving him proved difficult, but he made it clear from the start it had to be a secret.'

'So what's this ship for?'

Chayse takes over again. 'Long story short, someone on *Ares* has been poisoning Gryffin.'

'Similar to the poison used on Ultar?' Milla asks.

'Not quite,' Chayse replies. 'I mean someone tampered with his programming. I presume you can guess some of what happened to Gryffin as a child.'

Milla nods. 'I got the gist from his scars. It doesn't paint a great picture.'

'No,' Aleena confirms. 'He spent five years on an old station undergoing modifications. Rayde, the captain of *Ares* at the time, found him. Rayde and his crew nursed him back to health over many years.'

Chayse clears his throat and leans back in his seat. 'A few months ago, Gryffin started to lose control of his implants. The attacks came more frequently and each time he struggled to gain control of himself again. I've been looking into the reasons for his malfunctions and it all points towards a pretty big programming error. It started before the assault on Ultar.'

'The poison on the knife,' Milla suggests.

Aleena takes over again. 'That is what we thought, but whoever did that helped us. I received an encrypted message shortly after you left. It led me to a computer chip detailing a new implant which, when fitted, would completely counteract the primary one in his head. It would give him back the control he needs. Chayse has been able to begin simulations on a working model, but he estimates it will be approximately one year before he is confident enough to physically fit it to Gryffin's brain.'

'So, we're just expected to sit back and do nothing for the next year?'

'Of course not,' Chayse replies. 'This mysterious contact also said they have a temporary version available to load into the captain. Apparently, there is someone in place to do this once it's ready.'

'How temporary?'

Chayse shrugs. 'Days, weeks — no idea. It all depends on how long Gryffin himself can keep fighting for.'

Chayse activates the screen and brings up a series of schematics. It takes Roman a moment to realise one of the schematics shows Gryffin. 'The knife used to stab him on Ultar was loaded with dozens of microscopic chips. Our mystery helper gave us a live link to Gryffin.'

Milla whistles. 'This data is live?'

Chayse nods. 'It allows us to test our simulations.'

Milla points at a series of stats on the screen. 'His heartbeat is racing.'

Chayse's face drops. 'Yeah, he's in pain.'

'That's impossible,' Roman says. 'He's in Foundation custody.'

'Well, from the looks of his readings over the last few days, he's not receiving five-star treatment.'

Roman's chest tightens at the news. He can't tear his eyes from the screen. Milla examines the data. 'His heart rate is elevated and breathing laboured. The implants don't seem to be able to contend with whatever they're doing to him.'

Chayse crosses his arms and takes a deep breath. 'He's resisting whatever they're doing to him, but I doubt he can hang on much longer. He's no stranger to pain, but even he has his limits.'

'But why hurt him when they went to such lengths to get him? It doesn't make sense?'

'At the moment, Gryffin's brain is stronger than the control implant. He's learnt how to override its effects and — for the most part — decide when he wants to use it. That in itself was a bloody hard thing to do and took him years to figure out. The more he resists and fights the control implant, the harder it will be for them to control him.'

Roman licks his dry lips. 'They're trying to break him.'

Chayse nods. 'And it's working.'

Roman shakes his head. 'What does the Foundation gain from all of this?'

'They gain Gryffin.' Chayse loads a schematic of Gryffin's head onto the large screen. He points to a cluster of pea-sized chips attached to his brain. 'These form the primary control implant. At the moment, it doesn't work as it should. Some of the parts are inactive, but it wouldn't take much to repair it.'

'So why didn't you?' Milla asks. 'Why leave him like that?'

'Fixing the implant is the last thing we want to do,' Chayse explains. 'If it's working correctly, Gryffin becomes a weapon. Something to be controlled and used.'

'Could Klay have altered his programming over the last few months?' Milla asks.

'It's too complex for him — there's no way he could have written the program.' Chayse clenches his fists. 'But that doesn't mean he didn't upload the data. Every time the captain loses control, Klay runs, well, I suppose the best way to describe it is, a full systems check.

'He hooks the captain up to *Ares* so he can examine all his implants. I managed to get a look at the data and found something strange. The anomalies in the readings increase after each scan. Whatever the problem is with his implants, it's not accidental. But I can't detect any sign of a program or virus in the system. Whoever designed the software knows what they're doing.'

'Why would someone do this?' Roman asks. 'Why make him lose control?'

Chayse leans forward in his chair to rest his arms on his legs. 'You hit the nail on the head. Control. In the space of a few months, he's injured twenty-four crew, spent quite a bit of his time locked in a cage, or tranqed and being watched over by Klay. Then a series of attacks take place, a Foundation crew member is murdered, and another is missing. Gryffin thinks he lost control and killed Terra. Killed someone he cares about. He feels so guilty about that, he doesn't fight when the very people who made him what he is take him back. It's all little too convenient.'

'When you put it like that, I have to agree. Before Balfe took him, Gryffin spoke to me about his arm. The Foundation designed a band to disrupt the electrical current. They couldn't do that unless someone in the Foundation had intimate knowledge of his bionic arm.' Roman nods towards *Nemesis*. 'But that still doesn't explain this ship.'

'Whoever did this to Gryffin wants this Sector, Gryffin, or both,' Chayse explains. 'Without him in command of the Nomad, the group will split. It's already happening. *Ares* is the flagship, but Klay doesn't have the same level of support as Gryffin. All Gryffin's previous decisions will be overturned. That means colonies like Ultar may be left to defend themselves against another group coming in to take over. *Nemesis* is to bridge that gap.'

Roman looks back at the schematic on the screen. 'So, let me get this straight. You're saying the Foundation instigated this and have used my crew, the colonies, and Terra to get my son —who they kidnapped years ago — back, so they can torture him and turn him into a weapon?'

'I'm afraid so, Jensen,' Aleena confirms. She stands in front of him and looks up into his eyes. 'Help us. Please. Working together, we can get both Gryffin and Terra back safely.'

Helping Aleena could be his chance to make a difference. He can fight for something better, instead of filling the pockets of the Foundation. He looks over at Milla to gauge her opinion. As soon as their eyes meet, she nods, no hesitation. 'If we do this, we'll be disobeying a direct order. They want *Infinity* back at the border. They could very well come after us.'

Chayse looks back at *Nemesis* towering behind them. 'Then we'd better not waste any time.'

∞

Bray stands frozen to the spot beside his brother. 'I don't understand, sir.'

Rayde smiles. 'It's pretty straightforward. I wanted to make sure I could trust Sayber and his first officer, so I ran your DNA to check your details. Imagine my surprise when you popped up as a match for Gryffin. So, out of curiosity, I did a little further digging.'

Bray tries not to show too much emotion as Rayde quietly walks around Gryffin. He has a bad feeling about this. Without drawing attention to himself, he checks his gun is within reach. Luckily, Rayde's interest is with Gryffin rather than him. Sayber remains motionless at the door and keeps a close eye on events.

'I know your parents were Maggie and Dean. That you grew up in the large shadow of your missing big brother. I know you pushed yourself to excel at everything you did, even from a young age. But it didn't matter. No matter what you did, you felt you couldn't compensate for the fact your brother wasn't there. Then, to make matters worse, your parents died while trying to find him.'

Bray opens and closes his mouth a few times but can't keep up with his thoughts. How does Rayde know all of this about him?

'You moved out here to live with your grandparents, then things started to go wrong. You got in with the wrong crowd. Began to smuggle weapons across the border and got caught. Spent five years in a maximum security prison where you awaited a death sentence. Then you disappear. End up on his ship,' he says while he points at Sayber.

Bray subtly moves his hand closer to his gun.

Rayde steps closer to him. 'One question. How exactly did you get out of the prison?'

'My cell mate broke out. I hitched a ride with him,' Bray replies.

407

Rayde grunts. 'I see. I hear you earned quite a name for yourself in prison. All that pent up anger finally had an outlet. You violently attacked many of your fellow inmates. *Naughty Bray.*'

Bray finally finds his voice. 'Why am I still here if you know all that?'

Rayde shrugs. 'Your record on *Perses* is impeccable. You didn't seem aware of the truth, so I didn't see the harm in allowing you to stay. Besides, it's not like you have any feelings of loyalty towards your brother. You do blame him for your parents' deaths, don't you?'

Bray looks over at Gryffin — his brother. Rayde's right. He does blame him for their deaths.

'Just as I thought.' Rayde turns around and walks out of the room. 'Now, I suggest you return to work, Commander. You don't want to end up with your brother.'

Bray stands beside Gryffin, unable to move and unable to say anything. Before he walked into this room, he had a plan, but now he can't even remember why he's here.

'I didn't know.'

He turns towards Sayber. 'Sir?'

Sayber leans against the door jamb and runs a hand through his long hair. 'I didn't know about you and him,' he says as he nods towards Gryffin. 'Lock the cell and get back to work.' Sayber turns on his heel and marches out of the cell.

∞

'What the hell are you doing?' Sayber shouts as he enters the freighter.

Rayde barely looks up from the screen. 'What exactly didn't you get, Hunter?'

Sayber slams his hand down on the table. 'Gryffin and my first officer! Why the hell didn't you tell me? *Perses* is my damn ship after all!'

Rayde slowly swivels his chair around. 'Watch your tone, Sayber. I don't know why you are so upset. Nothing has changed as far as you're concerned.'

'I'm the captain. I should have known.'

Rayde turns back to the screen and waves Sayber away. Sayber storms out after fighting the urge to slam Rayde's face against the counter.

This whole deal is starting to get bloody irritating. *Perses* is his ship. His! Nothing to do with Rayde, yet he feels more and more like a guest on his own vessel. He should have known about Gryffin and Bray. Rayde's right; it probably won't change anything, but knowledge is key when in charge of the ship. When someone knows more than you, they have the upper hand. It is high time he got the upper hand again.

54

Avoca walks through *Perses* on his way to the freighter. He keeps his head up and tries to show an air of confidence, even though it is far from what he feels.

He's not comfortable on this ship, or among Sayber's crew, but he'd much prefer to be here than where he's going. The sooner this stage of the project is complete, the better, so he can get off this depressing vessel. Its dark, cramped corridors are a stark contrast to what he's used to on *Epsilon*.

He stops at the door to the lab and closes his eyes. He'd give anything not to go in there, but he has no choice. It is the landmark event they've all been working towards after all. All those years of dirty secrets and lies have come down to this. If he doesn't show, the others will find out and it could mean the end for him. Avoca takes a deep breath, puts on his best poker face, and enters the room.

Gryffin is naked and firmly locked to the table in the centre. They have cut his hair close to his head and hooked him up to various monitors. The Scientist works in the corner making checks, while Sayber quietly leans against the wall with a haunted look on his face. Avoca hides his sigh of relief when he sees Gryffin is unconscious.

Balfe looks over at him. 'Admiral Avoca. About time. We're ready to begin.'

'Very well.'

The Scientist turns Gryffin's head to the side and cuts into his skull. All of Avoca's worst nightmares come true when Gryffin's eyes fly open. He focuses on Avoca and locks onto him.

'Stop!' Avoca cries. 'He's awake!'

The Scientist doesn't hesitate for a second. Sayber pulls Avoca to the side, out of Balfe and Rayde's sight. 'What the hell do you think you're doing, Avoca?' he hisses.

Avoca can't tear his eyes away from Gryffin. 'He has to stop. The anaesthetic isn't working.'

Sayber sits on the edge of the counter. 'There is no anaesthetic; just something to paralyse him.'

Avoca looks back at the table in horror. 'But why?'

Sayber shrugs. 'He muttered something about anaesthetic ruining the results, or compromising the readings. Get yourself together. You don't want Balfe to see you like this.'

Avoca shakes his head and swallows. 'I wasn't expecting it.' The Scientist ignores his audience and continues drilling. 'What exactly is he going to do?'

Sayber hands him a tablet. 'All the technical stuff is in there. Short version: he's fixing the dud implant in his brain and adding a few modifications. He's also going to give him a new leg, or replace a part of it. I don't understand, or want to know what he's doing.'

Horrified, Avoca scans through the data. Sayber is right. The Scientist has found a way to cut away the top layers of tissue and muscle and replace it with cybernetic parts. Gryffin's thigh would be metal with flesh and blood underneath, leaving the bottom half of his leg as skin and bone. If not for the disturbing nature of the procedure, it would be ingenious.

Sayber looks away and curses. Before Avoca can stop himself, he turns towards the table. The Scientist is passing wires through a hole in Gryffin's skull. He pulls the knife through Gryffin's skin from his ocular implant, along the side of his head, to meet with the hole. Avoca has to turn away when the Scientist picks up the drill and screws things in place.

He wants to leave, wants nothing more than to run screaming from the room, but he can't. He couldn't live with himself if he ran to the safety and comfort of his room while Gryffin is going through this. The least he can do is stay and support him as best he can.

Avoca swallows back the bile that wants to come up, and stands firm as he tries to switch his brain off. It's no good. He knows he'll see Gryffin's haunted eyes in his mind for quite some time.

∞

Chayse checks the information for the third time before he calls the others. 'A Foundation ship has entered orbit.'

'Can you call up the signature?' Roman asks. He looks at the figures on the screen and frowns. 'It's *Epsilon*. Avoca's ship. What's he doing here?'

'Whatever it is, it can't be good.' Milla adds. 'He works in close collaboration with Balfe.'

'Can you contact him?' Roman asks.

'No need,' Chayse says. 'He's contacting us. Wants permission to land his ship and have a meeting. Apparently it's urgent. Hang on. According to this, he's transmitting on the same frequency as our mystery friend.'

'Could it be a coincidence?' Aleena asks.

Chayse shakes his head. 'Each ship's signature is unique to that vessel. The Nomad put a hell of a lot of effort into masking ours. While you can hide them with considerable effort, you can't duplicate them. It looks like Avoca has a secret he wants to share.'

∞

Gryffin groans out loud as the pain roughly pulls him back into consciousness. Instead of hanging from the ceiling, he's lying naked on a cold metal floor. After a moment of fighting the urge, he retches and vomits blood on the metal.

He screws his eyes shut as the room spins. The dizziness makes him throw up again, but the more he throws up, the worse the pain in his head gets which, in turn, makes him retch more. After what seems like a lifetime, his stomach stops churning, leaving no distraction from the pain in his head. He clenches his teeth to stop himself from screaming. All that exists is the pain. Wave after wave of unrelenting agony attacks his head. He forces his eyes open and blinks to try to clear his vision.

Shapes take form in the room and all he wants to do is scream. He's back in the lab where he spent his childhood. Bile rises in his throat. He knows this isn't the actual lab. It blew up years ago, but that doesn't stop the wave of memories from washing over him.

He suddenly remembers the other modification. Gryffin looks down and cries out when he sees his right thigh. The metal reaches from his hip to above his knee. Thin connectors stretch onto the remaining flesh of his lower leg and across his groin area. They snake down his other leg and connect to a band of metal in his skin above his left knee.

The modification is excruciating. The area where the metal and flesh join is oozing, the living tissue feels like it's on fire and the connectors pull painfully on his skin. He closes his eyes and lies back on the cold floor. As much as he tries to fight it, a lone tear escapes from his right eye.

He endured years of being slowly cut open and having bits of him replaced with metal. Years of seeing his humanity gradually sheared off so they could add wires, screws, and metal to his flesh. But, after two decades detesting himself, he had finally begun to accept his new body.

He opens his eyes and stares at his shiny new leg. No matter what happens to him, that flesh is gone forever. The large chunk of metal drilled into him will be a permanent reminder he can never escape his past. Rayde was right. He is their property and always has been. No matter what he does or where he goes, he has no say in what happens to his body. No say over what piece of flesh they will replace next.

He makes the mistake of moving the new limb slightly and can't hold back a scream as the pain explodes up his leg. The pain continues to assault him as he lies on the floor. He tries to breathe through it, but the collar seems to have grown tighter. His throat closes as the panic threatens to smother him.

He needs to keep calm. He needs to keep control of himself, but he can feel it quickly slipping away. It won't be long before the implant traps him in his head. Instead of the usual dull throb, the implant has roared to life. It fights to push his control aside and he feels his eyes shift, probably for the last time.

Gryffin forces his mind off the pain and onto Chayse. If all goes to plan, Chayse will lead the Nomad into battle against him, and he needs them to be successful. He doesn't want to live like this, but that's not what scares him the most. The damage he can inflict once he is under the implant's control terrifies him. The thought of hurting any of the colonies, or his people, makes his stomach turn again.

The room spins as a white hot blade of pain sears through his brain. With little strength left, he slowly rolls onto his right side. The pain from his leg helps to ground him for a few more minutes. He knows he should be fighting harder, he should at least be trying to get out, but he can't get his thoughts in order. His last independent thought is of Terra. He closes his eyes and then the implant finally wins.

55

Roman leans against the wall and watches Avoca as he fidgets in his seat. The Admiral landed fifteen minutes ago and, as with himself and Milla, had been escorted to the cavern in the dark by Lucan.

Although Roman has never met the man in person, he knows of his reputation. From what he has read, Avoca prefers to work from his ship rather than from behind a desk on Earth and is a straightforward, well-liked man who rose through the ranks by hard work.

Why would he risk everything to help a Nomad, especially one the Foundation wants so badly? Aleena hands Avoca a cup of herbal tea. 'Admiral Avoca. Why have you been helping us?'

He takes a long drink before he lowers the cup onto the table in front of him. 'I need to start at the beginning. Twenty-five years ago, Balfe came to me raving about a fantastic new project. He wanted me to complete the team of four. I thought it would be the perfect way to get noticed. Elevate myself in the ranks. Initially, I wasn't told what the project entailed. No excuse, of course. Balfe tasked me with helping to fund the project by siphoning funds from various Foundation accounts.'

He pauses and stares into his cup. 'What happened?' Aleena prompts.

'I saw Gryffin. Well, he wasn't the Gryffin we're familiar with now — he was just a young boy. Balfe took me to the station. They'd had a breakthrough. One of the subjects survived the first stage of the project.'

Roman looks across at Chayse. He could have sworn he heard a growl come out of him. Avoca still stares into his cup and doesn't seem to notice.

'I won't go into details, but what I saw will stay with me forever. By the time we visited him, he'd given up screaming. The boy just lay there while the Scientist cut him open. It was the silence that disturbed me the most. You don't expect that.

'The boy — Gryffin — had adjusted to all the implants, so Balfe and the Scientist wanted to take it further. They wanted to adapt the primary implant to allow mind control. I knew it had gone too far at that stage, and that I had to try and find a way to end it, but I didn't get a chance. The station blew up a year later. To be honest, I felt relieved. At least he wasn't suffering.'

The full-force blow from Chayse knocks Avoca off his feet and into the desk behind him. Roman immediately jumps up to help Avoca. 'Why did you do that?' Avoca exclaims. 'I'm trying to explain what happened.'

'No, you were explaining how you watched my captain, my friend, be tortured and you just walked away. You left him there for another year! You spineless—'

'Chayse, please calm yourself,' Aleena begs.

Milla takes his hand and leads him to the back of the room away from Avoca. Roman sits Avoca back down. 'As you can tell, emotions are running a bit high. Go on.'

Avoca glances over at a clearly pissed off Chayse in the corner.

Aleena hands him an ice pack, which he holds to his split lip. 'When we got a report of Lieutenant Rush being aided by a man with implants, Balfe started the project up again. As soon as I could, I put my plan in place.'

'The implant modification,' Aleena says.

He dabs his lip with a tissue and frowns at the blood. 'That's only part of it. I have a man on the ship where Gryffin is being held.'

That instantly gets everyone's attention. Chayse breaks away from Milla and forces Avoca to his feet again before Roman can stop him. 'Give me a name!'

'It's Brayden Sawyer. Gryffin's brother.'

∞

Bray steps aside to let Sayber into his room. In all the time he's been on board, this is the first time the captain has called to, let alone entered, his quarters.

Sayber slowly walks around the small space while he completely ignores Bray standing nervously at the door. Sayber finally comes to a stop beside the computer station and props himself up on the edge. 'I've been captain of *Perses* for quite a few years now. I've fought hard to get the ship and crew up to scratch. It took years to convince more ships to join us, but I finally succeeded. The Hunters are now a fleet I'm proud to lead. But, it's only possible because I can depend on every single crew member. They put their trust in me to lead and I, in turn, have to trust them.'

Bray doesn't like where this conversation is going. He glances over at his sidearm sitting beside Sayber on his desk. Sayber smiles and takes hold of the gun. 'You want this?'

'Do I need it, sir?'

Sayber crosses his arms. 'That depends. You see, I ran a full check on every single member of my crew recently. I wanted to make sure, as captain, I know exactly who is on my ship. Imagine my surprise

418

when I found communications hidden in the system to an unknown location near the Port.' He looks up and locks on to Bray's eyes. 'Transmissions sent by you.'

Bray's heart beats faster in his chest. It was inevitable this would happen sooner or later; he had just hoped it would be later. 'Sir—'

Sayber holds up a hand to silence him. 'I'm going to ask you a few questions. If I don't like the answers, or think you're lying, I will kill you. We clear?'

Bray nods.

Sayber gestures to Bray's bed. 'Take a seat, Commander. We may be here for some time.'

∞

'His brother? How the hell did you locate Gryffin's brother?'

Avoca sits back down again with Roman in front of him to create a barrier from Chayse. 'It was my job to destroy all evidence of the test subject's previous lives, so nothing would come back to implicate us. The name Daegan Sawyer always stuck in my head. Apart from the fact it was an unusual name, Daegan was the first one to survive the testing and alterations.

'When the station blew up, I put both him and the project to the back of my mind, but never forgot. Years later, I got a report of some new prisoners admitted to the penal colony in the Outer Rim. One of the prisoners was called Bray Sawyer. The name sounded familiar. After some digging, I found out that he was the brother of that poor boy I saw in the lab.

'I hadn't been able to save Daegan, but I could help his brother, so I paid to have him broken out of prison. I explained about the project, and he agreed to work for me. He felt in my debt. It took a year, but he got himself onto a Hunter ship.'

'How could you have known the project would start up again?' Roman asks.

419

'When I got a report from Tyrat prison where Bray was, I noticed something.'

'Gryffin,' Chayse offers from his corner. 'He spent three days there about four years back. From what I read, the guards interrogated him for the duration of his stay. He escaped and took out fourteen guards on the way.'

Avoca nods. 'More impressively, he did all that while injured. There was no name, just a description, but the implants said it all. I altered the report to hide his details but knew deep down, sooner or later, Balfe would discover him.'

'Okay,' Chayse says. 'But why a Hunter ship? Why not put his brother on a Nomad ship?'

'I took a gamble. I knew Balfe had a contact here to help him. As Gryffin was a Nomad, I figured, if captured, he would need to be given to another group. I gambled on the Hunters. I was lucky.'

'So, what are Brayden's orders?' Roman asks.

'As you know, I've been working on a modification to the main control implant fitted to Gryffin's brain. Bray stabbed Gryffin on Ultar a few months ago to release the nanoprobes into his body through the knife wound. Once the probes began to transmit, I passed all the information on to you. I needed your help to finish this.'

'We can see from your probes he's in a bad way. What happened?' Roman asks.

'He's had surgery to fully activate the implant. The Scientist also gave him a metal covering to his right leg. Cut out the skin and muscle and replaced it with his design. He survived, but he's not in control. Approaching him without having some way to block Balfe's signals will be fatal. Bray has a program to allow Gryffin to control himself again, but it is only temporary. The plan is to load this into Gryffin and get all three of them off the ship.'

'All three?'

'Your Lieutenant Rush. She's on *Perses* with Gryffin and Bray.'

Both Roman and Chayse curse in unison. 'Why wait all this time?

Why not get them all out before the surgery?'

'Then what? Bray and I have been gathering evidence against Balfe and the project. If we kill him, there's nothing to stop my other colleague and the contact here from taking his seat. A few weeks ago, Balfe murdered one of the original members, but there's still one in Foundation space and his contributor. What's to say there aren't more people out there being tested on? We need Balfe's files. And we needed to know who this mysterious donor is. Bray only found out after Balfe captured Gryffin.'

'Who is it?' Chayse asks.

Avoca pauses. 'It's Rayde.'

∞

Rayde attaches the handheld unit to Gryffin's head and checks the programming again. The Scientist assured him Gryffin would do what they needed him to, but he wasn't prepared to leave anything to chance.

Back in uniform, Gryffin looks every bit the threat he is. The collar fixed around his neck and a new metal strip screwed to the side of his shaved head do nothing to detract from that.

Everything seems to be in order. Nothing like a field test to make sure. He leads Gryffin through the ship. Any crew members they encounter quickly step aside to let them pass. Rayde glances over his shoulder and frowns. Gryffin is limping. The Scientist said the new leg would help improve Gryffin's lower body strength. The metal part of the leg would share power with the other leg through the connectors and band, but Rayde is doubtful. It sounds a bit too gimmicky to him. Hopefully, the limp won't be noticed.

Klay meets him with the rest of the landing team in the transport bay. The twenty men are all kitted out in uniforms with Gryffin's colours on the arm. The men are a mixture of his crew and a few from *Ares* still loyal to him instead of Gryffin. *Forty-Three* and his companions had quickly overpowered any crew loyal to Gryffin. They had been locked in the cargo hold until he decides what to do with them.

He knows some of the men personally and would prefer to have their fighting skills on his side. Overall, the *Ares* crew is the best in the fleet. It would be too much of a waste to kill them. Perhaps in time they would switch their loyalty.

He had pushed for this series of outings — starting with Ultar. Balfe wanted Gryffin back in Foundation space locked up in a lab, not doing what he is designed to do. The admiral had finally seen sense and agreed to use Gryffin to convince any of the undecided colonies to join the Foundation. It is no secret that Ultar is Gryffin's favourite colony. With it in ruins, the Nomad agreements will mean nothing.

Rayde can't help but smile to himself as the team run through their final checks. Everything is falling into place. It's only a matter of time until the Nomad are back to their original roots. Well, once he takes care of the Foundation matter, of course. He doesn't know what Gryffin was thinking when he entered into the deals with the colonies. The Nomad don't barter and negotiate. They take.

Something serious must have gone wrong with his programming for him to have ventured down that path. While it's not ideal having the Foundation involved, it helps get him closer to what he wants. Once things are in place, he'll remove them from the equation. Turn their creation against them. It would serve them right.

The bloody fools honestly thought they could duplicate what they had stumbled on with Gryffin. He was a fluke — nothing more. Rayde had seen the evidence of the failed attempts when he found Gryffin. The fact he survived the crucial primary implant in his brain was a one-in-a-million lucky shot. Unless they got that bit right, the rest of the implants are a waste of time and money. But, as it is their time and money and not his, he'll keep his mouth shut. While they're busy, he can continue with his plans uninterrupted.

First things first.

He can't help but feel slightly anxious about this test run. Gryffin performed well in the simulations, but this is real life. The Scientist programmed him to storm the very settlement he seems drawn to over any other.

He looks at Gryffin and tries to figure out what attracted him to the small farming world. He had asked him, but got no response. Apparently, there are some things even the implant can't do. Making Gryffin talk about his feelings is impossible. There's something special about this planet Gryffin is trying to protect. Maybe when they get him back after this outing, he'll see if the Scientist can convince him to tell.

Klay talks the team through their mission. Rayde knows they're less than happy having Gryffin tag along. He can't blame them, either. There's no way he'd go into a combat situation with him. Even going in as support for him doesn't mean they'll be entirely safe. If the implant fails, he could very well turn on them. Rayde stands in front of Gryffin and looks into his purple eyes. 'Orders clear?'

'Yes, sir. Kill. Everyone. In. The. Village.' Gryffin struggles to get the words out thanks to the collar and the control implant. The deep, emotionless, and almost forced way Gryffin speaks when under the implant's control has always unsteadied Rayde. It makes the young man seem completely devoid of humanity.

Rayde takes a step back from the primed weapon and nods. Kill everyone in the village. He couldn't have said it better himself.

56

Sayber lowers himself onto the chair beside Bray's desk. 'Let me get this straight. You work for Admiral Avoca? But I thought he works for Balfe.'

Bray shakes his head. 'He's going along with Balfe because he has no choice. He got tangled up in the project and by the time he realised Balfe had sanctioned the use of human subjects, let alone children, it was too late to back out.'

'Children?'

'He arranged for rogue groups to attack ships near the border. They took any children aged between ten and fifteen, then killed the rest of the crew.'

'So your brother, Gryffin, was ...'

'He was ten when he went missing. I didn't know what happened to him.' Bray blows out a breath and rubs the back of his neck. 'Avoca failed to mention he was one of the subjects. Could explain why he picked me.'

'He's trying to take down Balfe and his army of whatever those men of his are, all alone?'

Bray holds his hands out to the side. 'He's got me too.'

'What exactly is your part in all this? I presume he broke you out of the prison.'

Bray nods. 'He needed my programming skills. I've developed a program to help Gryffin control what's in his head — temporarily at least, but timing is crucial. If I loaded the programming before the surgery, the Scientist could have uncovered and removed it. I got the first one in on Ultar.' He looks down at his boots and frowns. 'That just leaves the second. It needs to be loaded ASAP.'

'You sure it will work?'

'It works in the simulations. We're confident.'

'Let me recap. You con your way onto my ship. Spend years working up the ranks. Assimilate into the crew. Make command decisions with me.' He moves closer to Bray and clasps his hands so tight his knuckles turn white. 'And all the time you're working to help our enemy?'

'That's not how it is, Captain.'

'I think you can drop the false formalities.'

'You are my captain, sir. Always have been. I may be working for Avoca, but until the Foundation found out about Gryffin, I operated as a sleeper agent. Apart from checking in every now and again, I'd no other mission. Avoca never made a request for information. I'm just here to stop the Foundation, not the Hunters. I consider myself a Hunter. Nothing I did independently, or on behalf of Avoca, harmed this ship or crew. I've always acted in the best interests of the Hunters.'

'How is helping Gryffin doing that?'

'Having the Foundation in the Sector helps no one. They'll use Gryffin to destroy the Hunters and the Nomad. Local groups will be forced to sign up or be wiped out.'

'So how exactly do you plan to get this programming into his head?'

'Break onto the freighter.'

Sayber snorts. 'You do realise it'll be next to impossible. Gryffin is chained up in the lab on the ship. The only ones with access to him are the Scientist, Rayde and Balfe. They've programmed him to kill anyone outside of their little group. He'll destroy you before you get anywhere near him.'

Bray gets to his feet and slowly approaches his armed captain. 'Sir, I know I have no right to ask, but what are you going to do?'

Instead of answering, Sayber raises his arm and strikes Bray across the head with the butt of his gun.

∞

'Shit.'

Aleena looks up from her screen, frowning. 'Is that necessary?'

Chayse stands up quickly. 'Too damn right it is! *Ares* just arrived in orbit.'

'Have they contacted you yet?' Roman asks.

Chayse shakes his head. 'No, but they've sent five carriers — each heading in a different direction. *Ares* only has three transports, so it's either Foundation or Hunters with them. We don't have long before they arrive in the village.'

Roman turns to Avoca. 'Admiral, with the greatest respect, can you return to your ship? Take Lucan with you. We need you to use *Epsilon* and *Infinity* to keep them at bay as long as possible. Buy us time to get the locals out of the way.' Avoca nods at Lucan and disappears down a side corridor. He turns to face Chayse. 'Fancy taking your new ship out for a spin?'

Chayse looks over his shoulder at the vessel. His ship. It's ready, but he's not so sure he can say the same about himself. The uncertainty on his face must show. Roman stands in front of him and puts a hand on each shoulder. 'You can do this.'

'What if I can't once I'm out there?'

426

'Trust your crew. They'll help you if you need it. Aleena, we need to get your people to safety.' He looks around him, but she's disappeared.

'Here.' Chayse throws him the keys to Gryffin's bike. 'Code is 556714. She'll head to the village.' Roman straddles the bike with a big smile on his face. He traces the purple griffin on the side. 'His bike?'

'Yeah, so look after it. I'd like to give it back to him.'

Roman revs the engine and takes off up the ramp.

∞

Terra wakes with a start when someone puts their hand over her mouth. She opens her eyes to see Sayber leaning over her. He puts a finger to his lips to silence her, then leans close to speak right into her ear. 'Keep quiet and do as I tell you. Follow me. Now.'

He helps her up before stuffing her pillow under the blanket. Sayber locks the cell door behind her and hurries her along the corridor. A few twists and turns later, he brings her into a small storage room. Sayber secures the door and pulls out a large trolley from the rows of empty boxes against the wall. He unlatches the lid and opens it. 'I don't have much time. I need you to trust me and get in there.'

She can't help but gape. 'Why would I get in there? What the hell are you doing?' she hisses.

He runs a hand through his hair. 'Damn it woman, get in the damn crate! I'm trying to save your life.'

Terra crosses her arms and returns his glare. 'Why would you help me?'

'You only got dragged into this mess because of Gryffin. You shouldn't be here, so I'm rectifying the situation. We're about to go down to Ultar. I need you in the crate so I can load you onto the transport. Once we're on the surface, I'll let you out. Time is against us, so please get in the damn box.'

She shakes her head and holds out her hand. 'I need a gun.'

Sayber's eyebrows shoot up. 'You what?'

'If you think I'm running away from here, you've got another thing coming. I'm not going anywhere without Gryffin, and nothing you say will change that.'

He curses and turns away from her. 'What the hell does he have over you?' He spins back around and folds his arms across his chest. 'Why are you risking yourself for him?'

'My reasons are none of your business. Now, you can either help me or get out of my way.'

Sayber looks at her for a moment, then slowly reaches behind his back and takes out a gun. He flips it in his hand and holds it out to her. Terra reaches for it, but he pulls his hand back a little. 'You do this, you're on your own. I will not help you get him out of here. I may not agree with what's happening to him, but that doesn't mean I'll willingly help him escape.'

She grabs the gun from his hand and points it at Sayber.

'I'm trying to help you.'

She smiles slightly at him. 'You've kept me captive on your ship. Forgive me if I don't entirely trust you.'

Sayber laughs and shakes his head. 'Fair point.' He gestures at a stack of crates against the side wall. 'Spare Hunter uniforms. If you're going to wander around, it might help if you blend in.'

'Thank you, Sayber.'

Sayber stops at the door and looks back at her. 'Terra, you need to be careful if you do find him. They gave him some pretty severe modifications. There's a high chance he will kill you.' Before she can respond, he opens the door and leaves her alone. Terra pulls trousers and a shirt from one of the crates. As she changes her clothes, she tries to come up with some plan. From what Sayber said, the odds of getting them both off the ship alive are stacked against them.

Aleena is in the middle of a nightmare. Everywhere she looks her people flee for their lives, running from the crew of *Ares*. The very ship they thought would protect them. She clutches the gun Roman gave her as she catches her breath behind a woodpile.

She steadies her breathing before she slowly emerges from behind her shelter and runs into Gryffin. She takes a step back and her throat goes dry when she gets a proper look at him. It's like she's facing an alternative version of him.

His once attractive face now borders on cold and cruel. His purple eyes are lifeless and the metal makes him look more deadly, especially since it stretches from his face to the side of his head. With his hair shaved off, nothing softens the scars and implants. Although it's quite clear he has been severely beaten, she cannot let herself feel any sympathy for him right now.

She clears her throat. 'Gryffin. Put the weapons down.'

He takes a step towards her.

'This is not you. Please, stop this now. You would not hurt me. You have to remember me.'

He continues to walk towards her until she's backed up against the wood stack. Gryffin strikes out and stabs her through the left shoulder. He drives his knife straight through her and into the wood behind. She screams out in pain as the metal pierces her flesh. Gryffin puts his hands on the wood at either side of her head and traps her even more as he leans forward.

'Please, stop! What do you want? Speak to me! Damn it, say something!' Tears stream down Aleena's face as she realises her words mean nothing to him. Gryffin suddenly slams his hand against her neck. The electricity courses along his arm. He looks straight into her eyes and slowly squeezes.

∞

Roman leans the bike to the side as another bullet whistles past his ear. He needs to find Aleena. Panic threatens to spill to the surface. He should have known she'd leave to help her people as soon as she heard the ships had arrived. She wouldn't be much of a leader if she hid away while her people fought.

He releases a few rounds and uses the machine's powerful engine to weave through the buildings. If it were any other situation, he'd take the time to enjoy the ride. The bike is a beautiful machine. He had to leave his own precious bike on Earth when he took command of *Infinity*. Being in the saddle again makes him realise it was probably the wrong decision. Seems he may have one thing in common with his son.

His radio sounds in his ear and brings him back to the task at hand. 'Roman, it's Avoca. *Ares* got away from us. We sustained minor damage. It didn't look like she was in the least bit bothered by us. She swatted us away and kept going towards Ultar. Where are you?'

'I'm heading towards the central square. Where's Chayse?'

'He should be with you in a few minutes.' As he finishes speaking, the ground shakes. He turns around to see the giant battleship rise from the cavern behind Aleena's house. He's got to hand it to the Nomad. *Nemesis* is impressive. Before the ship clears cover, her guns target the transports flying over the village. She fires on the unsuspecting vessels, using the element of surprise in her favour. Within minutes of her launch, *Nemesis* has destroyed the transports. 'Roman, it's Chayse. We're going after *Ares*. Your ground crew and mine are helping the villagers. Any sign of Aleena?'

'Not yet.' He pick up speed, praying he finds her in one piece.

Gryffin doesn't want to choke her. She's important to him. He screams at himself to stop, over and over in his head. *Stop! Stop! Stop!* But it does no good. His hand continues to slowly squeeze the life out of Aleena.

Without warning, sharp pain explodes through the flesh part of his arm. He turns to the side to find Roman pointing his gun at him. 'Let her go!' When he hesitates, Roman fires again and hits him in the shoulder.

'Stop!' Gryffin shouts.

Aleena's eyes widen when she hears him shout out loud. 'Gryffin?'

'Aleena?'

She releases the breath she was holding. 'Yes. You scared the hell out of me.'

Roman slowly approaches him. 'Let her go, Gryffin.'

Aleena puts her hand on his arm and gives it a gentle squeeze. 'Come on,' she sobs. 'Please let me go.'

His hand does what he wants it to. He has control again — barely.

It must've been the pain of the two gunshots.

He looks back at Aleena and his eyes lock on his large knife sticking out of her shoulder. Gryffin reaches out to touch it but pulls his hand back. 'I did this? Aleena, I'm ...' His voice cracks, unable to form the apology he desperately owes her. Instead, he reaches out for the handle again, hating the way she flinches as he gets nearer. He grips the knife firmly and pulls the blade out of her shoulder as gently as he can.

'Thank you.' She wipes her tear stained face and then gingerly reaches out to touch the discoloured skin around the band on his neck. 'What have they done to you?' Instead of pulling away, he allows the contact. He can't explain it; he needs to feel it. Blood oozes from both nostrils as he continues to wrestle the implant.

Roman pushes him away from Aleena. After checking her quickly for any other injuries, he stands between Gryffin and her. 'You need to call off your men.'

'I can't.'

Roman pulls off his shirt and wraps it tightly around her shoulder to stop the flow of blood. 'Can't or won't?'

'Gryffin, call them off!' Aleena shouts. 'Do it now!'

'I can't disobey my orders,' he says, as he grabs his head when pain explodes through his brain. 'Go now! Damn it, Aleena, move!' he yells.

'What about you?'

'I have a mission to complete. There's nothing I can do about that. They ordered me to kill everyone in the village. Go!' He grabs his head and cries out in pain. 'Go! I can't fight against it for much longer.'

Aleena hesitates, so Roman pushes her away from Gryffin. 'Go, get on the bike.'

She pauses briefly before she nods and runs over to the bike.

Roman turns to face Gryffin again. He pulls his gun out and points it at his head. 'Any bright ideas?'

'Pull the trigger.'

Roman looks down at the weapon in his hand. 'Any other ideas?'

Gryffin shakes his head. 'This won't end until I'm out of the equation. I can't do it myself — self-preservation programming. But if you're quick, you can kill me before I can stop you.'

'Your orders are to kill everyone in the village. What about outside the village?'

Gryffin wipes away the blood pouring from his nose. 'They'd be safe — for now. The other plan is better.'

'You're not going to die because of the Foundation. We'll figure something else out.' He slowly backs away from Gryffin towards the bike.

Gryffin struggles to get his mind back on track, but it's no good. He can't fight any longer. He stands up straight and looks towards Roman. With one last glance over his shoulder, Roman guns the engine. He disappears into the trees as Gryffin raises his arm and narrowly misses hitting him.

∞

'Where the hell did that come from?'

Rayde ignores Balfe and his whining. He has no doubts the mysterious ship is thanks to Gryffin. Even without seeing the enormous purple griffin painted on her hull, he still would have known. It seems he may have underestimated his protégé. 'Get Gryffin off the surface.'

Balfe's slightly red face turns to him quickly. 'Are you insane? This is the very test you have been demanding since the beginning. Why would you want to pull him out now?'

'Damn it, Balfe,' he spits. 'Do you really want your new creation splattered all over the surface? We have no idea what this ship's capabilities are. If I know Gryffin, he will have ordered this vessel to destroy him.'

Balfe laughs but stops when he sees Rayde is serious. 'His people would do that?'

Rayde shrugs. 'Gryffin will have given the order and he doesn't tolerate disobedience. We can't rule it out.'

Balfe immediately contacts *Ares* and orders them to evacuate. Rayde walks to the view screen showing the destruction on the surface. Balfe continues to complain in the background, but Rayde filters him out. Balfe may see the test as a failure, but Rayde couldn't disagree more.

Ultar lies in ruins below them. Gryffin has successfully reduced his precious little hideaway to ashes and blood, in the space of a few minutes. Rayde hopes there's a part of Gryffin's brain still his own. A small smile touches his lips at that thought.

∞

Chayse steps down off the loading ramp onto Ultar. Smoke curls up from the town centre from countless burning buildings.

Fifty-six people lost their lives in twenty minutes. Gryffin and the team he led were ruthless. He's thankful most of the villagers had been able to get to the tunnels before it was too late. He doesn't understand the reason behind it, but Gryffin did stick exactly to his orders and only targeted anyone in the actual village.

He heads over to Roman and Aleena. The Foundation captain is holding Aleena close to him, trying to offer her comfort. 'You let him go?'

'There wasn't anything else I could do.'

Chayse waves his gun in the air in frustration. 'That could have been our one shot to get him back! Just because you don't give a damn about him doesn't mean the rest of us feel the same.'

Roman gets right into Chayse's face. 'Please tell me how you would have expected me to restrain and hold him? He would have killed me without blinking.'

Tret pushes through the crowd. 'Sorry to interrupt, but *Nemesis* has picked up ten Foundation ships coming through the Port.'

Aleena cries out in despair. 'How can we possibly defend ourselves against ten ships?'

'Seems Balfe doesn't want to wait to take over.'

Chayse shakes his head. 'There's no reason to wait. Gryffin is out of the way and being used to destroy the colonies,' he says while giving Roman a dirty look. 'The Hunters are working with the Foundation, the Nomad are leaderless, and all the colonies are crying out for protection. He won't have any resistance.'

Roman walks around the group and faces *Epsilon*, *Nemesis,* and *Infinity* sitting side by side in the clearing. 'We'll just have to prove him wrong.'

∞

'Are you telling me you had no idea he was building a battleship on a farming colony?'

Rayde slams his hands onto the table. 'Of course I didn't know!'

Balfe isn't convinced. 'I've only been here a few weeks and I knew there was something going on with this colony. It's hard to believe you didn't even suspect.'

'Believe whatever the hell you want. It's done now. Can the Scientist not uncover any details?'

Balfe wanders over to Gryffin, restrained to the table in the centre of the room. The Scientist is running a full check, but so far everything appears to be working as expected. In spite of the mystery ship, everything else went to plan on the surface. From the readings, it seems like Gryffin pushed past the implant for a few minutes, but luckily it fought back and won. All in all, he deemed the test a success. Gryffin even killed quite a few of his precious colonists.

The Scientist moves away from the head of the table where he's working on Gryffin. The Nomad is conscious and staring at the ceiling; fine metal pins peek out from his ocular implant. Grimacing, Balfe has to turn away as blood oozes out of the corner of Gryffin's eye. 'I have asked. Apparently, Gryffin planned this all out in advance. He doesn't know anything about this ship. We're on our own.'

'It looks like we've underestimated him,' Rayde says. 'I'll send a team back to Ultar.'

'No point. I doubt you'll detect anything. Gryffin appears to have been planning this for a while. We can take care of Ultar with all the other loose ends later. For now, I need to rendezvous with the fleet. You stay here until the Scientist releases Gryffin.'

'What about Sayber? He's starting to get defiant.'

Balfe glances back at the operating table as the Scientist inserts a large needle into the side of the Nomad's head. 'Once the rest of the group gets here, the Hunters will be obsolete. Keep Sayber on a leash for now. He'll be out of the way soon enough. I have to ask: what exactly are you doing to him?'

The Scientist glances up briefly from what he's doing. 'Minor tweaking. There's always room for improvements.'

Balfe suppresses an involuntary shudder as he walks away.

∞

Bray fights against the churning in his stomach and struggles to open his eyes.

'Open your damn eyes.'

Recognising Sayber's voice, Bray forces his eyes open. His head pounds violently in time to his heartbeat. 'Sir?'

'Shut up and listen. You're on the freighter. I smuggled you in with some of the Scientist's supplies.' He points down the corridor. 'The lab is at the end of the first right turn. You should have about an hour clear. The Scientist just finished with Gryffin.' Sayber pulls a gun out of his jacket and hands it to Bray. 'You get caught, you're on your own, understand?'

Bray wants to thank his captain, but Sayber disappears down the corridor before he gets the chance. Using all his willpower, Bray manages to get to his feet with his stomach contents still where they belong. Surely Sayber could have found an easier way of smuggling him on board. Then again, he can't blame Sayber for his actions; he had just learnt his second-in-command had been deceiving him for years.

Bray takes a few deep breaths through his nose and out his mouth. After a minute, the queasy feeling has settled somewhat. With time against him, he puts one foot in front of the other and makes his way towards the lab.

As promised, the large space is empty. From listening to Balfe's conversations, Bray knows Gryffin is in a cell hidden in one of the walls. Seems the Foundation and the Scientist are a little anxious about someone stealing their project.

After a few minutes of searching, Bray uncovers a large panel behind the main computer bank standing proud of the rest of the wall. He runs his hand over the smooth metal and pushes against it. After a bit of trial and error, the large panel slides to the left, uncovering a cell hidden behind it.

Even though he is wasting precious time, Bray can't seem to get his limbs to move into the room. Monitors and displays beep and buzz in the background, carefully watching every vital sign of the man hanging in the cell.

His brother.

Well, what remains of his brother is hanging in the cell. All Bray can see at the moment are the metal implants and the wires. No doubt, each of those wires links to his systems. If Bray isn't careful, he could inadvertently trigger an alarm if he changes Gryffin's vitals in any way.

Bray clasps the small chip tightly in his hand. Years of hard work will either prove successful or a total failure, in the next thirty minutes. He finally forces himself to close the distance between them.

Without looking at his brother's face, Bray takes a screwdriver from his pocket and carefully opens the small interface at the side of

Gryffin's head. Bray slowly raises his hand and clicks the chip into place. The tiny LED on the chip blinks red as the program loads into Gryffin's control implant.

Bray wipes his sweating palm on his trousers and forces himself to breathe. The upload should only take two minutes, but a hell of a lot can go wrong in that time. After checking the still-steady vitals on the screen, Bray moves back to his brother. The LED changes to green, indicating the upload has completed, so Bray gingerly reaches out and removes it. He screws the interface closed again and steps back.

Without looking at his brother, he leaves the cell and reseals the metal door. Bray hurries across the lab and shoves the chip into the recycling unit, not leaving until he hears it being ground to dust. Bray quickly retreats from the lab and sprints back along the corridor.

He slows at the junction when voices echo along the hallway. It's Rayde and the Scientist. With no other option, Bray makes his way back the way he just came and comes face-to-face with Sayber. His captain raises his weapon and directs it at Bray's head. Sayber raises one eyebrow in a silent question. Bray nods once in response, hoping he is reading the situation correctly.

Seconds later, Rayde turns the corner and smiles at them. 'So, you were right to be suspicious of him, Sayber.' Rayde stops in front of Bray and searches through his pockets. He pulls out a chip and tosses it to the Scientist. The man catches it and loads it into his handheld. After a few seconds, he shakes his head. 'The data is still intact. He hasn't uploaded it to *Thirty-Five.*'

Rayde nods and turns back to Bray. 'What exactly were you hoping to achieve here, Commander?' Bray stays silent. Rayde scrutinises him for a moment. 'What happened to your head?' When he again gets no reply from Bray he gestures to the two security personnel behind him. 'Take the commander to the lab. Perhaps the Scientist can convince him to chat with us.'

Security knock Bray to the ground and fit restraints to his wrists. Rayde pats Sayber on the back. 'Seems I may have underestimated your loyalty, Sayber. Giving up your own second-in-command is a big step.' Rayde strolls down the corridor and after meeting Bray's eyes for a second, Sayber follows. They pull Bray to his feet and push him towards the lab.

Resigned to his fate, Bray feels almost calm. He has completed his mission after all. Years of hard work has finally paid off. He's glad he took the second chip with him. At least this way, they would assume he had failed and Gryffin is still under their control. Bray is confident the programming will be effective. The unknown factor is when it will be effective.

For this to work, they need Gryffin to wake up and destroy the freighter along with all the research into the cyborg program. If that means Bray and Gryffin have to die in the process, so be it.

∞

Terra creeps along the dark corridors, listening for any signs of life. She doesn't know what it is about this ship that makes it feel like death.

She suppresses a shiver and checks her handheld. According to the plans she stole from the system, the lab should be around the corner. She tightens her grip on the gun and peers around the corner. Whatever plan she had tried to form on the way here disappears as soon as she sees the inside of the room.

The first thing she sees is blood, everywhere. Moving in slow motion, she steps further into the room. The gun in her hand shakes slightly. A large table sits in the centre. Blood pools along the channels cut into the side and at the restraint points. The last person on the table had struggled enough to cut themselves.

She moves around to the head of the table and sees something that makes her heart lurch in her chest. Clumps of dark brown, blood-soaked hair litters the ground — Gryffin's hair. Terra crouches down and picks up a handful. Something shiny near the drain catches the light.

Terra brushes some hair away to uncover Gryffin's pendant. Blood smears the platinum griffin and the leather cord has been cut. Tears blur her vision and she angrily brushes them away. There'd be time enough to cry later. She quickly pockets the pendant for safe keeping.

A weak groan from her left brings her to her feet. She rounds the large computer console and gasps. Bray is lying on the floor of a cage; the left side of his face covered in blood. They have screwed a metal implant to the side of his face and three more to his bare chest.

Terra rushes over to him and tries to open the cage, but it's securely locked. 'Bray! Bray, can you hear me? Please open your eyes.' She reaches through the bars and tries to rouse him. After a long few minutes, he finally opens his eyes. 'Thank goodness. Bray, it's Terra. What the hell have they done to you?'

'Did it work?'

She shakes her head. 'Did what work?'

'Gryffin.'

'What about Gryffin?'

'By the sounds of things, Bray managed to fit his mod.'

Terra swings around and glares at Sayber. 'What are you doing here?'

'I'm here to get my second-in-command off this ship.' He pulls a tablet from his pocket and hooks it up to the locking mechanism on the cage.

'What do you mean he fitted the mod?' Terra asks.

Sayber doesn't look away from the tablet. 'Bray designed a mod to help Gryffin get control of himself again.'

'How do you know all this?'

He unhooks the tablet and pulls the door open. 'We don't have time for a back-story. Bray, where is he?'

Bray gestures over to a large door-sized panel in the far wall. Sayber lifts Bray onto one of the gurneys, hands him a gun, then joins Terra at the door, neither knowing what they are going to reveal on the other side.

Every single inch of his body aches.

Gryffin thought after being in pain for so long he wouldn't feel it anymore, but he's not that lucky. His physical body may not be reacting to the pain, cold, hunger, or exhaustion, but the section of his mind he still controls feels every bit of it. He wants to sleep, to fall into the darkness and never surface again, but he doesn't even have control over that.

He is an observer stuck in his body.

Gryffin's thoughts and memories are disjointed and confused, but he knows he attacked Ultar. Images of different faces — some familiar, some not — keep entering his thoughts. He can only assume they are people he murdered. From snippets of overheard conversation, he knows the assault didn't quite go to plan. He remembers Roman stopped him doing something, but he doesn't know what. Had Aleena finished the ship and used it against him? Another thought forces its way into his head. Did he kill Aleena?

He tries to concentrate on the faces, but he can't hold on to any of the images and memories long enough to identify them. Gryffin takes a deep breath and tries to keep control of his emotions. It takes him a minute to realise he took a breath. He tries his luck and repeats the act. Not only is he able to control his breathing, he can also move his hand.

The pain intensifies as he gradually gets control back. After a few failed attempts, he opens his eyes to meet darkness. In frustration, he tries to slam his head back against the metal frame, but his head is strapped down too securely.

The locks on the door release and a few seconds later the metal wall in front of him slides open. Light pours into the room and he squeezes his eyes shut. He hears light footsteps on the metal floor as someone approaches him.

'Oh my God!'

He must be losing his mind. He could have sworn Terra spoke, but it can't be her. Terra is dead; Klay killed her, on his orders. Gryffin pries his eyes open again and blinks as he tries to clear his vision. Even though the light still distorts what he sees, there's no mistaking the person staring at him.

'Terra?'

∞

'Aleena, a Hunter ship has entered orbit.'

Aleena and Roman glance at each other with the same worried expression on their faces, but before either of them can voice their concerns, Chayse interrupts. 'We're being contacted by a Hunter called Quinn. Says he needs to meet with us. He claims to have information on Gryffin, Terra, and the Foundation.'

Roman runs a hand over his hair. They've only just managed to secure the town again after the last battle. They can't face another one. He examines the satellite information. The ship arrived a few minutes ago, but hasn't made a move towards the planet. It's sitting

443

there transmitting the message over and over again. Even though it's probably a trap, they have to meet with him. If there's even the slightest possibility he is legitimate, they'd be fools to turn him away. He pulls Aleena to the side. 'Your call, but I think we should allow him to land.'

'You believe he has information?'

Roman shrugs. 'I honestly don't know. I don't think we're in a position to ignore the possibility.'

Aleena nods. 'I agree. Chayse, can you please take *Nemesis* and escort this man to the surface. If he does anything to alarm you, please do what you must to protect Ultar.'

Twenty minutes later, the two ships land side by side outside the town. A team from *Infinity* and some of Aleena's security line the landing zone to greet them. The loading ramps open on both ships, but there is no other movement from the smaller Hunter transport until Chayse has stepped onto the surface.

Quinn slowly walks down the ramp with his hands in the air. He stops at the bottom and turns in a circle. 'As you can see, I'm unarmed.' He lifts his shirt to show he doesn't have any concealed weapons. 'I have an urgent message for Aleena and Chayse.'

Aleena takes a step forward. 'A message from whom?'

Quinn smirks. 'I would have thought that bit was obvious. Sayber wishes to help you destroy the Foundation's hold on the Sector.'

∞

'Let go of me.'

Sayber keeps a firm grip on Terra's arm to keep her from getting any closer to Gryffin. 'He killed a village full of colonists. Take it slowly. We need to be sure he's in control first.'

Terra wants nothing more than to go to him, but she has to admit Sayber is right. She tries to rein in her emotions, but it is proving difficult, especially when she takes time to look at Gryffin. He's

444

chained to a large X-shaped frame in the centre of the cell.

Various wires snake out of computers lining the walls and enter his body via his implants. His close-cut hair offers no cover for the new metal screwed to the side of his head. Small cuts and bruises pepper his face, arms, and chest.

Sayber moves into the small cell and stops in front of Gryffin. 'Can you hear me?' Sayber unfastens Gryffin's head, letting it drop to his chest.

Gryffin raises his head slightly, before it drops to his chest again. Sayber grabs him by the chin and forces his head up. 'Damn it, look at me!'

Gryffin's eyelids flutter slightly before opening.

Terra moves further into the room. 'Is he okay?'

Sayber shrugs. 'Damned if I know.' Sayber examines Gryffin for a moment, then breathes a sigh of relief. 'His eyes are blue. That's got to be a good sign. They've been purple since they operated on him.' He turns back to face Gryffin and curses.

'What's wrong?' Terra asks, her voice trembling slightly. She doesn't know if she can keep her emotions in check much longer.

'His eyes are purple again.' He shakes Gryffin's head roughly. 'Stop being a coward. Fight against it.' Sayber lets go and takes a step back. 'We're already on borrowed time here. I came back to get Bray, not coddle my enemy.'

'There's no way I can unchain and unhook him alone. I need you to help. Five more minutes, please.'

He blows out a breath and waves his arms in the air. 'Fine, but I'm not letting him out of here until I'm sure he's back.'

Terra walks right up to Gryffin. She lifts her hand and places it gently on the side of his face. He turns his head to the side, putting more pressure on her hand. 'Gryffin, it's Terra. Look at me, please.'

'I killed you,' he says, his voice barely above a whisper.

Her thumb rubs against the stubble on his cheek. 'No, Rayde made it look that way. I'm all right, Gryffin.'

He turns his head away from her. 'I killed you and I killed the Ultarans. They're all dead ... because of me. Just like before. I killed all the others ...'

'Others? Any idea what he's talking about?' Sayber asks.

She shakes her head. 'Maybe he's confused.'

'Yeah, well, time's running out.' Sayber steps closer and runs his hand along Gryffin's thigh. Until then, Terra hadn't noticed the wires disappearing through a slit in his trousers. Before she can ask what's wrong with his leg, Sayber grabs on to Gryffin's thigh and squeezes hard.

Gryffin throws his head back and roars in pain.

'Stop it! You're hurting him!' Terra shouts.

'That's the point.' Instead of letting go, he increases the pressure.

∞

Gryffin quickly slams back into his body in fiery hot pain. He opens his eyes and the first thing he sees is Sayber squeezing his leg. He growls and lashes out, but the restraints hold his arm back.

'Down boy!' Sayber says. 'Keep that fist to yourself. I'm here to help. Show a little gratitude.'

'Let me out of these chains and I'll show you how damn grateful I am.'

Sayber moves back and shakes his head. 'He's all yours, Lieutenant.'

Gryffin looks towards her and Terra's piercing green eyes light up. 'You had me worried for a minute,' Terra says. 'I never thought I'd be so happy to see your blue eyes again.'

His brain tries to access and process everything, but it's struggling. 'How are you here?'

'It's a long story, one we don't have time for right now. We need to get you out of here.' She steps back and looks down at the series of wires attached to him. 'Are these safe to remove?'

Gryffin squeezes his eyes shut and tries to get his brain back in gear. 'Yeah, they're monitors. They'll pull out. You blocked the implant?'

'Actually, you have Bray to thank for that, with some help from Sayber.'

Bray. Why does that name sound familiar? So many names and faces swirl around his head, but he can't make sense of any of them. He shakes his head and gives up trying to remember. As long as this Bray doesn't get in his way, he couldn't care less who he is.

Terra turns to face the Hunter leader. 'Can you help unlock him?'

Sayber looks dubious. 'Only if he keeps those fists to himself.'

Sayber steps closer and crouches down to see to the restraints around Gryffin's ankles. Once they're off, he releases Gryffin's metal arm. As soon as the lock clicks open, Gryffin grabs Sayber around the neck and lifts him off the ground. Terra tries to help Sayber, but Gryffin ignores her. 'I'm going to enjoy killing you.'

'Gryffin! Put him down. He's here to help!' Terra says.

'He betrayed everyone in this Sector. For what? Money?'

Sayber's mouth opens but nothing comes out. Terra pushes herself between Sayber and Gryffin. 'I'd be dead if it weren't for him. I get you don't like each other, but if we're going to survive this, we need to work together. Once we're off this ship and have driven the Foundation out, you can go back to killing each other. Until then, can you please put your playground squabbling aside?'

It takes another full minute before Gryffin finally opens his hand and lets Sayber drop to the ground with a thump. 'I still don't get why you're helping me.'

Sayber rubs his neck. 'In spite of popular opinion, I think we were doing fine without the Foundation in the Sector. The Nomad and Hunters knew what was what. I wanted you dead and vice versa. We each had our place. What's going on now,' he gestures towards the metal on the side of Gryffin head. 'What they did to you ...' He meets Gryffin's eyes. 'They're not fighting fair. All the experiments — let's say they're not sitting so well with me anymore. Don't get me wrong, I still want your head, but not at the expense of the Sector.'

'So do you have a plan?' Gryffin asks.

Terra shakes her head. 'To be honest, no.'

'Plan is to get out of here,' Sayber offers. 'Shit's hitting the fan. Not quite sure where we can start.'

'Hitting the fan how?' Gryffin asks.

'Balfe has ten ships around the Port with another twenty due within the next day or so. We have to push the Foundation out so we can get back to tearing holes in each other. Common enemy and all that. To try and muddy the waters a bit I've sent *Perses* off. Made it look like I cut my losses and ran. Rayde sent *Kratos* after her.'

'He bought it?'

'Seems to have. It happened pretty quickly. Most of the crew were on board when they took off. Leaves us with a skeleton crew here.' He crosses his arms and nods at the final restraints around Gryffin's wrist. 'You going to be a good boy now so I can release you?'

'Call me *boy* one more time and I will kill you.'

Sayber shakes his head and unlocks the restraint from around Gryffin's wrist. He gestures at the collar. 'I'm not the right pay grade to have the code.'

Gryffin tries to keep himself upright but doesn't manage it. As soon as he puts pressure on his right leg, the pain explodes through the limb. He curses and falls to his knees. Sayber leans over him with an unfamiliar look of concern on his face. 'You okay?'

Gryffin nods. 'Forgot about my leg. Damn thing hurts like hell.'

'What about your leg?' Terra asks.

Sayber grimaces. 'They gave him a new thigh. Balfe and Rayde made me watch the op. I'm not saying there was any reason for them to do any of this to you, but your leg? That was wrong.' He holds out a hand and Gryffin allows him to help him up, while he keeps all his weight off the new leg. 'You going to be able to walk, or do you fancy hopping around after them?'

Gryffin ignores Sayber and slowly puts weight on his leg. It still hurts a hell of a lot, but he doesn't have any choice. He pushes the pain away and takes a few steps. He's limping badly, but he'll manage short-term. Gryffin tries to readjust the collar to make it more comfortable, but it won't budge. Only the Scientist, Balfe and Rayde have the code to remove it. He's going to have fun convincing them to cooperate.

'By the way, I need your command code,' Sayber says.

Gryffin looks at Sayber as if he suddenly sprouted another head. 'What?'

'As I said, one of my officers, Quinn, will go to Ultar after he destroys *Kratos*. He might already be there. I'm pretty sure either the Foundation ships, or your new-fangled vessel, will blow him up unless he can provide proof he's a good guy.'

Seeing the logic in what he's saying, Gryffin gives Sayber the code. 'Where's *Ares*?'

Sayber shrugs. 'I presume on her way to back Balfe up.'

'Rayde and the Scientist?'

'Still here. One of those guys is also on board. The rest are with Balfe. We need to take them down.'

'Don't forget about Bray,' Terra interrupts. 'We need to get him to a transport.'

Gryffin takes the offered gun from Sayber. 'We'd better get moving then. Sayber, you and Terra get Bray to a shuttle. I'll deal with Rayde and his friend.'

Terra grabs Gryffin by the arm. 'You think you're in a position to give orders? No offence, but you look like death warmed up. You take Bray back while myself and Sayber deal with Rayde.'

'You think I'm going to let you wander around this ship?' Gryffin replies. 'Get yourself to safety.'

'But I can help you.'

'You can help by getting yourself away from here.' He limps closer to her and leans against the wall. 'I thought I killed you, Terra.' His head lowers to his chest. 'I need to know you're safe. I can't do this unless I know you're safe.' He lifts his head again and his glistening blue eyes lock on hers.

Terra reaches into her pocket and pulls his pendant out. She ties a new knot in the cord and puts it around her neck, then rises to her toes to place a kiss on his lips. 'I know how important this pendant is to you. I'm going to hang on to it for safe keeping. Make sure you come back to get it.'

He straightens the pendant on her chest. Something stirs inside him he's never felt before. A knot forms in his stomach at the thought of not seeing her again. He'd kill for her without hesitation. Hell, he'd give his other arm and leg for her. Having never experienced feelings like love before, he has no idea how it should feel.

It doesn't matter what he should call this overwhelming feeling. What he does know is, if they survive, he wants Terra by his side. He needs her by his side. Gryffin leans down and kisses her with everything he has and then reluctantly pulls away. 'Deal. Now get the hell out of here.'

She smiles and turns away from him. Gryffin quickly pushes Terra to the ground when gunfire erupts from the central lab. Sayber crouches down to look out the door. 'Security team. Maybe five or six.'

'I could use some help here!' Bray calls from outside. Sayber and Terra rush out to Bray while Gryffin takes the other direction. By now, he knows the layout of this damn room like the back of his hand. He steps under and over various cables and machinery. Each step drives spears of red hot pain through his new leg. He is going to kill Balfe for his new leg alone.

He reaches the side door and cracks it open. He peers through to the corridor and smiles to himself. Damn fools didn't familiarise themselves with the layout before they attacked. That is going to be their last mistake.

Gryffin silently closes the distance between himself and the security team. He gets to within a metre before he catches the attention of the man nearest to him. Gryffin smiles at him, then shoots him between the eyes. He breaks the neck of the second while shooting the third and fourth. Bray, Terra or Sayber remove the last two which brings an end to his fun.

'All clear!' Gryffin reports.

Sayber meets him in the corridor and looks down at the bodies on the floor. 'Back on form, I see.'

Gryffin grunts, then bends down to relieve the team of their weapons. 'There'll be more on the way. Once you unhooked me, an alarm will have triggered somewhere.' He stands up and turns to Terra. 'You have to go now.' Thankfully, she doesn't argue with him. He hands her another weapon. 'You know where you're going?'

'I'll take her,' Sayber says.

Gryffin nods. 'Good.' With one last sad smile, she turns and pushes Bray away from him. 'Sayber.' Sayber stops and looks back at him. 'Remember how you tried to take *Ares* – what you did with her computer?'

Confusion crosses Sayber's face before his eyebrows shoot up. 'You serious?'

'Might be the only way to end this.'

Sayber nods slowly. 'Can't argue with that. I'll deal with it.'

Gryffin turns and climbs the stairs to the next deck. Time to have a chat with Rayde.

'Is this really necessary?'

Chayse locks the cuff around Quinn's wrist restraining him to the chair. 'Yes.'

'Man of many words,' Quinn says. 'Gryffin must have trained you. I get the impression you don't quite believe I'm honourable.'

Aleena sits opposite him with a gun in her hand. 'I am sure you understand why we must be cautious. The Hunters have hardly been friends to us.'

Quinn smirks. 'Fair point. The problem is the longer I take to convince you to trust me, the closer Balfe gets to destroying this Sector.'

Roman sits beside Aleena. 'Better start talking then.'

Quinn sighs. 'Balfe has Gryffin on an old freighter hidden in an asteroid cloud about an hour from here. The work the Scientist did on him was effective, as I'm sure you saw for yourself. Next step is to return him to Foundation space so he can be mass produced. Soldiers with his talents will mean the Foundation will be virtually unstoppable. Naturally, my captain and the Hunters as a whole aren't too keen on that happening.'

'Why the hell are you working with them then?'

Quinn shrugs. 'Sayber believed it was a good idea at the time. Balfe offered him an opportunity to get Gryffin out of the way. Unfortunately, the Hunters were a means to an end. Balfe moved some men onto our ships. A seriously dangerous group. By the time Sayber realised what was happening, it was too late. Sayber couldn't make a move without risking his crew and ships.'

Chayse snorts. 'So why send you here now?'

'You're not Gryffin, so you can drop the tough guy attitude,' Quinn snaps. He puts his feet up on the crate in front of him. 'Balfe called his modified men back yesterday. Last I heard, the six men are on the freighter, but that may have changed. Sayber's spotted an opportunity and we gotta act.'

Chayse gets up. 'We're wasting time here. The Foundation will be in the area soon. Let's lock him down until this is over. The priority is to stop Gryffin before they use him again.'

'They can't use him. Not at the moment.'

That gets Avoca's attention. 'Brayden added the modification?'

Quinn examines Avoca before answering. 'So, our traitorous commander is your man? Interesting. I have a transmission on my unit. I just heard it come in.'

Chayse pulls Quinn's radio out of his pocket and reads the message. 'This is Gryffin's command code.' He looks up at Roman. 'Seems like the Hunter is telling the truth. Bray managed to fit the mod and at the moment it appears to be working. The captain and Sayber have made a somewhat uneasy truce for the time being. Gryffin gave Sayber his code hoping it would help convince us. The captain wants *Nemesis* and any other available ships to go to the Port and stop the Foundation before more come through. He'll deal with Rayde and the freighter.'

Chayse lowers the unit and looks down at Aleena. Seeing the

continuing doubt on their faces, Quinn curses. 'We must act now!'

'What about Bray? We need to get him out,' Avoca says. 'He's in trouble because of me.'

'Sayber has secured both Bray and Terra.' Chayse says. 'He'll get them off the freighter safely.' Chayse throws the unit back to Quinn. 'That is, if we believe Sayber?'

'We must act,' Aleena says. 'Gryffin agrees.'

'How can you be so sure? I thought they've been attacking using those codes.' Roman says.

Chayse shakes his head. 'These are his personal ones. The code he uses for his unit.' He looks over at Quinn. 'By using these codes, Gryffin has given his verification.' Chayse leans back against the unit and crosses his arms as he glares at Quinn. 'So, Gryffin wants us to help you. What about him? How do we get him out?' Chayse asks.

Quinn shrugs. 'Gryffin's not my concern.'

Chayse storms up to Quinn and jams the muzzle of his gun against the Hunter's head. 'Well, he damn well should be!'

'Chayse, step down!' Roman commands. 'We don't have time for squabbling. Gryffin is more than capable of looking after himself. Our primary concern is keeping those Foundation ships from getting a foothold in the Sector. Once they break formation and spread out, the chances of us catching them decreases rapidly. Attacking while they're in the one location is our best chance.'

The young Nomad captain nods at what Roman is saying, but is far from happy about leaving Gryffin to look after himself. Even though attacking the Foundation is the most urgent task, Roman shares Chayse's concerns. He'll be no good to anyone if he can't push his personal feelings for his son aside.

'Sounds like we have a lot of work to do.'

∞

Nemesis, Epsilon, and *Infinity* come to a halt inside radio range of the ten Foundation ships led by *Omega*. Milla turns on the intercom when Avoca and Chayse contact them.

'So, Captain, what are we facing?' Chayse asks.

'Apart from *Omega*, the other ships are small patrol vessels. Manoeuvrable, but with a limited arsenal. One on one, it wouldn't be an issue. Ten of them, it's not going to be easy. *Omega* has the same capabilities as *Infinity*. What works in our favour is the fact that Balfe's rusty. He hasn't taken her into a battle for a decade.'

'Sir, we're all being contacted by *Omega*.' Milla hits the intercom linking the ships.

'This is Admiral Balfe. Admiral Avoca and Captain Roman. I can honestly say I am looking forward to getting you both back to Foundation space. I believe we have a lot to discuss, starting with treason. You've got five minutes to stand down and move away from the Nomad vessel. If not, you will be considered traitors and will face the same fate as the Nomad. I trust you'll make the right decision.'

Milla closes the channel and looks out at the small armada facing them. Three against eleven isn't bad odds. Roman leans on the back of Milla's chair and looks over her shoulder at the screen. He leans in close so no one else can hear him. 'We're all worried about Terra but I need to know you're with me on this.'

She clears her throat. 'Who's worrying? She'll be okay.'

Roman squeezes her shoulder. 'Well, how about we help her by occupying these ships?' He stands up and turns to face the Foundation armada. 'Right, people, let's get this started.'

Sitting back in his leather chair, Roman addresses his helmsman. 'Set an intercept course. All guns loaded. I want everything we have directed at that fleet. If we're to have a chance of getting out of this, we need to take them down fast.' He turns on the ship-wide intercom. 'Crew, brace for impact.'

The three ships break formation and move into weapons range. In the next few minutes, they'll either be dead or alive.

∞

Terra quietly moves along the corridor. She grips her gun firmly in her hand as she scans the darkness. God, she hates this ship. After seeing what they did to Gryffin, the feelings of hatred only intensify.

Her people did that to him. She pushes the shame and revulsion aside and climbs down the metal stairs. Terra pauses at the bottom and listens. She doesn't hear anything up ahead, so picks up the pace to meet with Sayber at the lift. Once she checks the area, Terra opens the elevator door and helps Sayber wheel Bray out.

Movement beyond Sayber catches her attention. 'Down!' Sayber instantly drops as Terra lets off a few rounds and kills the man.

Another turns the corner and shoots Sayber in the shoulder and Sayber takes him to the ground with a bullet to the head. 'We'd better pick up the pace.'

Terra slots a new magazine into her gun. 'Guess more crew stayed on board than you thought,' she replies with a slight smirk on her face.

Sayber shakes his head and gestures for Terra to lead the way. Terra slowly guides the two men through the ship. 'So, you still glad you didn't jump ship on Ultar?' Sayber asks as they continue along the dark corridor.

'I wasn't going to leave him behind. Like you didn't want to leave Bray.'

Sayber snorts. 'That's a bit different. Bray isn't a weapon. This misguided belief that Gryffin won't hurt you is going to backfire on you sooner or later.'

Terra glances over her shoulder at him. 'Thanks for the advice.'

'Your funeral, Lieutenant.'

Terra ignores him. She doesn't want to give his words any consideration, but can't deny the truth. When she saw Gryffin in the cell, she was terrified. It wasn't the man she remembered and the unknown modifications didn't help. He hadn't hurt her. Even though he was confused and in pain, he still recognised her. That means something. She has to believe that.

∞

Balfe curses as the three ships move towards them. Seems Roman and Avoca have decided to commit treason.

He's not overly surprised. He always considered them weak and emotional. Not traits he cares for in officers. Losing the ships is bothering him more. He'll try to keep the damage to a minimum, but if necessary he'll destroy the three ships. Rather that than let them fall into enemy hands. The most important thing at the moment is clearing the way so more Foundation ships can come through the Port.

'Power up the weapons. I want the Foundation ships disabled. No holding back with the Nomad vessel.'

The group holds their ground. Let the traitors come to them. A part of him wishes they were on the surface of the planet. He would have enjoyed sending Gryffin after them.

'Sir, *Ares* is here.'

Balfe laughs out loud. He thought she'd have been here before now, but better late than never. Having her here will help tip the balance in their favour.

Ares slows down in between the two groups, her guns facing the trio of ships. Feeling confident, Balfe sits back in his chair and watches the three ships approach. As soon as they get close enough, he orders all ships to open fire.

The three ships break formation and take evasive action. A lucky shot rocks *Omega*, throwing Balfe against the side of his chair. 'What the hell is *Ares* doing? Why is Klay just sitting there? Get him on the radio.'

'He's not answering.'

Before Balfe can respond, he notices *Ares* moving. The problem is her guns are moving in his direction.

457

Terra checks her watch for the tenth time in about a minute. It took ten minutes to get Bray back to Sayber's transport. She had hooked him up to the portable monitors on board and at the moment he's holding his own. That won't last unless he gets medical attention — sooner rather than later.

Sayber left four minutes ago to help Gryffin. Although she had argued and fought with him, she eventually agreed to stay and look after Bray.

Turning away from Bray's prone, too pale body, she walks to the back hatch. This is ridiculous. She can't wait here and trust Sayber has it all under control. What's to say he's not going to kill Gryffin instead? With her decision made, she checks Bray again and pockets more magazines for her gun. 'Sorry, Bray. I have to go. I'll be back soon.'

She brushes her hand through his damp hair and steps back onto the freighter, locking the transport door firmly behind her. Not knowing where to start, she retraces her steps until she can locate an interface. She hooks her unit into it and calls up the schematics.

Using the ship's internal sensors, she searches for them. It works; she picks up five heat signatures. Two are near Engineering, one a deck above moving towards Engineering, and another two near the lab where they found Bray. It takes her a second too long to realise she is one of the last two signatures.

She turns while pulling her gun out, but is too late. A man with a metal plate over his eye already has his gun pointed directly at her head.

'You seeing what I am?'

Roman isn't sure he believes it, but he does see it. He activates his radio to respond to Chayse. 'I wasn't expecting to see her.'

Before he can say anything else, the radio lights up with a message coming through from *Ares* to the fleet. 'This is Desyl. No time for details now. Short story, I've got command of *Ares*. How about we convince these ships to leave the Sector?'

For the first time since they started this, Roman can't help but smile.

∞

Every step feels like a battle, each second a struggle to stay focused and in control.

Gryffin forces one foot in front of the other until he reaches the door of engineering. According to the system, Rayde is in there. He lifts his gun and wills his arm to stop shaking as he steps into the room.

Rayde slowly turns to face Gryffin and raises his hands in the air in a mock surrender. 'So, back with us. Can't say I'm not disappointed. I liked you better the other way. What's your plan now, eh?'

Gryffin ignores the trickle of blood coming from his nose and moves closer to Rayde. 'I'm going to kill you.'

Rayde laughs harshly. 'Brief and to the point, as usual.' He leans against the unit and gestures at him with his gun. 'That would have been a lot more intimidating if you didn't have blood pouring out of your nose. Let go, son. You're only doing more long-term damage to your brain by fighting it.'

'Don't call me son — ever.'

The trace of humour leaves Rayde's face. 'Very well. Don't say I didn't try to do this the easy way.' He gestures over his shoulder and one of the modified men steps out from around the corner. That bit is bad enough without the man having his arm tightly around Terra's neck.

∞

'Have you heard anything from them?'

Lucan shakes his head and sits down next to Aleena. 'We don't have time to worry right now. We've enough to deal with here after Gryffin's strike. Focus on that.'

She nods, but says nothing. She does not want to think that they have not been in contact because something has happened. After what Gryffin did on the surface, she dreads to think what could happen with a fleet of ships involved. She had attended too many funerals and the last thing she wants is to lose any more people. The thought something could happen to Gryffin or Jensen makes her feel ill.

To take her mind off what is going on around the Port, she turns her attention to the defences. Gryffin had turned them off when he landed and as of yet, they have been unable to reactivate them. Until they can figure out how to restore them, they are completely defenceless.

In anticipation of trouble, Aleena has evacuated the people to the tunnels. It is crowded and not designed to hold so many people, but they will remain undetected for the moment.

Three hours ago, the sensors around the planet had picked up some rogue vessels showing a little too much interest. They had many of these ships visit before the alliance with Gryffin and each had been able to cause quite a bit of damage. They attacked quickly, with little regard for the locals.

Getting her mind back on the task at hand, she tries to link with the orbiting defences again. Lucan and a few of the engineers who helped put *Nemesis* together are also working on the problem from units next to her. By the looks on their faces and more importantly, the colourful language coming from each, they are having as much success as her.

∞

'She's not responding, sir.'

'Sir, we're within weapons range.'

Balfe falters for a moment as the reports keep flooding in. He planned everything to perfection. Nothing should have gone wrong. Having *Ares* taken from him was not part of that. He immediately starts to have concerns about leaving Rayde to transport the Nomad across the Port.

'Sir ...'

He snaps out of his daze and tries to regain composure. 'Protect the Port. Even if that means destroying every one of those ships. Any sign of *Kratos*?'

'Nothing yet.'

'Keep an eye out for her. Nothing is to happen to that ship.' He is too close for a disaster like that. If he comes back across the Port without Gryffin, the Council would have his rank, no question.

∞

Gryffin manages to grab onto the wall as his opponent kicks his uninjured leg from under him. His head smacks sharply against the console, splitting the skin on his forehead. Gryffin lands on all fours and the pain explodes through his new leg. He presses his hand to his leg and ignores the blood covering his palm.

Gryffin pushes the pain to the back of his mind and looks over at Rayde. His mentor smiles at him. Of all the things done to him over the last few weeks, the worst bit is the look on Rayde's face right now. He's enjoying seeing him being hurt. There's no other reason for him to pit Fifty-Eight, or whatever the hell his designation is, against him. It's for his pleasure.

As soon as Rayde produced Terra, Gryffin obediently put down his gun and complied. He didn't have a choice. He wants Rayde dead, but not at the expense of Terra.

Gryffin struggles to his feet and wills his metal leg to support his weight. Fifty-Eight pauses for a moment too long, so Gryffin lashes out and shatters the man's nose. Fifty-Eight screams in anger and retaliates by swinging the crowbar, which catches Gryffin directly on his ocular implant. Pain explodes in his head and drives him to his knees again. Fifty-Eight pushes the end of the crowbar against the damaged metal on Gryffin's face. He forces it further into Gryffin's eye and destroys it.

'Oh, that's got to hurt. One eye gone,' Rayde taunts from his position behind the console. 'What do you want to lose next?'

Gryffin ignores the stabbing pain from his eye. He grits his teeth and forces himself to his feet again. He doesn't have time for this if he's going to get Terra out of here. Problem is, he's not in the best condition for a brawl. All the operations are taking their toll on him;

he only has one eye, his reflexes are off and his brain feels like it's too big for his skull. Add that to the concentration needed to keep the implant at bay and it isn't the best day to rescue the damsel.

'Must be a bit embarrassing to lose a scuffle in front of your girlfriend,' Rayde taunts. Terra struggles to get away from him, but Rayde doesn't budge. 'You ready for more?'

Gryffin stands up straight. There's only one way he's going to get Terra out of this. He lets his control slip enough to help without being completely lost to it again — he hopes. Rayde's face drops when he notices Gryffin's purple eye. 'I'm ready for more. It's just you and me now.'

∞

Chayse grabs on to the arms of his chair as *Nemesis* dives to avoid being hit. Alarms screech from various different systems, but he ignores them. It's not like he can press the pause button on what he's doing and see to them right now.

He wipes blood out of his eye and glares at the two small Foundation vessels ducking and diving through their weapons fire. *Nemesis* has the power and the arsenal, but the smaller ships are far more manoeuvrable.

The Foundation ships break through and one manages to get off a lucky shot. The ship lurches to the side and throws some of the bridge crew against the consoles. Chayse jumps over the railings and pulls the unconscious officer from the helm. He lays him on the ground and takes the controls himself.

'Tret, when I bring us round, I want those bugs swatted.'

'Sir.'

Chayse swings *Nemesis* in the opposite direction, taking it around the outside of the Foundation ships.

'Sir, battle's the other way.'

Chayse ignores Tret and pushes her engines hard. The ships hold their positions as Chayse hoped they would. All of a sudden, he fires the reverse engines on the bow and port side. The ship groans and violently lurches to the side. He slams on the starboard and stern engines and pushes them to full capacity. *Nemesis* swings around sharply. Before she completes the turn, Chayse shouts at Tret. 'Fire!'

Taken by surprise, the smaller vessels don't have time to react. Tret's aim is true, hitting both ships. 'Again!' Neither ship can withstand the second strike. Chayse guides *Nemesis* through the debris and back towards the rest of the fleet.

'Open the intercom. Status?'

Roman is the first to respond. 'Impressive move, Chayse. Thought you were leaving all the fun to us for a moment.'

'Wouldn't dream of it. How are we looking?'

Roman responds with a sharp curse as a missile hits *Infinity*. 'We've got four of the smaller vessels left. *Epsilon* is down to one engine and we're down to two. Unfortunately, Balfe knows the best places to hit on our two ships.'

'I can't see *Ares*. She okay?' As he finishes asking the question, another of the small ships explodes when *Ares* bursts through the centre.

'Ah, you were worried about us,' Desyl mocks.

Chayse can't help but laugh. 'Try worried you'd break Gryffin's ship.'

'Don't worry. She's being looked after. Why's Balfe holding back?'

Chayse has been wondering about that himself. Since the attack started, the large cruiser held her position at the Port. The smaller vessels were running interference to keep everyone else away from her. If Balfe joined in, it would be a very different fight. 'No idea. Roman?'

'I don't know what he's planning. I have a horrible feeling he may be waiting for reinforcements.'

Chayse groans. 'Don't tempt fate.' The last thing they need now is more ships. But that's exactly what happens. The Port activates and another ten of the smaller vessels come through.

'Damn,' Desyl says. 'We need to close the Port. Who knows how many more are waiting to come through?'

'I agree,' Roman says. 'Problem is, it was built to withstand attacks from ships. We simply don't have the firepower to shut it down. Even combined we wouldn't do much more than scratch it.'

Chayse turns off the radio. No point talking about the problem at the moment. Unless they take out more ships, they won't be alive long enough to worry about it. He turns back to the task at hand. He needs to concentrate on thinning out the opposition.

∞

Terra watches in morbid fascination as the two men fight. She can barely keep track of their movements as each one moves faster than any ordinary man could. Unfortunately, both seem to be equally matched. Every time she thinks Gryffin has the upper hand, it changes again.

She understands why Gryffin was forced to use the implant to help, but it also scares the hell out of her. What if he can't get back afterwards? What if he's stuck like this forever?

The collision alarms screech to life throughout the ship. Rayde curses and turns to the screen, dragging her along with him. 'What the hell?' Large white numbers fill the screen as the computer counts down a thirty-minute self-destruct.

∞

Gryffin takes advantage of Fifty-Eight's brief lapse in concentration. With no other weapon available, Gryffin rams his metal fist into his opponent's chest.

Fifty-Eight's brows draw together in confusion. He looks down at Gryffin's arm embedded in his body. The man meets Gryffin's eyes again and a ghost of a smile crosses his face. Gryffin pulls his arm out, letting the man drop to the floor.

Gryffin looks at Terra and falters when he sees her expression. He fully expected her to be horrified by his actions, but he can only see relief. A small smile pulls at her mouth and she nods at him.

Her reaction hits him like a physical thing. She accepts him for who he is. It's the first time he feels like someone *gets* him. The pain in his head distracts him as the implant fights for control. He pushes his palm against the torn metal on the side of his head. The pain spears through his brain, helping to ground him. He'll pull all the damn metal off his face if it means he's in control long enough to deal with Rayde. He turns to face his old mentor and smiles. Time to finish this.

'How many are there?'

Lucan checks the screen again. 'Four ships. They're all short-distance crafts. Probably holding ten personnel each.'

In spite of her nature, Aleena curses. Forty, no doubt armed, men are making their way to the surface. 'There is nothing we can do but let them come. We have no way to stop them,' Aleena says. She cannot hide the despair in her voice even though she fights hard to keep it out.

Lucan stands up and unlocks the armoury. He takes two guns out and a box of ammunition. He cracks one open and looks down the barrel in an action so natural to him it confuses her. 'That is one option,' he says. He throws Aleena one of the guns, which she manages to catch in both hands. 'The other option is to stand our ground and force them out.'

Aleena looks at him in shock. 'Lucan, it is too much of a risk. We do not have the fighting experience. It would be like lambs to the slaughter.'

Lucan's mouth turns up into something resembling a smirk. 'It's a good thing I do then, isn't it?'

'You? I do not understand.'

He pulls down the front of his shirt to expose the swirling tattoo on his chest. Aleena instantly notices the purple tone to the artwork. 'You're Nomad — one of Gryffin's crew?'

'You didn't think Gryffin would leave you here unprotected, now, did you?'

Aleena tries to figure out how Gryffin had managed to plant one of his men on the surface. 'But I hired you. Personally. You have worked solely as my aide for the last three years. Gryffin had nothing to do with my decision.'

Lucan smirks. 'You discussed what you wanted with Gryffin and he made sure to send someone who fit the bill. You chose me because I was the best one for the job. The rest is history.' He grabs a bag of ammunition from the cupboard and fills a box with the guns. 'I'm sorry I couldn't do more when he attacked.' He slams the box on the ground and picks up another from the corner. 'He hurt you and I wasn't even there to protect you.'

Aleena takes a cautious step closer to him. 'Lucan, you were busy on *Nemesis*. You have nothing to regret.'

He looks over his shoulder at her and huffs. 'To be honest, I don't know what I would have done. He's my captain, but also my enemy. I know what happened isn't his fault but it's hard not to be angry at him.'

He closes the metal cabinet and places both boxes of guns on the wooden table. 'Ultar is my home, Aleena. This is where my loyalty lies and I'm damn sure no one is going to take this planet from you — whether it's Gryffin or someone else.' Lucan slips two handguns into his belt and picks up a rifle. 'Now, do you fancy defending Ultar or are you happy to hide and let them take what they want?'

She does not even have to think about it. Aleena opens her gun and holds out her hand for some rounds. It is about time she takes a leaf out of the Nomad's book.

∞

Sayber curses and pulls back around the corner. He's really starting to dislike this woman. She's as stubborn as Gryffin. Now, not only does he have to kill Rayde, but he also has to rescue Terra and by the looks of things, Gryffin too. Not exactly how he planned this. Then again, things rarely go to plan.

That's why Gryffin instructed him to alter the heading and set the self-destruct. Sayber had done the same thing when he tried to take *Ares* from Gryffin years ago, but his plan failed. Gryffin found out what he was planning and stopped him in time. They had fought each other and barely escaped with their lives. Sayber came close to losing his arm and Gryffin his head. If someone had told him a few weeks ago that he'd be working with Gryffin, he would have shot them.

The only way to prevent the Foundation from sending more ships is to make sure there's no way for them to get here. That means blowing the shit out of the Port. Evidently, the Foundation knew they would be unpopular at some stage in the future, so had made sure the Port's all but indestructible. Unless, of course, you have a flipping big freighter in your possession — which he just happens to have. The ship needs to be destroyed. No one else should be forced to spend time here.

But that only leaves thirty minutes to get the hell out of here. *Perses* is on her way to pick them up, but unless they are on the transport before the freighter nears the battle, they'll be stuck on her. Time to start the rescue part of his plan.

He braces himself against the wall, then slowly peeks around the corner. Gryffin is facing Rayde and Terra; Gryffin's right arm is covered in the blood of the man he was fighting. Unfortunately, from his position, he can't quite hit Rayde. With time running out, he takes the shot anyway, but misses anything vital, hitting Rayde in the shoulder instead. Rayde roars and releases Terra.

Before Sayber can react, Gryffin grabs her and holds her tight around her neck. He raises his metal arm and releases a shot of energy towards Sayber. Sayber narrowly manages to miss being fried by jumping out of the way at the last second. With no cover available, Sayber scrambles out of the room and sits with his back against the wall.

That part of the heroic rescue didn't exactly go to plan.

∞

Lucan activates his radio. 'Aleena, the transports have landed. It's Nera.'

The pause says more than any words. Nera is apparently hoping to take control of Ultar. He isn't surprised. Nera's a politician to the core. Lucan had been with Aleena when she was summoned to the impromptu meeting a few weeks ago. Nera's attitude at the meeting had pissed Lucan off.

'We go ahead as planned.'

'I was hoping you'd say that.' He signs off and crawls closer to the group. He signals to the villagers on each side, giving them instructions. Aleena had been a little surprised at how eager her people were to take arms. The children and older villagers remained in the tunnels, while Lucan armed everyone else and placed them in strategic positions throughout the village.

Personally, he hopes they won't have to take a shot. The plan is for his team of twelve men to take out as many as possible first. While the villagers are willing, he doesn't want to subject too many of the Ultarans to bloodshed. At their core, they're a peaceful people. Arming them doesn't sit well with him.

He watches as the rest of the men step off the transports. As expected, each is heavily armed but the Ultarans have the element of surprise. Signalling to his team, they zero in on their targets. Lucan steadies his breathing and pulls the trigger.

∞

'Kill her!'

Terra tries to calm her racing heart, but it does no good. All she can feel is Gryffin's metal arm firmly locked around her neck. Although it's a futile act, she puts everything she has into the glare she directs at Rayde. He points his weapon at them with a twisted smile on his face. Clearly, there are some significant cracks in his sanity. There'll be no negotiating with him.

'Quit delaying. Kill her!'

Gryffin's breath warms her ear. 'Trust me,' he whispers.

Terra's not sure if she heard him right. She certainly wasn't expecting him to whisper into her ear. To add to her confusion, he gently rubs his metal thumb across the back of her shoulder. Trust him to do what? Kill her?

She remembers the last time he said those words to her. She was hanging on to a ledge about to plunge to her death. He asked her to trust him before he saved her life. Whatever he's planning, she has nothing to lose. He'll either kill her or save her. Hoping for the latter, she nods as discreetly as she can.

∞

'What exactly do you think you're doing?'

Forty-Three takes a few steps closer to Balfe with his gun pointed at the admiral's head. 'We are taking this ship.'

Balfe snorts and leans back in his command chair. The rest of the bridge crew don't seem to share the admiral's optimism and appear to freeze on the spot. To emphasise the point, the other four men enter the deck, effectively trapping the crew. 'What about loyalty? I got you all out of prison. Or have you forgotten that small point?'

Forty-Three's red eye burns brighter for a second before it returns to normal. 'You must think we're stupid.'

Balfe swallows past the lump in his throat. 'What do you mean?'

'We were in prison on your orders.' He lowers his gun and walks casually around the deck. 'Don't get me wrong, we've all utilised what was done to us, but it's not something we ever asked for. Being cut open while still conscious isn't … pleasant.'

Balfe puts his palm on his gun but doesn't take it out. There's no point. He'd be dead before his hand even closed around the butt. 'This is all down to the Nomad.'

'Don't try to shift the blame,' he roars. 'The Foundation started the project.'

'But the Scientist and the Nomad—'

'The Scientist created us. We answer to him alone. As for the Nomad, he is the reason the experiment continued long enough to include us. He will suffer, but for now, we have other matters to tend to. Now, unless you want a blood bath in here, I suggest you order your crew to move to the conference room immediately.'

Balfe can clearly see he has no choice so makes the announcement. One by one the bridge crew leave him alone with the five men.

'Splendid, Admiral.' *Forty-Three* turns to one of his colleagues. 'Make sure they are secure.' *Forty-Three* moves to the navigational station and enters new coordinates.

'What do you think you're doing?' Balfe asks.

'Patience, Balfe.'

He grabs Balfe by the front of his jacket and lifts him right off his chair. After *Forty-Three* dumps Balfe unceremoniously on the floor, he sits down and slowly leans back in the warm leather. He drapes one leg over the arm and looks around him.

Balfe sits on the ground and glares up at *Forty-Three*. 'So you got my ship. What now?'

'Now we wait.'

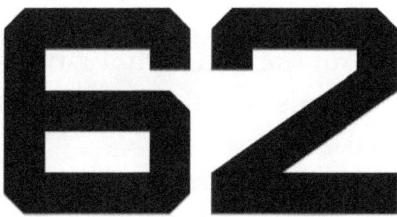

'Fall back!'

Lucan holds his position while the others make their way back to the village. The men and women had performed well. So far, they have taken out six of Nera's men before they could launch a counter strike. Lucan covers their backs and bursts through the trees, following closely behind the team heading back towards the village. Nera's men have split up, but their destination is clear. They'll want to capture or kill Aleena. Once she's out of the way, taking Ultar will be an easier task. Just a shame for Nera there isn't a chance in hell he'll get his hands on Aleena.

Lucan ducks under a branch as he races to catch up with the rest of the team. He glances up at the villagers he placed in the trees. They intently watch him as he passes underneath. Hopefully, they'll be able to reduce the numbers even more. A bullet flies by his ear, barely missing its target. Lucan turns quickly and fires behind him. A shout tells him the bullet hits home.

He passes the mile marker to the town and activates his radio.

'Aleena, they're heading your way — seven down.'

∞

Gryffin focuses hard to send as much power as possible into his arm. He's only got one shot at this, so it has to count. Gryffin can feel Terra's pulse race. She's scared.

Rayde stands in front of him with a large smile on his face. He holds his weapon towards Terra's head, showing that he'll shoot if Gryffin makes any false moves.

Gryffin concentrates and waits until the last minute before unleashing the full force of his power. It surges through his arm and explodes out in a deafening thump.

The force knocks him off his feet and throws them across the room into the bank of consoles against the far wall. A white hot pain shoots through his back. He falls to the ground but manages to twist his body to avoid landing on Terra.

Gryffin unwraps himself from her arms and drags himself towards Rayde's body impaled on the wall. The explosion had driven him back against the metal girders. A large piece of the ship sticks out of his chest, but he's still alive. Gryffin ignores the bucket full of protest from his own bloody and battered body and pulls himself to his feet.

Rayde looks up at him. The surprised expression on his face changes to confusion when he glances down at the rapidly growing patch of blood on his chest. He pulls his hand away and examines his blood-covered palm. Gryffin looks at him and feels nothing. No pity, no remorse. Nothing. It could be a complete stranger in front of him instead of the man he thought of as a father.

'I want the code to my collar,' Gryffin demands.

Rayde laughs briefly. 'Seriously Gryffin, you have more sense than to ask me that. Yet again, you disappoint me. I should have killed you when I found you lying in your own filth.'

Gryffin squeezes Rayde's neck. 'Code.'

474

Rayde coughs and blood dribbles out of his mouth. 'Or what? You'll kill me? You'll die with that thing around your neck, you stupid machine.'

'I'm not a machine. I'm your son.' Gryffin twists his hand and snaps Rayde's neck.

∞

Aleena pulls back from the edge of the stable roof. She hoped Lucan and his team would have taken care of a few more than seven, but that is more out of fear of what is to come, rather than disappointment at their performance.

Wiping her damp hands on her trousers, she picks up her gun again and gets into position. Never for one moment did she think she would be in this situation. Gryffin would be shocked if he saw her like this. She cannot help but smile in spite of the situation. How she wishes he were here in her place.

A whistle from her left signals they have company coming. Aleena activates her radio. 'Lucan, we have incoming. We are in position.'

'On my way.'

A team of men gradually break cover, moving slowly down the road. They scan the side streets but luckily seem to be disregarding the rooftops. She ignores the erratic beating of her heart and focuses on her target as Gryffin taught her. Aleena exhales and pulls the trigger. The man falls to the ground, the round having entered his chest. Not dwelling on the fact that she killed someone, she zones in on her next target.

Another of Nera's men drops down, but takes one of hers in return. Something changes in Aleena when she sees the body of her neighbour slump to the ground. Anger rises in her and explodes to the surface. Without an ounce of hesitation, she screams and opens fire.

Terra stares at the limp body of Rayde hanging on the wall. Gryffin saved her again. While she hates seeing anyone suffer, she can't muster an ounce of sympathy for Rayde. The man betrayed and tortured Gryffin. Rayde deserves his death. He deserves a hell of a lot worse.

Gryffin turns around, but that's as far as he gets. Sayber rushes to catch him as his legs go from under him. Sayber helps him lean back against the wall as Terra pulls the first aid kit from the wall. She crouches down beside Gryffin and stares at his injuries.

Blood seeps from countless deep gashes over his chest, arms and legs, and the left side of his face is completely unrecognisable under the blood and torn metal. Sayber lifts up Gryffin's shirt and sucks in a breath when he sees the large fist-sized puncture wound to his stomach. Terra carefully places a hand behind him. 'It goes right through.'

'Shit,' Sayber mutters under his breath.

'Not good?' Gryffin asks.

Sayber shakes his head. 'Bit of an understatement.' He pulls off his jacket and carefully presses it against the hole in Gryffin's torso. He looks back at the console Gryffin landed on and curses. 'The corner of the communication station stopped you. You're losing a lot of blood.' Sayber glances at the first aid kit beside Terra. 'Don't think that's going to do much good. Can you put pressure here?'

She swaps places with Sayber and gingerly applies pressure on the wound. 'Not quite your best plan.' She smiles to soften the words.

Gryffin smiles back at her. 'Seemed like a good idea at the time.'

'Any chance you can use your implants to stop the bleeding, maybe buy us more time?' Sayber asks.

'I can't access them,' he grinds out through clenched teeth. 'The new connector is damaged.'

Terra winces. That's putting it mildly. The shredded metal around his eye and along the side of his head is digging into his skin. Sayber pulls off his shirt to add to his jacket, as the blood continues to seep out. She's not stupid. The damage is too severe. His blood already saturates the coat. Unless he receives medical attention soon, he'll die. 'We have to get him back to your transport.'

Sayber nods. 'How about you head back and prepare the transport. Probably should check on Bray too.'

'Bray is fine,' Terra responds. 'I've linked the system to my handheld. His vitals are strong.'

Gryffin drops his head back against the metal wall. 'Did you alter course?' Gryffin asks.

'Of course I did,' Sayber replies. 'We'll get to the Port just as the self-destruct goes off. Now all we have to do is convince the others.'

'Others?' Terra asks.

'*Infinity, Nemesis,* and *Epsilon,*' Gryffin says.

Sayber gets up and studies the console. '*Ares* too. Desyl took her back. Terra, you think you can use my radio to contact your people? Someone seems to have landed on this one.'

∞

'How many?' Roman asks.

'Another ten,' Chayse confirms. 'Every time we take out a few, he calls more across. We're running seriously low on ammunition. We can't keep this pace up much longer.'

Roman nods even though they're only using radios. Balfe's playing with them, no question. He must be waiting for this Rayde person to bring Gryffin to him. He wouldn't risk crossing the Port without his prize.

He rubs a hand over his face and tries to remain positive in front of the crew. 'Sir, we've got a message coming in.'

He gestures at Milla to open the channel. 'This is Quinn. I've rounded up some Hunter ships to help.'

Roman shouts out in joy. 'How many of you are there?'

'Eight ships. Are there any left for us?' Quinn asks.

'One or two. Glad to have you back with us, Quinn.' He signs off and leans down to speak to Milla. 'I want you to link with *Omega*.'

'Sir, Balfe will have her locked down tight.'

Roman glances up at the Admiral's ship. 'It's worth a shot, Milla. Get into her system and get me something I can use. Files on the project, on Gryffin, information on whoever is behind the procedures, I don't care. Get me something to bury Balfe with.'

'My pleasure, sir.' Milla listens to the radio for a moment, then turns to face Roman again with a large smile on her face. 'Sir, I've got Terra.'

∞

'You want to what?'

Sayber licks his dry lips and tries to put more conviction into his voice. 'I want us to destroy the Port.'

Avoca clears his throat. 'You know what that means, right? If you destroy the Port, it will close the tunnel between the Sectors.'

'Of course I bloody well do.' Sayber tries to keep the patronising tone out of his voice. He doesn't have time to break things down for Avoca. Frustrated, he steps aside and puts Terra back on the radio.

'Listen, we'll be with you in a few minutes,' Terra explains. 'Sayber set the autodestruct, so the freighter's going to blow. Balfe equipped it with state of the art cloaks that we've managed to get up and running. If we keep Balfe's lot occupied, it'll give the ship a good chance to slip through.'

Desyl pipes up. 'I agree with Sayber.'

'It'll also buy us some time,' Roman agrees. 'Without the Port, it'll take the Foundation up to a year to get here.'

'I'm in too,' Chayse agrees. 'Whatever we do, can we do it pretty damn quick? Don't fancy our chances with another twenty ships. Did you locate Gryffin?'

Terra looks down at Gryffin bleeding on the floor. 'We've got Gryffin and Bray. They're both seriously injured and need medical attention as soon as we get to you.'

'We'll let you know when we get there,' Sayber says. 'We'll jump ship as soon as we can.' He signs off and leans back against the console. It's a shame not everyone will get off the freighter.

63

Lucan pumps his arms and forces himself to move faster. He heard the gunfire and Aleena's scream over the radio, so orders his team to take his place as he races ahead.

Gryffin ordered him to protect Aleena. It's his one and only task and he's managed to screw it up. If anything happens to her, no punishment from Gryffin will be worse than what he'll do to himself.

One of Nera's men bursts out of the trees in front of him. Without even pausing for a breath, he puts a bullet in the centre of the man's forehead. Using a low hanging branch, he grabs on and swings himself around the corner, but freezes when he sees the path ahead of him.

There are bodies littered along the road, their blood staining the pale shingle. From the looks of their clothing, they seem to be Nera's men but there are some Ultaran bodies too. Then he sees her. Aleena is still alive. Some of her long blonde hair has broken free of its tie and frames her face as she stands at the side of the road, firing across at the group hiding behind a house.

Even though it's not the time or place, he can't help the smile that spreads across his face. She could be a Nomad looking as she does. He wipes the smile off his face and moves through the trees around the back of the group. Before he gets too close, he spots a sentry. Luckily, the man is looking in the opposite direction. They must be more worried about trouble coming from the town. Lucan moves into stealth mode. As he nears the group, he pulls his knife out. He needs this to end quietly if he's to have any chance of getting to Aleena.

He manages to get all the way to the man's back before he turns around. Before he can react, Lucan grabs him and holds him close to his chest while he quickly draws the blade across the man's throat. He lowers the body to the ground and takes out his gun.

Using the undergrowth as cover, he peers out at the team. Someone must be smiling on him today. Preoccupied with the Ultarans, they don't even notice him moving closer. Lucan raises his gun, fires, and counts to four as each man drops to the ground.

∞

Sayber crouches down beside Gryffin and tries to focus anywhere but on the bloody hole where his eye should be. 'How are you doing?'

Gryffin glances sideways at him. 'How do I look?'

'Shit.'

'That's your answer.' Gryffin's laugh dies when his broken ribs protest. 'How are the mods coming along?'

'I've put the finishing touches to the cloaks and Terra needs another few minutes until she can mask the ship's signal. She's confident we'll be able to creep up without the Foundation knowing we're there.' Gryffin nods and turns his attention back to Terra. 'So, when are you going to tell her?' Sayber asks.

'Not yet,' Gryffin says. 'She needs to be focused.'

Sayber snorts. 'Better you than me, mate. She's not going to be happy.'

Gryffin closes his eye and smiles briefly. 'I don't care as long as she's alive.'

Terra stands up and wipes her hand on the front of her trousers. 'Okay, that should do it. The ship should be able to fly right past Balfe.'

Sayber gets to his feet and claps his hands together. 'Right then. As much as I've loved every minute of my time on this dump, I think it's time to bid it farewell.'

'We should get a gurney to transport Gryffin,' Terra says. The look passing between Sayber and Gryffin doesn't go unnoticed. 'What's wrong?'

Gryffin meets her eyes. 'Terra, I can't go with you.'

∞

What the hell is taking Sayber so long?

Sayber should have been back with Terra and Gryffin by now. Desyl targets another Foundation vessel as *Ares* swings around. They're still holding their own but the Foundation keeps coming. Even with the added help from the Hunters, they're slowly getting ground down. The Foundation knows exactly where to hit to cause the most damage. *Nemesis* is the only ship still faring well thanks to Gryffin having no knowledge about her.

Desyl grips the arms of the worn leather captain's seat. Gryffin's seat. He has to make sure Gryffin has a ship to come back to. Lieutenant Kellyn climbs up the steps and shakes his head. 'Klay doesn't know anything. Whatever Balfe and Rayde had planned, they didn't open up to Klay.'

'How hard did you try?'

Kellyn looks down at his torn fists and smiles. 'Fairly damn hard. I'm pretty sure the commander is regretting his actions, unlike me. Don't think I've enjoyed myself so much in a while. All he knows is there are a number of ships waiting to come through. They want the

Sector bad.'

'What about Gryffin?'

Kellyn shakes his head. 'Rayde is pissed at the captain for betraying the "actual path" of the Nomad or some bullshit like that. Rayde reeled Klay in hook, line and sinker. Rayde used him as his eyes and ears on board since Klay first became commander. Klay arranged the hits blamed on Gryffin. He even planted the programming behind all the captain's malfunctions.'

Desyl shakes his head. 'Explains why he got so pissed when Gryffin appointed Chayse to help.'

Kellyn nods. 'Makes sense. If the captain found out, he would have skinned Klay alive, literally.'

'Yeah, if he was lucky.' He can't believe Klay fooled them all for so long. Their conversation is cut short as an alarm sounds and *Ares* shudders. Desyl checks the system and lets out a string of obscenities. 'They're targeting the masts. Evasive moves. I want that ship destroyed. Now!'

As ordered, the large guns target and destroy the Foundation vessel.

'They were hitting the deck below, focusing on the support beams for the masts. Sir, I've got Chayse,' Kellyn reports.

Desyl nods. 'What's up, Chayse? We're a bit busy.'

'We've picked up two Foundation ships that somehow slipped through unnoticed.'

'You must be losing your touch,' Desyl replies. 'Where are they heading?'

'Ultar. *Ares* is the fastest. Fancy reeling them in?'

Desyl smiles. 'We're on it.' He turns off his radio and orders the helm to alter course. 'Give it everything she has. Kellyn, we've got about ten minutes before we catch up. I need the masts to hold up.'

'Sir.'

Kellyn takes two crew members from the command deck and heads towards the top level. Desyl watches out the window as they race towards Ultar. He hopes they get there in time.

∞

'What do you mean you can't go with us?' Terra asks. 'Are the mods wearing off?'

He shakes his head and looks over at Sayber. Sayber gets the hint and clears his throat. 'I'll just check... over here.' He walks to the far corner and turns his back on them.

'What's going on, Gryffin?' Terra asks.

'I can't leave the freighter. The collar connects to the primary system. If I leave, it will blow.'

Terra looks at him in disbelief. 'As in blow up?' He nods. She crouches down beside him to examine the collar. 'Why didn't you say sooner? We could have got it off you. How is it powered?'

'Need the code. Balfe, the Scientist and Rayde have it.'

She looks over her shoulder at Rayde's body. 'No problem. We've still got Balfe. I'll turn off the autodestruct. Our ships can buy us some time.' She stands up to leave, but Gryffin stops her in her tracks by grabbing her gun. He fires it at the control console and puts a large hole in it.

'What the hell did you do that for?' Terra shouts.

He throws the empty gun on the floor. 'Have to protect the Sector.'

Terra turns to face Sayber. 'You knew about this, didn't you?'

He stays with his face towards the corner. 'Greater good, Terra.'

She turns back to Gryffin. 'There has to be a way of doing this without sacrificing you. There has to be another way.'

He shakes his head and squeezes his eye shut in pain. 'No. Go now.'

She angrily wipes a tear from her cheek. 'I can't leave you.'

He slowly raises his metal hand to wipe another tear from her face, confused by her reaction. 'Why are you crying?'

'Isn't it obvious, you damn fool? I love you, Gryffin. I can't ... I won't leave you here to die.'

He brushes his metal hand through her hair as she cries. She carefully shuffles beside him and tucks against his right side. He closes his eye and lets himself enjoy the feeling of her against him. For the first time, he wishes he hadn't spent years dismissing his emotions.

Rayde always told him to embrace the machine and ignore the man. For twenty years, he had taken it a step further by hating both sides of himself. If only he'd listened to his feelings, maybe he would know if he loves her or not. Painfully aware time's running out, he forces himself to let her go. He locks on to her with his functioning eye. 'Go with Sayber.'

She squeezes Gryffin's hand. 'Stop talking like that. We're all getting off the ship together. Aren't we, Sayber?'

Sayber's shoulders sag. 'Terra, it's just not possible.'

'No! You both listen! The four of us are leaving together, understand?'

Gryffin pushes away from her. 'I can't physically leave, and the ship is going to crash into the Port. It doesn't matter what you say or do — this is happening. You need to understand and get the hell out of here.'

'Damn it, Gryffin!' Terra beats her fist against his shoulder. 'You can't give up. I won't let you.'

Tears flow freely down her face, but her eyes show her real emotions. She's angry and clearly won't back down. He runs his fingers down her cheek. 'I'm sorry, Terra.' Her brows draw together a split second before Sayber hits her on the head with his gun.

64

'Doesn't really look like you needed me.'

Aleena manages a small but satisfied smile. 'Nonetheless, I am glad you are here. Have you seen Nera yet?'

Lucan shakes his head. 'He got off one of the shuttles. He must be here somewhere.'

As if hearing their conversation Nera's voice sounds over the town's loudspeaker system. 'Aleena, you have five minutes to come into the centre before your people continue to pay for your foolishness.'

Aleena walks towards the centre until Lucan grabs her by the arm. 'Where the hell do you think you're going?'

She pulls away from his grip. 'I am going to help my people.'

Lucan shakes his head. 'You seriously think Nera is going to let them go once he has you? No, he's going to kill you and them.' He signals to the surrounding locals. Waiting until they are all within earshot, Lucan continues. 'We're going to do this my way. That means getting your people and you out of this in one piece.'

Aleena frowns. 'What exactly are you planning?'

Lucan smiles.

∞

Sayber carries Terra's limp body down the corridor back to his shuttle. Knocking her out was the only way she was ever going to leave that ship. There isn't a chance in hell she would have left voluntarily. As Gryffin said earlier; she'll be mad as hell, but alive.

Sayber's boots squeak on the metal floor as he rounds the final corner too fast. He remains on his feet and bursts through the door of his shuttle. He quickly fastens the harness around Terra's torso. Sayber glances at the equipment monitoring Bray and then takes his seat behind the controls. He starts the engine's ignition sequence and manoeuvres the transport out of the hold.

There isn't much time left to evacuate the freighter. The engines roar as he pushes them hard. The small craft speeds away from Gryffin and the ship towards the rendezvous coordinates. Once clear of the freighter, he activates his radio. 'Quinn, this is Sayber. Prepare the med bay. Two injured coming in. You'd bloody well better be at the meeting point.'

The only reply for a moment is static, but finally Quinn responds. 'We'll be there in one minute, sir. We've had another influx of Foundation vessels.'

'Make sure you're there to pick us up. Sayber out.'

Quinn will be there. He has no doubts. Sayber checks the sensors and is relieved to see the freighter has disappeared. Looks like the cloaks and signal mods worked. His relief is overshadowed by regret when he sees Terra's face. She looks so at peace at the moment. He knows he's somewhat to blame for her involvement in this. If he hadn't brought her back to *Perses* in the first place, she wouldn't have had to deal with leaving Gryffin behind like they did.

He pushes any regret away as *Perses* suddenly appears and comes to a halt in front of him. He guides the transport around the back and docks in the bay. As soon as he opens the doors, three medical personnel climb on board. After they check that Sayber himself is unharmed, they wheel Bray away to try and do something with him. It's certainly going to put their skills to the test. Terra follows after Bray. He hopes he didn't hit her too hard.

Sayber leaves them in the capable hands of his crew. He has a fight to join. Sayber runs through the winding corridors. He can't wait to destroy his fair share of Foundation ships.

∞

Lucan crawls to the end of the building and presses his body tight to the concrete wall. He slowly peers around the corner towards the town centre.

A group of twenty or so intruders have converged around the main well, each one heavily armed. He moves out from the safety of the building to gain a better view of the alleys leading to the square. Guards block each path.

He moves back to the rest of the team, divides the group, and sends them on their way. Through his earpiece, he waits for confirmation they've all reached their target. Once satisfied they're where they should be, he pulls himself up onto the crates leaning against the back of the building and hauls himself onto the roof. Luckily the men in the square are concentrating on the main paths instead of above them. He needs to find the locals before he orders an assault.

Lucan crouches on the straw roof, runs to the edge, and clears the gap between the two buildings with ease. Three buildings later, he silently lands on the roof of the main town hall. Lucan slowly peers through the nearest skylight into the room below. Twelve Ultaran men are being held in the one building with eight guards. He's glad the rest of the villagers are in the tunnels.

Lucan examines the rest of the room and suppresses a growl when he spots six bodies covered in cloth at the side. Nera's taking things too far. Lucan needs to end this now.

Without taking his eyes off his targets, he opens a channel to his teams. 'Let's go.'

He forces himself to stay put as Aleena slowly approaches along the main path to the centre. Nera apparently doesn't trust anyone, so stays safely hidden inside. His men search her and guide her inside. Lucan grimaces. He's less than happy about the next part of the plan. Lucan quietly slides off the roof and empties what he needs out of his bag. He's only going to get one shot at this. If he gets it wrong, everyone in the building is going to die.

∞

Sayber looks out the window on the command deck on *Perses*. He received word from the medical bay. Apart from a rotten headache, Terra should be all right. Bray is another story. They managed to stabilise him, but no one has the first clue what to do about the bits of metal on him. It will have to wait. At the moment, they have bigger problems.

'Quinn. Get the fleet on the intercom. Tell them to back away from the Port. We need to give the freighter room to get through.'

'Sir.'

Sayber lowers himself into his chair and clenches the armrests. Two minutes until they reach the fleet, but it might as well be two days. Time slows down for Sayber as he mentally prepares. He's vaguely aware of Quinn relaying the message. One by one the confirmations come through. Sayber stands up and walks closer to the main window. 'Anything yet?'

'No, sir.'

Sayber paces at the front of the deck. A few seconds later, it appears. The large freighter uncloaks past Balfe's ship. 'Right, everyone. Let's give her some room. Keep those other vessels away from her.'

∞

Balfe stares in confused fascination as the freighter appears. 'What the hell is that doing here?'

'She is here as I instructed.'

Balfe spins to face the Scientist. 'Get the hell off my bridge!'

The Scientist smiles gently. 'You asked a question and I responded. We are expecting the freighter.' The man walks to the front of the deck flanked by *Forty-Three* and another of the men. 'Balfe, tell your ships to let her through.'

'Let her through? I don't understand.'

Forty-Three grabs Balfe by the neck and lifts him off the ground. The Scientist ignores Balfe's protests and gazes out the window. 'It is a simple request,' he says. *Forty-Three* drops Balfe to the ground. The Scientist clasps his hands behind his back and glances down at Balfe. 'Now, Admiral, have you outlived your usefulness?'

Balfe coughs and rubs his neck. 'Very well.' The Scientist instructs *Forty-Three* to activate the intercom to the rest of the Foundation fleet. 'This is Balfe. Let the freighter pass unharmed.' *Forty-Three* nods and turns off the intercom. 'You planned this?'

The Scientist sits back on Balfe's chair. 'I am merely following the plan as laid out by my employers.'

Balfe's face turns red. 'What the hell are you talking about? I am your damn employer!'

The Scientist removes his glasses and begins to clean them on the hem of his shirt. 'Actually, I work for the Foundation directly.' Balfe's mouth opens and repeatedly closes as he struggles to speak. 'Did you really think I would work so hard so you could produce one cyborg? Really, Balfe. Where is your ambition?'

'But I funded you.'

The Scientist slams his hand down on the armrest in the first real display of emotion Balfe has ever seen. 'You're small fry compared to what I have planned. Replacing limbs and enhancing organs is all well and good, but so much more can be achieved. You may not be able to see that, but the Foundation realises the true potential. They are more than happy for me to modify as many subjects as I wish. *Thirty-Five* will serve as the blueprint for a new breed of compliant and programmable cyborgs for the Foundation. The Council have granted me as much funding and time as I need to make this a success.'

Balfe gets up to his knees. 'It is a success, you fool! The prototype did as ordered.'

The Scientist sneers. 'He broke through the programming. That should never happen. I had no choice but to rush his procedure and as a result, he's faulty. Given the time, *Thirty-Five* can be a formidable machine. His strength and endurance is vital to the final stage of the project.'

Balfe snorts. 'You're completely insane. You really believe you can replace an organic brain with a computer, don't you?' Balfe shakes his head. 'Just because he survived the control implant doesn't mean he'll survive that. Face it. That woman you carry around like luggage is dead. Dead!'

The Scientist clenches his jaw as he fights to remain composed. He slowly turns to look at *Forty-Three* and nods once. Forty-Three twists Balfe's head around sharply. Balfe's lifeless body slumps to the floor. The Scientist focuses on the screen in front of him. 'Let's collect your brother, *Forty-Three*.'

∞

Gryffin watches the details of the battle on the small screen beside him. From what he can see, the Nomad and Hunters seem to be holding their own. They may make it out without many losses. As long as the freighter annihilates the Port, they'll be safe — for the moment at least.

He drops Sayber's blood-soaked shirt and jacket to the ground. They land in the growing pool of blood surrounding him. It isn't as if the makeshift wadding can help anymore. He sits and watches for a minute until he notices something. Balfe's ship is stationary near the Port. The smaller Foundation crafts aggressively protect it from the attacking ships. He grinds his teeth together. Damn Balfe is hiding behind those ships. *Forty-Three* and the others are on *Omega*. They must be waiting for Rayde to deliver him.

Gryffin looks at the secondary controls on the far side of the room, then back at Balfe's ship. He slowly lowers himself onto his right side, and screams as the pain spears through his stomach. His head drops onto the floor with a dull thump as he tries to breathe through the agony. After he takes a few deep breaths, he clenches his jaw and forces his metal arm out in front of him. His fingers find purchase on the rough floor and he pulls himself forward. He roars in pain as he drags his torn body along the floor.

He takes a few more breaths and reaches out again. Balfe and *Forty-Three* have to die. And he is damn well going to kill them.

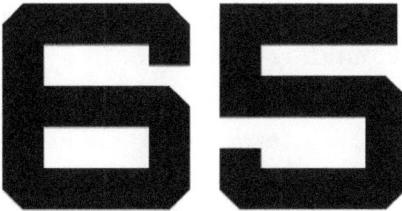

65

Aleena stands tall in front of Nera. He is sitting in the main chair at the banquet table, his back ramrod straight as he looks down at her in disgust. 'That was not a friendly welcome, Aleena.'

'You are not here under friendly circumstances. Did you really believe I would stand by and let you take Ultar?'

He shakes his head as he sits up straight. 'To be honest, yes. With Gryffin preoccupied as he is, I felt you would be open for a discussion.' He gets up and walks around her. The way his eyes travel over her body makes her feel very uncomfortable. He stops in front of her and smiles. 'Are you going to fight against this or will you step aside?'

'I will not step aside.'

He laughs and shakes his head. 'Are you still anticipating a rescue from Gryffin? I believe he visited recently. How many did he kill? You must face facts, Aleena. The Nomad is all but disbanded. Once Gryffin showed his true colours, the rest of the thread holding the Nomad together unravelled. We must join the colonies and sign with the Foundation in order to survive.'

'Under your leadership, of course.'

He shrugs. 'It would probably be best. After all, your reputation has taken a bit of a hit after your misguided faith in Gryffin.'

Aleena glances at the clock on the wall behind Nera. As Lucan had instructed, timing is imperative if they are to succeed. 'I believe you are misguided. Do you really think Gryffin would not have prepared for something like this?' She signals for her people to take cover as the side wall of the building explodes.

∞

Desyl spits out a mouthful of blood and pulls himself to his feet. They caught up with the Foundation vessels as they entered orbit around Ultar.

Before they can fire towards the surface, *Ares* attacks. In spite of the two-against-one odds, *Ares* is holding her own, but the battle is taking its toll. Two masts are down, which in turn blew their main engine. They're sitting ducks with no way to avoid what the Foundation is throwing at them. He has to accept facts: *Ares* is going down.

'Shut those damn alarms off!' His head is sore enough after it hit against the railing. A sore head will be nothing compared to how this will end if the tables don't turn pretty damn quickly. Even their defences are working against them, allowing the Foundation to sail right past.

That's it!

Desyl pushes an unconscious crew member from the console and links in with the defence system. The defences aren't letting them through. Someone had deactivated them, which means he can activate them again. Without Gryffin's override code, the defences will target *Ares* as well as the Foundation, but at least the enemy ships will go down. That's the most important thing at the moment.

Kellyn steadies himself against the wall. 'You thinking what I'm thinking?'

Desyl nods. It's suicide staying here. 'Abandon ship.'

∞

'Sir, the freighter just launched tethers at *Omega*.'

Chayse gets up and checks the console. 'I thought Sayber emptied the freighter?'

Tret shrugs. 'Don't know what to say. Someone has tethered the two ships together and the freighter is reeling her in.'

Chayse knows exactly what's going on. 'Get Sayber!' he roars, surprising the command crew. Chayse glares down at the screen as Sayber appears. 'You left him on board, didn't you?'

Sayber at least has the decency not to lie. 'The collar they locked on him will remove his head from the rest of his body if he leaves. We didn't have a choice. He even blew a hole in the nav system to make sure we couldn't do anything to interfere.'

Chayse curses and runs a hand through his hair. 'So we just leave him there?'

'Gryffin wants this,' Sayber sighs. 'I feel the same about this as you do. There's nothing we can do.'

∞

Gryffin lies face down on the floor beside the console. It's just about finished him off, but he managed to direct and launch the tethers. At least he can die knowing Balfe and his men will die along with him. Cold seeps into his body and works its way along his limbs. Death is close. Not surprising really — most of his blood is smeared across the metal floor.

He uses the last of his strength to tip himself onto his back. The pain of the open wound hitting the metal floor doesn't register. His body's lost all feeling — something he's grateful for. Even the damn implant is silent. It's done its job and helped to keep him alive this long. With hardly any blood left in his body, it is only a matter of minutes before he dies, implants or not.

Gryffin stares at the emergency lights trailing the ceiling. Various machines beep and hum in time to the louder shriek of the collision alarm. He closes his eyes. It's probably the first time in his life when he's not in some kind of pain. An image of Terra jumps into his mind and he smiles. Even if only for a short while, she made things better for him. She may have screwed him over too many times to count, but she cares about him, loves him like no one else ever has. And he believes he cares about her too, in his own way.

With an image of Terra firmly in his mind, he lets himself drift away.

∞

'You ready?'

Kellyn smirks and nods at Desyl. It took five minutes to evacuate everyone, except himself and Kellyn, from the ship. His friend flat out refused to leave him alone. Desyl's finger hovers over the button. In theory, it should take thirty seconds to reactivate the defences once start-up is initiated. It takes over a minute to get to the final escape pod. That leaves a very noticeable thirty seconds of big fat unknown. Thirty seconds could be plenty of time depending on where the missile hits, or it could just blow them to pieces.

Desyl hits the button and they both run. The two men jump down the steps to the command deck, race past Gryffin's quarters, then clear the two flights of stairs down to the transport bay. Their boots thump on the metal floor as they get closer to their destination.

The ship suddenly jolts as the defences hit again and again. The alarms he silenced earlier scream to life again. The wall behind Kellyn explodes and throws lethal shrapnel at them. Kellyn roars and falls to the ground with a piece of bulkhead through his chest just below his heart. Desyl skids to a halt and clambers back over to him.

With no time to do anything for him, Desyl grabs him under his arms and drags him along the corridor. The ship shudders violently and tilts as her stabilisers shut down. Desyl fails to keep his footing. He drops himself and Kellyn against the wall with a thump. Desyl pulls himself to his feet and ignores the sudden dart of pain in his ankle. Desyl holds onto the wall with one hand and leans over to pull Kellyn up again. Kellyn refuses Desyl's help and pushes him away.

'We need to keep moving, Kellyn. This whole place is going to blow.'

Kellyn smirks and shakes his head. 'We won't make it out. You have to go.'

Desyl ignores him and reaches out again. 'I'm not going to leave you.'

'You have to, Captain.'

Desyl looks down at his friend. He's right. It kills him to admit it, but there's no way he'll be able to carry him up another three flights of stairs before the ship blew.

'Do me one favour?' Kellyn asks.

'Sure.'

'Don't try to shift the blame to me because I'm not around. I did not break Gryffin's ship,' he says with a smile.

Desyl can't help but smile back. 'You have my word.' With little time left to save himself, Desyl stands up. With one last look at his friend, he turns and races up the stairs towards the transport bay.

∞

'All engines at full power!'

'We're at full power. She's going to pull us in.'

The Scientist thumps the arm of his chair. Apparently, *Thirty-Five's* self-preservation programming is malfunctioning. He looks out at the last three Foundation ships being destroyed by the Nomad and

Hunter ships.

'Time to go.' He gestures at *Forty-Three*. 'Get your men on the transport. We'll rendezvous with the others once we're through the Port.'

The Scientist follows *Forty-Three* to the shuttle bay and sits towards the back. The large stasis pod and his equipment fill the back of the craft. As *Forty-Three* starts the launch sequence, the Scientist runs a finger along the glass covering the woman's face. He places a kiss on his fingers and presses them to the glass. 'There's been a little setback. Don't worry, Maggie. We'll get him back.'

∞

Using the confusion of the explosion, Lucan orders the attack. Whether on the ground or the rooftops, the Ultarans open fire, striking down anyone unlucky enough to be out in the open. Lucan loads another magazine into his gun and kicks down the door into the hall. 'Aleena!' Seeing movement to his left, he takes down another one of Nera's men. 'Aleena!'

'Over here.'

He breathes a sigh of relief and moves in the direction of her voice. Lucan picks his way through the rubble and helps a few injured Ultarans to their feet. Eventually, he finds her standing in front of Nera with her gun tight against his head. While Lucan himself would have no hesitation killing him, he knows it's not how Aleena does things. 'Aleena, I got him.'

'Do I not deserve a chance to take care of him myself?'

'Not like that. You've got the upper hand. Ultaran law should take over now.'

Aleena shakes her head. 'We have gone beyond that point. He killed some of my people for mere greed. He wanted Ultar, so damn everything else.'

Lucan hesitates, slightly thrown off track for a second by her curse.

'I know you, Aleena. Killing people in combat is going to weigh heavy on you. You know you had no choice though. It was them or us. If you kill him now, you won't be able to forgive yourself. You're not a murderer.'

'Gryffin would kill him.'

Lucan nods. 'And you'd be furious with him for doing it. Most of your arguments have been about him pulling the trigger before looking at other alternatives. If you do this, it will change you, change who you are as a leader. Put Nera in a cell. Deal with him according to your laws.'

Aleena slowly lowers her gun. Nera's shoulders immediately sag. 'Thank you. You've done the right thing, Aleena,' Nera says.

She steps up close to him and strikes Nera full force across the face with the butt of her gun. 'You may live to regret my decision.'

Lucan puts his arm around her shoulder and squeezes her tight to him. 'Remind me never to get on your bad side.'

'Lucan, Aleena!' One of the Ultarans hurries through the building, waving a radio at them. '*Ares* is in orbit.'

'Friendly?'

'Seems to be. Someone on board reactivated the defences and destroyed two Foundation ships.'

Aleena blows out a breath. 'That is good news.'

'Not really. The defences also hit *Ares*. She's about to crash onto the surface.'

66

Nemesis, *Infinity*, *Perses*, and the rest of the Hunter fleet turn to face the Port as the freighter enters the large tunnel towing *Omega* behind it. Roman knows Balfe and the crew are still on board, but there's nothing he can do now. It's too late to plan a rescue.

If he's honest with himself, he can't arouse any feelings of regret for Balfe. The crew, yes, but Balfe deserves to go down with the ship. In fact, he knows of quite a few people who would have enjoyed seeing him put through the same things he put the innocent children through.

Roman counts down the last few seconds until the ship self-destructs. The force of the explosion inside the entrance does the trick and tears apart the Port and freighter, scattering debris in all directions.

It's over.

Not only is the Sector free from Foundation interference for a year, but so is he. The explosion acts like a cleansing ritual for him. Without the Port, the crew of *Infinity* have no choice but to call this Sector home. He stole an expensive vessel and used it to battle against the Foundation. Not exactly how he saw his career going.

Instead of feeling anxious or worried about the repercussions, he's strangely relieved.

He activates the ship-wide intercom and addresses his crew. 'The Port has been successfully destroyed. Due to our actions today, we have no doubt been labelled traitors by the Foundation. I cannot do anything to change that. What I can do is assure you your actions here will not be in vain. Together with the Nomad and Hunters, we have helped thousands of colonists in this Sector. Be proud of that.'

'Sir,' Milla says. 'I managed to link with *Omega* very briefly.' Milla purses her lips and looks away from him. 'Sir, I think ... Sir, I have a bad feeling about what I heard.'

Roman sits at the station next to her and holds out his hand for the earpiece. Milla slowly hands it over, but the look on her face worries him.

'Sir, I was only able to patch in to one of *Omega*'s transports. The ship was powered up, but no one had locked the system. It's three sentences.'

Roman keeps his eyes on Milla as he plays the message. Initially, it's not the content that drops his stomach to the floor. It's the voice from the grave that echoes loudly in his head.

'There's been a little setback. Don't worry, Maggie. We'll get him back.'

It's a voice he'll never forget — his best friend, Callum Rush.

Terra's father.

∞

Aleena shields her eyes from the sun as she scans the sky. Thanks to Lucan's help they rounded up any of Nera's men left on the surface. Nera is confined to a cell awaiting trial as per their customs. She is so glad Lucan talked her out of doing something she would regret the

501

rest of her life. It frightens her how close she was to ending his life in cold blood.

If Lucan had not entered when he did, she would have killed Nera without hesitation. After experiencing such feelings herself, she can somewhat empathise with Gryffin. In the past, his actions always seemed so rash and heartless. Now, she sees his actions are anything but. They both do whatever is necessary to protect her people and the colony. The only difference is, Gryffin has taken the step Lucan stopped her from taking.

They arrive at their destination and Aleena gets off the transport with Lucan and Desyl at either side. All but two of the pods made it to the surface unharmed. Again, the Nomad have sacrificed themselves to protect her people. It is not something she will ever forget.

Lucan scans the landscape and whistles. The remains of the Nomad flagship litter the field. She landed on her side with her hull buried deep in the ground. One mast is outside the town, the other in the lake, and the majority of the rest of her lies in pieces over and in the ground.

Desyl walks towards the wreckage. 'Captain for a few hours and I've managed to destroy Gryffin's pride and joy.'

Aleena puts a hand on his shoulder. 'You helped keep the Foundation from taking over the Sector and saved Ultar from the Foundation ships. I'm sure Gryffin would approve of the sacrifice.'

Desyl turns to face her. 'Crew members are dead and the ship is scrap metal. He's going to kill me.'

Aleena holds her hair out of her face as the wind rushes around her. The three battleships fly overhead and lower in the meadow in front of her, beside the remains of *Ares*.

Seeming to be faring only slightly better than *Ares*, *Nemesis*, *Infinity*, and *Perses* show many scars from the assault with the Foundation. One by one the hatches open and the three captains step onto the surface. Roman walks up to her and she cannot contain herself. She closes the distance and throws her arms around his neck.

Surprised by her reaction, he freezes for a moment before wrapping his arms around her. After a minute, she pulls away looking slightly embarrassed. 'I apologise, Captain. I do not know what came over me.'

He brushes some hair from her face and smiles. 'I'm glad to see you too. I heard you had some trouble. Is everything all right?'

She nods and smiles over her shoulder at Lucan. 'Thanks to my personal Nomad bodyguard.'

Chayse looks at the remains of *Ares*. 'You were damn lucky to get out, Desyl.'

'Yeah, well, we weren't all so lucky. Does Gryffin know about *Ares* yet?'

Roman's face immediately drops. Aleena's eyes fix on each of the people in front of her. Roman, Chayse, and even Sayber look extremely troubled. It is then she catches sight of Terra standing on the loading ramp of *Perses*. Even from this distance, the tears are clearly evident. 'Where is he?' she asks again.

Roman takes her hands in his. 'I'm sorry. He stayed on the freighter.'

∞

Terra closes her eyes and turns her face to the spray. The hot water doesn't help to warm the chills wracking her body. She can't get warm, can't sleep, all food tastes like cardboard, and there's a large, gaping hole where her heart was.

Tears spill down her face and she squeezes her eyes shut tighter, but they keep coming. She didn't get to say goodbye to him. The tears subside slightly at the thought of Sayber at the end of her gun. The Hunter leader had the good sense to avoid her since they got back to Ultar. Next time she sees him, she will shoot him.

Terra gives up on the shower, dries quickly, and dresses in plain black combat trousers and a white vest. Her small room in the village

503

makes a nice change from the ship. Since the battle, most personnel have moved into the community for a proper break. The link to Earth was severed when the freighter destroyed the Port — it would take time to accept this Sector as home.

She draws her long hair into a messy bun and sits down to pull her boots on. The box of drawings under the table catches her eye. She gingerly takes a page out and turns it over. The image of Gryffin swims as her eyes tear up again. Cursing herself, she shoves the box further under the table and leaves her room. Milla and Roman tried to convince her to draw again, but she refuses to pick up a pencil. The last drawing she did was the one she gave Bray on *Perses*. Her inspiration and love of drawing died along with Gryffin.

The moon hangs low in the clear sky. She wraps her cardigan tighter around herself as she shuffles along the forest path. The large lake comes into view and as expected, so does Roman. She lowers onto the seat beside him and reaches up to hold Gryffin's pendant in her hand. It hasn't left her neck once and never will. It's the only part of him she has left.

'I gave that to his mother.'

Terra turns to look at him. 'Sir.'

Roman gestures at the pendant. 'It was his mother's.'

'I didn't know.'

Roman stuffs his hands into the pockets of his jacket. 'I don't think he did either.'

Terra nods and watches a bat dart in the air at the lake edge. For some reason, people seem reluctant to say Gryffin's name. Everyone refers to him as 'he' almost like, by not mentioning his name, he is somehow still alive. 'Can't sleep, sir?'

Roman scratches his newly-grown short beard. 'Can't switch off. You?'

'Same.'

They share a comfortable silence for a moment before Roman sighs. 'I let him down, Terra. I was too wrapped up in Foundation rules and regulations to accept he was my son.'

'It was an awkward situation, sir.'

'But I didn't even try. I could have told him.' Roman kicks at a stone next to his boot. 'He died without knowing the truth and there's not a damn thing I can do about it.'

'That's not true.'

Roman turns to face her. 'What?'

'You're working with the Nomad to help protect this Sector. The colonies are his legacy. He... he...' She falters. She'll never be able to say he's dead. 'Sir, he did what he did on the freighter to save them. We can honour him by making sure the Foundation keeps away.'

∞

Roman nods and looks back over the lake. Terra is right. He had let Maggie's son — his son — down and he can't fix that. All he can do is ensure nothing like that happens again to anyone else.

He closes his eyes and takes a deep breath. In the peace of the evening, he can pretend, for a short while at least, none of the horrors of the last few weeks took place. Pretend all the betrayal, pain, and death are fragments of a dream and that his son didn't die thanks to his lack of action.

He still can't quite accept the Foundation had orchestrated all of this. Well, if the Foundation thinks they can waltz into the Sector and take what they want, they'll be in for a shock. As he sits here, *Infinity* is being overhauled, Nomad style. With the threat of the incoming Foundation, the Nomad and Hunters need as much help as possible.

In the two weeks since the Port blew, Sayber called in all his Hunter ships. For the moment at least, the Nomad and Hunters are working together with *Nemesis* and *Perses* at the forefront. Neither side feels comfortable with the new relationship, but beggars can't be choosers. They need every ship they can get — *Infinity* included.

Desyl had reluctantly taken the captain's seat on *Ares* — or her remains at least. They had already begun piecing her back together. If they were in Foundation space, she wouldn't even be salvaged for scrap, but out here they can't turn their back on the ship, no matter the condition.

Apparently, the Nomad have rebuilt ships in far worse condition, but he's still sceptical. He suspects neither Chayse nor Desyl is willing to give up on her. It appears *Ares* means a great deal to them and the Nomad as a whole.

Chayse had tried to execute Klay and the crew loyal to him, but Aleena had put her foot down. Instead, they would spend their lives in a cell on the surface. It went against Gryffin's 'no second chances' rule, but Aleena had refused to back down. While killing the twelve men wasn't something Roman condoned, he understood Chayse's eagerness to seek revenge. Things are dealt with very differently out here and he can fully understand why.

'We've got a tough fight ahead of us, Terra. We all need to concentrate on our jobs. As my second-in-command, I need you to have my back.'

Roman takes her completely by surprise with his statement. She looks at him with her eyebrows raised. 'Your second-in-command?'

'You're the obvious choice. It'll be a very different role to Stanner's position. *Infinity* is a very different ship now.'

'That sounds good. I accept, sir. Thank you.'

'I thought you would.' He looks back at the setting sun. 'So, how's Bray doing?'

'He's holding his own. Milla won't know exactly how the implants will affect him until he comes around — if he comes around. She's removed what modifications she can, but feels it's too risky to touch the plate over his heart and the implant along his hairline. Avoca's still with him. He's refusing to leave.'

Avoca hasn't left Bray's bedside since Sayber brought him in. Roman still isn't sure what to do with the admiral. Without the implant he helped design, Gryffin wouldn't have been able to get

506

control again, but that doesn't exonerate him. He still knew about the project for decades. There's no making up for that.

He tries to clear his head and enjoy the sunset, but it doesn't work. There's too much to think about, to worry about and feel anxious about. Milla and Chayse had tried, but they couldn't resurrect any more transmissions from *Omega* or the freighter. Callum's voice from the grave continues to haunt him. And what Maggie was he speaking to? Evidently not Gryffin's mother. She died over a decade ago.

Roman searches the night sky for an answer, but all he finds are more questions. He does know one thing for definite. Terra will never know of his suspicions. She has too much to deal with without adding ghosts to her problems.

He knows without a doubt the Foundation won't forget about *Infinity* or the Sector. They're more than likely already on their way out here with a full battle contingent. If that isn't enough to worry about, a lot of smaller rogue groups are appearing. Due to what Gryffin did, the Nomad have lost support along with their main deterrent. Without the Nomad leader's reputation, they're just another group.

He puts his arm around Terra and pulls her close. They huddle in companionable silence as the large red sun drops behind the mountain range. Both take time out to enjoy the moment before they have to leave and fight for a Sector they each would like to call home.

Both thinking about Gryffin, hoping, by some miracle, he is still alive.

EPILOGUE

Three months later

Gryffin's eyes follow the small bird as it flies over the lake towards *Ares*. He can't help but smile when he sees his ship in the middle of the field. The Ultaran sun reflects off her sails as his crew mill around her, working on repairs.

Terra playfully pulls on the stud in his ear. 'You're a big softy underneath your tough shell,' she mocks.

'What?'

She moves her hand up to his hair and twists the locks around her fingers. A few months ago, he would have instantly recoiled from the contact, but not anymore. He trusts her and her touch. 'The fierce Nomad leader just went all googly-eyed when he looked at his ship.'

He playfully swats her hand away and lies back on the grassy bank. 'She's mine.'

She tucks in against him, her small body fitting perfectly against his. 'What about me?'

He shrugs. 'What about you?' He grunts as Terra punches him in the arm. 'Fine. You're mine too.'

'Too damn right I am.' She runs her finger along the crescent-shaped scar on his cheek and his short stubble rasps under her fingers. Terra takes a deep breath and releases it slowly. 'Thank you.'

He opens his eyes and rolls over to look at her. 'For what?'

Her deep green eyes lock onto him. 'For trusting me enough to let me in. I'm really glad you did.'

He smiles. 'Me too.'

Gryffin lies back down and pulls Terra close to him. The warm sun shines on them and the gentle breeze blows through his hair as the birds sing in the trees. Everything is perfect, yet he can't shake the feeling that something is off.

Flashes of memories pop into his head: fighting another cyborg, working with Sayber, saying goodbye to Terra. He pushes the memories aside. They must be from a dream.

He tightens his grip on Terra. She sighs and snuggles closer to him. He just needs to switch off and stop worrying. Terra is safe and with him, Ultar is thriving, *Ares* looks better than ever and he's not in pain. For the first time in his life, he's free and happy.

He gets lost in the moment until a sharp stab of pain pierces his left eye. He opens his mouth and screams, but no sound comes out.

Gryffin opens his eyes and Terra is gone, along with the sun, breeze and birds. He tries to move his head, but nothing happens. It suddenly comes back to him. It's just his imagination running wild. Another in a long line of dreams he's had since he woke up in this place.

There's nothing to do but dream; make up shit that didn't even happen. As if he isn't going through enough torture without inflicting it on himself by imagining being with her again and again. It's a sure sign he's losing his mind. Who knows, maybe he'll completely lose it and marry her in the next one. Not that he'd mind. Any fantasy is better than his nightmare of a reality.

He doesn't know how long he's been locked into this glass box, unable to move anything except his lone functioning eye, unable to talk, or to turn away from the reflection of his naked and dissected body in the metal ceiling above him.

His last memory is of tethering the freighter to *Omega*. After that, everything goes blank. The collar is still around his neck and so is his head, so whoever got him off the ship must have had the code to deactivate the detonator.

He looks at his roommate in the reflective ceiling. The dark-haired woman has been by his side since he woke up. Like him, she's trapped in a life support case. Whoever she is, she means something to the Scientist. When he isn't working with *Forty-Three*, he remains by her side. Seeing how caring and attentive he is with the woman only makes everything he's doing more disturbing.

Forty-Three steps up to him and pushes cables and connectors into Gryffin's torn flesh. With no other way of blocking out the image, Gryffin closes his eye.

It doesn't work.

He can still see the rib spreaders holding his chest open exposing his internal implants, his heart beating steadily, his lungs inflating and deflating, the tubes and wires snaking in and out of his body, keeping him alive. It doesn't matter how many times he sees his reflection; he'll never get used to it. Blocking out the sounds of his life support, he forces himself to think of Terra.

His captors are careful not to talk about anything except their work. He hopes she made it through the battle. The only thing that makes what he's going through remotely bearable is the belief they all survived. Imagining Terra sitting by the lake on Ultar helps him block out the sounds of whatever is being done to him.

He puts himself next to her again and hopes he'll lose consciousness.

Maybe this time his luck will change and he won't wake up.

If you enjoyed *Ares*, please leave a review and tell somebody about the book. Reviews and shares are always welcome.

Thanks for your support!

K.A. Finn

Next in the Nomad Series.

NEMESIS

NOMAD SERIES – BOOK 2

K.A.FINN